MARGARITO AND THE SNOWMAN

REYOUNG

MARGARITO AND THE SNOWMAN
A NOVEL

DALKEY ARCHIVE PRESS

Library of Congress Cataloging-in-Publication Data
Names: REYoung, 1950- author.
Title: Margarito and the Snowman / REYoung.
Description: First edition. | Victoria, TX : Dalkey Archive Press, 2016.
Identifiers: LCCN 2016009404 | ISBN 9781628971446 (softcover : acid-free
   paper)
Subjects: LCSH: Motion picture producers and directors--Fiction. |
   Storytelling--Fiction. | GSAFD: Humorous fiction.
Classification: LCC PS3568.E94 M37 2016 | DDC 813/.54--dc23
LC record available at https://lccn.loc.gov/2016009404

Partially funded by a grant by the Illinois Arts Council, a state agency.

www.dalkeyarchive.com
Victoria, TX / McLean, IL / Dublin

Dalkey Archive Press publications are, in part, made possible through the support of the University of Houston-Victoria and its program in creative writing,
publishing, and translation.

Printed on permanent/durable acid-free paper

MARGARITO AND THE SNOWMAN

EVERYTHING, THE HOT WIND roaring in the open windows and the tires whining over the asphalt and that big screen panorama unfolding before his eyes, that vast ochre desert scattered with cactus and scrub brush, adobe, cinderblock and weathered wood and tin shacks and cantinas, cattle skulls, rattlesnakes coiled like poisonous ropes, scorpion tails crackling like tiny, electric cattle prods, and above it all the sun burning in the thin blue sky like an acetylene torch, the sun flaring up in a million, billion grains of sand, the sun the way he'd never conceived of the sun before—it all came out of Margarito's mouth, out of Margarito's voice, out of that hot lava flow of language, that cornucopia of papayas and guavas, pistoleros, caballeros, serapes, señoritas and sombreros out of which he struggled to pick words, phrases, to penetrate that other tongue by constantly nagging, cajoling and demanding of Margarito, how do you say *ice*, how do you say *snow*, how do you say *it's so fucking cold I'm freezing my balls off*? Watching Margarito's lips move beneath his shiny black mustache as if he were pronouncing secret incantations that unlocked the doors of ancient mysteries, then attempting to reproduce those magical utterances himself until sound and meaning fused in tiny detonations of comprehension. Of course! *Hielo! Nieve! Hace un frío de puta madre, se me están helando los huevos!* And then the confirmation, Margarito's face glowing like a terra cotta sunburst of surprise and delight, *Tú sabes*, Snowman! *You said* eet *right!* If all teachers were as good as Margarito, if all teachers were captive, held prisoner, imprisoned by poverty, fear, the color of their skin, the foreignness of their tongue, desperate to survive in a hostile environment where every word, every gesture betrays you as alien, where you can never just walk into a convenience store or fast food joint and ask for a pack of cigarettes or a hamburger because when you try to speak all that comes out are these horrible noises, you have to contort your face, you have to gesticulate and wave your hands around like a raving lunatic to get your message across. It's like communicating from behind the plateglass window of another dimension. Worse, the other customers are staring at you, at your funny looking clothes—*you're* funny looking, your face, your features, hammered and molded out of bronze, out of copper and terra cotta. And on top of that you have this crazy snowman digging into your brain in search of words, thoughts, *secrets*. And in exchange you get nothing, nobody's teaching you anything, you can't put a crowbar to a snowman's skull and pry out of it words, knowledge, the key to this mystery of cold and snow. *El Norte*.

1

Avalanche

Now what the hell was he doing, getting lost in the goddamn desert? Whose bright idea was that? Boone's, most likely, that evil genius hurling his thunderbolts from the clouds, writing wrong turns and nonexistent road signs into the script and scattering obstacles in his path like thumbtacks. And he didn't even realize, did he, poor Snowman? He was mindlessly trudging back into the cactus and scrub on a sandy, rocky path littered with sun-scorched cans and bottles, plastic bags, wads of toilet paper smeared with tarry black shit, human shit, like desiccated carnations from a long ago wedding party. His boots jingled like harness bells on a plodding draft horse. Blinding white patches of caliche flared up in the graphite glare of his sunglasses. Rivulets of sweat streamed down his face and soaked the synthfur lining of his parka. Spectral waves of heat rose around him, flooding his nostrils and all the bony and cartilaginous cavities of his skull with the rancid, choking smell of death. He scanned the fire-blackened pile of garbage in front of him, simultaneously expecting to see and hoping not to see the decomposing carcass of some large animal, bovine, porcine or hominine, bloated body split open like a rotting sofa, the fetid stew of internal organs boiling with maggots. His perfectly normal mind at work, replaying a hit parade of all the lurid tabloid covers he'd perused in the clinical fluorescence of convenience store checkouts at two, three, four a.m. Rape, murder, unspeakable acts of depravity, the worst nightmares of a well-fed society dumped on a simple refuse heap and makeshift rest stop.

He peeled open his parka, unzipped his pants, dug through sweat-sodden thermal underwear and cotton Jockey shorts, untucked and released a toxic yellow stream that splashed on the ground, partially collapsing the earthworks of an abandoned anthill. Bladder deflating, abdominal muscles sagging gratefully, eyes raised to some unspecified deity, he stared at the black specks drifting in lazy circles high overhead, retinal fragments of last night and all the other nights dislodged by alternating bursts of caffeine, nicotine, alcohol and various other stimulants and depressants ingested more or less in an assembly line continuum throughout his *waking* hours. He took off his sunglasses, wiped the sweat from his eyes (in an odd kind of camera close-up, they look like pale blue patches of arctic sea ice skimmed with frost, and frighteningly bloodshot). The black specks were still there, wheeling and turning in the thin blue atmosphere. Buzzards. In his mind he saw a man spread-eagled on the ground naked, his hands and feet staked, writhing against the blistering sun, against insect bites, cigarette burns, knife wounds, nearly mad with pain and helplessness. Not that he really expected to end his life here in the desert, a piece of jerked meat waiting for the ants and coyotes to pick him apart and haul him off. All he had to do was shake, tuck away, rezip and Velcrotize and tramp back through the cactus and scrub to the Coupe crouched on the side of the road like a big black cat and pull onto the highway in a cloud of yellow dust. And then it's like he never stopped, like he's been driving forever in the celluloid river of time, the cracked, recapped and dangerously bald white walls he's been meaning to replace for the last six months whining over the worn gray asphalt and the hot sirocco roaring in the open windows whipping his dirty blond hair around his face, his mouth's as dry as the sun-blasted desert he's driving through and nothing to whet his whistle but the tepid dregs of coffee in the thermos next to him. Add to that, he's down to one, maybe two cigarettes in the crumpled pack on the dash and worse still, the sarcastic little tongue of the gas gauge is flickering ever closer to empty, a nagging reminder of his decision to get off the toll road for this *scenic route* an hour ago and not a sign of another car or even a house since. Now this white van appears out of nowhere, which reassured him at first, but increasingly annoys him the longer it hangs on his tail, and, finally, his anxiety returning (mother rapers, *father* rapers, etc.), causes him serious concern, especially when the van swerves out alongside him and a man with a bony skull, oval sunglasses and a black pencil mustache leans out the passenger window and points something at him that under the circumstances he naturally assumes is—*a gun! I'm going to die!* That horror and absolute certainty of death contorting his face for a fraction of a second captured in the indifferent lens of a videocam. Because it isn't a gun, is it? It's just a photo-happy tourist filming everything in sight, cactus, wandering cattle, this old classic Coupe rolling down the highway like a derelict of time and neglect, a big, blundering barge of a boat drifting and floating over the road like an outlandish vacuum cleaner sucking sand, dust and crawling centipedes into its chrome-plated turbo charger, majestic black shark fins shearing the airstream in back, big silver bumper and grill gleaming Cheshire-like in front, and him, the Snowman, grinning like a fucking idiot behind the wheel, so glad just to be a guest star in somebody's little home movie instead of a bloody, mutilated corpse dumped on the side of the road like a worn-out and abused old yard dog. Next family reunion Mom and Pop drag out the video from their big trip south of the border and there he is, a ghostly presence behind the windshield of that old black bomb. *Mercy, Elmer, what on earth is that?* Poor befuddled Elmer peers over his bifocals. *Good lord, Helen! I think it's a Sasquatch! Driving a '59 Coupe du Jour!*

But, the Snowman's fifteen seconds of fame already up, a warm sea surge of relief floods his body as he watches the van disappear into the desert ahead. Easing back on the gas, he extracts a thin paper pod of cannabis from the pencil pocket of his left sleeve, scratches a red-and-white-tipped, strike-anywhere kitchen match across the dash, raises the sulfurous-smelling

flame to his joint and inhales deeply, drawing the smoky ambience of an opium den—Persian carpets, hookahs, incense—
down into his lungs just as the radio comes on, sprung to life by
a wire-jiggling bump in the road. Blaring brass, the hurdy-gurdy
of an accordion, a chorus of male tenor voices crooning of heart-
break and undying love for the wild-eyed Carlita. *"Ai-ai-aiiiii!"*
the DJ breaks in with the ubiquitous Mexican coyote cry, *"Así
es, damas y caballeros! Acabamos escuchar el éxito numero uno!"*
Then, total disconnect, a doleful bell tolls and a woman's voice
reads the names of the recently deceased in alphabetical order—
Anita Arquebus, Ezequiel Epazote, Pedro Páramo, followed by
birthdays—*feliz cumpleaños, María!* Matrimonies—*con mucho
orgullo los padres de Juanita Empanada anuncian . . .* somebody
searching for somebody else in some distant town—*por favor, si
tiene noticias de nuestro hermano Pablo . . .* then music again, *este
es el Corrido de Santo Del Año, el más guapo de todo México*, the
story, as he understands it, of the drug-running legend, whose
appellation "Santo Del Año" is a nod to the limited longevity of
those who ply his trade. North of the border, the presidentially
appointed Drug Czar, Marvin Morefein, who appears in these
laughable TV spots in the full regalia of an eighteenth-century
naval officer (the whole shebang, bi-cornered hat, powdered wig,
blue serge frock coat with gold braid and frogged buttons, white
satin breeches, knee-stockings and buckled shoes), has personally
sworn to put this "Damn Del Santo" (*sic*) away for life in one
of those dreary maximum security prisons in the arctic tundra
whose sole purpose is to irreversibly reduce inmates to drooling,
incontinent imbeciles as an example to the rest of the bad boys
in the world. Said war against drugs in which he, the Snowman,
is what? A peon, pee-in-the-cup-son, PFC, infantryman, foot
soldier? For the other side. In fact, unhappy coincidence, he's just
blown a small cumulonimbus cloud of marijuana smoke out the
window when he drives smack into an unwelcome mirage trembling in the heat waves rising over the highway ahead. Humvees,
deuce-and-a-halfs, soldiers in olive drab uniforms, most of them

young, high school age, copper faces, Indian features, hostile expressions, eyes gleaming like splinters of coal beneath the cave openings of their helmets, automatic weapons gripped at their chests—and what if they pull him over, find his stash? Goodbye Mister Snowman, right? Disappeared down some bottomless black hole of a hoosegow and never heard from again. But, who knows, maybe they'd just laugh, *hahaha*, whoever heard of a greenghost smuggling drugs *into* Mexico? and send him on his way, *bye-bye*. In a movie maybe. The whole time he's frantically snuffing out the joint and trying to stuff it in some convenient hidey hole *they'll never think of looking in* while his boots jingle and jump between clutch, brake and gas pedal in an effort to slow the Coupe down without appearing too obvious—flashing red brake lights alerting some atavistic trigger mechanism buried deep inside the soldiers' brains, the splatter of hot lead shattering safety glass, puncturing ten gauge steel, shredding vinyl, flesh, smashing bone, the Coupe turned into a bullet-riddled tin of canned meat leaking blood, oil and gasoline. Fortunately these soldiers don't have any beef with him. It's the guy in the white van. Crazy tourist, he's actually gotten out and is filming everything in sight. He's pointing his camera right in the soldiers' faces. The soldiers don't seem to like that. They're shouting and wrestling with him for the camera. Suddenly the guy gesticulates at *him*. Then the soldiers are turning and gesticulating at him too, but—*bwahahaha!* giddy, fiendish laughter escapes his throat—he's already past and picking up speed, his eyes jumping back and forth between the road and the rear mirror, expecting to see the convoy roaring after him in a cloud of dust, soldiers clinging to the vehicles like Keystone Kops, which is probably a combination of pot paranoia and too much TV as a kid.

He instinctively hangs a left at a fork in the road and immediately regrets it when the blacktop deteriorates into broken asphalt and then orange dirt and blinding white caliche. He passes a man in a straw hat, coarse brown serape and bare feet that look cartoonishly oversized with huge, mud-caked toes, leading a scabby, sad-eyed donkey, then a squat yellow adobe church. In the arched cupola a heavy iron bell waits silently, malevolently, with hand-wringing glee for the Sunday morning swing when it clangs and bangs across sandy desert and winding arroyos, sounding the call of worship, of alarm, of the death and internment of whatever passes for life in this barren land, that contingency accounted for by a small cemetery enclosed by a rusty wrought-iron fence and cluttered with crude wooden and cement crosses, homemade monuments constructed out of brick and mortar and decorated with pieces of colored glass and tile and drably festooned with faded plastic flowers. Shortly after that, a small black bundle of cloth perched on a large flat rock, an old woman hunched buzzard-like in an all-encompassing black shawl, her wizened face like a small brown nut, her black currant eyes unmoving, watching out of centuries of desert, of drought, of endless sun, her head bent slightly as if she were receiving messages from some distant place, maybe even (his all too vivid imagination again?) alerting someone of his passing, *yes, he's here now, the Snowman.*

The dirt road reassembles itself into asphalt. He passes unfinished houses with rusted rebar sticking out of the tops of gray cinderblock walls, pastel blue or red, yellow or green stucco houses with terra cotta tiled roofs sprouting prickly pear cactus and colonies of alien-looking kalanchoes. Scrawny, disease-ridden chickens squawk and flap in bare dirt yards enclosed by living fences of ocotillo, their spiny green wands bursting at the tips with crimson stars. Barefoot pubescent girls in stained cotton T-shirts and short skirts revealing pointy breasts and narrow hips and prematurely aged women with missing teeth, tired eyes and babies at their flaccid breasts watch him go by from open doorways. Mangy mongrel dogs curled up in patches of shade lift their heads. Scrawny cats lie sphinx-like on windowsills next to cracked terra cotta pots of pink and red geraniums. A lean black pig runs out of a house. In every dwelling a TV screen flickers on a wooden chair or the dirt or cement floor. *An informed populace is a warm populace.*

The asphalt turns into cobblestone and the Coupe rumbles past conjoined houses, shops, a bakery, a hardware store, a mini-mart. An old man with white hair and mustache, almost luminous in white cotton shirt and trousers, watches him from the shadowy archway of a small white chapel, his lips moving as if he's mouthing a prayer, although it could just as easily be a curse. A young woman in red stilettos, a shimmering green dress and hair like spun copper materializes on a street corner like a model in a fashion shoot, her face hidden behind oversized sunglasses, her plump pillowy red lips parted in a pouty, surprised *oh*—who knows, maybe subconsciously reenacting the blowjob she gave her pimp an hour ago *and now I gotta fuck this weirdo?* Assuming, as he does, briefly, that she must be a prostitute, otherwise what's a classy dame like that doing in a tiny pueblo like this? On the other hand, what *is* a classy dame like that doing in a tiny pueblo like this? Maybe this is the answer on the next corner—a couple of seriously bad-looking mofos clad entirely in black and flashing bling like a Vegas marquee, slightly less conspicuous, the poisonous gleam of short-barreled, heavy weaponry inside their open jackets. The one guy's short, stocky, looks to the Snowman like someone who tosses around sacks of cement and dead bodies with equal ease. The other's a stringbean, tall, lean, hair tied back in a ponytail. A black eye patch partially conceals the jagged scar that slashes the left side of his face from his hairline to his jaw. Their heads roll sideways as he cruises past and he thinks, *uh-oh*, but then it occurs to him they're probably just checking out the Coupe. Everyone loves a classic.

He comes to a sun-splashed plaza. A concrete obelisk with a black iron ring at the top and a copper spigot oxidized into a greenish lump at its base stands like a pillory in front of a tiny stone municipal building, half-hidden by a giant prickly pear cactus. A hand-painted sign says *Cerrado*—closed. Outside a butcher's shop, reddish-brown slabs of flyspecked meat hang from steel hooks. A small, whitewashed cinderblock building is plastered with red, white and green political posters in the middle of which a single word in gold sends an ice-cold saline rush through his sinuses and into the center of his brain. *Cerveza!* Barley malt, hops, yeast and spring water in a tall cold bottle of foaming carbonated suds. *Beer!*

Promising the Coupe a lump of sugar later (he actually says this aloud, mostly to reassure himself), he ties his mount at the hitching post and, hitching up his shooting irons (the way he's holding his hands it does look like he's adjusting holsters on his hips), he jingles through the saloon-style swinging doors and stops, stunned by the radiant glory of a dozen or so votive candles glowing in tall red, green and orange drinking glasses among an ossuary of age-yellowed white plastic Madonnas and Messiahs draped with rosary beads and colored lights. This lambent menagerie is arranged around a faded poster of a beatific female figure. Head bowed, hands pressed together in prayer, wearing a green star-splashed shawl over a maroon robe embroidered with lotus blossoms, she's emerging from the center of a giant spiky desert plant surrounded by a golden aura. What the heck? Did he go through the wrong door? Intrude upon some kind of religious sanctuary? A small black and white TV, sound off, flickers in the dim, smoky light, on the screen a haggard apparition in dark glasses and hooded parka that sure looks an awful lot like . . . *me*, or rather, *him*—absolutely certain he's enjoying another fifteen seconds of video anonymity in a security camera when the title and opening credits begin to scroll down the screen. *Ohhh* . . . now he gets it. It's a *movie*. Boone Weller's campy sci-fi western, *The Abominable Snowman of the North*, starring Billy "Plum" Bob Bengay, who appeared on the Hollywood scene as a twenty-something hotshot—before, that is, he nosedived in a debacle of drugs, alcohol and sex scandals, followed by stints in rehab, relapses, after which (his entire life history serialized in celebrity columns, fan zines, and on talk shows) he morphed into the more sober-sounding William Bengay in an effort to jump-start his career.

The Snowman's field of vision widens to include an old man standing behind a rough wooden countertop. Creased and seamed brown paper sack face, coarse salt-and-pepper beard stubble. Mossy white tufts of hair sprout from his ears and nostrils. His small, rheumy eyes gleam like distant candles. At the end of the counter, a pair of paunchy middle-aged men in straw Stetsons and pearl snap, western-cut chambray shirts stare at him as if he's just stepped out of a flying saucer. Two younger men in wifebeaters and skinny black jeans stand over a miniature pool table. One is sighting along his cue stick, although his eyes have clearly registered something out of the ordinary in their periphery. The other, chin resting on the back of his hands, which are cupped over the tip of his cue stick, has just picked up on this because he's got a kind of *uh-oh* look of apprehension at what he will see if he rotates his head five degrees to the right. Everyone, the Snowman included, momentarily suspended in this same hallucinatory vision. He, the abominable snowman from outer space, destroyer and prophet of God, his awful, unseeable eyes hidden behind opaque lenses lest they cast into blindness and ruination all mortal creatures that look upon them, walks out of the wilderness of the TV screen and into the up until now totally banal lives of the local inhabitants. Do they call him crazy, loco, holy, insane? Fall to their knees praising God or whatever heathen deity they pray to in these torpid climes and all the saints as well while lifting up their hands to receive the deluge of gold and silver coins pouring from his mouth like a slot machine? What if—just as possible and probably even more likely—they rush at him, fists knotted, knives flashing, spitting out their hatred and disdain in an incomprehensible barrage of curses? *&%$!# greenghost! &%$!# yanqui!*

A fat iridescent green fly buzzes and bangs into dusty bottles, drinking glasses. A small metal fan in a black wire cage whirrs back and forth, futilely pushing warm air around the room.

Hot rivulets of sweat trickle down his face. The synthfur lining of his parka clings to his neck like a drowned squirrel. It would probably be a good idea to say something but at the moment he can't conceive of anything in Spanish more than Neanderthal grunts. *Me Snowman? Me want beer? Me sorry for bad entrance? Me go now?* An explosion of trumpets blares like the midday sun and the jukebox in the corner spontaneously glows into life, a glass and chrome affair crash-landed in the middle of the desert like a rocket from the planet Krypton bearing its precious little super baby cargo. The music stops, the lights go out, the corner goes dark. The old man behind the counter squeezes his rheumy eyes shut, his moist, beard-stubbled jaws creak open, revealing a black cavern hung with rotting, stalactitic stumps, and he breaks into a loud cackle that sounds like a serrated knife sawing through a plastic milk carton. Then everyone's laughing, the Snowman and the old man behind the counter and the two middle-aged men at the end of the counter and the two young cholos bent over the pool table. Encouraged by this turn of events, he points at himself and says in his *peccable* Spanish, *Duh may una cerveza, por favor?* For a second the old man looks like he's been hit over the head with a loaf of artisan bread, but then, with the alacrity of a seasoned bellhop hustling tips, he grabs a pink plastic pitcher and sloppily pours a frothy white liquid into a glass jar while chortling toothlessly, *No, no, no, amigo. Hoy no bebemos cerveza, hoy bebemos pulque, porque es el Día de la Santa Agave.* The Snowman digs a little finger in his right ear. *Porque? Sí, amigo,* the old man nods vigorously. *Pulque! Agave! Trinkst du! Versteh?* Remnants of high school German echo in his brain.

> Dieter: *Guten Tag,* Paul. *Wie geht es Ihnen?*
> Paul: *Es geht mir gut, und dir?*
> Dieter: *Ausgezeichnet! Aber wer ist denn das da drüben?*
> Paul: *Das ist ein Freund von mir. Willst du ihn kennenlernen?*

Perhaps the old man has mistaken him for an intrepid German

tourist trekking off the beaten track in search of a sighting of the rare ring-necked desert cuckoo. Oh well, when in Bavaria . . . he raises the jar to his lips for a cautious sip, convinced he's ingesting a whole slew of unwanted congeners, dirt, insect parts, machine oil, disease-bearing bacteria. *How do you say germs, microbes, bacteria?* And, ooo, yuck, it's thick and slimy and tastes kind of sweet and sour like overripe fruit. His mind fills with images of giant, sword-shaped plants with tall, candelabra-like spikes of waxy white flowers. He distinctly hears bat wings flutter close to his ears. Hmm, not bad actually. *Tome!* The old man raises his hands in encouragement. He takes another swallow, wipes his hand across his mouth, *Moy bwayno!* Another swallow and he's feeling great! And these guys, they're friends! He can trust them! Look! He spreads a ragged road map on the counter and pokes at a spot marked with a big red X. Mi amigo, Margarito! This is his pueblecito! I'm heading there now! It's only another four–five hundred miles as the crow flies, a thousand if you take the shortcut. And holy Mother of God, they understand him, they know what he's talking about. Sí, sí, Margarito! Four–five hundred miles a vuelo de cuervo, mil if you take the shortcut! But for now, have another glass of pulque, *Meester Snowman,* it's on the house, *Meester Snowman.* Amazing, not only do they understand him, they know his name. Wait a second—*they know his name?!*

At the back of the room a cloud of smoke hangs like a cotton boll over a small round table. A cigarette smolders in an ashtray next to a half-empty jar of pulque. Uh-oh. He's getting that unpleasant feeling again. Why is he always so goddamn stupid? Why did he mention Margarito's name, and even worse, his destination? These guys are probably in cahoots with every desperado in the territory, a simple call ahead and the notorious Jewish Mexican bandit Eli Wallajon and his gang are waiting just out of town to dry-gulch him. But the old man's smiling toothlessly and pouring more pulque and repeating, *Sí, sí, todos amigos,* and of course he doesn't want to appear ungrateful, only—*what ho?*—at that very moment he spots a small refrigerator case and glowing like molten sunshine behind its frosty glass door a solitary six-pack of bottled beer. *Quiere cerveza, señor?* The old man waves at the case as if it contains an entire warehouse of beer and, at the Snowman's nod, extracts the six-pack and places it on the counter. A dusty gleam, like a guttering kerosene lantern, draws the Snowman's eye to a narrow shelf on which stands a single bottle of—*Quiere tequila, señor?* The old man turns in anticipation. A brief and slightly inebriated conversation ensues in the Snowman's brain. Now wait a second, do you really need that? No, but I want it. Of coursh you *want* it. Look, I'll give it to Margarito as a present. Yeah, shure ya will, *Snowman.* He nods and the old man clunks the bottle down on the counter. But, *Kay Milagro!* Is it possible? Among the tantalizing POS display of candied scorpions, pickled rattlesnake eggs and fried chicken feet he spots a pristine, cellophane-wrapped package of chocolate cupcakes topped with white buttercream icing. Geez, he hasn't seen Kay Milagro cupcakes in years. That big shtink in the States, falsh labeling, unsafe ingredients, consumer groups whining about heavy metals, carcinogens. After all, Snowman, you'll need some solid food in your belly to soak up this alcohol. A balanced diet for an unbalanced mind, right? Oh yeah, don't forget cigarettes. How 'bout a pack of those intriguingly oval-shaped smokes? And throw in some foshforosh from the Boshporush—matches, I mean. He surveys his bounty. How much? The old man flaps his hands open and shut four times and the Snowman digs in his pocket, pulls out a wad of paper currency and, grandiose as a grandee, dumps fifty thousand on the counter. Keep the change, I think you're cheating yourself on the cupcakes. And gathering up his purchases, he backs out of the dim little cantina and into the sudden scorching reminder of too much sun and too much heat.

But—what in the blessed name of Santa Agave? The empty, sunblasted plaza is coming alive. Women in billowing red, green and orange ruffled skirts and blouses emerge from beneath shadowy archways and men in sombreros, ruffly white shirts, toreador jackets and knee-length trousers appear out of dark doorways, and together they begin to whirl around the plaza, the women spinning like windblown marigolds and chrysanthemums, the men prancing up and down as if on horseback, while an orchestra of mandolins, violins, guitars, guitarróns and trumpets performs a rousing rendition of *El Jarabe Tapatio* (yes, it's the Mexican hat dance song). And look—it's the guy in the white van again. Christ, he's got an entire film crew with him. They're filming everything. They're filming *him*. They're advancing on him in a crowd of lights, boom-mikes, track cameras. The white van guy (who, in addition to his oval sunglasses, is now sporting a black beret and clenching an ebony cigarette holder between his teeth) is holding his hands before his eyes in the shape of a box while chanting like a high school baseball coach, "All right, all right, all right, Billy baby, you're starting to get it now. Your entrance was a little weak, a little more dialogue next time, a little more interaction with the cast. Remember, you're daydreaming, Billy. You're flashing forward to this grand reception you imagine when you arrive in Margarito's village. You know the cues, right, Billy?"

Cues? And whazh thish *Billy* bizhness? And how the heck's he know 'bout Margarito? "Look, pal, I think, you got me confused with shomebody elsh."

Sweating like a pressure cooker, the white van guy yanks out a handkerchief and mops his brow. "C'mon, Billy! Don't drop the ball on me now! You've read the script! You know the scoop! Hey, Billy, are you okay?! Your agent swore you were off the juice!"

"Hey, Boone! Telephone!" A cell phone appears stage right, held out as if it were somebody else's dirty sock by a skinny, potbellied young hipster guy in a fedora, goatee, polo shirt, plaid shorts and pink rubber bathroom slippers.

"Weller here! What?! No! I told you I won't talk to that sleazebag! Goodbye!"

Wait a minute, Boone Weller? The movie director dude? The Snowman does a quick two plus two equals five in his head. Of course. Now he sees. Everything, the town, the desert ambience—it's all fake, cardboard cutouts, portable cactus on wheels. Even the dancers, whose beefy physiques and clumsy, bovine steps should have been a dead giveaway—locals Boone has hired for a few pesos a cabeza.

"Geez, Billy," Boone looks him up and down, "you lose weight or something? You look *gaunt.*"

"The name isn't Billy," he says more testily than intended, a sign the pulque is wearing off.

Boone's brows knit together over his sunglasses. A venomous hiss issues from his lips. "After that little scandal you pulled in LA, I wouldn't want to be called *Billy* either." Suddenly Boone smacks himself on the forehead. "Of course! Now I get it! You're in character! I forgot you took this method stuff seriously, Bill—*Snowman.* Boy, get a loada that outfit. I hope Costume didn't exceed budget." The camera pans over the Snowman again, for the first time actually showing his black rubber boots with the metal buckles running up the front like railroad tracks. "*Ha!Ha!Ha!* That scene when you stopped to take a leak was great!"

"You filmed me with my pecker out?!"

"Heyyy! Whatsa matter, Billy Boy? I thought you were such a goddamn exhibitionist. Besides, it's a great opener. You're wandering in the desert, in a daze, reduced to your most basic instincts—we'll screen it tonight."

"But that's the *point.* I don't want you to screen it! What about my rights?"

"*Ha!Ha!Ha!*" Boone's dry hacking laugh crumples his face like newsprint. "We're in *Mexico*! No one has any rights, *Snowman*!"

"We'll see about that," he mutters, an idle threat he knows even as he utters it. He crunches open the door of the Coupe, sticks the beer in the ice chest in the back, dumps the rest of his groceries on the front seat and slides behind the wheel. Yee-oww! The seat's red-hot! The Coupe's an oven! He turns the key in the ignition, desperate to get back on the road and get some ventilation going. But wait—he sticks his head out the window. "Hey, do you know where I can get gas around here?"

"*Gas?!*" Boone snorts with disdain. "It's a goddamn movie, *Snowman.* You don't need gas! Eat a can of beans, *Ha!Ha!Ha!*"

Then, the Snowman's beard-stubbled scowl framed in the window for another second (to be used, without his knowledge or consent, in a publicity still the very next day), the scene's over and he's barreling down the two-lane blacktop again, in a pleasantly stoned state after smoking down to his fingertips the roach that, following a frantic search, he found incautiously tucked under the thermos and puffing on one of these unexpectedly and possibly just a little too sweet oval cigarettes. Only one thing's lacking to make this picture perfect. Fumbling open the ice chest behind the seat, he tears an ice-cold bottle of beer from the pack, one-handedly pops the top on the rim of the ashtray and, like a glimpse of the December sun through a frozen windowpane, tilts the bottle overhead, sending a slug of cold, carbonated effervescence flooding down the sandpaper dry gulch of his throat and—*epiphany*, in that moment the true purpose of beer makes itself known, the sponge of vinegar on a dying man's lips, the ice-cold charge of alcohol and electrolytes re-injecting life into a Frankensteinian corpse. Although there's also this faint but disturbing aluminum taste, and an even fainter taste of mildew that makes him think of blue-green molds blooming inside the dingy white vegetable compartment of a shuddering, worn-out refrigerator. But what the heck, it's beer, and it's cold, and he can already feel that wonderful pulque buzz coming back. He guzzles the rest in two swallows, belches like a frat boy. He's feeling better and better. He thumps his hand on the dash and shouts, Whoo-eee! He laughs maniacally *hahaha! hohoho! heeheehee!* and congratulates himself. You fucking idiot, Snowman, they're gonna put you in the movies! They're gonna

make a big star out of you! And all you gotta do is act naturally!
Maybe you'll even get paid! Ha! Wait until that dumbass Boone
finds out he fucked up! He thumps the dash again, beeps the
horn at a herd of goats. He did it! He's really here, south of
the border, in ol' Mexico, the land of bullfights, señoritas, piña
coladas. He wants to shout out loud, tell someone. He wants to
mail off picture postcards. He can see the gang at work, everybody bundled up like Eskimos, teeth chattering, blowing steam,
rubbing their hands together and stamping their feet, M'Shaka,
Hanktheredneckasshole, Jippi Jaime, Evelyn and the girls, even
Mister Gastreaux crowding around, hahaha, is that really the
Snowman next to that cactus? Why's he still wearing his parka?

Okay, now he's done it. Raised the very question he's been
scrupulously avoiding. Why *is* he still wearing this stupid thing?
Because he just can't get that nagging, lifelong chill out of his
bones? Because Boone thinks it'll make his cheesy B-grade production even weirder? That alone's enough to make him take
the damn thing off. Although he does kind of enjoy in a slightly
pathological way this heat insinuating itself around him like
the hot sloppy tongue of a very large warm-blooded creature.
Besides, he isn't ready to take it off yet, he might need it. For
what, Snowman, the next ice age to push south of the border?
A frozen asteroid to crash down in your vicinity? Wait a second,
Snowchump, you aren't thinking of going back? How long have
you dreamed of getting out of that life and away from those people? You're just feeling guilty for walking out on them. Yeah, but
it's true. All he's gotta do is turn around and head back home,
call in as soon as he crosses the border, make up some lie, an
emergency, his poor old mother. But listen to you, Snowman,
whining, making excuses. If you really wanta crawl back home
with your tail between your legs, go ahead, turn around, be my
guest. Big loser.

Okay, now what's he doing? Digging himself into a cannabis
funk, second-guessing himself and getting depressed? Another
foot deeper and he'll need a fireman's ladder to climb out of this

pit. At least a plausible plot shift, like the dust storm rapidly approaching in the opposite lane. Wow, what the hell's that, a fucking ocean liner? No, he sees now, it's a goddamn semi-tanker and it's got a big blue I on the spoiler. I-ching, he says aloud, which, due to an underlying goofy streak, he pronounces *Aww . . . cheeng*, in the west Texas drawl of a rangy young cowboy just off the ranch and immediately afterwards corrects himself like an irate grammarian, No, you idiot, not I-ching, *Icine*. And then the next question: what the hell's an Icine truck doing on this cattle track? Definitely not taking a shortcut, as he's learned himself. More likely, the driver's avoiding the toll road ten or twenty miles thataway. Regardless, in a kind of nostalgic reflex, suddenly he's beeping the horn bee-bee-beep! and waving his arm out the window, Hey! I'm one of you guys!

Wham! The semi roars past, rocking the Coupe on its chassis and wrapping him in a wintry chill that infuses his brain with the cool, anesthetizing smells of ether and eucalyptus, accompanied by the dry whisper of pale blue gossamer wings and a choir of cupid-like angels calling to him in an androidal, computerized voice, *you haven't forgotten us have you, Snowmannn?* No, he hasn't forgotten, which is precisely why he isn't going back.

2

That Damn Donkey

THERE'S SOMETHING IN THE ROAD. *There's something in the road!*
Slow out of the station, the ocular freight train suddenly picks
up speed and slams into the Snowman's brain and, inches to
spare, he jerks the Coupe around something in the middle of
the highway that, in a flash, looks like a piece of furniture but in
his rear mirror resolves itself into the knobby legs, moth-eaten
gray upholstery and floppy bedroom slipper ears of a small donkey insouciantly munching dry brown grass sticking out of the
cracked asphalt. Not so surprising in itself, he's in the country
after all, except that in another of those odd camera close-ups,
the damn donkey actually winks a big brown eye at him and
peels back its rubbery black lips in derision, *hee-haw-haw, you
missed me, Snowman, better luck next time!* Of course it's all a
trick, more cinemagic, Boone, the perennial cheapskate, splicing
in shaky, hand-held frames of a donkey at a children's petting
zoo. But the way Boone plays it, this isn't any old hick donkey
just off the hacienda. It's a very brainy burro with a highly developed human emotive quotient. It's also the prototype for the
flop-eared, sad-eyed, hyper-phlegmatic talking toy, *Brucephalos
Burro*®, or "Brucie" as he will become better known, that Boone
intends to sell to the public in a media blitz of picture books, virtual games and *action*-packed cartoons (specifically aimed at the
five-year-old market, a growing consumer base). Boone doesn't
seem to care in the least that *Brucie* is probably one of *the* most
detested male diminutives in the English-speaking universe, or
that Brucie's future success will be due entirely to the unusual

22

delight children take in taunting, tormenting and abusing him, not to mention that another foot and all of this would have been moot because *Brucie* would have been burritos. In fact it was here, before the commercial angle occurred to him, that Boone had originally planned to work in a dramatic scene in which, through one of those clichéd (albeit tragically in this case) cinematic devices that infuriate critics but drive the viewing public wild, the Snowman, as he is now, more or less an adult, that is, crossed paths with Margarito as a boy, with Boone's gardener's son, Miguel or Manuel *or whatever the fuck the little wetback's name is*—Boone's words exactly—playing Margarito, and even though Boone ended up cutting the scene altogether, a pirated copy must have gotten out because the Snowman clearly remembers glancing up in the rear mirror one last time to make sure the damn donkey really was all right when he spotted a dart of red, a bouncing black mop of hair, a little boy running wide-eyed up from the ditch on the roadside. Margarito, of course, in an impossible film flashback, impossible because there was no camera, no audience, no one there to see or record the horror on his face, that resounding crash of the universe fallen down upon his seven-year-old head when he found the still convulsing wreckage of the donkey lying in the highway like an absurd piece of broken furniture, pink ribbons of flesh torn from the crushed gray velour of its heaving flanks, scabbed and scarred legs splintered like matchsticks, bright red froth bubbling from its nostrils, pale pink tongue flopped between its big yellow chompers and, like a Magritte painting, white cotton puffs of clouds drifting across the pale blue patches of sky reflected in its bulging eyeballs.

Eet's my fault, Snowman, I keeled heem. Moist with brandy, Margarito's lower lip trembled beneath his shiny black mustache. His eyes gleamed like wells of sadness. His face partially hidden in the shadows of his hood, he resembled a penitent monk. Yeah, he was a great actor—he'd read the script anyway, the story of his impoverished childhood, the harsh conditions, how he had to work from an early age, how Papa'd tell him, Margarito, go down to the stream and get a bucket of water. Margarito, *deed* you hoe the beans like I *tole* you? Margarito, take the donkey across the highway and gather some firewood. All that responsibility Papa gave him, all that work Papa expected him to do, never once questioning that it was work, that in another time in another place they'd call it child abuse, slave labor, they'd drag Papa off to jail, split up the family, send the children into foster homes, orphanages, and finally the street. But *eet* wasn't like that, Snowman, Papa *deed* love me, he was trying to teach me the best he could, the way *hees* father taught *heem*. Help me hoe the corn, *mijo*, fetch the water, *mijo*, chop firewood, *mijo*. (Of course the film's in English so the Mexican actors all speak with what is intended as a Spanish accent—*Ed*.) How else are you going to learn about work and life and struggle? In school? What will they teach you there but words for things and not the things themselves? And who's going to pay for the books? The pens and paper? Are you going to make ink out of bird berries, tablets from corn husks? Papa demanding this of him like a priest a catechism over a breakfast of refried pinto beans, corn tortillas and hot chile peppers, seated at the rough wooden table in the middle of the one-room, dirt-floored adobe hut, his still sleeping younger brothers and sisters piled together like a litter of puppies on a blanket in the corner, Mama kneeling in front of the small mudbrick oven, patting and patting the wet, lime-smelling masa into perfect round tortillas between her strong brown hands, her thoughts, her entire mind locked in ceaseless prayer, an invocation to God and the Virgin and all the saints, including the most recently canonized, as well as those awaiting vacancies in the limbo of theological bureaucracy, for the protection of her family, for the well-being of her people, for—if not prosperity, something more than this crushing millstone of poverty. Education's a fine thing, Margarito, Papa continued, but more eemportaunt ees a chob. Everyone muss have a chob. Even that cucaracha scurrying across the floor,

Margarito, even he hass a chob. He cleans op the tortilla crombs and dropped beans, he keeps away disease.

Of course it's Carl Cockroach, a long-time character actor who, following a string of hits during the blattaria vogue, fell into disrepute after his last movie, a disturbing—in fact pathologically twisted, many would say—Sid Ney production that completely traumatized the movie-going public, a generation of kindergarteners turned into thumb-sucking vegetables, their parents haunted by endlessly looping hallucinatory flashbacks of unsettling events, real or imagined, in their own childhoods, CEOs of vast and powerful corporations breaking down in tearful, gasping sobs during annual shareholders' meetings as they recalled long-lost but deeply treasured teddy bears, tricycles, toy trucks, cars, baby dolls, sleds. Now Carl's trying to lift his career out of the dumps. (And, folks, that's no joke. Though a crafty punster in his own right, Carl's current residence is the twenty-fourth plot of the southeast quadrant of the San Soya County landfill—*Ed.*) In fact, Carl's agent has been trying to reposition him in the public eye through his promotional work on behalf of the Federal Department of Sanitation, Hygiene and Healthcare's new "Keep Our Communities Clean" campaign. It was a pure stroke of luck he landed this gig. The script originally called for some cricket dude, but the cricket had just signed on to a singing role in the new Sid Ney flick that the producers promised in a blatantly self-promoting full-page ad in the *New Yorkshire Times* would restore the public's faith in the decency, the integrity, the platitudes and attitudes *ad Excedrin* of the film industry. Besides, crusty Carl's got a heart of gold and he's especially happy to help a hardworking father get his homely homily across to his thickheaded son. Work hard, stay alive, that's what yer old man's trying to teach ya, kid—how t'stay alive.

Ah yes, but our little naïf didn't appreciate the lesson Papa was teaching him, did he? It's all there in the script, worked and reworked by a constantly morphing staff of screenwriters, that big black pot of tragedy and beans bubbling over a crackling, aromatic fire of piñon and ocote. How he went out at five a.m. and climbed up on the donkey's bony back and clopped along the narrow rocky path out to the highway, overhead the stars wheeling away in the west and the black of night fading into lilac and then nacre in the east and that thing starting in his chest, not just the faster beating of his heart with the approach of day and grandfather sun's big beaming terra cotta face beginning to appear over the ragged line of mountains, but his nascent manhood and the weight of all this responsibility Papa gave him, which he felt even more as he neared the worn, two-lane strip of blacktop. Crossing early in the morning wasn't as bad, not much traffic yet, maybe a truck piled with crates of scrawny, defeated chickens, or a crazy greenghost eager to get from one tourist destination to the next. But later in the day, the traffic heavier, strings of cars roaring past, the donkey loaded down with bundles of firewood, picking their way through the rattlepods and jaguarbush on the roadside, impatient for an opportunity to cross, knowing Mama and Papa, his brothers and sisters were waiting for him at home, in that dreary little adobe hut with the sickly yellow prickly pear next to the front door, hungry, shivering—an unusual cold front had come down from the north— Mama kneeling in front of the cold mudbrick oven, working her hands, patting and patting the damp tortillas, Where is that boy? Do you think he got rrron over and killed on the highway? And Papa shouting, that leetle bastard, sawn-off-a-beech, if I catch heem I'll keel heem! Papa! You don't mean that! But, alas, she knew Papa was right, the boy was dawdling again, picking at things the way he did. While the donkey chewed at dead brown weeds and grass the little Entomolgaritogist turned over rocks on the roadside, collecting scorpions, spiders, grasshoppers, mice and other poor little creatures in a jar where they engaged in horrific mortal combat or else sat motionless, paralyzed by the shock of displacement, until they succumbed from heat and asphyxiation. Sometimes he found aluminum cans or sheets of cardboard or pieces of electrical wire Papa could take into town to sell to the junk man for a few pennies. One time a paper cup clattered at his feet, scattering strange, glasslike cubes on the ground. He squatted on his heels and picked one up. Ouch! It burned! He threw it down and stared at his fingers. They were red, but rather than being hot, they felt cold, wet. He touched his forehead, his lips, his bare chest, and shuddered. Of course he'd heard of ice, he knew that the little people who lived in Tia Fecundia's television put ice in everything they drank, but that world was very far from his. He picked up another cube, put it in his mouth. His tongue burned, the cold flooded his sinuses, pounded in his head. A vast expanse of frozen whiteness stretched out before him and a word echoed in his skull, *el Norte*. He bent down for more ice but it was gone, melted into the sandy soil, nothing left but a damp spot, and soon that too had evaporated. He hurried the donkey across the highway and ran home, shouting, Ice! Ice! He tried to tell Mama and Papa but they looked at him funny, they called him crazy. The brewhag came in a rustling of skirts, sashes and scarves, in tinkling strings of beads and bangles and gold earrings, her pockets stuffed with amulets, bags of potions, herbs. She laid a thick, calloused hand on his forehead and stood motionless, her liver-spotted face like a death mask, her blind eye like the gibbous moon in a starless night, her good eye black, fierce, blazing down at him hawk-like. Her yellow talons tightened against his temples. She inhaled deeply, her eyes rolled back in her head and she hissed through missing teeth and lipstick as thick as paint, *Ayyy, Diablo! He's seen things that weren't meant to be seen.* Mama and Papa shivered, blessed themselves. After the brewhag left, Mama tugged his ear, Papa whacked him across the back of the head, You deedn't see nawteeng, you hear? There ees no ice!

Margarito raised his glass again. Sí, Snowman, I know, you theenk eet ees all silly supersteetion, the fears of uneducated peasants. We only had to wait a while longer to see how such superstitions work.

For weeks he was heartbroken, distraught. He prayed to God

to relieve him of this burden but when he said *God* his mind filled with frozen whiteness. When he took the donkey to gather firewood, he searched the ground for wet spots, signs of ice. Maybe that's why eet happened, Snowman. Margarito's voice, always full of boundless hope and even joy, barely rose above a whisper. Because he wasn't paying attention to the highway, nor the highway to him, all those cars roaring by, never seeing him, or, who knows, maybe they'd seen him too many times before, in the tourist shops, in the picture postcards, in the cheap hand-painted ceramic statues, a pudgy little Butterballrito in a sombrero and serape astride his trusty burro Sancho. That's what the original script called for, anyway. But somewhere along the line a new character began to emerge, a skinny, barefoot little boy in a faded red shirt and torn trousers, with a thatch of shiny black hair falling over his big brown eyes.

And then, that fateful moment, the screeching tires, the loud thud, the donkey's desperate wheezing, gasping, braying *heeeee-haw! heeeee-haw!*

Margarito took another drink, transferring the moist sheen of brandy from the rim of his glass to the soft pink swelling of his lower lip. Eets my fault, Snowman, I keeled heem. Maybe I deedn't keel heem with my own hands, but I let heem wander out on the highway and get rrron over by that carrr (this scene was filmed when the studio still had Margarito doing sound tests for a rum commercial—"So why doan' you rrron the rrrisk with el Riesgo rum?!"—*Ed.*). Why did he do that, Snowman? He wasn't dumb, it was always a struggle to make him cross the road. I had to yell at heem and pull on the reins, Come on, donkey! Horry op! Les go! No way. That donkey wouldn't budge. He'd dig all four hooves into the ground, lie back on his haunches and go *huh-uh! huh-uh!* A second later a car or truck'd roar past and the donkey'd look at me as if to say, stupeed leetle boy, deed you want to keel us both? You see, Snowman, that donkey was always careful, and then he wandered onto the high-way and got heemself keeled? I refuse to believe that, Snowman.

There must have been something else. Maybe he was depressed. Poor donkey. He'd been pulling the plow and carrying bundles of firewood and jugs of water his entire life and he'd probably have to work like a donkey until the day he died. And why not? In the shadows of his monk's cell, Margarito made a sardonic smile. He *was* a donkey.

He never imagined how hard it would be without the donkey, never realized how much work the donkey did. And now, no more donkey to carry firewood, no more donkey to pull the plow or take to market the baskets, blankets and rugs, hammocks, sweaters and serapes Mama stitched and wove together out of dried reeds, goat hair and bad dreams, sitting on the dirt floor of the dim little casita late at night, dead tired, working in darkness, trying not to wake the others with her cries of pain every time she stuck herself with the needle, her own spilled blood the secret ingredient among the yellows, greens, oranges and blues extracted from roots and berries, from the red dye of the fuzzy white cochineal scale on the prickly pear cactus, to obtain the bright crimson red she wanted to ignite the blanket or rug with a flame that'd catch the eye of some greenghost tourist lady who could just imagine the blanket filling her bedroom with sunshine and warmth during the long cold nights in the north. Two dollars, the tourist lady says, holding up her fingers. *No, señora*, Mama shakes her head. *Es mucho trabajo. Bway-no, trace*, the greenghost lady says, knowing how much the natives love to barter. But no way she's going to pay another penny for this dirty rag in which she now notices insinuating itself among the rather pleasing scent of wool and lanolin, the stronger odors of sweat and urine, which somehow bring to her mind the image of a pair of leering goats engaged in grunting, humpbacked fornication on a rocky mountain slope. *No, no, no, es mucho trabajo, señora!* Mama shakes her head emphatically. *Bway-no!* The greenghost lady sneezes into the red rose woven in the center of the blanket before dropping it back on the pile. I'm allergic to wool anyway.

Aiií, poor Mama. Margarito's hand gripped the edge of the

table (the camera zooms in on his fingers, oddly more like those of a pianist or a surgeon than someone who has grown up on hard physical labor). It was too much for her after the donkey died. She tried to carry the water and the firewood and pull the plow. She was much bigger and stronger than Papa, Snowman, but she couldn't do eet. Besides, it drove Papa mad to see her struggling like that. He had to whip her and drive her even harder when she stumbled over a rock in the field or got too tired to pull the plow. I know, Snowman, now you are thinking, yes, but people don't really live like that. But we are not people, remember, Snowman? We are *Zolmen*. We don't feel pain the way you do. We don't suffer the way you do. Isn't that what you greenghosts say, Snowman?

Soon they had no source of income, no more pinto beans or hot peppers, no corn meal for the tortillas. Mama sat at the table, her empty hands endlessly patting and patting. Finally she lost her strength and died. After Mama died, Papa lost his mind completely. He sat around the house all day and drank turpentine, coal oil, gasoline, anything he could get his hands on. He'd fly into a rage at the slightest sound, tear out clumps of hair, his mad eyes staring around the room, searching among the rickety wooden shelves for the cause of his misery, find it at last huddled in a dark corner, scratching a stick figure of a donkey in the dirt. You! *Diablito!* You've keeled us all with your evil! It's because you found the ice, you put it in your mouth, it filled you with the greenghost's curse. Now I weel keel you!

Papa came at me as if he really would kill me, Snowman. I had never seen him so angry. But his rage was too great. It struck him down dead on the floor. No wonder he hated me so much, Snowman. He was right to hate me. Eet was my fault, I keeled them all. The donkey, Mama and Papa, his younger brothers, who went off to work like donkeys for the rest of their lives on other men's farms and ranches, his younger sisters, who went off to be cooks and maids in other women's kitchens and bedrooms, to be raped, whipped and beaten by other women's drunken husbands, who burst into their cells at night reeking of tequila, slobbering and slurring the words *love* and *God* in a frantic desperate coupling that ended with a growled threat, you leetle beech, I keel you eef you tell anyone.

Margarito poured brandy until their glasses brimmed with orange firelight. And then, greatest irony of all, he who should have suffered all the flaming torments of hell, who should have been orphaned into the streets to live a life of filth and beggary, instead went to live in comfort with his grandfather. He always had plenty to eat, he had a real bed to sleep in. During the day he wandered over the rugged hillsides, keeping an eye on Grandpa's sheep while his mind filled with the mute, inarticulate poetry of ancient shepherds. The hawks, buzzards and eagles soaring in the vast azure sky overhead. The rattlesnakes, scorpions, lizards and other desert denizens peering at him out of rocky crevices. The waxy pink, red and yellow flowers that appeared on the spiny cactus in spring. The already aerodynamically challenged honeybees so laden with golden kernels of pollen they bumbled from flower to flower like drunken little drones.

You see how God punishes sinners like me, Snowman? Not weeth death but weeth life. Margarito's voice was thick with brandy, swallowed salt water. This is a stupid story, Snowman, I shouldn't tell you this. Eet says right here in the screept that Zolmen are stoic, like the mountains in winter. They endure hardship, pain, but they don't show their feelings. Which, as the Snowman can attest, is more or less a universal standard for the male population. So how to explain this concurrent urge to offer comfort, to place a reassuring hand on Margarito's shoulder, to say words he hadn't formulated yet and would probably never say. Easier, instead, to take another drink, to swallow the sweet fire down into his belly and look away, shaken by that intimate and prolonged contact with another man's eyes, to feign interest in a car that has just started up outside and even surprise as its brake lights flood the frosty window with blood red ink.

3
Snow Country

IN A CLICHÉD BUT CLASSIC DISSOLVE, a pair of murky red orbs vanishes from the screen and immediately afterward another pair of red-hot cherries flares up before the Snowman's eyes. Fire alarms! Klaxons! Warning bells! All systems on alert! He slams on his brakes and comes to a screeching halt mere inches from the rear end of a battered horse trailer rattling and banging and creeping along in front of him at about nine miles an hour (everything's in kilometers here, so you get these odd conversions). His field of vision shrinks from vast desertscape to the skinny brownish-gray butt and stringy, shit-crusted tail of a donkey, which, in yet another of those odd camera close-ups, glances over its shoulder at him, its black rubbery lips peeled back from its big yellow chompers in silent equine laughter, *hee-haw-haw, you are so dumb, Snowman!* Of course it's Boone again, with a final plug for *Brucephalos Burro®*, but the Snowman doesn't know that. He's groggy, dazed. Normally this time of day he'd be curled up in a tangle of bedcovers like a gerbil in a nest of wood shavings with another three–four hours of sawing logs still to go and the cold and snow and long, dark night ahead nothing but a bad dream in the alcohol slurry of a second-rate scriptwriter's sleeping brain.

But now he'd done it, started thinking about the cold and the north again, due in part, no doubt, to these subliminal images he's been getting from the sparkling white mountain range to the east, its serrated peaks strung out like giant piles of sugar or big-top circus tents or even the snow-covered hills outside Osberg. Which in turn triggers another image. A sleek red sports car speeding around winding curves, Judith driving, her eyes fixed like a fighter pilot's on the road ahead, her black kidskin gloves slipping over the steering wheel, he slouched in the passenger seat in a red thermal hoodie and faded denim jacket, stoned, slightly dazed, completely out of his time zone, but also wired on psalt and caffeine and fascinated by this (for him) daylight phenomenon of snow-covered villas, townhouses, condos and gated communities, a confusion of pride for work well done and despondency over the nature of that work roiling the already turbulent waters of his psyche. In his memory he carries a kind of *National Geographic* photograph of the hill country when it was still prairie grass, scrub oak and prickly pear cactus inhabited by a vivarium of coyotes, whitetail deer, bobcats, javelinas, armadillos, fox, possum, raccoon, scorpions, tarantulas, lizards, rattlesnakes and a multitude of other creatures, all banished now by the advance of civilization, all buried now beneath the snow. And still there's something beautiful about it, beautiful and barren, the sunburnt prairie turned into snow-white tundra. Only the shaggy green cedars like dark green flames roaring over the frozen white quiescence, those cedars everybody hated so much—ranchers, developers, allergy sufferers—the sole reminder of life as it had been, as if these dark brooding evergreens had taken the very last of the living green into their ragged survival folds, like ancient monasteries that held and protected all the knowledge and learning of the great civilizations through the dark ages when famine and plague, tyrants and barbarian hordes ravaged the known world. Is it all dead? Or has it just been sleeping all these years? A thirty-year hibernation, is that possible? Can anything survive so long buried beneath the ice and snow? Like those science fiction films where they revive some Neanderthal monster they've hacked out of a glacier? Oh *Snowman*, you're consumed with nostalgia like all the rest. Why weep for the sins of ghosts when we have our own sins to deal with now? Judith, patience tried beyond reason, interrupting his stoned soliloquy. This recent habit of his, talking to himself, out loud, in public, is at the very least embarrassing, potentially even dangerous. Which is the only reason he might seriously consider acquiring a cell phone—so people think he's talking to *it* and therefore isn't crazy, a faulty supposition if there ever was one. Besides, at least when you talk to yourself you usually get an answer, sometimes even the answer you want to hear. (Right, *Snowman*?) How can it be like this? How can he be sitting in this hundred-thousand-dollar fuck machine next to this woman he has fucked, made love to, lived with, at times felt conjoined to? And now they're total strangers. It's like he stayed down on the farm in his little hick town where nothing ever changed and no one ever did anything but grow old and die while she flew off into outer space and came back a Martian and now that strange, almost radiant, cobalt blue of her eyes, which he had finally more or less gotten used to, seems even stranger than before. Definitely something about her ears, exposed—you could almost say carved—by the close cropping of her once gloriously luxurious and untamed mane. They're even kind of pointed. Her lips, too, which approximate the classic bow shape, not like on a Christmas present, or even a Victorian schoolgirl's archery range, but the bow of an Amazon queen, Pallas Athena, a bow made out of rams' horns, or hewn out of hickory, oak, or the aptly named bois d'arc, a bow designed and constructed to launch mortal arrows and which, no longer exclusively his domain, he ached now to kiss, taste, explore as passionately as if she were a stranger.

It was Judith's idea to climb Mystic Mount. The pink granite dome swelling against the blue sky like a giant mammary gland. Thin lines of hikers in brightly colored winter outfits stretching up and down its face like columns of insects. Scattered here and there, small, ice-skimmed catchpools gleaming like tin foil. Judith's butt in black leggings shifting up and down like bowling balls at about eye level in front of him, sculpted by an intense sixty-minute Marine boot camp regimen she pushes herself through at five a.m. every morning. He's staggering and gasping for breath behind her. His lungs burn, his legs are rubbery, he just wants to get to the top of this damn thing and smoke a cigarette. On the summit, they stand silently, the immense expanse of whiteness stretching out below strewn with pink granite boulders and survivalist clumps of prickly pear cactus, the distance between here and the horizon grown immeasurably greater.

By late afternoon the temperature was in the fifties and they drove with the top down, the azure sky stretched overhead like plastic wrap, the breeze cool, springlike, the sunlight brilliant and warm, the wet black asphalt steaming, the snow beginning to slump and melt on the roadsides, Judith's finely tuned little machine caressing the curves like a velvet glove on a champagne glass.

And then that other change that occurred driving back into the city, putting the top up against the growing chill, the purple and gray shadows spreading, Osberg's silver, green and gold glass towers turned a lurid, fiery orange by the setting sun, the Eye's unblinking, dispassionate gleam watching over everything like a strange sentient beacon, the fainter beacon of the evening star already visible in the cerulean blue sea of the eastern sky, signaling the approach of night and that old melancholy and despair that always came with the approach of night. That despair he woke into when he woke out of the darkness of sleep and dream into the early evening darkness of winter at five-thirty p.m., post-modern time, post-mortem time, when he extricated himself from the warm, hibernational cocoon of his bed expelling a miasma of bean and whiskey farts, exhaling frosty white cartoon breaths without any words to express the horror of the night ahead. But he couldn't allow himself to think that, not for one second, or the whole thing'd collapse, he'd sink back into an oblivious sleep during which his stupid job and his drafty little shack of a house and the Coupe and anything else of any value in his life slipped away and was gone and it almost wouldn't matter for those few extra minutes of sleep.

Groaning, cursing—it's the mantra, the litany, the morning prayer of the workingman, his muscles stiff as jerked beef,
his spine crunching like broken glass, he rises to his feet like a
rusted farm implement and staggers-stumbles to the bathroom,
his white thermal underwear an ectoplasmic doppelgänger in
the gelid pools of bare oak he hurries, splashes, tiptoes across
in his damp wool socks. The icy bathroom tiles under his feet
send a jolt of electricity shooting up his spine into the back of
his brain. He indifferently pees a heavy, splashing stream into
the stained toilet bowl and stares out the small square window
at the blood-streaked yellow blob of sun sinking behind the
shotgun shacks and bungalows across the street, igniting into
orange flame patches of dirty melting snow and icicles dripping
like translucent carrots from gutters and eaves, contemplating as
he always does this transformation between day and night. Do
you call it dusk, Snowman? Do you call it dawn? Your sunrise
and sunset become one?

Sunrise . . . sunset . . .

(A chorus of seriously world-weary male and female voices
repeats a melancholy refrain in the movie theater next door.)

Afterwards, he stares at himself in the mirror. Nothing new.
He looks like shit. His face is pallid, tallowy. Bruised half-moons
droop beneath his bloodshot eyes. An uneven platinum blond
nap sprouts from his jaw. He thinks about shaving but doesn't
feel like waiting for the hot water to work its way through the
calcified plumbing. He splashes a couple handfuls of cold, sulfu-
rous H_2O on his face, shivers, stumbles out to the kitchen, puts
on water for coffee, scrambles some eggs, dumps some canned
black beans in the frying pan, pours spicy salsa over it, burns
some toast—and that, Snowman, do you call it breakfast? Do
you call it dinner? Do you just call it fuel for the night ahead
and don't think about the foment of holy terror in your belly
that comes later? Meanwhile Me'th's rumbling against his leg
and looking up at him meaningfully with those wide, jade green
eyes and making encouraging *mrrrt mrrrt* sounds that turn into

an urgent meow accompanied by a violent waving of his stumpy, moth-eaten black tail as the Snowman dumps half a cup of dry crunchies in the bowl on the floor, adds a few catnip and fish-flavored treats, then sits down at the small kitchen table to eat his own grub (which seems appropriate for what he's got on his plate) while gazing out the window. Purple and gray shadows fall across the street like deflated hot air balloons. A young woman in a red beret and ankle length camel hair coat talks into a cell phone while dragging a small black-and-white dog behind her on a leash. A car starts up in a cloud of vapor. A streetlight flickers in anticipation of its overnight gig, that always discombobulating dawning of incandescent day, artificial day, a day of streetlights, car lights, lights in restaurants, convenience stores, laundromats, twenty-four-hour grocers.

He finishes breakfast with a second cup of coffee and his first cigarette of the night while scanning the newspaper for breaking news even though the news in his hands has been in print over fourteen hours. It's just this obsessive/compulsive habit of his, he voraciously consumes the details—wars, earthquakes, pandemics, terrorist strikes—all that happening out there in that fabric of existence he's somehow a part of and apart from. Plus, he's the only house on the block that subscribes, he kind of feels like he owes it to the old guy who delivers the paper, he's seen him a couple of times in the morning, fat, bald, tufts of white hair sticking out over his ears, the guy always gives him this desperate look like he depends exclusively on his lousy seventy-five cents a day, dollar fifty on Sunday, for his meager diet of canned cat food and white bread sandwiches. Afterwards he adds his dirty dishes to the rickety pile of chipped, cracked and mismatched bowls, cups, saucers and plates in the sink and heads back to the bathroom to brush his teeth, take another pee, a dump, whatever the censors allow. He pulls on a clean or at least dry pair of wool socks, jeans, flannel shirt, wool sweater, thermal hoodie, denim jacket and watch cap, laces up his insulated hightops and steps into his black rubber boots without bothering to buckle them up, pours the rest of the coffee into his thermos and jingles out the door and down the walk to the Coupe and—yes, there is a benevolent god, the vinyl seat is still welcomingly warm from the afternoon sun. He turns the key in the ignition—there's a lapse, a lacuna in the forward flow of time as the gelid stream of electrons struggles to push lazy old Elmer at the front of the line across the synapse between cold quietus and a hot, revitalizing spark and *vrooom* that big V8 roars to life, then settles into a steady rumble as he pulls into the street and cruises past the yellow house, the green house, the blue house. Outside the Pink House, Moses is stumbling around in an almost matching Pepto-Bismol® pink bathrobe, his ratty black beard and dreads sticking out everywhere, his eyes, even from this distance, a disconcerting milky white— *zombie* eyes. He makes a left, a right, a left again on Maynard, which for some reason is pronounced *Mannered*, and joins the bumper-to-bumper line of evening traffic trickling past drab, dingy restaurants, apartment buildings, auto repair shops, gas stations, barbecue joints, a tiny strip mall agglomeration of a beauty salon, laundromat, storefront Pentecostal church, window-service-only taquería and mini-mart, a Mister Valet's dry cleaners, the Eight Ball motel, everything made tawdrier by the dusty, drooping, put-up-once-upon-a-time-long-ago-and-never-taken-down-since strings of threadbare gold and silver tinsel, burned out Christmas lights and faded plastic evergreen boughs. *So this is Christmas.* A cynical, snarling refrain loops through his brain as he crosses the railroad tracks and turns onto Aero (the indigenous population pronounce it *Arrow*) Boulevard and, ignoring the threatening gestures, angry frowns and mouthed obscenities, he kind of squeezes—forces his way, actually, and of course everybody makes room because nobody in his right mind wants anywhere near this old bomb—into four lanes of honking horns, flashing brake lights, angry, crazed drivers trying to get out of town, get home, get some dinner, watch some TV, drink a coupla sixpacks, do a coupla lines, plot bank robberies, mercilessly beat the wife and kids into whimpering submission before passing out in a drooling, contented stupor, or, conversely, like this pale, frightened school teacher, tech writer, housewife, whatever she is next to him, hurrying home to deadbolts, chains, burglar bars in a darkened living room with a strong drink in her unsteady hand and the TV terrorizing her with another day's horror stories; *an informed people is a warm people.* But what the fuck does he care about their miserable little issues? He's shooting them the bird and shouting *get the fuck out of my way you fucking losers!* Don't these sorry-ass deadbeats realize? Can't any of them fathom? While the rest of this federated mass of so-called humanity is going home to eat dinner and watch TV and sleep and fuck and do whatever else normal people do, he's just now, as the clock cruelly ticks away the vital hours, minutes, seconds of his life, *tick tick tick*, never to be lived again—he's just now going to work, the job, *the raison d'être*, which (his job) actually *is* on everyone else's mind, at least in an abstract way as the melancholy yellow lights begin to come on in closely nestled together red brick and wood-frame houses where dusty, cobwebbed and nearly needleless Christmas trees strung with faded tinsel and mostly burned out colored lights glow feebly and—eager, youthful spirits still unbroken—boys and girls watch wide-eyed at kitchen or living room windows for the night's first burst of snow flurries, even Mom and Dad, who should know better by now, are getting excited, even old Granny Donut up the street, her aging, dementia-tainted brain steeped in memories of cast iron stoves, crackling wood fires—*Mercy, Ebenezer!* she declares to the gray tabby curled in her lap, *I b'lieve we'll see some snow tonight!* And oh yeah, it's going to snow all right. He knows it's going to snow because he's the fucking Snowman and he's going to make it snow. Because now—he unscrews the cap from his thermos and pours his third cup of coffee, digs out a kitchen match, unzips a hot, sputtering flash of phosphorus across the black metal dash, and lights his second cigarette—now he's really beginning to wake up, he's starting to think about the night and the job ahead and how much he really doesn't want to face the night ahead, in fact he's already scheming to take off in the sled later and cruise the back roads by himself for a couple hours when a whiny, nasal voice in the back of his brain reminds him, *yeah, but Snowmannn . . . the sled ain't working, remember? The new guy Hector crashed it last night?* And then you wonder why I get so goddamn nervous. Nervous? I'm losing my fucking mind. Hey *Snowmannn*, you're doing it again, you're talking to yourself. Yeah, well tough shit, just don't tell anyone.

The Coupe bounces-bangs over a pothole and the radio comes on, a lone speaker emitting fuzzy, staticky chunks of the VBS theme music. Then, Uncle Bob, the grand old man of the airwaves, intoning in his gruff baritone, *Good evening, ladies and gentlemen, this is Uncle Bob with VBS nightly news*—which stands for verifiable bullshit, right, Bob?—the Snowman trying to disguise his grudging affection for the venerable Uncle Bob with a thin veneer of cynicism unconvincing even to himself. Good old Uncle Bob's been doing the news since some time in the last millennium, and even though the Snowman's never even seen a picture of Uncle Bob, he's certain he'd recognize him on the street, just like he'd recognize Santa Claus or God. Who knows, maybe there isn't an Uncle Bob, just a machine programmed with Uncle Bob's weary, pipe smoke- and bourbon-roughened avuncular voice, the disembodied Uncle Bob floating through space, filling cars, homes, warm, supper-smelling kitchens, cozy cluttered dens and damp shivery basement workshops with the wisdom of the ages. You can actually hear Uncle Bob's mustache scratching against the microphone as he leads his legions of loyal listeners down a litany of tonight's top stories. There's been a little crime in the streets, a little killing across the country, a little unrest around the world, but Uncle Bob's not concerned, he's just reporting the facts in that reassuringly matter-of-fact tone that suggests, don't worry, folks, we've got it all under control.

Yeah, sure, we've got it under control, don't we, Snowman? As he turns off Aero onto the much calmer Valle Dulce, he extracts a previously rolled joint, lights it with a kitchen match and exhales a cloud of blue smoke that eerily resembles a genie emerging from its lamp. The smoke drifts for a moment as if undecided of its next move, grant three piddling wishes to this mortal fool or destroy the world—what the fuck, three wishes, then the world—before a draft from the cracked window vent tears it to shreds. Another hit and he's drifting in a pleasant narcotic state as he tops Caliche Knoll from where he watches the final red crescent of sun sink in a moiling orange, purple and red Martian swirl behind the darkening blue hills west of Osberg. The city gleams like a towering eruption of crystalline structures in the dusty pink light. At its very pinnacle, radiant, unwavering, ensconced in a translucent green pyramid like a diamond in an emerald pendant, the Eye floats just above a much larger (if truncated) pyramid that appears to be built entirely out of solid gold bricks. Maybe it's the pot (*Of course it's the pot!* the tokers in the audience shout with childish glee) but the Snowman would swear the usually phlegmatic eye just winked at him. His gaze travels thence to the east where the dark hulk of the ice factory looms on the dusky horizon like the head and shoulders of some monstrous golem emerging from the earth, its twin smokestacks, dotted with blinking red beacons to warn away low-flying aircraft, spewing their foul black entrails into the indigo sky, and in only a few minutes that toxic cloud of smoke and ash will magically turn snow-white, *Habemus papam!* In fact, at that very instant a powerful blast of wind rocks the Coupe on its chassis, one second the wipers are beating back a spatter of sleet and freezing rain, the next heavy clots of wet snow. The boys in the control room are really cranking it up now, which reminds him again of how unready he is for this night ahead, which also means it's time for another boost. He takes the cut glass psalt shaker from the dash, sprinkles white crystals on the back of his left hand, raises it to his nose, inhales sharply, once, twice, a white-hot jolt of lightning strikes him between the eyes, throwing open all the electrical circuitry in his brain. His teeth clench, his eyes shrink into shiny black pinpoints, his mind races like a food blender. Then it passes. There's a kind of pleasant saline burn in his sinuses, a numbness in his brain, but otherwise he's normal again (relatively speaking), just more *awake*. (And, yeah, *psalt* does sound kind of like cocaine, but it's actually just a variant of smelling salts, pretty much the same stuff (*sal ammoniac*) alchemists fooled around with in the thirteenth century and ancient Romans got a rush off more than a thousand years earlier.) He lights another cigarette, inhales deeply. Ah, even better. Then he's cruising at seventy miles an hour across the barrens, a winding section of two-lane blacktop that once acted as the sole arbiter between the quietude desired by the habitués of the former municipal golf course and the requisite noise of the former municipal airport, the cold wind screaming in through that crack in the side vent, as well as myriad pinholes, mouse holes, *bullet* holes, that big old Dyno V8 awash and agush in thick black oil pounding away under the hood of this oversized behemoth exhumed from the neo-plasticene age, from the rust and decay of Tommy's Repurposed Automobiles and Parts after his last piece of shit, a little foreign economy model with three hundred thousand miles on the odometer, broke down on him for good halfway across the railroad tracks on Maynard (it's *Mannered*, remember?) at five-thirty a.m., just about right on schedule for the first commuter express of the day, which hurtled past a mere thirty seconds after he managed to push the car off the tracks, followed by fifteen minutes of fooling around under the hood before he finally gave up and staggered homeward, his body beat, his brain a fog, his thoughts vaguely suicidal and even more so when his gaze fell on the eight-foot-tall chain-link fence topped with razor wire surrounding the very establishment where he'd purchased the abovementioned vehicle. And speak of the devil, at that very moment Tommy, the host and impresario himself, a chemically orange splat of hair shellacked to his skull with motor oil, appeared at the front gate in a pair of torn tennis shoes and greasy orange coveralls from which a tangle of black and copper chest hair sprouted at his throat. Morning, *Snowman*, Tommy purred, stopping in the middle of unlocking the gate to leer at him, the milky blue-gray discs of his severely bloodshot eyes staring madly, infused with hydrocarbons, THC, methamphetamine, nicotine, malt liquor, *Ice*. In reply, he glowered significantly. If Tommy got the message he didn't show it. Taking the bus today, Snowman? Tommy growled through a frosty breath. Grr, that did it. He started to convey his severe disappointment regarding his previous purchase but, beneath Tommy's mad, unwavering, one might even say psychotic gaze, his complaint quickly deteriorated into a rambling sort of apology for his own incompetence with auto mechanics, because of course if he'd thought to take the distributor cap off right there in the middle of the railroad tracks and lightly sand and blow-dry the contact points and rotor as Tommy suggested, he probably wouldn't be here right now to press his case. Which was probably true, he wouldn't be here. He'd be smashed flat under a train. Tommy, whose attitude until now had suggested nothing but utter contempt, suddenly beamed as if the light of true understanding had cast a narrow shaft into the bedlam of his brain. In a single instant he had not only assessed the Snowman's current car-less status, but also remembered the nature of his own business. Hey! Tommy growled, jabbing a thick, scarred, grease-blackened finger in the Snowman's face. Maybe you'd like to take a look at some of the little beauties I got sitting out back. Oh, come on, Snowman, don't give me *that* look. What? You're still sore about that wuvable wittle VW bug? Or was it a—HaHaHa—Honda? Don't tell me it was a *Yugoslo*?! Look, Snowman, I know times are tough, your paycheck's never enough, just have a look around, get some ideas. Remember, at Tommy's, no money down until you sign on the dotted line. I'll do you right, Snowman. *Trust* me. Tommy's pushing open the gate and

chattering away in a friendly, jocular tone while clutching the
Snowman's elbow in a greasy black claw and forcefully steering
him into an elephant's graveyard of car parts, engines, chasses,
front ends stacked like empty eye-socketed Neanderthal skulls,
piles of tires, racks of gleaming hubcaps, a colony of dislocated
car doors, they're splashing through chocolate milk mud puddles
skinned with thin sheets of ice, tripping over bumpers, grills,
Tommy kicking at snow-covered radiators, rear axles, growling
disdainfully, *goddamn junk*, then fixing him with those mad,
staring eyes—it's a *joke*, Snowman! Of course it's *junk*! Tommy's
bending under the hoods of Chryslers, Plymouths, Fords,
Chevys, Pontiacs, he's urging and cajoling him in a gravelly,
boozy, tobacco-worn voice. What you need, Snowman, is a
vehicular apparatus, a motorized appliance, I mean to say, an
automobile! Hey! smacking his forehead again, completely
stunned, stopped dead in his tracks by the holy throes of another
epiphany. What about that one? Tommy's blasted eyes focus on
a dully gleaming black hull half-buried in a snowdrift like the
wreckage of an alien spaceship, adding to this impression the
tall black tailfins stacked with brake, back-up and parking lights
that do kind of look like the rocket ships in old sci-fi films.
Before the Snowman can say or even think to say, *what, are you
crazy?* Tommy's leading him forward and earnestly purring, Oh,
she runs, Snowman, she runs. She's got a motor in her that'd
power a tank. Love, Snowman, that's the key. A little love, a little
black magic, a quart of elbow grease. Tommy the raconteur, fast
talker, snake oil salesman and back-alley sleight-of-hand magi-
cian, he's on a roll now, he's a card shark warming up his mark,
he's a carney barker beckoning a country bumpkin to his booth,
he's talking and gesticulating and coaxing the Snowman's eyes
past the rough spots, the rust spots, the dings, dents and snicker
doodles crumbled on the dash, not to mention the pattern of
bullet holes like a distant flock of geese winging their way across
the left front quarter panel. But Tommy has a tune for that, too.
A crazy deer hunter, Snowman! It's the last day of the season,

two minutes before sundown, he's got a wife at home, children—sons, Snowman, he's got sons! He's gotta show them he's a man, he's gotta bring home the meat, he's gotta fill their bellies, the old lady's already got the frying pan on the stove, the boys are out back chopping the last quarter-acre of forest into firewood. Our citizen's cold, he's shivering, the sun's just dropping below the horizon, it's past the legal hunting hour now but he doesn't care, it's no longer the noble hunt, the struggle between man and beast, it's outright poaching, it's a violation of some civil code amended to the laws of nature, but he's got the itch now, it's crawling under his skin like a caffeine overdose, he's twitching and blinking, he's trembling so hard he can't even hold the damn gun straight, and there it is, thrashing around in the thicket, a fucking bear! Keee-rrriist, it's a big motherfucker! He opens up on full auto, empties half a clip of steel-jacketed armor-piercing shells into the beast. He approaches his kill, chest heaving, adrenaline flooding his veins, ready to tear out the monster's throat with his unsheathed Bowie knife. Too late he realizes his mistake. But it's nothing, Snowman! Just a flesh wound! It doesn't even pierce the interior. This baby's built like a fucking battleship, Snowman. The previous owner was apparently some kinda safety nut. You could crash head-on into a semi hauling *Icine* and come out as clean as any unbaptized heathen. And the appointments, Snowman! Phone, mini-fridge, kitchen sink. *Kitchen sink?* The whole time Tommy's watching him, gauging him, Tommy the simpleton turned sinister, lynx-like, oozing ninety weight gear oil. Oh, I don't know, Snowman, maybe you're right, maybe she's not the one for you. It takes a unique sort of *in-da-vi-jool* to appreciate a classic like this. Tommy's grabbing him by the elbow again, escorting him toward the Asian market, Hondas, Hyundais, Toyotas, Banzais. But . . . hey, wait, hold on a minute, the Snowman interrupts Tommy's spiel. I wanta take a closer look at that coupe. A closer look! Tommy roars, reeling around in mid-step, his eyes rolling a full revolution in their sockets before stopping at 13 o'clock.

And actually grabbing the Snowman by the collar, he drags him back to this automotive classic, creaks open the heavy black door, slides his lanky frame behind the wheel and, with a conductorly flourish, turns the key in the ignition. The engine coughs, a cloud of black smoke pops out the tailpipe and *va-va-Vooom!* a powerful throbbing roar reverberates in the Snowman's eardrums and chest, suggesting possibilities of both very high speed and acceleration—should one ever need them. How much? Grinning like a fox licking egg yolk from its chin when into the chicken coop struts a big fat hen, Tommy climbs out of this hoary pride of Detroit, feels around in his coveralls, pulls out a TV remote and furiously starts punching buttons. A thousand bucks, Snowman, it's the best I can do. I'll have to think about it, he says. Tommy makes a face like he's suffering acute indigestion. Yeah, sure, think about it, Snowman. The thing is, I got this guy coming by later, see, I think he'll go one-and-a-half Ks. Let's face it, Snowman, it's a fucking classic! It's in demand! I gotta think about business! Go to the Salvation Army if you want a fucking handout! That's the problem with society today, everybody wants something for nothing! Nobody takes no goddamn responsibility! Look at me, Snowman! I built this thriving enterprise with the sweat of my brow and my own two hands. (As well as the proceeds from several profitable years of dealing Ice without getting busted.) The only thing is, he really hadn't planned to drop a thousand bucks right now. But what if someone *was* coming by this afternoon? Tommy kicked a loose distributor cap, sending it tumbling across the snowy yard. Look, Snowman, I'll tell ya what. I'll knock off the cost of registration and plates, and all the special appointments conveyed at no extra charge. And what could he say but okay, I'll take it, at which point Tommy was already leading him back across the yard and up the creaking wooden steps to his office, a small, cramped hut, kind of like a glorified deer stand, but stifling hot from the kerosene stove in the corner as well as the narcotizing smells of several gallons of spilled hydrocarbons, oil, gas,

transmission fluid, antifreeze, etc. that have dangerously satu-
rated this shack over the years, further adding to its combusti-
bility, the walls papered with automotive calendars, big-breasted
women in tiny, cutoff jeans and overflowing polka-dot bikini
tops, the desktop a sprawling landfill of greasy invoices, bills,
business cards, burger wrappers, pill bottles, cigarette packs,
packed ashtrays, a half-empty bottle of whiskey. In the middle
of this firetrap Tommy's trying to light a cigarette and throwing
still-burning matches on the floor while he forages through a
pile of vinyl cleaning fluid-soaked papers, finally extracting a
transfer of title and shoving it at him to sign, which he does
swooning in waves of petroleum fumes. *Snowwwwmannnn.*

Then he was back outside in the cold, keys in hand, still
convinced that the Coupe, uppercase *C* now, really was a beaut
and he really was going to fix it up and take care of all those
little dents and dings and other things that from the very minute
he pulled out of Tommy's junkyard began to nag at the back of
his brain like an incipient toothache, not only that high-pitched
whistle and whine of cold air streaming in through the cracked
side vent, or the heater that came on at its own caprice—just
enough to get his hopes up before it conked out again—and
the lush pile carpet on the floorboards long ago worn away
revealing corroded sheet metal, and the white vinyl seat pocked
with tiny brown volcanic craters from dropped or carelessly
stubbed-out cigarette butts, or that the special appointments
Tommy had mentioned turned out to be: 1) an old black rotary
phone plunked on the dash; 2) the kitchen sink literally a sink
Tommy'd dumped in back and never bothered to dispose of;
and 3) the fridge—a vintage green metal Coleman 54-quart
ice chest, actually in pretty good shape. Even worse the barrels
of gas and oil the Coupe guzzled, spewing half of it back on the
pavement through endless leaks in the gaskets, tubes, cracked
hoses and connectors, the whole creaking, rattling, rusting and
banging cacophony of springs, popping rivets and sheet metal
screws gradually uniting and blending into an almost pleasant

background noise in which his thoughts roamed like a mouse
in a boiler or, in this case, ice factory. He came around a bend
and there it was, an enormous, roaring, clanking, floodlit, black
corrugated metal building, lightning rods, weathervanes, giant
spinning fans, squalls of fluffy, powdery snow flurries blowing under sheet metal doors and out of gill-like louvers, and
towering above it all, the two huge smokestacks gushing great,
semen-like clots of snow. Like a plague-ridden black freighter
washed far inland by an apocryphal tidal wave everyone speaks
of but no one clearly remembers, the ice factory casts a permanent industrial pall over the dreary, impoverished and ironically
named neighborhood of SunnySide sprawled around its base,
an agglomeration of sagging, soot-blackened hovels, shacks and
shanties, although the newly falling snow has already transformed this wretched, festering shithole into one of those starkly
beautiful black-and-white nineteenth-century woodblock prints.
The place reeks so much of downtrodden bathos you can hear
Tiny Tim's faint consumptive cough over the melancholy strains
of a timeworn church hymn. (In fact, here Boone had intended
to introduce a segment of life in the Meekly Mouse family, an
animated dystopia of poor little mousies living in their poor little
housie brazenly copied from trailers for Sid Ney's newest release,
except in Boone's version things never get better, no wealthy
benefactor arrives on the scene, little Timothy Stillwagon doesn't
recover from his tumble down the well, people continue to get
sick and die, or they're horribly maimed in work accidents,
or brutally murdered in the street, or their homes burn down
around them.) Even the once brightly colored murals of ancient
warrior kings and goddesses, blossoming flower gardens, overflowing cornucopias of fresh farm produce and happy looking
barnyard animals painted on the walls of cafes, bakeries, corner
grocery stores and meat markets have faded into drab, decomposing advertisements against themselves.

And then that second or is it third waking when he drives
through the gate, gives an informal salute to the stiff, unsmiling

guard shivering in his little tin-soldier booth, floodlights and security cameras everywhere, coils of razor wire, twelve-foot chain-link fence, over the entrance in stark gray iron, **ARBEIT MACHT WARM**, which, Old Dave once explained in his slow Texas drawl, remained from the original power plant, built and privately owned by an industrious immigrant family. He surveys the latest crop of job seekers hanging off the chain-link fence, their hair runneling like black snakes in the blowing snow, their terra cotta faces ashen from the cold, all dressed in variations of the au courant illegal immigrant costume, blue-and-white New Yorkshire Yaks letter jackets, red cummerbunded tuxedoes, white dinner jackets with black velvet lapels, jodhpurs and riding boots, baggy checkered clown pants and floppy, size twenty-four clown shoes. He's barely turned off the engine and climbed out of the Coupe when—floppy clown shoes, baggy checkered trousers, squirting daisies and polka-dotted bow ties still clinging cartoon-like to the fence—the eager job seekers jump down, dash past the guard and crowd around him, smothering him in a spice-laden simoom of broken English, *Hey Snowman! Lookee me! You gottee work today? You gottee chob?* which sounds, oddly—suspiciously, one may even say—like the Pidgin English spoken by Chinese coolies, cooks and clothes launderers in old movies. How's he supposed to know they're simply recycling phrases from the tattered old classic *Beginning English for Success* phrasebook passed down by successive generations of Native Americans, African slaves, yes, Chinese coolies, Irish cops, Mexican *mojados* and Italian guappos? He's furiously puffing on a cigarette and making every appearance of ignoring these guys as he trudges across the snow-covered parking lot, which, of course, only makes them more insistent, they're clutching at his arms, poking him in the ribs, blows are landing, *You gimme work, Snowman! You gimme goddamn chob!* He struggles up the icy concrete stairs, pries open the heavy metal door, forces it shut against a hydra of flailing arms and legs and jingles down a narrow passageway, iron girders, catwalks overhead, valves and gauges and hissing steam pipes everywhere. He enters the locker room, the cement floor littered with candy and chewing gum wrappers, crumpled Kleenex, crushed cigarette butts, piles of melting snow. An empty tin of mint-flavored smokeless tobacco sits on a wooden bench—Hanktheredneckasshole. His locker door sticks so it always bangs open, resonating each time with adolescent male shouts, laughter, the smell of sweaty gym clothes, tennis shoes shrieking on polished wooden floorboards. At the back of his locker, wrapped in a clear plastic dry cleaner's cover, hangs his long unused Class A dress uniform (midnight blue cotton-polyester jacket and pants, twilight blue shirt and standard issue midnight blue wool sweater with brown leather elbow patches—midnight and twilight blue are the official color codes in the company's thousand-page compendium of rules and regulations). Teeth still chattering from the well-ventilated drive in, he steps into his puffy midnight blue coveralls, pulls the suspenders over his shoulders, shrugs on his bulky midnight blue parka with the kitchen mitt-like gloves dangling from the cuffs. He glances down at the bottom of his locker where his mukluks should be, and then at his black rubber boots, and shakes his head as if reconsidering a hasty decision. He appraises himself in the small, cracked rectangular mirror in the door, applies drops to his eyes from a small plastic bottle *WiteOut®* *gets the red out!* Back out in the hall, he punches his card in the time clock (you'd think they would have updated this thing by now), stops at the coffee counter, dumps sugar substitute and powdered creamer in a Styrofoam cup, infuses it with a stream of steaming black coffee from the commercial-size thermos, burns his tongue tasting it, despite a posted prohibition, lights up yet another cigarette—although didn't you already have one going, *Snowman?* And besides, weren't you going to quit smoking and change your life, change your habits, change into an anchorite subsisting on a diet of brown rice and Spartan denial?

Accompanied by scratchy, mechanical strains of "Have a Holly Jolly Christmas," he enters a large bright reception area, where a patina of hoarfrost covers glass doors, plateglass windows, track-lit walls, the framed photographs of past company presidents, vice presidents, managers, the very first snow crew standing in front of a prototypal SnowBile. In the corner, an aluminum Christmas tree droops beneath dusty gold tinsel and red and green glass balls. A bell rings and a small detonation goes off in the back of his brain, a plosive, hungover little epiphany he experiences at the start of every evening. *Okay, now I'm really here, now it really is time to go to work.* Spilling coffee and dropping cigarette ashes, his clinking, jingling rubber boots depositing crunchy white wedges of snow on the linoleum floor, he approaches the barge-like receptionist's desk behind which sits a small, middle-aged woman, her hair a Brillo pad of wiry black and silver curls, her bright blue eyes birdlike behind the gold-rimmed bifocals perched on her small button nose in her small button face, her slightly hirsute upper lip crimped like a bottle cap, her small mouth pinched in a slight moue anchored at the corners by deep dimples, tonight modeling a taupe ladies office-wear parka with black frog buttons, accessorized with a green plastic sprig of holly on the lapel, the hood fashionably splayed in back to reveal faux ermine lining, Evelyn, the formidable executive secretary, receptionist, radio dispatcher, coffee maker, bookkeeper, goal and gatekeeper, furiously tapping away at a computer screen, the methodical staccato of her high school prize-winning typing skills long ago transformed into the quiet patter of the much more forgiving computer keyboard. In fact, in one of his trademark digressions that drove critics batty, Boone had originally planned to extrapolate Evelyn's life outside the office through a photo gallery of gilt-framed memories accrued over the years on her otherwise impeccably organized desk. The black-and-white Polaroid of a chubby young guy in horn-rimmed glasses, black sideburns and greased back hair, his arm around the shoulder of a rhinestone bespectacled, anxious-looking and clearly pregnant young woman with an outsized bouffant, kind of like a very large chocolate ice cream cone,

in front of a nondescript family sedan. A color photo of the first
baby, a boy, swaddled like a papoose. Then a second, also a boy,
red-faced, screaming, in diapers. Finally the third, a girl this
time, maybe five months old, in a pink bunny suit. These are
followed by a succession of color photos. First grade, sixth grade,
the boys with crew cuts, missing teeth, the girl with blond
braids, pink cats-eye glasses. Then junior high, high school,
proms, yearbooks, graduations, the kids scattered across the
country in colleges and universities that required two incomes
and a second mortgage on the house, in wedding tuxedoes and
gown, the first grandchild, a girl, Evelyn and Fred (was that his
name?) again, Fred bald, overweight, Evelyn—well, this Evelyn
before him, in the final throes of menopause, an enormous soupy
storm of roiling, boiling hormones and frustration she unstint-
ingly applies to the job, endlessly processing spreadsheets, schedules, invoices, time sheets, on top of her stack, the yellow Form
361 accident report he filled out on the sled this morning—in
fact, she's half-rising from her keyboard, blinking at him over
her glasses, imploring him with those bright blue bird's eyes,
flirting with him, commanding him, *Snowman!* Stop tracking
snow all over the clean floor! Somebody's going to fall and break
their neck and it'll be your fault! And what are you doing with
those ridiculous rubber boots? Where are your mukluks? You
know it's company policy! And how many times have I told you
not to smoke in here? Through the glass partition behind Evelyn
he can see Elsie's broad back in an ill-chosen black-and-white
Holstein-pattern office parka. From the movement of her head
and shoulders he guesses she's working her way through her
fourth breakfast taco of the evening while narrating a food-slob-
bering gossip column to her co-worker, Clarisse, whose cubist
arrangement of nose and mouth he finds attractive in a kinky
way, despite the fact that she's also a capitalist fashionista and a
tad skinny even for his tastes, although the swelling of her small
high breasts in her sleek, silver-gray faux sealskin parka does
kind of turn him on, not to mention those large brown,

obscenely commercial puppy dog eyes he briefly and drunkenly gazed into during the last debauchery of a company Christmas party, everybody, all the employees, from the janitors to the clerical staff, snowtechs, accountants, motor mechs, the bevy of secretaries, who, despite advances in gender equality, still occupied the many cubicles jammed like chicken hutches throughout the building, even Evelyn, even *Gastreaux*, drunk, singing corrupted Christmas carols—*God blast ye merry gentilemen*. He came to his senses in a clutch in a corner with Clarisse, saying to himself *Snowman, Snowman, Snowman, what the fuck are you doing, Snowman?* And more prosaically to Clarisse, excuse me, I gotta take a pee, and went out the back door instead, wiping lipstick off his mouth and feeling disgusted with himself even as he wondered what it would have been like to wake up next to Clarisse the following morning. *Snowman! Are you listening to me?* Evelyn, still half-risen over her desk, demanding his attention. By the way, *Snowman* (is it his imagination or does everyone pronounce this sobriquet with a certain irony?), Mister Gastreaux wants to see you ASAP. I don't know what it's about but you better get your behind up there. And he's rolling his eyes and muttering under his breath yeah, yeah, yeah, while sneaking a furtive glance up at the frosty green-glass window of Gastreaux's mezzanine office, picturing the fat, greasy bastard staring down at him, rocking on his heels, cracking his knuckles, can't wait to interrogate this insubordinate shithead *Snowman* over some bullshit citizen's complaint, or, who knows, maybe it's more missing inventory, or he's already heard about the sled. Only thing is, we're not going to oblige the fat sonofabitch, are we Snowman? Avoidance being the better part of valor, right? Listen, I'm in a hurry, I'm behind schedule, I got stuff to take care of. Tell Gastreaux I'll talk to him at the end of my shift. Evelyn scowls, rolls her bright bird's eyes. Okay, *Snowman*, I'll tell him, but you know he ain't gonna like it. And find those damn mukluks! And stop smoking in here! You're killing people! And he's mumbling yeah, yeah, yeah, all right, okay, fumbling with the lint-packed Velcro liner of his parka, and splashing coffee everywhere as he scoops up printouts, invoices, requisition forms and weather tracking data from his in-box when at that very moment a bunch of grinning, jack-o'-lantern faces pop around the corner stacked one on top of the other like a pre-Columbian totem pole, their eyes wide, mouths gaping with childish delight as if to say, Aha! There you are, *Snowman*! We caught you! *Zip!* A faint, liminal trace of their totemic masks hangs in midair as they descend on Evelyn's desk like a tribe of gnomes, dwarves, knotty, muscular, otherworld creatures come up out of labyrinthine caverns in the earth, incongruously dressed in mismatched immigrant haberdashery culled from flea markets, thrift shops, Goodwill and Salvation Army racks, plaid and sharkskin pants, checked shirts, powder blue tuxedoes with ruffled blouses, satin brocaded matador and flamenco outfits, pirate costumes. They're making a big show of scraping their muddy shoes on the carpet. They're tugging at mustaches, doffing golf caps, top hats, fright wigs and sombreros while repeating in that fake Chinese accent, *You gottee chob, nice lady? You gottee work?* And Evelyn's officiously reciting the company's hiring policy while handing out pens, applications—of course it's all in English, these guys don't understand a word, they're blinking and bewildered, they're shrugging their shoulders and making the beseeching hand gestures of exasperated mafia dons. The next instant he finds himself involved in an absurd charade in which he and Evelyn are running around her desk with lampshades on their heads, they're waving letter openers, staplers, bottles of liquid paper, paper clips, paper weights and potted paper whites, they're miming and mimicking in sign language and shouting (as if that helps) in English while leading the prospective employees through a kind of bilingual catechism, You're all here legally?! *Sí! Todos legales!* And you're absolutely certain you all have green cards?! *Sí! Tenemos cartas verdes!* Social security cards?! *Sí, seguridad social!* Drivers' licenses, proofs of insurance, birth certificates, Visas, Mastercards and PhDs?! *Sí, sí, sí, licencias de manejar, prueba de seguro, certificados de nacimiento, cartas verdes, rojas, blancas, cartas de papiro y higiénicas.* They're nodding and gesturing and jabbering in an unintelligible babble that blows through the office like a warm, spicy tradewind. The ceiling is actually dripping. Rivulets of ice water trickle down the walls and windows. The big moment has arrived. Before them lies a vast white landscape covered with indecipherable bird tracks, and all they have to do is make their mark at the bottom and follow these tracks into the greenghost world of big cars, beautiful homes, vault-loads of money. It's like some kind of communion. They're waving the applications in the air like diplomas, proclamations of citizenship, proof of purchase, they're whistling, shouting, howling like coyotes *ai-ai-aiiiee*. And then it's over, the moment passed, nothing more than a little communication gap, certainly no cause for all this hoopla. Amid embarrassed coughs, shuffling feet, they file out stage left and, as if by magic, Evelyn is back in her seat, head bent over her screen. And the Snowman? Rather than follow the labyrinth of overheated halls and corridors along which there is always the danger of an unwelcome encounter with Gastreaux, he heads back down the ship's gangway whence he came, out a rear door and into the maelstrom.

4
The Crew

CLUTCHING A FISTFUL OF FLAPPING papers in front of his face, splashing coffee all over the place, he shuffles *jink jink jink* along an asphalt walkway cobwebbed with blowing snow, that premonition of disaster that precedes the beginning of every night growing as he pushes through a metal door into the relative warmth and narcotic petroleum smells of bay number nine, where a spectral swarm of heat rises from the ancient kerosene stove squatting in the corner like a fiery black hobgoblin, and wakes yet again to another little detonation going off in the back of his brain, another sleep-deprived, hungover epiphany superceding the last little epiphany, trouble with a capital Z for Zolman, or rather *men*, half a dozen of them, slouched like sullen S-hooks against the tires of the SnowBile crouched like an enormous white jumping spider beneath the grimy overhead shop lights. Yeah, sure, they were always so eager to get the damned job when they applied, if he said, look up there, boys, can't you see that old sun a'shining in that big bluebird sky and all them angels are a'singing, and it feels like paradise, they'd tear off their shirts, rub themselves down with tanning lotion, throw their bronze bodies on the snow, and intone in a totally inappropriate shuckin' and jivin' minstrel voice that definitely isn't going to make it past the Cultural Sensitivity Board, *Whooooeee! Sho is hot today, ain't it, Mister Snowman, suh?* Now that they've been hired they watch him from beneath sleepy eyelids, their pupils tiny solar flares of resentment in their hammered bronze faces. They haven't even been issued mukluks and

56

parkas yet. They're wearing street clothes, shirts open, exposing bare chests, hard muscular bellies to show their disdain for the work, for the cold and snow, for the snowmen who make the cold and snow. And that's him, right? Out of all the thousands and possibly even millions of snowmen across the nation, he's *the* fucking Snowman. But that wasn't always true, was it? He wasn't *the* Snowman until the Zolmen arrived on the scene. He didn't even know what a Zolman (or rather *Zoltec*, to be precise) was then. It wasn't until he actually worked with them, talked to them, spent most of his waking hours with them that they began to exist.

In yet another of Boone's heavy-handed transitions, the screen fades to black accompanied by a descending scale on an upright bass to signify we're going back in time as, once again, the Snowman enters bay number nine to find a strange pantomime acted out by a troupe of gnome-like creatures in knee-length midnight blue parkas and knee-high Nanook of the North faux caribou hide mukluks. Carroteeno's nodding and smiling, in fact, almost leering at him with those bright, cunning, slightly oriental eyes in a broad, sweet potato face topped with an incongruous orange mop of hair that actually looks like one of those stringy yarn mopheads. Maybe someone told him it makes him look Irish. Only thing is, he can't get the brogue down, he's muttering some mumbo jumbo that sure doesn't sound like Gaelic much less Spanish and methodically pushing a stiff-bristled broom back and forth across an oil-stained patch of concrete the size of a grave. Little Nico, who has been frantically waltzing his push broom around the bay with a maze-maddened ferret look in his eyes, stops long enough to greet him through a chattering mouthful of too many teeth, *es muy frío, no, Snowman?* before he whirls away again like a dervish. Bombástico, who has probably put on ten pounds since yesterday—his huge bronze belly bursts through the velcrotized bonds of his parka like an enormous butterscotch pudding—is bouncing up and down like a weather balloon with a bladder problem, a wide-eyed *ooh . . . ooh . . . what's-going-to-happen-next?* expression on his big round pumpkin face as he neurotically, methodically consumes the contents of a family-size bag of caramel-coated fried pork skins. Raf-I-el is seated on the floor in a lotus position pretending to levitate even though it's pretty obvious he's just sitting on his heels, his eyes rolled back in his head like crescent moons to demonstrate his contempt for earthly travails, which, with his short henna dreads, makes him look kind of like a yogic voodoo zombie (which, let's be clear, is nothing at all like these stupid, staggering, brain-eating rotten corpses that are all the rage; cf. *White Zombie* (1932), *Revolt of the Zombies* (1936), *I Walked with a Zombie* (1943), etc.). But the really scary one is Xuan Carlode, who looks like a medieval executioner with his pointed parka hood and bare muscular arms locked like tree trunks across his massive chest. In flagrant violation of company policy forbidding modifications to the official uniform, Xuan, whose name the Snowman hears pronounced alternately as Juan, Sean or Shu-ahn, has chopped the sleeves off his parka, which also makes him look a little bit like a pre-Columbian Viking (think about it). Even more unnerving, the red plasticized scars that run vertically down his face, as if a large jungle cat had slashed him. A ten-pound sledgehammer lies conspicuously at his feet. Meeting the Snowman's gaze, Xuan's upper lip curls in a bemused sneer that reveals the blue gleam of a sapphire in a gold front tooth. He reaches down the front of his pants, slowly extracts a large and very scary-looking knife with a gleaming black blade and insouciantly begins to pare his fingernails. (The Snowman will later learn this fierce blade is over a thousand years old, knapped out of obsidian, brittle, not made for prying, but frighteningly sharp. When, also later, Evelyn confides to him that Xuan pulled the same trick with her, little fishhooks tug the corners of her mouth upward into a naughtical smile and she says, I wondered what he had in his pants.)

His eyes shift to the pile of junk Carroteeno and Nico have

been sweeping up, among which he clearly identifies the barrel and trigger mechanism of an ice gun. Aiiee, muchachos,
whot hoppen to thee gon?! he says in a ridiculous accent that
is somehow supposed to convey his meaning in Spanish, even
as he vaguely remembers that before clocking out last night—
this morning—he had instructed *los guys*, as he calls them, to
break down the old ice gun and clean it, which, in his mind
anyway, sounded something like *romper la arma day yellow ee
limp-ee-ar lo*, to which, he also remembers now, said *guys* had
responded with unusual enthusiasm, *Sí, Snowman, vamos a
romperla*. Someone snickers and he whips around but everyone's completely straight-faced, although he can see a tremor
in Xuan's lower lip and Bombástico has this *who, me?* look,
Raf-I-el is surreptitiously peeping through closed eyelashes
and someone Nico?—is whistling *abre, abre, abre* through
his nose. By now he should be used to this but every night's
a shock, he still can't accept that these alien beings are actually here and that by some further accident of time and place
he's responsible for getting them organized and motivated for
work. Depending on how much he drank this morning—last
night—and if he had another fight with Judith, with himself,
with his conscience, soul, whatever it is that constantly nags,
scolds, reminds him, You're wasting your fucking *life*, Snowman,
he enters with clipboard in hand, head down, like he's lost in
thought, so don't anyone bother me now, okay? If, rarely, he's
early, or even on time, and he actually managed to stay relatively
sober and get some decent sleep, he enters loud, laughing, full
of neurotic nicotine and caffeine madness, waving his arms,
shouting orders, chiding *los guys* with the latest in a litany of
complaints from management in a mix of English and badly
mangled textbook Spanish augmented by that absurd accent
which contributes absolutely nothing to anyone's understanding.
Hokay, amigos, *escootcha* me good! No more pee pee in the *boh-
nee-toh* snow, hokay?! No drink *ser-vay-sah* in pooblic, no *ra-sor*
blades, hauntink naïfs or *ma-chet-tays*—hokay?! *Sí! Sí! Machetes!*

Xuan smiles widely in affirmation, the sapphire in his gold tooth
gleaming like a blue dwarf star, the scars down his face shining like war paint. *Final-mentay!* You absolutely must not say
bad teengs to *las muchachas de—en?—las kii-yas* (calles—*Ed.*),
hokay?! But no matter how much he threatens, cajoles, coerces
and exhorts them, they stare at him blankly, their faces bronze
and terra cotta masks of incomprehension, their eyes glazing
over as if he were speaking to them across a vast chasm of space
and time when the first campfires licked at the edge of night
and the smell of cooking meat filled their minds with delirious
visions of God, some god anyway, and something yet to come
called civilization, and now, here it was, speaking right at them
but the only problem was it didn't make any *pinche* sense. Finally
he says in a pretty fair John Wayne voice, Hokay, boys, *cagamos
el kah-meen-yone* (he's pretty sure this means *let's load up the
truck*) and get this sorry-ass show on the road, I need a drink.
To which the guys reply, again with unusual enthusiasm and
a lot of snickering and even a few hand-in-the-armpit farting
sounds—which he doesn't get at all—*Sí, Snowman, lo cagamos*,
followed by a mad scramble as everyone rushes to load ice guns
and hoses on the truck and climb up in the cab (in the official
Operator's Manual, issued back in the days before the snowbiz
was privatized, this is referred to as *mounting* the vehicle, which,
usually good for a laugh among new hires, is lost in translation
with these *caballeros*). Everyone's assiduously buckling seat belts
and scrunching their butts around in the cracked brown vinyl
seat. The Snowman sambas and rumbas his own butt into its
customary place behind the wheel, which reminds him a little of
the sweet spot in a baseball glove, even though the last time he
played baseball he was twelve years old and half a foot of snow
covered the ground, not to mention as reassuring in its familiar-
ity as this simple act is, it also horrifies him when he remembers
he has done this at least three *thousand* times before. He slams
his door shut and is engulfed by an olfactory bombardment

of diesel fumes, petroleum-based lubricants, stale cigarette and marijuana smoke, embedded farts, spilled food, booze, soda and the musty odor of ancient skin magazines mouldering under the front seat. And penetrating those smells, cold, ether-like, *Snowwwmannn*, the insidious creeping smell of Icine, because no matter how perfect, how tight, how hermetic all the seals, gaskets, O-rings, washers, silicon, latex, osmotic and prophylactic measures to prevent any leakage, seepage or otherwise escape of Icine, infinitesimal quantities of this highly volatile (ert?) gas slip free of their molecular shackles and quietly infiltrate the atmosphere of the cab, penetrating every pore, crevice and orifice, whether plastic, vinyl, leather or human. He lights a cigarette, reaches forward and turns the key in the ignition. The engine chugs a couple times and then roars to life, setting in motion a constant underlying vibration in the cab. Again per standard operating procedure, he checks the onboard computer screen, the curb sensors, parked car radars, pending seismic and/ or political event meters, as well as power reserves, hydraulic, electric and pneumatic systems, Icine volume and pressure. It's like an industrial era engine room, a WWI submarine. Glass dials and gauges glow dimly through coats of dust and grime, in some cases partially wiped clean so the vital numbers and data are nominally visible.

And then that next waking, the bay door opening and the headlights' phosphorescence tunneling through the blowing snow and the windshield wipers slapping back and forth as they rumble out of the motor pool, through the factory gate and down the main street of SunnySide. (By the way, for you motorhead guys and gals, the technical specifications of the PeterMackInt M-440 Mobile Snow Dispensing Vehicle—commonly referred to as a Snow Truck by the general public, SnowBile by the crews that operate them—are as follows: converted drum-type cement truck, height 180, length 240, width 120, two-thousand-gallon capacity, 62,000 pounds fully loaded, ten-speed transmission, six 8-foot wheels with independent suspension and drive trains, 650 horsepower hybrid diesel and electric engine, six cubic yard displacement carbon-titanium alloy V-shaped plow blade with front loader conversion capability.)

They turn onto a ramp and enter the crosstown Expressway and here the Snowman belatedly performs another routine task, also per Operator's Manual ("Prior to entering any public thoroughfare, highway, boulevard, avenue, expressway, street, road, lane, etc."): lighting up the arcade, which is SnowBile lingo for turning on the banks of pulsing red, blue and white running lights, blinding orange fore and aft sodium halide fog lights, amber hazard flashers and green and yellow rotating beacons on top of the two-thousand-gallon Icine tank. And while the guys love this moment—everything they pass, other vehicles, bridges, buildings, explodes into a psychedelic light show—it drives him crazy because he doesn't see it as something happening *out there*, he sees it as this great big flashing marquee pointing to something happening inside here. *Him.* His face, his mind, body, life, his desire for solitude, privacy, violated, put on display for the whole world to see. Right here! Dumbass motherfucker! Willing to work twelve hours a day, seven days a week for lousy pay and no benefits! Witness: Here comes the Murphy family, Mom and Pop both exhausted from a full day on the job, from harried, hurried grocery shopping, financial planning, auto repairs, picking up Junior and Missy from daycare, ballet, play dates, pediatric appointments, chess and piano lessons, tutorial sessions, pre-K pre-college interviews, the kids by now thoroughly tired and wired in the back seat from their own pharmaceutically enhanced chock-full-of-nuts daily grind and here comes the SnowBile, bouncing down the highway with all its lights blinking and flashing like a carnival on wheels. Mommy! Daddy! Look! Look! It's the snow truck! A perfect PR opp, right? Camera comes in for a close-up (was there a camera even then?), the Snowman smiles, waves to the kiddos, Hey, there, little folks, it's me, jolly Mister Snowman! Only thing is, Mister Snowman's not feeling particularly jolly this evening. Perpetually beat, hungover, plagued by this ongoing existential crisis bordering on agoraphobic—most of the time he just wants to nail shut the doors and windows of his little hovel and curl up under the bedcovers like a caterpillar in a pile of leaves while civilization crumbles around him. And then, not only to not be able to hide from that world, but instead to be made the ineluctable object of its attention, all those invisible eyes watching him from the anonymity of their glass and steel containers, most likely harboring their own seething resentment toward him, and if not him, certainly the SnowBile, as if it were a sentient beast, the bellowing, wooly mammoth avatar of their misery, the unrepentant purveyor of the unrelenting cold and snow. The irony of his situation, the hypocrisy of theirs, fills him with irrational rage and he snarls, Just wait, motherfuckers, you want snow, you'll get snow. And, wow, it's like he's been appointed chief sorcerer. A huge snow squall immediately, almost magically, begins to blow around them, it's a total whiteout, cars crashing into each other, skidding off the highway. He doesn't give a shit. The SnowBile's about as immune to hazards of the highway as an elephant to a mosquito bite. The great gleaming maul of the plow blade shoves aside mountains of snow and barricades of stalled cars with equal ease. The damn tires have six-inch thick, steel-reinforced treads embedded with titanium spikes for extra traction on snow and ice—which also mercilessly tear up asphalt and concrete and turn the highway into a nightmarish minefield of potholes, adding significantly to the cost of street maintenance and further taxing the nerves of the taxpaying public, which definitely means somebody's making some big bucks somewhere, and it's all thanks to the genius of Roger Wilco, ICIN's top R&D guy, who also came up with the brilliant idea of filling the tires with a colloidal mixture of antifreeze and strawberry Jell-O that makes them impervious to punctures or penetrations of any sort. And, at eight feet in diameter, and with a suspension system like a rocket launch pad, these tires also place the SnowBile's occupants a full story above the rest of traffic, which is how they spot the car upside down in a ditch, its wheels spinning happily, inertially, the driver probably in there with his head split open, blood pouring out like hot transmission fluid. Despite his generally dyspeptic personality, the Snowman keys the mike, says in a practiced radio voice, *KNBC 219, number nine to base*, listens for Evelyn's crisp snippet of nasal sibilance to come back at him, *Yesss, Sssnowman?* and relays the location and pertinent information to her. *Ten-four, Snowman*, she signals confirmation (in the background he hears a lispy refrain of the perennially annoying "All I Want for Christmas is My Two Front Teeth"). He can picture her at her desk, the earnest determination in her bright little bird's eyes, the resoluteness in her slightly tremulous voice, as if she were dispatching a rescue mission to a downed airliner. If the bastard's lucky, his number'll come up in the daily MedCareless lottery, they'll send out an ambulance, and he gets a brief mini-vacation in the hospital while they repair his plumbing, put in new wires, gizmos, gears and a highly durable plastic pelvis. Otherwise the poor schmuck's left to his own resources. Desperate family members down at the morgue bartering for used body parts, negotiating kitchen tabletop surgery with ghoulish Doctor Frankenstein types. At the very least, let's hope the guy's drunk, which will not only anesthetize him against the trauma but get him off the hook with the law, who, at this stage of the game (the national highway system is commonly referred to as the Winter Olympics on wheels) refuse to accept any excuse for reckless driving *except* DUI, a subject that has been on his mind from the moment he got behind the wheel of the SnowBile this evening—not the DUI but a drink. C'mon, Snowman, it's a reward for doing your civic duty. He reaches under the seat, extracts a bottle of tequila from the rabbit warren of garbage, food wrappers, newspapers and porn magazines, deftly unscrews and removes the cap with one hand, takes a stiff belt that sends a ball of fire roaring down his throat, and passes the bottle to

Carroteeno, who has been fumbling with multiple strings of beads and chanting to himself in a low electric hum that definitely does not sound like Spanish. Carroteeno shrugs, gulps tequila as if it were spring water and passes the bottle to Nico sitting shotgun. Nico's been puffing on a crooked brown twist of raw tobacco and neurotically combing his shiny black pompadour into a towering promontory, but now his strangely beaked face—an unfortunate conjoining of prognathic jaws and tomahawk nose—widens into a surprised ferret grin. He takes a quick swallow, makes an exaggerated grimace, blinks furiously, smiles widely again and passes the bottle over his shoulder to Bombástico seated directly behind him. Bombástico, who has probably already put on another two pounds this morning, at this very moment is solemnly, methodically stuffing a soft flour taco as big as a rolled-up throw rug into his mouth. Bombástico squeals as if he's seen the devil himself and bobbles the tequila like a hot potato to Raf-I-el, who, though an avid spiritual practitioner, also believes that temperance means *including* in his diet a wide range of stimulants his more orthodox brethren eschew, and duly takes a righteous swallow before he passes the bottle on to Xuan, whose brutal, scarred face the Snowman can see staring directly back at him in his darkened computer screen, and even more unnerving, he's smiling as if he were contemplating a good meal. At least he isn't carrying a whaling harpoon and wearing a bunch of shrunken heads around his neck. Despite drinks on the house, the level of conviviality remains flatlined and once again the Snowman thinks to himself, What the fuck am I doing here, in this truck, in this world, with these strange people I can barely communicate with? How do you say alien, Margarito? How do you say different? Weird? Beyond my ken? What do you call a world that time forgot? A people and a way of life divided from yours by a wall bricked up over the centuries by language, culture, the color of skin, by abject poverty, ignorance, by the unrelenting heat of the sun?

Arriving at such impasses in the dark canyons of his mind

usually signals it's time for some herbal enhancement, a tradition
dating back to the first snow crew he served on: Old Dave, the
Commander (official title in the OM), a west Texas Buddhist-
bubba who spoke with such a slow drawl he sounded brain-damaged, until you realized he was quoting from Herodotus or
Tacitus or Pliny the Elder, Hanktheredneckasshole—his name
says it all but to give you a clearer picture, he's this scrawny,
skinny (he kind of looks like a ruined twelve-year-old kid),
devious, lying, thieving (the Snowman's pretty sure Hank's the
one who walked off with his wristwatch, a high school gradu-
ation present and the only personal, portable timepiece he has
ever owned), a hardcore alcoholic with an abused wife and two
or three undernourished kids at home (so the story goes), Jipi
Jaime, the ponytailed space cadet, antique smoked sunglasses,
D'Artagnan mustache and soul patch (the company's unofficial
pharmacologist, he carries a modest drug store of bottles, phi-
als and ampules under his parka), M'Shaka N'Baka, this big
black dude, dreads halfway down his back, thick black beard,
apparently served several tours in that endless hellhole of a war
in that unpronounceable shithole of a country, which probably
explained his tendency to sit as silent and aloof as one of those
giant Easter Island heads, and of course, him, the not-yet-but-
soon-to-be anointed *Snowman*, also playing his cards close to
his chest in this unfamiliar element—ah, but pot, the common denominator, they weren't even out of the factory gate and
everyone was rolling up joints, spliffs, fucking industrial-sized
marijuana smokestacks, everybody laughing and talking manic
stoned bullshit and the hell with the lone Mexican guy smiling like a frog in a snake den because, completely excluded by
the icy tongue, he has no fucking idea what anyone's saying,
which is probably best for international diplomacy considering
Hank's almost nonstop redneck *bons mots*, Hey, Pedro, don't
get the seat wet, okay? Hey, Pedro, you no get paid for siesta,
okay? Now the crew's all Mexican (or rather, *Zoltec*, a distinction he still isn't clear on), and he's the one who feels excluded,

and if he smokes dope he feels even more alienated, not that *los guys* frown on cannabis usage, *au contraire*. The first night they came on board, he lit up a spliff, offered it all around, I mean, what pothead in his right mind could refuse, right? This stuff's supposed to be primo. Grown in one of the many secret grow houses around the city, reputedly run by a venerable old Vietnamese immigrant, a genius of marijuana cultivation, he won one war, now he's winning another. But not only did the guys express no interest, they shook their heads in disgust. Oops, major faux pas, right? He's probably violated all kinds of cultural and religious beliefs, offended their sense of decency and, in a nutshell, essentially accused them of criminal drug abuse. About thirty seconds of awkward silence passed and then a sweet, spicy aroma, like a cross between grandma's fresh baked apple pie and grandpa's pipe tobacco, filled his nostrils and Raf-I-el handed a huge smoldering spliff over the seat. He remembered nothing of the next several minutes except that *los guys* seemed to be engaged in a fairly animated conversation and yet no sound came out of their mouths. Instead they exhaled clouds of smoke or steam, like cartoon word balloons without any words in them, and—maybe it was the light—they looked like they were wearing elaborate headdresses decorated with feathers, jade, colored twists of cloth. Other than lapses like this, however, usually they sat silent, brooding like warriors preparing themselves for battle, or, rarely, laughed and cackled among themselves like grackles and of course he just knew they were talking about him. Occasionally he caught words or even entire phrases in Spanish and strung them together into alternate sentences that most likely bore little resemblance to their original. *When the moon at night is big and bright and the snow is on the cactus?* What the heck's that mean? Wait—did Nico say *película*? That's *movie*, right? That was something he could talk about. He'd seen plenty of movies. But by the time he patched together a tattered fabric of words and syntax that barely made sense in his own mind, and even had the temerity to interrupt the guys' conversation with this vital commentary, he was already five minutes behind the current topic and the guys were scratching their heads in puzzlement. Was he talking to us? Come on, Snowman, out with it. What did you want to say? On even rarer occasions, his tongue loosened by weed, he'd forget he didn't know how to speak Spanish and just start saying anything that came into his head, the guys'd forget too, they'd start talking back at him and for a moment it clicked, they were actually communicating with each other. Then he'd realize and they'd realize. They'd look at each other out of the corners of their eyes, like, hey, was that the Snowman talking just then? Then that great wall of silence was up again, that great Paleolithic bridge arching across continents of time and space. What if he actually spoke their language, understood all the nuances, innuendoes, puns, jokes, tropes, word play, double entendres and hidden meanings, would everything they said and did, their whole way of life and being, suddenly become perfectly pellucid to him and conversely his world to them, not just the simple naming of things, *árbol*— tree, *puerco*—pig (*Puerqui* Pig?), but the ability to convert snowdrifts, bobsleds, sleigh bells and icicles hanging from the eaves of candlelit Currier and Ives Christmas cottages into desert, cactus, sombreros and adobe and back again? He'd erupt out of the labyrinths of his own thoughts, demanding, Hey Nico, how do you say *gnat, nitpick, nothing*? Hey Bombástico, how do you say *Porterhouse steak, prime ribs, pork chops*? Hey Xuan, how do you say *murder, mayhem, mass destruction*? Hey Carroteeno, how do you say *porridge, panda, hockey puck*? Hey Raf-I-el, how do you say *trippin', cosmic, out there*? Hey anyone, how do you say *crowbar, crescent wrench, platypus, marmoset, magneto*? To which the guys invariably shrugged, *Quién sabe*, Snowman? *Pregúntale a Dios. Tal vez Él sabe.* (Who knows, *Snowman*? Go ask God. Maybe He knows—*Ed.*) Followed by a determined silence. How do you say *boring*? *dull*? *disinterested*?

One night he was adjusting a valve on the compressor, snow blowing around him, grit in his eyes. He yelled for someone to get him an *araña*. A crescent wrench appeared at his side and a soft, throaty voice said in heavily accented but otherwise perfectly good English, *here ees a rrrench, what deed you want the espider for?* He turned and found himself staring into a pair of mocking brown eyes in a smooth, youthful face alloyed out of bronze, copper, terra cotta. The soft, full lips pendent beneath the bristly black mustache like pieces of exotic fruit were curled in a bemused smile. It was a familiar face, possibly even a famous face, a face that made his own traitorous face collapse into a goofy, rubbery grin like a bashful adolescent boy who's just bumped head-on into his super high school crush. He barely suppressed an urge to say something stupid like, Hi! Are you the new guy on our team? I'm so excited to meet you! Embarrassed, he looked away, made a pretense of extracting some large obstruction from his eye, like a log or a camel, and in the same moment remembered that only recently Nico had approached him, shuffling, shivering, rubbing his hands together and blowing into his fists, his eyes darting about like feral creatures and that sidelong ferret grin on his face as he launched into a rambling spiel. (As mentioned earlier, subtitles being abhorrent to the American film audience, speech in Spanish is represented by a horrendously fake Spanish accent—*Ed.*) Whooeee! Ees colder'n a weech's teet, no, Snowman? We gottee mucho trabajo tonight, no, Snowman? Ayyy, my back ees horting me too much, do you know ees there some kind of medeceen, Snowman? By the way, Snowman, you gottee chob for mi amigo, Margarito? He ees one very smart chocolate cheep cookie, Snowman. (Was it Nico who first identified him as *the* Snowman?) He also remembered now the twinkle in Evelyn's eye when she said, oh, Margarito, the *handsome* one. But—*Margarito*? What kind of name was that?

Nevertheless, suddenly he had a translator, interpreter. Everything he had tried to say before, all his inarticulate gesticulations, all his futile explanations, all his unheeded commands were apprehended in an eye blink. He ordered the guys to load up the SnowBile and prepare for departure and his words passed through Margarito like an icicle through a coal furnace. Two seconds later the SnowBile was ready to go and the guys were strapped in their seats like eager kindergarteners. Even better, Margarito seemed amused by his "how-do-you-say?" game. They'd barely left the Ice Factory and he was already shouting over the engine, How do you say *house, cat, stove*? How do you say *hand, foot, nose*? His eyes incautiously leaving the road to focus on the position of Margarito's lips and tongue (both, he noticed, pink and healthy, unlike his own crusty *labios* and fuzzy, cottage cheese-coated *lengua*) as he pronounced each word, then struggling to repeat the words himself, to reconstruct the sound and the meaning of the sound until they burst from his mouth in a plosive fusion of understanding, of course! *Casa, gato, horno! Mano, pié, nariz!* And then the confirmation, Margarito's face glowing like a terra cotta sunburst of surprise and delight, Tú sabes, Snowman! You said eet right! And just like that—this gap bridged? this bond established? this intimacy, understanding, camaraderie between himself and Margarito? Margarito always so enthusiastic, so encouraging. How do you say *one, two, three, four*, Margarito? How do you say *east, west, south . . . north*? Who would have guessed that a single word could unlock so many doors, a word that, on one hand, simply indicated a cardinal direction on the map, but, on the other, brought to mind Jack London vastnesses of frozen whiteness.

5
Crossing the River

EL NORTE! THAT WAS THE DREAM, Snowman. Margarito placed the bottle of brandy back on the table. He heard it from the time he was born, from the time he was first able to distinguish one word from another. He heard it in the adult conversation babbling over his head like a brook, he heard it echoing in church in the louvered shadows of the confessional smelling of wood polish, cologne, cheap perfume, disinfectant, urine, incontinent old ladies weeping, seeping, confessing their anger and hatred at husbands' long ago infidelities, ungrateful grandchildren, a merciless god, on the feverish lips of the young parish priest Father O'Jalajan himself, in that hurried whisper, more conspiracy than chastisement, *el Norte es,* my son, go, seek your salvation, God will protect you—*I hope.* In the cantina late at night the drunks passed out at their tables slurring a single word from a song on the jukebox sung in a golden tenor voice both plangent and ecstatic *el Nor-tayyyyy.* The women passed the word among themselves in the market, taught the word to their daughters while they sewed and cooked and tilled the tiny plot of rocky soil behind their homes into a tortured patch of green. *El Norte es, mija.* In the bakery where they sold *bolillos* and sugar cookies for ten pesos a sack the word was leavened, fattened and sweetened with yeast, lard and sugar, kneaded, rolled and baked in the hot oven into a thing to fill the hunger that gnawed at his stomach when he lay down on the floor among his brothers and sisters at night. *El Norte.* It was a breath of cold winter freshness after every fiery bowl of red-hot chiles, beans and tortillas mama put on the table for dinner. *El Norte*. Working, playing, making love, the ice and snow crept into their words, their thoughts. *El Norte*. At night they looked up at the stars blasting out of the sky and the vast, shimmering draperies of blue and green and red in the north. (It's worth noting that Boone's twelve-year-old niece, Dawn, put together the faux aurora borealis in about five minutes on her EyePhone®—*Ed*.) When he was still a child he thought it must take great wealth or the magic of a very power-ful brewhag to go to the north. Of course he didn't know then that the passage was much more mundane. You simply bought a ticket on the coyotl express. The train leaves at midnight. Sometimes it's late. Sometimes it never arrives. Sometimes the train pulls into the station with a boxcar of dead Mexicans. Somebody forgot they were in there. Maybe they didn't forget. The train dropped the car off on a desert siding. The sun beat down on the metal roof. At first the men laughed, nervous. Then they began to worry as the vital liquids slowly drained from their bodies and the temperature inside rose to one hundred, one hundred ten, one hundred twenty degrees. Their eyes filled with terror, they cried out to God, they tore at the hot metal with their bare hands until their fingers bled. It was futile, the hot air filled their lungs, sucked away their oxygen, they couldn't breathe, they sank into lizard-like lassitude, their bodies dry and clammy, a last ditch effort to conserve precious resources, to shut down all but the most vital functions, in their diminishing sentience they thought of their loved ones back home, prayed to God, please let me see Mama's and Papa's faces one last time and tell them I love them. Or, who knows, maybe it wasn't in the desert. Maybe it was in the mountains. The train jerked to a halt on a siding, followed by another jolt and then the sound of the engine gaining momentum as it chugged away. They waited, nothing happened, no one came. One of them tried the door, it was locked. A draft of bitter cold air poured in through a hole in the floor. The metal siding of the boxcar turned to ice, they started to shiver, it was so cold, they couldn't stop shivering, they huddled together to keep warm, but one by one they felt the warmth slide out of the man next to them, his body turned cold and stiff, and they knew he was dead but it didn't matter as long as they lived. Someone lit a match to a small pile of straw on the floor of the boxcar, but there was nowhere for the smoke to escape, they were coughing, choking, tears streamed from their eyes, the boxcar had been used to carry nitrates, the salt had penetrated the wooden floorboards, then the explosion. But those are just stories, the ones who didn't make it, somebody's brother, cousin, nephew, father, son, but there are lots of others who do make it, they get good jobs, earn a lot of money, they buy houses, send their children to school, support their families back home. Listen, *mijo, el Norte* is calling you. Go, my son, to the north.

Then the camera was swooping over rugged mountain passes and cactus-strewn valleys washed in powdery white moonlight on the wings of an eagle, on the belly of a drone following a battered, tarp-covered, blue pickup as it bounced and banged over a rutted dirt road, rattling the spines and pummeling the kidneys of the dozen men slumped against each other on the metal bed, their legs and arms carelessly entangled like those of lovers or callously discarded corpses, snoring and farting obliviously in their sleep, exhausted by the trip through the interior in hot cramped buses, on top of lurching, screeching trains, while deep in the marrow of their bones, in the blood pulsing through their veins, in the never-sleeping part of their brain, that biological data processor ticked away, culling shards of information from a constantly fluctuating matrix—time of night, temperature, humidity, the chance of much-needed rain tomorrow or, more likely, another brutally hot day—although that was all going to change soon, their body gauges and instruments knocked out of whack by an onslaught of alien data from the world they were about to enter.

While the other men slept, Margarito sat rigid, upright, staring at a point in the darkness where, a moment ago, a match had flared, followed by the glow of a cigarette, the smell of tobacco. The cigarette glowed again, long enough for him to glimpse a leathery face, hook nose, a single bright eye aimed directly at him, the other dark, as if covered by a patch. Suddenly his fifteen-year-old body was too big, it took up too much space. If only he could make himself less visible, shrink back into the body of a little boy who could cry out Mama! I'm scared! There's a bad man! And get what in return? Consolation? Reassurance? Of what? The certainty of death? The mercilessness of life? He tugged at the necklace of dried field corn and a rattlesnake tail the brewhag gave him.

Someone coughed. The men stirred around him. Details began to emerge in the spreading light. The canvas strap next to his face, a boot pressed against his ribs. He forced his head to turn, to confront this man who had kept him awake all night with such fear. The man stared back at him, a paunchy, middle-aged, beat-up donkey, the patch he'd imagined over one eye just a shadow. Relieved, but angry at his own fear, he snarled like a vicious little mutt, What are you staring at, *viejo*? The man didn't blink or look away. He said, *You*. I was staring at you, *mijo*. Why? What about me? Margarito demanded. The man shrugged. I was wondering what will happen when the border patrol catches you. Will you wet your pants? Will you fall on your knees weeping like a little girl and name all the names of those who crossed with you? You think it's easy, don't you? You'll make it across, get a good job, earn a lot of money? Margarito shrugged. He wasn't going to work for free. No, not for free, the man agreed, but almost free. Yes, you will make more money than you could in Mexico, but still less than the least of all greenghosts, less than it costs to buy rice and beans and tortillas and pay the rent and maybe even send something home to your family. But don't say anything, not a word. If you protest, you'll be lucky if they only fire you. Just shut up, work hard, endure the hatred, the contempt. But if it's so bad why are you going back? Margarito asked. The man scoffed. Someone has to show the greenghosts how a real man works.

Margarito raised his glass. That man may have been a beat-up donkey, *Snowman*, but he was a real man after all. And still I hated him, because he made me afraid.

The truck stopped on a bank above the river and the men climbed out. Another man was supposed to be waiting for them with a rubber raft but there was no one. The men demanded their money back from the pickup driver but he pointed a gun at them and drove off. Most of the men turned and started to walk back the way they had come. A few ran down the riverbank, pulled off their clothes, stuffed them into plastic garbage bags and waded into the water. Margarito followed their example. The warm black muck sucked at his feet. The stench of sewage and chemicals rose around him. A snake undulated toward him through the tall reeds. He'd never learned how to swim, never been near enough water to learn how to swim. He pushed his plastic bag of belongings before him and began to kick with his feet. Halfway across, the dark water turned colder. The cold penetrated his arms and legs, he felt his *huevos* shrink into a hard little package (a funny, embarrassed smile). Chunks of ice floated past. Suddenly the water was breathtakingly cold. He started to panic. He couldn't breathe, the current was pulling him under. His body felt heavy, fatigued, he didn't want to struggle anymore. Somehow he kept going. Ahead of him the water turned into blue-black undulations of ice. He had to break through it with his bare hands. Naked, gasping for breath, he dragged himself out of the water into knee-deep snow. Half a mile down the river he saw a dark form break through the thin ice and climb ashore. There was no sign of the others. By now he was shivering violently. He had to move, get his blood flowing or freeze to death. He fumbled his clothes out of the plastic bag. Fortunately they were dry and had even retained some of his body warmth and he quickly pulled them on, as well as the sweater, hoodie, jacket and gloves he had been encouraged to buy, then stumbled up the riverbank through the deep snow. A metal wall approximately twenty feet tall and topped with razor wire stood before him. Black, impassive, impassable, it stretched into infinity in the east and in the west. A network of cameras, infrared sensors, drones, helicopters, aerostat radar and satellites observed every square inch of this barrier and environs. The chances of getting through undetected—of getting through at all—were nearly zero. And yet it happened. Somebody looked away from the screen, someone misinterpreted a signal, the power went down, fire ants chewed through a cable. Miraculously, he found the small hole he'd been advised of at the base of the wall and squeezed through. On the other side a vast barren whiteness lay ahead of him. He began to walk. He trudged across snow-blown desert, forced his way through waist-deep snowdrifts, miles of dense, ice-coated nival scrub brush, watching for the mutant snow serpents and ice scorpions he'd heard of. He stared up at the brilliant sun overhead and wondered how it could be so cold. Sometimes he encountered menthol-blue pools of ice from a long ago thaw. He continually searched the blinding white seam of horizon for the flash of binoculars or a gun scope. Once he heard a faint whirring overhead and, suspecting a drone, buried himself in a snowdrift. Another time he watched a jet airplane streak across the vast blue sky like a silver needle, dense white contrails shooting out behind it like strands of cotton yarn. He imagined the jet full of greenghosts, eating warm food, drinking hot beverages, playing games, staring at screens. What if one of them happened to look down thirty thousand feet below and spot the tiny figure moving across the vast frozen whiteness like Frankenstein's monster? Would he point him out to his neighbor. Look, down there, it's a man, maybe he's lost, he needs help. Should we tell the flight attendant? His legs felt heavy, numb, like logs. He ordered them to move but his own words seemed to come from a distant place in his brain. He wanted to lie down in the snow and sleep but he knew he'd never wake again. He trudged onward. He didn't care anymore if the border patrol caught him, if they beat and interrogated him and sent him back across the border in a cage. He swore that if he survived he'd never be so foolish again, never question his destiny. His boots struck something hard. He had stumbled onto a narrow, snow-blown blacktop. He started to walk. He didn't hear the car until it crunched to a stop next to him. He turned and saw the star on the door and the red and blue lights on the roof. The window went down and the sheriff said in Spanish *vámonos.* The sheriff poured hot coffee for him from a thermos and gave him a sandwich. The warmth in the car was like a soft wool blanket he wrapped himself in. He fell asleep with the sandwich in his hands and woke in a small town. The sheriff let him out in front of a convenience store. They don't pay me to arrest *mojados.* He went inside and asked for water. The man said in Spanish, *Solamente agua, nada más?* He woke lying on a cot. A woman leaned over him, spooning hot, spicy soup into his mouth. When she saw that his eyes were open she only said, *Dios mío.* He stayed with them three days. They gave him food, warm clothes, and drove him another thirty miles north to a large town.

The car had barely pulled away when a gang of greenghosts, kids his age, started harassing him. He picked up a chunk of ice and drew back his arm as if to throw it at them. The guys ducked and he turned and ran. He found his way to the rail yard and caught a slow-moving freight train. Huddled in the corner of a boxcar, he shivered and occasionally drifted into restless sleep while the train clanked and clattered another two hundred miles further north to the fabled city of Osberg. He had been given a street address. The same day he arrived he had a place to stay, in a room with six other men. Soon after he found a job in a restaurant washing dishes, and then another job at a health spa, first mopping floors and then as an attendant. Everyone liked him—the other employees, the customers. He was handsome, charming. His English improved quickly. His salary too. He was even planning to go to school. Then the economy faltered, followed by another crackdown on illegals. He returned to Mexico. But even as he crossed the border he was looking back over his shoulder toward *el Norte*.

6
The Job

ON A SMALL PLATEAU ABOVE Loop 360 the Arctics and the IceBergs are facing off in the Osberg Memorial Stadium's inaugural event. This is the city's obsession with ice hockey at its peak. The parking lot's packed, every seat sold out, the crowd's excitement palpable even outside the great coliseum, the fans' stomping and shouting so loud the stadium actually seems to be expanding and contracting like a giant pressure cooker. The Snowman can feel this deep throb in his chest even shut up inside the roaring SnowBile. Into this pagan clamor seeps the eerie, ethereal harmony of pipe organs, choirs of angels. On a hill on the opposite side of the highway, The Church Of Jesus Christ Warrior-Redeemer's great cathedral spirals into the dark heavens like a giant conch shell, at its pinnacle a towering solid gold cross illuminated from below by a dozen five-thousand-watt carbon arc spotlights. The undulating asphalted terrain around this holy bastion is aswarm with thousands of shiny, beetle-hulled, snow-dusted cars. The town seems equally divided between the two forums tonight, the legions of loyal ice hockey fans, and the multitudes of faithful who have braved the highway's icy terrors to hear the great oracle of God, the Right Reverend K. James Fallible, proclaim unto them the promise of eternal abundance here on earth as it is in heaven. The good reverend's in his dressing room right now, a cadre of minions primping, pomading and perfuming. A tortoiseshell comb slides through the golden waves of hair, the head is gently tilted back so drops can be administered to make those ol' blue eyes sparkle, the golden tan radiates the health and vitality of a South Pacific islander. A final dusting of skin toner, an invisible mouse-whisker of lint plucked from his powder-blue lapel. The time is here, his moment arrived. He strides out of his dressing room, down the short hall, up the stairs, stage left, the curtain rises, applause signs flash, the announcer's voice, *Laaaadies ann- nnd gennntlemennn*, the Reverend! K! JAMES!! FALLIBLE!!! YAYYYYYYY!!! A pipe organ the size of a small cruise ship and a thousand-voice choir combine in an eerie angelic roar projected into the night sky for miles around by mammoth loudspeakers. Heavenly strains resonate in the ears of crew Number Nine as they roll down the exit ramp to the *très* tony SilverSpoon district ablaze with lights, holiday decorations, ultra chic shops, restau- rants, boutiques, high-end department stores and boxy, color- ful condos stacked like children's building blocks. On Western Avenue they pull up to a one-third scale marble reproduction of the Brandenburg Gate, floodlights, razor wire, security cam- eras perched like ever-watchful owls. A pair of heavily armed guards exhaling frosty cartoon balloons and stamping tall black jackboots waves him through. He flips on his console screen. A network of cul-de-sacs radiates outward like spider legs. First on tonight's agenda, Canyon Drive. The SnowBile's stained glass kaleidoscope of flashing lights crashes against Tudor, Tuscan, Georgian, Greek Revival, Victorian, none of which have any- thing to do with each other, this climate, terrain or part of the world. *The . . . ghetto . . . of . . . the . . . rich*, Old Dave called it. Further highlighting the incongruity of all this, many homes now sport the latest miracle of nival horticulture (plants that grow in or under snow—*Ed.*). Birds of paradise, plumeria, poin- ciana, bougainvillea, all in startling neon orange, purple, red and yellow, emerge from the snow like a ski slope fashion parade.

It's simple, Snowman. Through particle bombardment, research- ers are able to transfer specific genes from one species (in this case soil bacterium) to another (horticultural plants). Genetically altered plants are resistant to disease, as well as temperature extremes, both hot and cold. By adding to the mix chloroplastic polymers grown from Arctic Sea-ice algae and the stem cells of whale blubber, tropical flowers can survive and even thrive in extremely cold climates. Prohibitively expensive, of course, like everything out here in these gated burbs.

To highlight this point, Boone insists on a ridiculously surreal minstrel skit bound to offend everyone, with Nico and Raf-I-el in blackface but speaking with a heavily nasal Mexican accent that sounds like dueling chainsaws: Hey Raf, how much *dozz eeet* cost to *leeeve* here? For you, *Neeeco*? Another lifetime and a change of *skeeen*. But *theeese* pretty snow lilies like us *geeengerbread* men. We got soul. *Ayyy, Neeeco*, you are talking about los *Neeegros*, like *EeeM'Shaka*. We're hot-blooded, remember? That's what I'm *sayeeeng*! *Theeese* cute little snowdrops gonna like my red-hot *cheeeluy*. Forget *eeet, Neeeco*. Your *cheeelay* ain't *driveeeng* a Maserati. Hey Raf, did you hear about the Mexican guy who joined the NFL? Yeah, they got a new position—wet back. *Booooo*.

Against this background chatter, the Snowman presses a bright red *ARM* button glowing on the dash like a ripe cherry and in a tone that has morphed from genuine schoolboy enthusiasm when he first took *command* of Number Nine about ten or eleven years ago into sardonic battle cry, he mutters *yee-haw* under his breath and squeezes the trigger on the gearshift—and this moment the guys almost seem to hold holy, a complete silence overcomes them, and they stare with wide-eyed fascination as the port and starboard deck cannons begin to shoot out huge, loopy ropes of white latex-like substance that immediately fluffs up into great woolly blankets of snow and floats to earth, burying fire hydrants, stop signs, bare brown front yards, Culture Commission-approved Seasonal Holiday Trees, sleds, skates and hockey sticks carelessly left in driveways, poor shivering little yappy mutts forgotten on front doorsteps. The SnowBile screeches to a halt at the end of the cul-de-sac in front of a classic Cape Cod (dormers, shutters, shake shingle, clapboard, etc.). The guys *dismount* pulling up hoods, adjusting bulging bluebottle-fly night goggles, tuning mikes—of course they immediately have to start acting like a bunch of children, making farting noises, whistling and heckling each other. Heyyy Bombástico! Sí, Nico? I got a Creesmass carol for you, Bombástico! *Cheengalay, cheengalay, cheengalay cabrón!* Ooh, Nico, that is not a nice thing to say! In their midnight blue parkas and pointed hoods, they look like brethren of an esoteric religious order, like giant lawn dwarves. When the Snowman was a kid, he and his friends believed the snowmen were giant smurfs. Parents had zero discipline problems. *If you insist on whining like that, Johnny, I'll let the smurfs in.* (By the way, it should be mentioned that both the coveralls and parka are constructed of a lightweight hemp fiber and duck down synthetic, 1/2" of perfect climate controlled blue-collar comfort, yet another ingenious byproduct of the defense industry's R&D, so don't give those guys a hard time—*Ed.*) (It's . . . kind . . . of . . . like . . . walking . . . around . . . in . . . an . . . inflatable . . . igloo—*Old Dave.*)

The wind has picked up. Snow flurries blow around them. *Now, now, now it really is time to work.* He's not sure if he said that aloud or only thought it. The guys unrack guns and roll out hoses, tighten down connectors and adjust valves. He pushes a button and the compressor coughs and chugs into a steady roar. Through his night goggles' blue lenses, the snow is a pale, luminous blue, a red car looks cobalt, dark objects appear purple or black, kind of like black-and-white TV. He watches Xuan, Bombástico and Carroteeno shuffle up the walk with the bazookas, dragging behind them cherry red high compression hoses like industrial-sized IV lines. Xuan raises his bazooka, his massive bronze biceps knot like ships' hawsers and, totally impervious to the cold, he sends out a big bloopy white ovoid that expands like a parasail and completely buries a Mercedes sedan. He launches another ovoid over the front porch, inundating stairs and railings in white cotton fabric. Each time Xuan fires, his shoulder jerks backward. The bazooka's kick is frequently compared to a twelve-gauge shotgun's. The Snowman has never fired a shotgun of any gauge so he doesn't know, but after his first night with this blunderbuss, his shoulder felt like it'd been pounded with a sledgehammer. He was soaking in a hot bath, a glass of whiskey on the edge of the tub, cigarette smoldering in an ashtray when Judith clomped in in her shaggy yak skin clogs, waves of raven black hair tumbling around her white thermal top. She pulled down her bottoms, sat on the toilet to pee, yawned widely, the cobalt blue gleam of her sleep-slitted eyes slid over him like laser beams. Oh my god! she gasped, momentarily scaring him senseless. Like, what, am I bleeding? Did I grow a penis in the middle of my forehead? Then he noticed the massive purple-and-yellow bruise covering his right shoulder like a monstrously botched rose tattoo. After a while the pounding became normal. He learned to meld plastic and metal alloy with muscle and bone until he didn't feel the kick anymore. Bombástico, who also seems indifferent to the cold, has the butt of his bazooka lodged against his huge bronze sumo-Buddha belly and casually fires off rounds one-handed while munching on a pillow-sized soft taco. Carroteeno, stolid, methodical, a campesino to the bone, fires his bazooka as if he were lobbing potatoes to a herd of swine. After all, they're just doing basic grunt work, covering large areas the deck cannons have missed. It's up to the Snowman, Nico and Raf-I-el, wearing three-gallon backpacks and carrying torches, to take care of the fancy stuff. He raises his torch, squeezes the trigger and pukes out a splat of yogurt that fluffs up and falls to the ground like damp cotton batting. He fiddles with his nozzle, tightens the spray into a hissing white stream and begins to sculpt lacy filigree and arabesques under eaves and over windows in the front of the house while Nico and Raf-I-el work their way around back. Five minutes—ten tops— and the house looks like a crystal palace in a children's fairytale. A final touch here and there and they back down the drive spraying over their tracks and leaving behind a pristine winter wonderland to greet the happy homeowners first thing in the morning, courtesy of the Snowman and his band of merry elves. *It's beginning to look a lot like Christmas.* They repeat this process at one residence after another, the SnowBile making a plaintive *bee bee bee* sound each time the Snowman jumps up in the cab and backs another fifty yards up the street, taking advantage of these mini-breaks for a couple furious drags on a cigarette and another blast of psalt *yeowwww!* and, sure, why not half a cup of hot coffee and maybe another gulp of tequila and, oh yeah, that's good, that hit the spot, he's starting to warm up now, he's getting in the groove, he's right on the cusp of that synaptic leap, one second all his thoughts and energy are totally focused on shooting out this perfect stream of frozen white cursive and the next second he's in the zone and the whole snowmaking business goes on automatic pilot and the world outside disappears while his thoughts plunge like a bathysphere into the oceanic depths.

The smell of snow reminds him of damp laundry, aluminum ice trays in frosty refrigerator freezers—he's thinking of his grandmother's now, which invites further, sometimes conflicting images, tubs of ice cream, a quiet green farm pond beneath a spreading willow tree, the blood-red meat of a ripe watermelon, a chicken running around with its head cut off.

The snow makes a sort of ticking sound as it sifts down from the sky, the sound of the individual snowflakes, rigid, crystalline, not soft at all, colliding with each other.

There are people in arctic climes who are said to have over a hundred different words for snow, each with its own particular connotation, from the shades of whiteness (or blueness), degree of wetness or dryness, the texture, whether soft- or hard-packed, whether too treacherous to travel or easily traversed on skis or snowshoes. There is granular and slush, frozen and refrozen, neve and firn, graupel, corn and crud. There are also types of snow-flakes, the classic stars and dendrites, the more prosaic prisms, plates, triangles and rosettes. And of course there is every skier's delight, champagne powder.

He learned all the names for snow one bitterly cold night early in his career when Jipi Jaime gave him a hit of acid by accident. (Or not. He remembered Jaime said, Try this, it'll give you a little buzz for an hour or two. Wrong. Whatever the fuck it was, he walked the plank and dove right into Scylla and Charybdis, after which Jaime hemmed and hawed and muttered something about the wrong pills.) One minute he was diligently icing up a front porch with the torch, the next he was unraveling skeins of white satin into the velvet blackness of night. He felt like a celestial interior decorator hanging draperies from the high heavens. He felt like a symphony conductor leading an orchestra through a John Cage production that had to be seen to be believed. He felt like a mad genius physicist composing an elaborate mathematical equation that explained the origin of existence. He pondered for what seemed hours the impossibly unique and never again repeated architectonics of a single snow-flake as it lazily drifted to earth among an incalculable mass of extraordinarily similar but equally unique crystalline structures.

The real ones, anyway. That's how you can tell 'em apart. Icine, every single flake's exactly alike, billions and trillions, *centillions* of snowflakes exactly the same, perfect little gothic ice cathedrals that interlock with all the other cathedrals into this contradictorily soft, fluffy blanket of snow.

He didn't realize he had been babbling aloud until Old Dave said in his understated Texas drawl, We . . . all . . . know . . . what . . . snow . . . looks . . . like.

To which he replied, as if it had just occurred to him (which, oddly, it had), Yeah, but why do we make snow?

And then Old Dave, snow blowing around him, snow-flakes clotting his reddish-black lumberjack beard, mouth open and hands raised as if he were about to speak to an althing council . . .

Various Theories on the Origin of Snow:

Initially, the Federal Department of Sanitation, Hygiene and Healthcare touted the snow's salubrious effects and the promise of a clean, sterile environment free from the taint of communicable diseases. Which, of course, was an invitation for the Reverend K. James Fallible, his young star already shining brightly in the Religious Community, to expound on his philosophy of guilt and atonement for sin that could never be expiated completely, that required that you spend your entire life bearing on your shoulders this great burden of culpability and self-loathing, because you—because *We!*—weak creatures that we are, could not resist temptation, because we forfeited an *eternity* in edenic paradise for a few moments of wallowing in the *filth* of carnal pleasure, and so it is that the cold and snow have come to insulate us from sin and more than that, *thoughts of sin*, which we witness far more often among the unwashed heathen in the lower latitudes and torpid climes, for whom life does not have the same meaning as it does for us. *Amen.* The atavists, Luddites and survivalists, while not entirely in accordance with the Reverend, advance their own quasi-religious interpretation. The cold and snow remind us of the dark void whence we came and whither we must return if the unholy entropists of science have their way. We must never forget how pure life was when none of this was understood, when none of it had been explained, before everything was translated into mundane things like molecules and atoms, internal combustion and central heat, when the howling was real and near, when you could never show weakness if you hoped to survive the terrible cold and misery you were born into, when you had to wrastle with fire-breathing dinosaurs as big as office buildings and your only hope was Jesus H. Christ and your AK-47. Always the optimists, the Business community seized upon a whole raft of possibilities. We're talking about money! Big money! And nothing says money like nostalgia! TV commercials show couples cuddling romantically in front of crackling fireplaces, families riding sleds and toboggans down the hill in front of the Capitol building, marshmallows floating in hot chocolate. The scientific community, in the face of overwhelming distrust from the public and crushing criticism from all the parties mentioned above, and fearing a catastrophic loss of funding, conceded the snow's very slight potential effectiveness in countering the still not universally accepted concept of global warm—*mmmph!* Criminologists commended the snow business for tamping down crime. Or, as Police Commissioner Brick Wallace stated, *Nobody feels like going out and causing trouble when it's twenty below zero and there's two feet of snow on the ground.* There's also the more banal explanation for the snow, to cover up all this goddamn garbage. It's piled everywhere, in fields and vacant lots, in drainage ditches and dry gulches, outside condos, apartment buildings, private residences, it fills driveways and alleys, spills over sidewalks and curbs and into the street, the old TV from the den, rusty, banged up kids' bicycles, mangled sleds, Tommy's broken robot, little Sis's headless dolly, big Sis's little unhatched baby chick, its amniotic arteries and veins visible in a clear plastic produce sack with a complimentary coat hanger attached, old bed frames, space heaters, kitchen stoves, washing machines, refrigerators, worn-out and even brand new, never used recreational devices, job-savers, time-savers, work-savers—all sunk into rust and disrepair. Elmo, operating the route six garbage truck in the seventeenth district, puts it this way: Ya can't burn this shit because the air's already full of pollution and ya can't bury it because the ground's already full of dead bodies and ya can't throw it in the ocean because the sea's already a moribund cesspool (Elmo's been working on his vocabulary).

Your obsolescence is our future, Snowman. We can build hospitals, schools, houses, factories, machinery out of the stuff you throw away. You should lobby your lawmakers, Snowman, let us cross the border with our pickup trucks, donkey carts, wheelbarrows, bicycles, buckets, we'll gladly cart away all your junk for free.

After all the failed anti-litter campaigns, after the adopt-a-highway programs, after the recycling and environmental awareness efforts, after the armies of boy scouts, trash bags in hand, earning their community service badges in the mean streets of suburbia, after the return to road gangs, convicts in black-and-whites and leg-irons humping the roadsides, after all that, the powers that be realized it'd be a whole lot easier, not to mention phenomenally cheaper, just to cover up the mess where it lay and pretend it didn't exist.

And how do we do that, professor?

A modulated male baritone narrates: In ultra-secret but later much-ballyhooed laboratory tests (here Boone has spliced in clips from a B-grade sci-fi flick, test tubes, beakers, boiling alembics, lightning crackling Van der Graaf machines), scientists made an amazing discovery. A molecular variation of a biofuel alternative extracted from a common desert plant produced a substance with unique (and patented) freezing properties, similar to the methane hydrates that form around oil wellheads on the seafloor, which they dubbed Icine, a relatively inert substance in liquid suspension (but a volatile gas in its evaporative state) that, when combined with moisture in the atmosphere, produced snow, even at temperatures well above freezing. It only took a small leap of the imagination to envision introducing Icine to the steam vapor rising from cooling towers of existing power plants to produce masses of snow that, with the aid of giant fans, covered large urban areas.

And on the eighth day it began to snow.

He remembers when the snow began. It was his fifth birthday. His mother set up a table outside in the warm sunshine with paper plates and glasses of pink lemonade, balloons and streamers and in the middle a big round cake with lots of icing and his name on it and five burning red candles and all the other little kids from the neighborhood were invited and came dressed in their good clothes with presents wrapped in ribbons and bows and pretty paper. In a matter of minutes the sky turned from robin's-egg blue to a dark purple and gray torment of clouds and big wet snowflakes began to fall. He still remembered the pained expression on his mother's face, as if God Himself had betrayed her. Without a word, she bunched up all the place settings, the plastic forks and spoons and paper plates and the big beautiful cake in the tablecloth, heaved the improvised Santa Claus sack over her shoulder, marched to the garbage container, dropped it in, then dragged him inside by the arm and shut the door. The snow quickly melted but the damage was done.

Thanksgiving saw a dusting of dry powdery snow, followed by a record snowfall for Christmas and a particularly hard freeze that had all of Osberg out on skates on City Lake in a reenactment of a sixteenth-century Dutch oil painting (you know the one). The week after New Year's there was a brief thaw and period of sunshine, then continuous snowfall until Easter, when, with a reluctant nod to the religious holiday, the authorities shut down the system for general maintenance and a performance evaluation, setting in motion another kind of resurrection. The snow melted away, the sun shone, a warm, balmy breeze blew, the grass turned green, the trees leafed out, flowers bloomed. The summer, too, was pleasant, the days sunny and warm, tomatoes and peppers grew in the garden, the kids splashed in the kiddy pool, Mom made Kool-Aid and iced tea, Dad ran the lawnmower on the weekends—things still seemed somewhat normal. It was the last real summer anyone remembered.

On the first day of autumn the skies turned gray, the temperature dropped, snow began to fall from the sky. The snow fell night and day, a wet heavy snow that broke tree limbs, brought down power lines. The snow buried gardens, flowerbeds, filled up birdbaths, cat dishes. As the snow stayed on the ground longer, the temperature plummeted. A hard freeze clamped everything in its icy grip and with it a death and dormancy that was going to last far longer than any normal three- or four-month season in hell. Otherwise known as the Big Freeze. Pipes burst, swimming pools cracked, farms and gardens died, summer clothing was packed away in attics and a big chunk of the paycheck assigned to new winter apparel and fuel bills. Driving on the highways was like playing Russian roulette with three loaded chambers.

Of course the system wasn't perfect in the beginning. The snowfall was erratic, sometimes the snowflakes were as big as kites, sometimes as small as grains of salt. Tons fell on a single block, on a single residence even, a hundred-foot-tall column of snow packed on top of a two-story brownstone, while next door, nothing, rooftop and tiny yard bare. A rare thaw sent melting snow waters rushing down city streets, inundating homes and businesses. In the southern latitudes the snow business was particularly tough in the summertime, the snow an illusion that collapsed every day as the temperature inexorably rose. The legendary beaches of Florida, for example. The jet stream warmed the coast so much you couldn't keep a decent blanket of snow down. Palm trees, mangoes, bananas, sweet flowering plumerias dripping with this yucky slush. Municipalities resorted to spray foams, shaving cream made a big comeback, they tried powdered coconut, popcorn, styrofoam peanuts, soap flakes, confetti, excelsior, various meringues—key lime was the most popular—they even recycled cotton batting from the mattresses at old folks homes, but the indelible yellow tint and the unmistakable smell of urine put an end to that. Here, too, in the southwest, where the hot summer sun mercilessly beat down on the city and all that concrete gathered up the reflected, convected and collected heat and the temperature soared above a hundred, the snow rarely lasted until evening.

On top of which, the coverage produced by the ice factories was subject to the caprices of wind, high and low pressure cells, thermals rising off escarpments, mesas, mountain ridges. The greater the radius from the ice factories in the urban centers, the less snow that fell. Entire suburban neighborhoods were left bare. The Mobile Snow Dispensing Vehicles arose to fill the gaps, the fiscal responsibility to be borne by state and municipal tax-ing agencies. But with the second great depression and ensuing budget cuts across the spectrum of public services, the snowbiz entered the hands of the private entity International Cryogenic Industries Network. In a kind of You scratch my back, I'll scratch yours arrangement, ICIN lobbyists and Congressional committee members agreed to certain standards, to be defined individually by state and municipal governments, to ensure the citizens' well-being (a wink and a nod) and the business's profit-ability (indeed). For the Snowman, this meant a loss of all health and retirement benefits, an increasingly grueling schedule and a basically take it or leave it contract. For the citizens of Osberg, this meant yet another form of extortion. Zoning required a minimum four-inch snow coverage in all private residences, with subsidies and rebates for senior citizens and lower income housing. In an ironic twist, this also meant that for once it was the upper crust out in the gated burbs who footed most of the tab. Of course, if they were going to pay for it, they wanted the works. In fact, here's good citizen Edward Wrothrock Whitis in a green velvet evening gown over classic red-and-white striped pajamas, with a matching green nightcap and red kidskin slip-pers—every night upon the SnowBile's arrival, citizen Whitis flings open the huge oaken door of his faux Scottish Castle, steps outside and salutes the Snowman and his crew with a steaming crystal mug of hot buttered rum and his standard greeting, *Looks like snow tonight, eh, boys? Fa la la la la!* So pleased is he with his tired old joke that he coughs up cheerless chunks of Christmas carol laughter through perfect white dental implants, his eyes blazing like zirconium lasers behind military-style steel-rimmed glasses. He's had his fun, re-established ties with the working class, now it's time to get serious again, show the untermensch who's in charge here. Let's get this place looking *tip-top*, eh boys? he barks like a company commander. *Tip-top!* he repeats, closing the door behind him. Yeah, we'll get it tip-top, the Snowman mutters, even as he notices a nasty brown trickle in the fresh snow. More burst pipes, the plumbing too shallow, laid in the days when the sun reigned. Now the permafrost wraps everything in its pythonic embrace, copper, ceramic, PVC, galvanized, doesn't matter, pipes expand and contract until they rupture, laundry suds bubbling out of the ground, raw sewage spreading across front yards, bearing insidious little agents of destruction *germs, microbes, bacteria*. But you don't have time to fill out the twenty-five page maintenance report no one will ever look at, Snowman. Let the homeowner take some civic initiative. He opens his nozzle wide, shoots out a flubbery white glop of Icine that flops down on top of the mess and seals it up like medical glue (2-octyl cyanoacrylate, *not* Krazy Glue but pretty close).

In a further irony, with little or no government oversight or safety inspections, ICIN quickly laid off more-experienced but higher-paid employees and started hiring Mexicans. Which seemed like an enormous joke perpetrated upon the citizens by their own government, because even though unspoken (this great big white elephant in the room) by now everyone knew the true purpose of the snow was to (*shhhh*) KEEP OUT ILLEGAL IMMIGRANTS ("We'll make it so damn cold and nasty no wetback will ever want to come here again"—Clyde Crushcup, Chief of the Bureau of Security for the Homeland and Territories), principally those from that *torpid* country south of the border, i.e., they were hiring Mexicans to keep Mexicans out. (Inside sources subsequently revealed that much of the original funding for Icine's development came from BSHT's "secure borders" program—*Ed.*) Equally ironic, given their more temperate provenance, Mexicans, many of whom viewed the snow as—if not magical, at least unnatural, would seem the least likely candidates to work in the snow business. *Los guys* almost seemed contemptuous of the snow. They carelessly spat in the perfect little snow scallops he worked so hard to craft in the prayer-cupped hands of stone cupids. They sat down in the soft white comforters of snow blanketing front lawns and got up again leaving wide, blueberry-stained butt prints. They unzipped their trousers and scrawled their signatures in ornate yellow ribbons, then listened, uncomprehending, their copper faces all schoolboy innocence, when he scolded them. If the snow melted and froze again in eccentric patterns, giant phalluses, humpbacked camels and long-necked giraffes, they shrugged their shoulders and made resigned *tsking* sounds through their front teeth while he muttered and cursed and stomped up and down. Because even though he hated people telling *him* what to do, and yeah, he did come across as kind of a fuck-up, he still demanded order, the rigid geometry of borders, he wanted symmetry in his lines and edges, he wanted the snow to sit perfectly on porch railings and window ledges. Because a job worth doing is a job worth doing well, right, Snowman? Because if you're gonna spend practically every waking hour of your life on the damn job, you gotta make it mean *something*, right, Snowman? *Right?*

What deed you say, Snowman? Bluebottle night goggles gleaming over his tomahawk nose, mouthful of yellow teeth stretched into a funny, curious smile behind his mike, Nico is staring at him like a strange beetley insect inside the carapace of his parka. He makes a sort of head-rolling, *Sorry, I must have been out of it for a minute* expression, gives Nico a thumbs-up and shoots out another skein of Icine. Making snow is largely an insular business, which suits him fine. The guys, already taciturn at best, talk even less over the radio. At most there's this redacted conversation. *You missed a spot, cabrón! Watchalayyy, putoooo! Qué padre!*

In the midst of this comedy of errors and unremitting drudgery, Margarito appeared on the scene like a golden glowing numen, illuminating the dark shadows with his boundless optimism and radiant smile. No matter how cold or how late or how bad, when he himself was feeling down in the dumps and it seemed like there was no way they could possibly get the job done that night, Margarito laughed in his face and cried with heart-aching earnestness, *Vámonos*, Snowman, we can do eet! We can feeneesh! And if he had thought of himself as a kind of Zen master of snowmaking, Margarito was the Buddha. He tuned his gun with the finesse of a master glassblower. He made snow the way he spoke, like a flautist issuing creamy layers of satin, bolts of liquid sound that spread out into the night and settled to the earth like gossamer. Within a week he knew every aspect of the snowmaking business, he had their entire schedule down pat. Say Evelyn paged him, Got a special job for you, Snowman. He'd jump down from the SnowBile shouting, Let's go! Let's go! We gotta finish up and get outta here! But—what the *fuuuudge*? Everything's already snowed under, bare brown yards buried beneath perfect wedding cake swirls and curlicues, dark green cedars wreathed in sugar frosting, shutters, eaves and trellises draped with mantilla lace, and here's Margarito lecturing the guys on the finer points of tool maintenance. Soon he felt not only unneeded but even in the way. He'd sit in the cab and sip coffee, smoke another cigarette, read the newspaper, worry about things he had no control over but which somehow had control over him, the war and the economy and some new disease out of Africa. Ah, but don't worry about the world, Snowman, it's not in your hands, just do your job, make all the ugliness disappear—that's your purpose in life. After all, the night's going reasonably well, they've already finished Canyon, Cuernavaca and Mirabelles, they're only half an hour behind schedule.

His attempt at a more positive attitude sinks when they turn down Chivas and he sees that the New Bedford Falls neighborhood just across the narrow Bull Creek is already blanketed with snow and Number Seven, Hanktheredneckasshole's SnowBile, flying a tattered Confederate stars and bars from the cab, is pulling out. The radio crackles and Hank's high-pitched Texas twang comes over the airwaves, *Uh, Ah-ser Seven to, ah, Ah-ser Naaahn, Say, Naaahn, you boys runnin' late again?* Fucking Hank, trying to make him look bad in front of Gastreaux who's probably back at the shop monitoring the radio right now. He can hear Gastreaux's voice in his head, Tell me, *Snowman*, why a college-educated guy like yerself can't keep up with an ignoramus like Hank? And, yeah, sure, he could do like Hank, crank up the pressure, pump molecules of Icine and water together into swollen little bladders that burst in the frigid air and fell to earth in a soggy blanket that quickly began to slump and melt and trickle down the sidewalks and driveways and into the gutters. In the early a.m. when the temperature sinks into the single digits and even below zero, this slush freezes again into threatening ridges, and what happens if little Johnny running for the school bus falls and cuts his forehead? Another lawsuit, malfeasance, violation of the public trust. He keys the mike but before he can speak, Nico leans across Carroteeno and gleefully yells, Fok you, Hunk! Great, now he's definitely going to hear from Gastreaux. Meanwhile Nico's smiling at him with that beakful of yellow rodent teeth, like, Wasn't that the right thing to do, Snowman? Thankfully, they only have to finish this street and then it's—lunchtime. He's not the only one thinking about food. Bombástico leans forward and whispers to Carroteeno, who glances over his shoulder at Xuan, then whispers back in a fearful tone, You deedn't eat hees lonche too that I packed for heem? Sí, hees lonche too (at least, that's how the Snowman understands this exchange). Bombástico, whose character is rapidly embraced by the sentimental viewing audience, solemnly nods his big round pumpkin head up and down, his enormous brown puppy dog eyes brimming with tears. Then Nico and Raf-I-el have to add their two centavos and, uh-oh, now Xuan's eyes are rolling sideways suspiciously.

7

Lonche

SOME TIME AFTER MIDNIGHT they take lunch, dinner—he can never get that straight either—which usually includes a stop at a convenience store. Everybody tramps inside, tawny, faux reindeer mukluks depositing melting wedges of snow on the black-and-white checked linoleum floor (*Piso mojado!*), their hoods thrown back, night goggles pushed up on their heads, raccoon eyes blinking against way too bright fluorescence. Tinny Christmas music assaults their ears, *It's beginning to look a lot like*, waves of pine and cherry-scented industrial disinfectant and air freshener flood their nostrils. Everyone's been acting pretty casual up to this moment but suddenly eyes dart sideways like a colony of bats exiting a cave and a mad scramble for the bathroom ensues, which, despite his girth, Bombástico, making desperate little *wee wee wee* sounds, reaches first, followed almost immediately by a fairly loud explosion that actually blows open the door and leaves a malodorous cloud looming outside like an evil jinn to dissuade other mortals foolish enough from entering (Boone thinks this scene is hilarious; his staff, a bunch of young hipsters, *juvenile*). Meanwhile everybody else is already at the cash register clutching armloads of fruit pies, candy bars, corn chips, sodas and TexMex Christmas Burritos. The guy behind the counter, this limp piece of protoplasm with a lifetime of flipping dead meat ahead of him, gives the Snowman a conspiratorial wink and proceeds to loudly count out their change in particularly bad Spanish, *Oo-no! Dose! Trace! Quah-troh!* Which elicits plenty of grumbling and murderous looks from the guys,

96

but, ever mindful of their non-legal status, they swallow their pride and head out to the SnowBile. But where the heck has Nico gotten? Out in public, the Snowman watches over his crew like a mother hen her chicks. He finds his lost boy in the back of the store, furiously chewing a rustic stick of tobacco, unlit, and bouncing up and down in front of a video game, his eyes gleaming like LEDs, his fingers moving like spider legs. Saint Nicotino, saint of wired, high-energy nicotine madness, saint of nickels, dimes and quarters. He's ringing and jingling like a gunslinger in buckles, bangles and spurs, like a highrolling gambler slinging five-hundred-dollar chips at a gaming table in Vegas. Raised on a hardscrabble sheep farm, education completed in third grade, he's nevertheless invested with the zeitgeist of his generation. He plays every game or electronic device he encounters—soda machines, pay phones, parking meters, weigh-yourself-scales in pharmacies, cigarette machines, condom dispensers proffering boundless and prolonged pleasures in Technicolor latex. The Snowman has to forcefully drag him out to the SnowBile, spidery fingers still trembling, clutching at phantom buttons and knobs. But what's going on? The rest of the guys are slouched down in their seats, pointed parka hoods comically conspicuous like a coven of witches. Across the street a Silverspoon police car is parked in front of *Dorothy's Devilishly Delicious Donuts*. Ever fearful of *la Migra*, the guys shrink into invisibility in the presence of anyone in uniform, cops, postmen, UPS drivers—a nerdy, bespectacled eagle scout once sent Nico diving under the seat. Truth is, the guys don't need to worry about the local constabulary as long as they stick to the script: Do your job and get your brown ass out of Dodge before daybreak and we won't fuck with you.

But this is all background chatter. By now everyone's digging into their tin-foil-wrapped TexMex Christmas Burritos, juicy cornucopias of roast turkey, chestnut, sage and giblet stuffing, and gravy, cranberry sauce, sweet potatoes, pinto beans, green peppers, tomatoes and jalapeños slathered with hot salsa and

rolled up in a huge soft taco still steaming hot from the microwave, a culinary innovation that caught on with the guys like
hotcakes ever since the night Bombástico asked in a shy little
voice, *Can you pleese geeve me a leetle taste of your Chreesmas,
Meester Snowman?* (As you have probably noticed by now,
Bombástico is anything but—bombastic, that is.) In fact, he's
already finished his own Christmas burrito and is cadging everyone else's. Hey, Xuan, eef you geeve me haf of your Creesmas
today I weel gladly geeve you a whole Creesmas tomorrow.
Hey, Nico, are you goeeng to feeneesh your Creesmas? Because
eef you aren't I can probably help you weeth eet. On several
occasions the Snowman has witnessed tears streaming down
Bombástico's cheeks as he consumes enormous quantities of
food. Apparently he's eating for his entire family back home.
Once a month he sends them a photograph so they can see how
much he's grown. They go to bed with empty stomachs but
their hearts full. Nevertheless, the emotional toll this takes on
Bombástico is clearly overwhelming.

In reciprocity for introducing the guys to the TexMex
Christmas burrito, they introduce him to the *polvo rojo*.
Everything the guys eat they sprinkle with this red powder
they carry around in small leather pouches. Sometimes he'll
see them put a pinch on their tongues, or even snort it like
snuff. They've all got red flecks around their mouths and noses.
Their eyes have a strange vermillion glow, like tiny solar collectors brimming with sunlight. One night Nico handed him
his pouch with an enthusiastic nod. He raised it to his nostrils, inhaled—a little musty, faintly spicy, hmm, intriguing.
He sprinkled a liberal dose on his burrito. The dark red powder
looked like dried blood—okay, maybe that's too dramatic—
paprika. He took a bite. Not bad, kind of smoky, slightly sweet,
not really that spi—*yeeeoww!* Paisley flames roared from his
mouth, incinerating his lips and tongue. A wildfire ravaged his
sinuses. An inferno raged in his brain. Desperate, he gulped half
a Good-God-It's-A-Gallon® root beer soda. A white-hot ball of

gas surged down his throat, scorching his esophagus and setting off a firestorm in his belly. Huge, oily drops of sweat burst from his forehead. Waves of heat radiated from his body. He felt like Sam McGee sitting inside a red-hot furnace. He felt like he *was* a red-hot furnace. But what the heck? He was burning alive and the guys were clutching their stomachs and screeching like hyenas *Ha!Ha!Ha!Hee!Hee!Hee!* Bombástico was laughing so hard milk squirted out his nose. Carroteeno tried to maintain his composure but a wheezy, asthmatic *whee! whee! whee!* still escaped his throat. Even worse, when he took a leak afterwards and somehow managed to transfer vestigial traces of the red powder onto his dick—it was like a new kind of STD, it burned, it raged, it was enflamed. The rest of the night he kept tugging at his crotch and trying not to be too obvious about it. The biggest joke came the next time he took a shit. His asshole felt like a foundry extruding red-hot slag. His hemorrhoids popped out like a slew of Vesuviuses. His rectum ached for two days. All the more ironic, then, that the guys referred to the powder as *medicina*. Sí, *Snowman*, Margarito assured him, eet keels the leetle animals in your food. You know, *germs, microbes, bacteria.* Which did give him pause—not so much about the red powder's medicinal value, but Margarito's word choice.

(By the way, the viewer may have noticed a bit of awkwardness in the shift between past and present tenses, as well as obvious cases of dislinearity. Boone's struggle with chronology will never resolve itself. On the one hand, the simple past would—well, simplify things. On the other hand, Boone is striving to capture the immediacy of life and the natural disorder of the human thought process. Apparently this is somehow tied to his vision of the old cold war in a new epic format that is both retro and prophetic—*Ed.*)

The repast (no pun intended) over, everyone thoroughly stuffed with a ton of calories, the cab's warm and cozy, the air redolent of diesel fumes and flatulence, the guys are dozing or talking quietly, he's savoring a cigarette with a cup of coffee,

and sure, why not a toke or two, and a hearty belt of tequila
from the magically self-replenishing bottle under the front seat
(before the guys arrived on the scene it was usually bourbon
or scotch and once even a generally despised Pernod), but this
time everyone, even Bombástico, takes a belt. And call it the
Eucharist or taking communion or just another kind of reality,
another waking. You've gotta stoke that furnace. You've gotta
get your head right. You've gotta prepare yourself body and soul.
Because now, when the cold wind is roaring outside and rocking
the SnowBile, now, when all the good citizens are home asleep
in their warm beds, and all their doors and windows, cat and
doggie flaps are securely locked and sealed against the storm,
now, *you*, Snowman, are going to go back out and work in that.

8
Back to Work

AND THEN THAT NEXT WAKING shock when he climbed down from the SnowBile and the blowing snow slashed his face and the cold wind penetrated his parka and sent him into a paroxysm of shivering that tore at his already sore muscles and made strapping the three-gallon tank on his back excruciating, even the ten-pound torch felt heavy in his hands and he still had another four-five hours of this shit ahead of him. And of course there's always something, a break in a main or bad connectors, ice-cold water splashes everywhere, soaks your mittens, swamps your mukluks. The hoses are stiff and heavy and caked with ice, the couplings freeze. You try to get things working again but the wrench slips in your hand and cracks your bare knuckles because you stupidly took off your mittens to get a better grip and now you're staring at this white gash of subcutaneous and fatty tissue oozing bright red blood. Then you feel the pain. It doesn't seem possible such a tiny tear in your upholstery could cause such absolute and crushing pain. It's that invisible whack to the white plastic hardware of cartilage and bone beneath the epidermal Naugahyde that does it, compounded several times over by the cold that is both ally in the business of making snow and enemy in the business of survival. It hurts so much tears well in your eyes, you simultaneously blaspheme and appeal to the mercy of some higher authority to release you from this torment. Finally the pain does ease, fades into some distant place, but the rest of the night it's going to remind you, every time you forget and bang your knuckles again and another lightning bolt surges along its neural highway and explodes in your brain. And of course you can't say anything about it to the guys because they don't feel pain, they don't express pain. If you ask, Are you tired? Are you cold? Does it hurt? they deny everything, noooo, Snowman, you muss be eemagineeng eet.

Where we come from, Snowman, pain is a useless consideration. You swallow your pain, turn it into its own medicine, that bitter balm distilled out of scorpion tails, cactus spines and rattlesnake fangs. It makes everything else—extreme heat, cold, hunger, sickness, pain, whatever troubles you—less important, the pain becomes just a thing you carry around with you, like a comb or a pocketknife. And if you cannot do that then you cannot survive. Show no weakness, admit no injury, because if you do, you are prey to the predators, the scavengers, to anyone who is only a little stronger than you.

To further make this point, Boone includes one of his trademark shock scenes, which occurred right after Moll Flowers became the first woman in company history to be hired onto a snow crew. Square-shouldered, rawboned, good-looking in a kind of rough outdoors way, sun-bleached chestnut curls, aristocratic nose, eyes the leaden green of deep rivers, ruddy skin, former ski instructor, whitewater guide, mountain climber, bi- and tri-athlete. She took the work in stride, laughed off the guys' hi-jinks, even when things went badly awry. Xuan, putting on his macho display for Moll's sake (everyone could tell right away he had a crush on her), reached down in his pants and slowly withdrew his obsidian blade, and didn't even seem to realize what had happened until Nico let out a kind of girlish scream *eeeeeee!* and pointed—and here Boone mercilessly sent the camera zooming in for a gruesome and protracted close-up of the actual event, the gleaming black blade slicing across bronze flesh, separating layers of epidermis, dermis, fatty tissue, tendons, nerves, veins, muscles, cartilage and bone, sending a bright red geyser gushing from the stump of Xuan's left thumb, which now hung by a shred like a toppled Easter Island head in miniature (and yes, you astute film students, Boone's ambiguous camera work was intended to make the audience initially believe it was Xuan's penis that had been guillotined). Xuan stared at his decapitated thumb in bafflement, as if it were a traitorous homunculus. Without blinking an eye, Moll stepped forward, doused the wound with tequila, gave Xuan a drink, took a belt herself, pulled a needle and a length of nylon thread out of the nerdy all-purpose utility kit she wore on a belt and in a husky voice said, I ain't too proud to do a little stitchin' now and then, and in a trice had sewn the thumb back in place. Carroteeno ceremoniously dusted the wound with red powder and tied a dried cornhusk around it and Xuan, who had never once flinched or demonstrated the tiniest indication he was in pain, shrugged and went back to work. In a week the wound had healed completely and Moll had won an ardent admirer. Xuan was an adolescent in love, a virgin in lust, he was puppy dog eyes, head in the clouds, he was a barbarian brought to his knees by the tenderness of an Amazon. Only one problem. It had not escaped anyone's attention that a golden pigtailed, western fringe jacketed Annie Oakley type (the TV version c. 1950s, but with myopic, wire-rimmed glasses) in a humungous fourby often dropped Moll off at work in the evening and picked her up in the morning, accompanied, rumor had it, by a very fond kiss. Unable to bear it any longer, Xuan pointed a brown tree limb of a finger at Moll. You been keeseen gorls, Moll? At which Moll laughed like a barmaid on the Barbary Coast and said, Don't you wish you were? Which caused the other guys to point and jeer with uncharacteristic temerity at Xuan, who, even more befuddled by this turn of events, could only smile like a country fool and generally act like it didn't bother him one whit, although the observant Snowman was pretty sure he saw a few tears roll down those ghastly cheeks. No surprise then that a universally glum mood descended on the crew when Moll gave her two weeks' notice to go roustabout on an oil rig in the Arctic Circle. Months after her departure, Xuan could be seen lovingly stroking his restored thumb.

By now, megadoses of sugar and fat, caffeine, nicotine, tequila and pot coursing through his veins, augmented with a couple blasts of sinus-opening and head-clearing psalt, he's starting to warm up again, get back in the groove, he's on a roll, his senses alert, his thoughts keen, his mind working like a steel tarp—*trap*—in fact, he's feeling just a little bit crazed. Maybe it's his heritage, scion of men in steel helms and animal skins, Viking warrior striding through the cold and snow to do battle with a mighty enemy or great beast, that urge and yearning for the clash of iron and steel, of stone battleaxes crashing against leather shields, to shout aloud, to raise the ram's horn of victory to your lips, to smash and chop and destroy your opponent with the merciless wrath of God. Which is the perfect attitude for the task ahead. 1306 Cavendish Drive. The Simpsons' rooftop, front yard, sidewalk and driveway have remained woefully bare of snow on several occasions, repeated complaints from the neighborhood committee. Oh, but they've got an excuse, plenty of excuses: radiant heat from concrete pavement and other hard and impermeable surfaces; residual chemical buildup from previous decades of lawn care; subterranean uranium deposits. The zoning commission isn't buying it. The authorities have given the Simpsons ample warning—now it's time to act. The crew climbs down from the SnowBile and approaches the house like a gang of hopped-up *hashashins* on a mission of murder. Shadows move behind the curtains. He knows the Simpsons are in there peeking out at him, terrified, hating him. It makes him hate them in return for forcing him to do this. The deadbeats have got the money, that's clear enough. They just don't wanta ante up their fair share for the snow show. At the first bazooka blast the shadows disappear from the curtains, the lights go off inside. Xuan knocks out a garage window with his bare elbow and, biceps bulging like gorging pythons, shoves his bazooka barrel inside and releases a blast that breaks out doors and windows and causes snow to gush out everywhere like the proverbial porridge. Bombástico's got the barrel of his bazooka stuck up a dryer vent and is packing the laundry room with basket-loads of frozen lint. Carroteeno lugs his bazooka around back to seal off the rear entrance beneath a small avalanche. Nico and Raf-I-el mischievously bury the front windows under layer after layer of frosty snowmen, reindeer and Santa Clauses as if they were embroidering winter wool sweaters. His target is the car Mr. or Mrs. Simpson foolishly left parked in the drive. He sticks his nozzle under the front grill and inserts a thin stream of Icine that penetrates carburetor, distributor and crankcase, frosts over electrical contacts, freezes shut valves and switches, immobilizes pistons, flywheel and drive shaft, locking the car's engine in the frozen hibernation of ice-age beasts. He finishes by coating the entire car in a solid inch of ice. For the coup de grâce he moves up the walk to the front door, tightens down the nozzle of his torch and inserts it in the keyhole, which is easier than one might think. The Simpsons are into the retro thing, so they've got this glass-paned, wood-framed, authentic Victorian-era door from about a hundred and fifty years ago that rattles when it's opened and bangs when it's closed and one of those big see-through keyholes that looks something like a miniature train tunnel and—you wanted Victorian, you got Victorian—he shoots out a spray that disperses through the darkened house like a cloud of spores, covering walls, ceiling, floor, mirrors, tables and TV screens with an intricate lacework of hoarfrost. Poor fat, frightened Mom, whimpering, almost hysterical with fear, rocks back and forth on the couch, wrapped in a blanket. Fat, ineffectual Pop paces back and forth on the icy carpet, knotting his fists with trembling, impotent rage. Pudgy, pimply bespectacled Harold, fearing he's busted, promptly stops doing whatever it is he's doing in his bedroom. Plump, pimply Sis, under the covers, poring over a teen fanzine, is just now realizing the shame and humiliation she'll face at school tomorrow. In a final insult, Xuan, Bombástico and Carroteeno launch a heavy volley that plomps down on the roof, damaging shingles and gutters and causing the eaves to sag visibly.

Following the Simpsons, there's damage control on an inde-
pendently minded citizen's attempt at personal home-snow-con-
ditioning run amok, the result of one of ICIN's most successful
ever money-making schemes—er, marketing campaigns, thanks
again to the genius of Roger Wilco, who came up with the bright
idea of selling to the public a line of "Home Snow Blowers."
Touting its appeal to the individualist spirit, the campaign is
pretty obviously directed at the man of the house, the club carrier, meat getter, authentic card-carrying XY guy who immediately senses a manly challenge in the works, especially when this
snow-blowing marvel is presented on big screen TV by a buxom
young lass in a green velvet elf costume with enough cleavage to
make a blind man interested—the camera's certainly interested,
it plunges right down that crevasse of décolletage as the elf purrs
to the viewer, "The Wolverine 4000 puts *you* in control of your
snow conditioning. Are *you* ready to ride this beast?" (In a rad-
ical leap, Boone has inserted an actual TV commercial in the
film, hoping to offset any lawsuits with royalties to be negotiated
later.) For a cool thirty thousand clams, the Dadster can have his
own Wolverine 4000 Home Snow Blower delivered to his door,
sign on the dotted line and he's ready to settle his ever-broaden-
ing butt on the faux leather tractor saddle, fire up that eighty-six
horsepower engine, grip the molded rubber steering wheel in
his hands and confront the elements like a man. *Yeehaw!* Yeah,
but Mister Gastreaux, isn't this going to cut into our business?
This sick stakhanovite quirk of the Snowman's, loyal employee
to the hilt, nothing but the company's best interests at heart,
after all these years that dewy innocence in his eyes. *Snowman,
Snowman, Snowman.* Gastreaux, shaking his head with a mix of
condescension and genuine incredulousness, lays it out for him.
Haven't you figured it out yet, *Snowman*? Yeah, sure, the first
coupla nights Dad's gonna be only too eager to get out there
with his new toy, just to try it out, to prove he's up to the task,
don't want Mom and the kids to think he's a frightened little
worm. But how long you think that's gonna last, *Snowman*?

How long you think these overweight, middle-aged slobs—and I admit I speak as one—are gonna wanna go out on a freezing cold night and muck around with some loud, scary machine? And this thing's a holy terror. It's big, it's loud, it's really frightening, especially that huge spinning screw thing in front. Just like a city dude on an ornery bronco, Dad never quite gets a handle on it. Yeah, sure, maybe he drags the charade out a couple of weeks, months even, out of nothing but stubborn determination. He's out there at night, after work, a recently purchased, ill-fitting anorak pulled on over his business suit, clumsily maneuvering this damn machine back and forth across the front yard, ploughing up dead turf, spurting out a pathetic stream of runny, greenish-white faux snow at eaves, gutters (there's no way they're going to put industrial-grade Icine in the hands of the public, even with the NRA and Tea Potty lobbying). By the time Dad's done for the night, it looks like someone dropped a giant pile of pigeon shit on the house. Then there's the unforeseen costs. Deliveries of "Domestic Icine" soon mount up to thousands of dollars. Maintenance for this machine is over the top. New bugs pop up every week that the warranty never seems to cover. At this stage of the game, Pop wants nothing more than to quietly park his toy behind the ping-pong table in the garage and hope Martha never mentions the damn thing again. *Georrrruhhdge*, whatever happened to that snowhickey you bought? And bingo! We're back! We even offer them a special discount to renew our services. No hard feelings, pal. Great to have you on board again. You can see the warm tidal wave of relief wash over them, they've practically got pee running down their legs. They're absolutely ecstatic to turn the reins over to us. And you know why, *Snowman*? Because we make the trains run on time.

By the end of Gastreaux's spiel, the Snowman's feeling pretty warm and tingly himself, just the thought of all this commerce, all this genius at work, this massive symbiotic thing that draws to its bosom millions of disparate human beings who only want to be good little worker bees and do as they're told in exchange for a modicum of security, some decent TV programming and plenty of good (i.e., sweet, fat, alcoholic) stuff to eat and drink. And he—he's a part of it all, he's a distinct cog in the machine. Just like a cute little cheerleader at a home basketball game he practically shouts, I think it's a terrific idea!

To reward the Snowman's enthusiasm, Gastreaux assigns him and his crew special duty—a promotional gig for ICIN's newest line of Home Snow Blowers. Dealers from all over the country are flying in for the big shindig, the Pacific Northwest contingent in black-and-red checked mackinaws and fur-lined caps with earflaps, the Southwest in chaps and Stetsons, West Coast, tees and baggies, East Coast, fedoras and sweater vests. Buffet tables, punch bowls, everything hung with red and green velvet ribbons and bows, Christmas trees everywhere, buxom girls in jingly, green elf costumes, a full orchestra backing up the legendary crooner Frankie Sinestra (yes, intended wordplay on Sinatra-sinister) in a medley of the top one hundred Christmas carols. The Snowman and his crew have been ordered to show up in full regalia, midnight blue parkas, faux reindeer skin mukluks, headsets, mikes and big bluebottle-fly night goggles. Gastreaux gives him the pregame spiel. No fuck-ups, okay, *Snowman?* I don't want your crew acting like a bunch of gorillas. And please, *Snowman*—Gastreaux leans in close with those chilling dead fish eyes—let's see if we can stay sober for one night. So is anyone really surprised when the SnowBile bounces to a halt outside the ever expanding (one might even say metastasizing as it eats up block after block of prime real estate) Convention Center and the Snowman and his merry crew tumble down in a pungent cloud of marijuana smoke and tequila fumes (it's worth mentioning here that the Zolmen, a.k.a. *los guys*, usually of somber demeanor and sober temperament, are also given, at times—one might even say ritually—to getting very trashed) and stomp inside like a bunch of mad Siberian monks, the guys gibbering and laughing in a language that, the Snowman's sure now, is definitely not Spanish. All these dealers, distributors and vendors in orange or green or red or blue company aprons and gimme caps are already three sheets to the wind, they're calling out, Keep up the good work, *Snowman*! Great to see you guys! Drinks are on us! Which is all the invitation the crew needs to plunge into the goodies. The punch bowls are drained in minutes, the buffet tables stripped clean, Bombástico alone methodically consumes an entire side of barbecued beef. When Gastreaux appears on the scene to bask in his success, he finds the Convention Center trashed, conventioneers passed out everywhere, the guys driving snow blowers all over the place, knocking down displays, crashing into each other like bumper cars, and the Snowman himself dancing the Mazurka solo on a table top. Hey, chief! Great job, huh? The camera pulls in close and you can actually see Gastreaux's head trembling with rage, his eyes bulge, his teeth are clenched and he's making inarticulate straining sounds *nn! nn! nn!* like a car engine trying to start on a cold morning. His face twists into a deranged smile and he says, Yes, *Snowman*, great job, absolutely wonderful, I couldn't have asked for anything more, and just because you and your crew did such a goddamn great job tonight, *Snowman*, I've got another special assignment for you.

They spend the following week on shit detail. Literally. Covering up sewage spills, refuse management mishaps, a semi hauling hospital waste turns over on MoPark. They've gotta spray down mounds of soiled diapers—adult and infant— blood-, urine- and feces-stained hospital gowns, used syringes, black plastic sacks of amputated limbs, cancerous, oozing, rotting, necrotic, sclerotic, cirrhotic internal organs. Bury the whole damn mess under starched white sheets of snow and stamp it with the imprimatur of the Federal Department of Sanitation, Hygiene and Healthcare.

He shivers awake from another fifteen, twenty minutes, half an hour at most, submerged in the zone, repeating to himself, *This is your life, Snowman, your fucking life!* And he asks himself again, as he does every night, at least twenty times a night, How the fuck did you end up here, Snowman? What are you doing in this lousy job working these crazy hours for such crummy pay? Yeah, but just try and bitch about it to the guys. Lousy job? Long hours? Crummy pay? Are you crazy, Snowman? You theenk ees bad here? Noooo, ees verry gooood! Ees a lot of chob (like the snowbiz), ees a lot of mawney (five–six dollars an hour), ees plawney to eat an dreenk (rice, beans and light beer). Why do you think we leave Zol? (Note: this is the first actual reference we've heard to a place called Zol—*Ed.*) Just so we can come here and work like donkeys? We are not stupeed, Snowman. (More like desperate.) Every time he backs up the SnowBile (*bee bee bee*), he takes a couple more furious drags on a cigarette, does another blast of psalt, gulps more hot coffee, maybe takes another toke of weed, another shot of tequila, trying to either numb himself, or bring himself to an even higher state of wakefulness or being that makes this all mean something more or other than it does.

It's now about three a.m.—the coldest, darkest precinct of night when the temperature falls below zero and the roar of ice factories all across the country has agglomerated into a single monstrous howl people in the snowbiz call the Arctic Roar, which, to his ears, sounds like an unceasing exhalation of torment from the void. It penetrates his parka and headset and echoes inside the cavernous hollows of his skull so that he can think of nothing else, his mind become a vast expanse of arctic whiteness across which a dark form struggles, pursued by a howling that may have been wolves or only his own voice when he shouted out half an hour or an hour ago, *Hey! Hello!* just to hear his own voice, to remind himself there was a world out there, and now half an hour or an hour later he keeps hearing his own voice echoing back *Hey! Hello!* Although, oddly, he's no longer struggling across an arctic snowscape, he's crawling across a blinding white desert on his hands and knees, the burning white sand sifts through his fingers, his lips and mouth are parched, he's desperate for a drink of water.

He snaps awake again, the last half hour a complete blank, snow eddying around him, the wind biting at his throat, the SnowBile's party lights crashing against houses. The clouds break apart and the full moon appears, cold, distant, watching from her haughty heights, and in Diana's thrall, the temperature plunges another ten degrees and the heat exchange between his body and the ambient atmosphere begins to slip out of balance. The cold seeps osmotically through the molecular mesh of cotton, wool, synthfur, hemp and nylon polymers and like a negative heat pump begins to drain him of his last reserves of energy, he's so cold he can't make his fingers work, his toes have passed from burn to numb, he's shivering uncontrollably. How do you say ice, Margarito? How do you say snow? How do you say Jesus Fucking Christ and Holy Santa Claus, it's so fucking cold I'm freezing my balls off? *Hielo! Nieve! Hace un frío chingón, se me están helando los huevos!* As if naming the ice and the snow in that other language would somehow transform it, make it something other than what it really was, not cold and crippling but warm and comforting, like a fluffy down quilt you could pull over yourself and go to sleep forever. *Snowwwwmaaaan.*

Huh?

For the rest of the night he keeps waking up and thinking, Now I really am awake, I really am here, before sinking back into that zone when he's thinking about nothing and everything, and the growl of the SnowBile engine and the monotonous rise and fall of the compressor and even the Arctic Roar subside into the background in a kind of machine-mantra repeating *snowmansnowmansnowmansnowman* at four thousand RPMs, turning him into an inertial and by now largely insentient dynamo. He staggers around the job site, trying to make his mind focus. The icy backlash from his torch slashes his face. A fiery little hobgoblin of insubordination sits on his shoulder and snarls in his ear, *Aww, c'mon, Snowchump, just fire off a few blasts and let's get the hell out of here.* At the same time he can hear Margarito's earnest voice perched like a little white-robed, brown-faced angel on his other shoulder urging him, *Don't geev up Snowman, we can feeneesh it!* as earnestly as if he were pleading for his life before a high tribunal. Next to him Nico's swaying on his feet, still lost in battle, his copper face like that of some strange rodent god. Nico is the exception to the Zolmen's rule of stoic silence. It's like this shtick of his. He complains constantly about the cold, about how much his back hurts, but then he works all night until you have to tear the gun out of his hands and he looks at you with that mad ferret expression and says through chattering rodent teeth, *Es muy frío, no, Snowman?*

Finally the job's done to the Snowman's satisfaction, the SnowBile's loaded, hoses rolled up, guns racked, valves closed, compressor shut down, everyone's settling their sorry asses into their seats and buckling up. But what's this? Like a gnarly old grandmother of yore, worn out by years of unceasing labor, her body a pincushion of aches and pains and still she cooks and cleans and puts food on the table every day, here's Carroteeno handing around cups of steaming hot chocolate and the guys are pushing back their hoods and pulling off their giant puffy mittens with their teeth and laughing and joking as they gratefully take the hot cups in their hands, because this isn't your grandma's hot chocolate. It's thick as mud, with a rich, dark chocolate flavor that tastes like it's been distilled out of the earth, out of the night—a little on the bitter side, and tempered with cinnamon, honey, a good dose of tequila and a fairly hefty pinch of *polvo rojo*, and at the moment it's the perfect balm for some pretty tired souls.

9
Quitting Time

AND SO THE LONG BLACK RIVER of night once again having wended its way through the wintry white landscape to the beginning of day, the Snowman and his merry band head back to the shop, their barrage of warning lights flashing like a sad little sideshow carney, the deck cannons blorping out final soupy spurts of pancake batter. Company regs require that all Icine tanks be emptied before returning to base, a directive he's only too happy to comply with. He drives around a tank load of this shit every night and he doesn't even know what it is. Yeah, sure, Icine is *supposed* to be inert in liquid suspension, but nobody quite believes that, there's always this big *what if?* Sometimes he hears this plosive burp coming from the tank and apparently there's something called *dissociation*, or spontaneous demolecularization, whereby an outside agent, an electrostatic discharge, for example, or a sudden percussive force, causes molecules of Icine to separate from water molecules, potentially turning this tank into a huge bomb. Another reason he should have paid attention in high school chemistry.

His extremities have begun to thaw, his feet burn as they extract themselves from the blocks of ice he's been stomping around in for the last two hours. His body aches all over. His shoulders and back are so sore he can't sit up straight. His hands are cracked, chafed, raw. Even wearing his inky blue goggles all night, his vision's blurry from staring at the highly reflective snow for twelve hours straight. His brain's in tatters from the constant assault of stimulants and depressants, his thoughts drift

113

like rudderless dinghies. Everyone's beat. Nico sucks the picket fence of his front teeth in contemplation. Carroteeno is either snoring or chanting a mantra. Xuan, Raf-I-el and Bombástico, still clutching a half-eaten burrito in his hand, are all conked in back. He feels a wave of affection for these guys. He has absolutely zero in common with them, but working together night after night in this forced intimacy in this shitty job produces a strange sense of—what, camaraderie? Friendship? What do you call a relationship that is mostly tacit, unspoken, stretched across a chasm between one dimension and another? How do you say *ladder, bridge, causeway*? As if Margarito or anyone else for that matter could give him the words, the phrases, the oracular keys to that other kingdom. Because even after he began to strip away the latex and nose puddy, fright wigs and rubber clown masks he had constructed for *los guys*, he still didn't know if he was seeing their real faces or just another set of even more inscrutable masks. And when they spoke, why was it never their own voices he heard, but the voices of buffoons, cartoon characters? *My name José Jiménez. My name ees Speedy González.* Why is there such a distance between them and us, Uncle Bob? Because they aren't like you and me, Snowman. Remember? They don't have the same values, life doesn't have the same meaning.

His gaze shifts to the monolithic UT tower, still glowing burnt orange against the crepuscular sky. Apparently the varsity glazed-donut eating team has triumphed against the hated Aggies. And yes, *hate* is a harsh word, and in the case of college sports pure hyperbole. Nevertheless, these are some serious competitors, their rivalry harkens back to the age of football, the Hail Marys, the clash of helmets and pads on the gridiron—all in the past, of course, gone the way of the dinosaur, nobody throws the old pigskin around anymore, kids today are all about virtual, and eating.

Rrruhnnn! Rrruhnnn! A familiar sound returns him to the here and now, car tires spinning futilely, icy streets, two feet of snow, angry commuters, late for work, more hassles, bills to pay, they're shaking their fists at him, flipping him the bird, mouthing horrible things they wouldn't say to a drunken sailor. He's mouthing his own anathema back at them, fantasizing about crushing their puny little SUVs under the SnowBile. And meanwhile here's this incredible show happening right in front of them, Osberg in all its morning manifestations as the first sunlight emerges from an oystery clot of clouds and a dull yellow gleam strikes the blue and silver, green and gold glass walls of office towers, condominiums, hotels, municipal buildings, and then, as the sun rises incrementally higher, the whole city erupts in orange and red flames, and hovering over it all, watching all, the Eye, which—maybe it's the light—looks just a bit jaded, sleepy.

At the shop, half a dozen semi-tankers are lined up outside the motor pool, the familiar turquoise blue I on their air foils, their long white egg cases full of cool blue Icine. The drivers mill around their rigs in white thermal HAZMAT suits, sucking desperately on unlit cigarettes, faces gaunt, eyes spectral behind wraparound shades. Red warning triangles everywhere are a reminder of what we're dealing with here. They can't wait to dump this load and get some downtime before they pick up the next rolling bomb. (So there must be some truth to that spontaneous demolecularization thing.) Most of the other crews are already in, Jipi Jaime's SnowBile covered with plastic appliqué flowers and peace signs in bay six, Hanktheredneckasshole in bay seven, M'Shaka N'Baka pulling in just ahead of him in Number Eight, his crew's all in dreads, do-rags, his Snowbile's pulsing with this booming bass and growling lyrics, *Shaka Zulu, kill the Buddha, yo, bro, Buddha ain't dead, he just foolin'*. The motechs are wandering in, smoking and drinking coffee and prepping themselves for their day gig, which includes pressure washing the SnowBiles, performing general motor maintenance and refilling the Icine tanks. While the guys trudge off to the locker room, the Snowman heads to the front office to file paperwork, along the way kind of forcefully bumping elbows with a couple of guys from Public Works. In a slightly strained relationship, the City Public Works division runs the Power Station but shares their territory with the private ICIN consortium. As a result the snow crews don't get any respect from the CPW, to whom they're a bunch of bottom feeders on about the same level as garbage men. The snow crews, of course, think the CPW guys are all fat-assed button pushers. Mofos wouldn't last one night on the job. They be puking up their guts an' stuff. I mean, they have, like, zero idea of the craftsmanship, the *artistry* that goes into this work. His resurgent pissy mood exacerbated by this stupid *I'm dreaming of a white Christmas* he's only heard ol' Bingo croon about forty thousand times this year alone as he tramps into the front office, where Evelyn gives him this eye-rolling look because as usual he's the last one in and she's waiting for his report so she can close her books and go home. *And stop tracking snow all over the floor! And how many times do I have to tell you to stop smoking in here?* To which he responds over his shoulder Yeah, yeah, yeah in a tone not entirely unlike the classic Beatles' tune and heads off to the locker room, where he dumps his parka, coveralls and mukluks in his locker and, finally, clocks out.

Shivering, he hurries across the snow-covered parking lot and slides behind the wheel of the Coupe. The ice-cold seat sends a sciatic lightning bolt shooting up his spine, setting off a barrage of aches and pains throughout his entire body. The windshield's got about a quarter-inch of frost on the *inside*. He uses an empty beer can to scrape away a jagged tic-tac-toe crosshatching he can barely see through, fires up the engine, pulls out of the factory gate and cruises through the streets of the now completely snow-entombed barrio of SunnySide. Amazingly, the heater's actually blowing out warm air. Damp black lakes spread outward across the frozen white windshield. He lights a cigarette and the smoke mingles with the smells of leaking gasoline, oil, transmission fluid, *Icine*. He can't escape the smell of Icine. It penetrates his clothes, skin, envelops his brain like a cloud of ether *snowwwmannn*. He takes a drag on his cigarette and the ash's bright orange glow makes him wonder if it's possible to absorb enough Icine in your body to spontaneously combust, a notion that has stuck with him ever since he read *Bleak House*, even though Dickens himself may have been just a little too credulous regarding the scientific theories of his day. Which is probably also why the company doesn't bother to administer drug tests. They figure anybody who works in the snowbiz long enough is bound to have Icine in their system, which, by the way, is only something like one carbon atom short of being pure Ice (also called at one time or another cane, candy cane, candy, sugar cane, sugar sticks, ice cream and jizz), something nobody talks about much. In fact, one of the long-term hazards of the snowbiz is *white eye*—the pupils and irises turn snow white, which is what gives Ice junkies that spooky zombie look. They can still see but there's this white aura around everything and a permanent sense of otherworldliness. The Snowman's been in the snowbiz a long time but not that long. (I suppose we should clarify. At this point he's been shooting snow maybe eleven–twelve years, not at all long by most standards, but it is one third of his life, and it is the snow business, where people usually don't last six months—*Ed.*)

Halfway across the barrens, the fields of snow drifted like whipped egg whites, pinkish-orange tea light illuminating dry brown weeds that appear sporadically during rare "warm spells." (The term "nival plant" comes to mind again. Certain species seem to have adapted to the hibernal climate. For example, the ivory white wild foxglove and snow lilies that grow on the roadside, almost invisible against the winter landscape. Their flowers age and blow away like dandelion fluff or snowflakes, seeding and reseeding themselves according to the whims of the wind.) He taps the gas and the speedometer briefly leaps past seventy miles an hour as the Coupe surges forward, then slows inertially as he climbs Caliche Knoll and rolls over the top from where the city appears before him again in all its blazing red and gold, orange and green glory (like something you'd expect to see in the *Martian Chronicles*) at the same moment the Coupe bangs over a pothole and out of nowhere Uncle Bob says in his gruff, warm, reassuring voice, *It's another beautiful winter day, folks.* That's right, Bob, he repeats, *Another beautiful winter day.* His own words are meant to sound sardonic, dismissive, but even as he says them aloud, his only audience himself, his voice cracks on the word *beautiful* and a hot, saline wash of tears rises up from the subterranean sea of lachramae in his soul and floods his already snow-blinded, bloodshot eyes. He tells himself it's nothing, just the light reflected off the dazzlingly white snow, just exhaustion from, what is it now, like twenty-six nights in a row of this fucking madness, he's strung out on physical exhaustion and a lack of sleep, not to mention a fairly heavy regimen of self-medication. But maybe it's pride, didja thinka that, *Snowchump*? The manly tears that come with the pride of a job well done? The pride you feel for sacrificing, for giving up, for utterly *wasting* another fucking day/night of your life, *that* kind of pride? And all these *motherfuckers* (he's now converging with, or, rather, barging into, morning traffic on Aero), all these *losers* with their resigned, defeated faces, the faces of boiled cabbage and potato eaters, of groveling, toadying shiteaters, they don't give a damn about *your* issues, Snowman, they're preparing themselves for their own suffocating horror, performing all their rituals of deferral, putting on makeup, lighting cigarettes, eating donuts, Danishes, bacon and egg waffle sandwiches, drinking coffee, bottled water, soft drinks, whiskey, texting, talking on the cell phone, listening to the radio, to audio texts, playing word games, mind games, jerking off, nodding off. He turns on to Maynard, bounces-crosses the railroad tracks and starts up the hill past the frozen brown mud and snow-covered raw timbers where they're building a new apartment complex, the Savage Vanguard Theater, Juanita Chavez's Tax Services, Tommy's Repurposed Automobiles and Parts, Kamel's Pawn Shop, the tiny strip mall composed of the Iglesia Pentecostal de la Virgin Sanctimonia, coin-op laundromat, Wuendy's Hair

Salon, window service only Micro-Taquería and super-mini-mart, the BO gas station, a string of Mexican eateries, Borracho's Burritos, Chilito's Chalupas, Enrique's Enchiladas, Tu Madre's Tacos, all dressed in their tawdry, late for the ball, droopy, dusty, sagging Christmas decorations. From here his line of sight travels straight down Maynard, past stop signs, traffic lights, light poles, maintenance buildings, beneath the upper deck of I-35 packed with morning traffic, across equally packed Red River, onto the University of Texas at Osberg campus and smack into the green glass walls of the long, low Johnson Hall flaring up in a burnt orange explosion of solar energy. He makes a right on Lafitte, left again on 31st, past the red house, the yellow, the blue, the green. Outside the pink house Moses is wandering around in a faded pink bathrobe and pink bunny slippers. Good God, has he been out here all night? Moses is the neighborhood's notorious Icehead, skinny as a licorice whip, never sleeps, looks like he never bathes or changes clothes, his hair and beard resemble a briar patch, he's completely wigged out, eyes white as eggs, you can almost see the little stars and planets and fizzy, squiggly retinal fragments circling his head . . . definitely a poster child for the anti-Ice campaign.

He pulls up outside his house, a fact he still can't quite accept, that, however modest, it is *his* house, he's the *owner*. That was a coup, right, Snowman? At least you thought so then. The market collapses, suddenly his normally absent landlord's on the phone, Look kid, I'll make you a great deal. Oh yeah, and he just happened to have received a small inheritance from his Aunt Ethyl—she really spelled it that way—his mother's estranged sister, so estranged he never actually met her and only infrequently heard her referred to and even then only as *her*. His newly acquired homeowner status one more improbable link in a long and insidious process of entrapment planned and laid out to look like pure coincidence by some minor god of consumer capitalism. Because now instead of just rent and utilities and a college loan for one degree he finished and another he didn't, he's

gotta pay a mortgage, admittedly nominal, homeowner's insurance, fire, flood, blizzard, tornado and earthquake insurance,
and on top of that, property taxes, which, he knows—a nod to
the Social Contract—are supposed to pay to educate the little
kiddos and turn them into productive citizens, but it still irks
the hell out of him that every year he's gotta turn over more of
his hard-earned ducats to support this ever-growing population
of rug rats who just keep popping out of these hordes of poseur
Madonnas who march up and down the increasingly gentrified
neighborhood streets with their climate-controlled baby car-
riages soliciting homage from an adoring populace for having
done their theological, biological and sociological duty. And he's
going to be held in bondage to this extortion for the rest of
his life? Adding insult to injury—larceny's a better word—the
municipal government gives away half this money to entice even
more of these corporate entities who don't give a shit about the
city or its quality of life. Every a.m. he enters this cold, dank
hovel, looks around at the peeling yellow wallpaper, the worn
floorboards, the water stains on the ceiling, the torn linoleum
in the kitchen, the corroded and leaking faucets, and thinks,
man, what a dump, I oughta fix it up. An *idée fixe* that, while
it recurs on a daily basis, remains fixed in his mind no longer
than it takes him to bend down and ignite the space heater—
that minor thrill and presentiment of death when he strikes the
kitchen match and instead of the damn thing exploding in his
face *ka-Boom!* it simply goes *whoomph* and the orange-blue flame
appears like a ghost in the little ceramic Angkor Wat grillwork.
He runs water for a bath, kicks off his boots, drops his clothes
on the floor and, groaning with anticipatory pleasure, slowly
lowers himself into the steaming hot tub and immediately all the
chills, the aches and pains and chilblains, begin to subside, aided
by the anodynes of whiskey, weed and a cigarette smoldering
in the ashtray on the edge of the tub while he drifts away in a
little sailboat on a warm turquoise sea with palm trees rustling
in the breeze and the sun glowing molten and golden overhead.

10
The Whole Sad Story
(A Melodrama in Passato)

HE WAKES FROM HIS DREAM vacation with the bathwater gone cold. He nudges the hot water on again with his big toe but it's hopeless, the ratio of cold to hot too great to overcome. He gets out of the tub shivering, towels off briskly and dresses quickly in clean socks, thermals, flannel shirt, baggy, comfortable corduroys, brown wool sweater and hoodie and a big clompy pair of work boots. Meanwhile Me'th's been lobbying for dinner (breakfast?), which is pretty much a repeat of breakfast-dinner for both of them, except instead of coffee he washes down his meal with a bottle of dark ale, the latest batch from the Hangin' Tree brewpub that's recently opened on Maynard. Afterwards he crashes on the couch, sipping whiskey and smoking cigarettes in an increasingly pleasant daze as the warm yellow sunlight spreading across the fresh snow fills the room and the space heater finally begins to own up to its name. In a symbiosis of shared body warmth, Me'th has climbed up on top of him so now he has this big black feline slop stretched out on his chest and purring so loudly his own body is vibrating like an electric motor. Inevitably his eyes shift to the black Rorschach blotch of calligraphy printed on a luminous white square of handbeaten paper tacked to the wall and as always he sees a cold winter day, Judith running toward him like a fucking television commercial, her wide smile and her hair crashing around her face and shoulders like waves of India ink and her tits bouncing beneath a brown rag wool sweater, behind her protestors shouting, waving comically staid signs, *DON'T BE LOYAL TO BLIMPFORD OIL!!* Somehow they ended up back at his place, a little one-bedroom shack he glommed onto by answering an ad in a funky, randomly published street rag, their clothes strewn everywhere, stoned, laughing, fucking violently, sloppily on the floor, on the couch, against the bathroom sink, in the kitchen, knocking over chairs, the cinderblock and pineboard bookcase, empty wine bottles crashing to the floor, naked except for socks, Judith's bracelets ringing and jingling like a belly dancer's, exhaling clouds of steam in the cold air, gasping at exploding orgasms and snorting with laughter in a wanton bacchanalia of lust, possibly already in love. Pretty amazing considering that until only an hour ago they'd never spoken a single word to each other. And yet neither as precipitous nor as preposterous as it might sound, keeping in mind they'd already entered into some kind of social contract via those lightning leaps of connectivity when their eyes locked across the chasmic but packed auditorium in Professor Hugh Hieroglyph's wildly popular Political Calligraphy seminar (Signs, Symbols and Significance from Cuneiform to the Fall of the Qing Dynasty), especially on those rare occasions when Professor Hieroglyph deigned to direct a question, usually of a rhetorical nature with no clear right answer but many possible wrong, to his audience of five hundred graduate students and one hand, heavily ringed and braceleted, always shot up first, hers, the girl with the moiling black sea storm of hair down in row two, who, acknowledged by a scowling lift of Hieroglyph's sandy brows, answered the proffered koan in her usual rapid-fire, precise (and, he noticed, accented, e.g., e-cu-*meen*-i-cal, *seemp*-to-mah-*teec*) manner, which usually extracted a smile of bemusement from behind the bulwark of Professor Hieroglyph's bushy, sand-colored mustache, but rather than bask in the warm waters of Hieroglyph's unspoken praise, she turned her head and raised her eyes—their preternatural blue gleam visible even at that distance—to where he sat in the obscurity and near

anonymity of row Y seat forty-two and smiled what he probably would have described as a mischievous, possibly even elven
smile (too much Romantic Literature?), almost as if she had
been performing for him rather than Hieroglyph. Even more
unsettling, when those same strangely blue eyes began to greet
him at the entrance of the auditorium each day with a funny,
puzzled look, like some kind of hamadryadic creature who had
just encountered a man in her forest, although more prosaically,
she may have just been thinking, What are you waiting for,
silly? And then at the protest when she ran toward him bouncing and smiling, he thought she was just happy she recognized
somebody, until she threw her arms around him and kissed
him on the mouth, then laughed and said *Thees ees wonderful!*
and he didn't know if by *Thees* she meant the protest or kissing
him. That barely suppressed manic energy, that enthusiasm for
everything she did, the rapid hand gestures, hyperkinetic body
language, the quick but precise speech, the way she smoked a
cigarette in convulsive jabs, the sudden laughter, the wide mouth
and beautiful white teeth with oddly pointed canines (something to do with a purification ritual in a remote tribal region
of western Somalia. Apparently her father, a big muckety-muck
in an international corporate entity, divorced from a mother
she never met, moved her and her nanny, who, she suspected
in hindsight, may also have been her father's lover, throughout Asia, Africa, the Middle East, Europe and South America.
Which may have explained why he was never sure of her country of or-*ee*-gin, much less her native tongue, complicated by
the fact that she apparently spoke several languages fluently).
Above all her eyes, the color as mutable as her moods, that
strangely radiant Mesopotamian blue, apothecary blue, the blue
of ancient glass, sapphire, cerulean, cobalt blue, the *wine dark*
blue of the Aegean Sea (the way it looked in *National Geographic*
anyway), the coastal regions of her irises a lighter turquoise and
even the impossible chemical blue of toilet bowl cleanser. All
of which, to his woefully provincial eyes, made her seem not

only foreign and exotic but almost otherworldly. What she saw in him he had no idea. Well, sure, he was a handsome guy with rugged good looks, wavy blond hair and a big dick, right? One . . . out . . . of . . . three . . . ain't . . . bad, Old Dave used to say. Although his hair wasn't even that blond, or wavy, except when he neglected to wash it. Of course there was always the possibility that she was part of some enormously complex international conspiracy he could never begin to guess at that indifferently used and threw away whatever players appeared on the board, professional spies, hardened criminals, psychopathic killers, naïve graduate students who, all evidence to the contrary, still believed life should be fair.

We are always happy to bring on board people with unique talents such as yours who also share our philosophy.

At the beginning of the spring semester, Judith moved in with him, an occasion she ceremoniously noted by tacking up the rough square of paper she herself had beaten and pressed out of papyrus and inked with a Japanese ideogram so perfectly rendered (Hieroglyph reportedly had said) that it suggested years of tutelage at the hands of a Zen master and which apparently meant something like *the path to harmony is strewn with tacks.* He loved to watch her run through the cold little house in her bra and panties, exhaling clouds of steam, her hair like a black paintbrush moving across a broad canvas, the artist's dynamic composition having managed to create a tripartite focal point: the white triangle of cotton between her thighs, her erect nipples and the cobalt blue gleam of her eyes fixed, almost creepily, on his (she clearly expected to see him watching her). And sex, tectonic, tsunamic, volcanic, oceans crashed, the world tilted on its axis, the earth split asunder and new mountains arose where old mountains collapsed. Masturbation and a few clumsy, fumbling, mutually unsatisfying sexual encounters hadn't prepared him for coital bliss such as this. Ahead of him lay a Kama Sutra of carnal pleasures, a thousand and one nights on the flying carpet of eroticism, dalliances beyond the imagination of Casanova,

Lothario or Don Juan. Or so he had envisioned. Unfortunately, these earth-shaking unions of the flesh quickly diminished in number the deeper into the spring semester they sprang and he began to realize that to call Judith a dedicated student was at best a gross understatement. She was obsessed, she was driven, she was mad, she was—*brilliant*. Like a machine even, think think think, work work work. It was like she had some vital agenda, time is of the essence, etc. Her work exceeded anything her professors expected or were even capable of executing themselves. She spent hours in the lab, she read all the literature in the field, she led her peers in discussion groups, she had papers accepted for publication in professional journals. She called herself an orthological ecology warrior, swore her life to protecting the integrity of the text.

While Judith's star soared, a sun to all the aspiring planets within her sphere, his astral body plunged below the horizon like a burned-out satellite, his face an ever more sullen lunarscape at the back of his classes, his presence ever more spectral as his absences exceeded his attendance. A sense of meaninglessness pervaded his every action, he felt enervated, defeated, his motivation motorless. True, his mood may have been tainted slightly by current events, i.e., a quarter of the world's population lived in abject poverty, guys—*girls*—he knew in high school were getting blown apart (You mean like Napoleon?) in a brutal and most likely illegal war, as if "legal war" made any more sense, and he was engaged in juvenile wordplay and jurisprudent acrobatics or else arguing with his peers over *The Effects of Plasma Turbulence on Orthology and its Application to the Construction of Meaning*. Keeping in mind that each one of them was carrying at least a quarter-million dollars in debt they'd never be able to pay back in their lives, a financial burden their children (presumptive) and their grandchildren (also) and (who knows) even great grandchildren would assume as it became ever more unpayable, and for what? The illusion that they were doing something of profound importance for the rest of humanity? All of which—his purported concern for humanity, that is—may have been a lame excuse for the chronic cycles of procrastination, apathy and lassitude that had dogged him his entire academic career, punctuated, it should be noted, by manic bursts of joy and exultation when he felt this urge welling up inside him and he felt absolutely convinced he was going to do something really great, he couldn't wait to get home and get started on this new venture right away. Except that by the time he got home his inspiration for this unspecified but urgent project had mysteriously dried up, fizzled out, disappeared down the dark, damp labyrinth of plumbing where his mood was just as suddenly spiraling because, really, what was the point? Why try to do anything when it was all meaningless, school, life, the world—everything? This depression that overcame him, so monstrous and heavy and debilitating, as if he were encased in a lead sarcophagus and set adrift in the empty vacuum of an ever-expanding space with no hope of ever again encountering another human being (still not sure about Judith at this point—those alien eyes, that androidal intellect). Which also may have explained, at least partially, how something that had lain nascent in his being began to coalesce into—if not exactly a strict vow of poverty and hermetical retreat from the world, then at least a resolve not to participate in the machinery of greed and corruption, which, in its earliest manifestation, meant he stopped going to class altogether and hung around the house, smoking pot and devouring offbeat fiction, most recently a novel in which every sentence, while clearly following upon the sentence before it logically and grammatically, also served as the beginning of another novel, so that by the final page, the reader had read a novel about the possibility of novels, in the process, out of a sheer need to fill the abhorrent vacuum, creating his or her own unique plot, characters, theme and any other elements of fiction deemed essential by the illiterati.

There was also the issue of money. No longer enrolled in school, he had a loan to pay back. Of more immediate concern—when he came up short on the rent and the formerly laissez-faire landlord *I'm just an old hippie* showed up at their door, after which he began to compulsively scroll through job listings of even the most obscure employment opportunities (copy editing canned salmon labels in Fairbanks, Alaska, manning a fire tower on an uninhabited and vegetally barren island in Micronesia) while chain-smoking, a vicious habit he disinterestedly glommed (*again?*) onto one night in front of the screen when he felt a strong urge for *something* and the closest thing at hand happened to be a pack of Judith's cigarettes and from there on out he was on board that train, even though, ironically, Judith quit cold turkey the following week. Meanwhile his job search was going nowhere, he apparently wasn't qualified for anything but entry-level burger flipping. Then he saw the ad on the local rag's website: Snow Services Technician.

And so he started in the snowbiz convinced he was some kind of blue-collar hero, a titan of labor, that he, the job he did, was somehow noble, even vital to the well-being of mankind. While the population at large slept comfortably in their warm beds and visions of sugar plums danced in their heads, he went out and worked in that cold black night, he tucked the world under a protective blanket of snow that kept it safe and secure from the threat of disease, rampant crime and invasion by locust-like hordes of undocumented barbarians. And yeah, maybe he did believe that at first, maybe Judith even believed it at first. Maybe she was just preoccupied with her own life. He'd come home at six, seven a.m., fingers and toes still frozen, his mind vacant as a cave, his body a minefield of detonating aches and pains, find Judith in a hoodie, rag wool sweater, thermal leggings and sheepskin moccasins bent over her screen at the kitchen table, her coffee cup situated in a honeycomb of brown carbon rings on a paper mat, her eyes exuding a manic blue radiance, her fingers running over the keyboard like amphetaminic spiders, the 3-D MakerBot happily humming the same monotonous tune over and over again as it perfectly produced one conical, volcanic-like structure after another, a recent obsession of hers and apparently not one she wished to discuss. In response to his casual *what are those?* she muttered in a guttural tone unsettlingly similar to that of the little girl in *The Exorcist, Hollow furnaces.* Fifteen minutes later, soaking his weary bones in a hot bath, she'd come in, drop her clothes on the floor and climb into the tub, leading to frantic, clutching, slippery sex in clouds of steam, her back arched, moisture-beaded breasts and hard flat belly pushed out in a yogic paroxysm, her black bush awash against his blondish pubic hairs, that otherworldly cobalt blue flickering of her eyes as she disappeared to her own planet. Afterwards hurriedly toweling off and crashing together in bed in a slumber of profound exhaustion. He'd wake in the afternoon, groggy, dazed, his inchoate thoughts teetering on a frayed rope suspension bridge over a bottomless chasm separating a swampy primordial island of sensual pleasure from the frozen white tundra of another cold, black night ahead. Judith just then coming back from a seminar, wired on caffeine and conversation, she and Jon—*Jon?*—this guy in Hieroglyph's Heroic Hermeneutics class—so how long had she and Jon known each other? Wait—Judith's incredulous double take—are you jealous? What? Him? Jealous? Oh no no no, he wasn't jealous. Jealousy was a thing of the past, a self-indulgence of the petite bourgeoisie, an artifact of the helplessly romantic sentimental masses. And he, an enlightened exemplar of egalité among the sexes, jealous? Like hell he wasn't jealous! He was jealous of her male friends, he was jealous of her female friends, he was jealous of her confidence and drive and certainty of her path in life. Yeah, sure, he knew the academic scene was lame, it was bullshit, it was all a bunch of hypocrisy (la la la, I can't hear you), but she was thinking, she was using her mind, while he—his work was totally mindless, he functioned in a corrupted Zen state, a perfect dynamo of industry, his working-class hero status rapidly diminished to that of a barely cognitive cog in the wheel, all his time, his energy, his life devoted to this meaningless donkey labor with a bunch of grunting troglodytes.

The utter pointlessness of existence, his and everyone else's, all the more evident on the rare occasion he accompanied Judith to one of her colleague's *au courrant* bikram parties, the thermostat set at a steamy ninety-eight degrees, every light in the place blazing, all the electronic appliances and devices, stove, microwave, toaster oven, hair blower, electric toothbrush—and especially all those sneaky little LEDs gleaming malevolently everywhere—radiating additional heat and light, everybody hanging out in surfer shorts and bikinis (even though they really shouldn't), all these pallid, hipster-posturing pudding bellies and lard butts sucking down mai tais, piña coladas, frozen daiquiris, hurricanes, each and every one of whom believed with the absolute confidence instilled throughout a childhood and adolescence of triumphs and awards for giving it their best (more or less), for trying (but not succeeding), for sharing (who cares?) that the world was their oyster and it came with a million-dollar pearl to boot, or at least enough to pay off their student loans. And inevitably someone was going to ask him what he *did* and he would have to grudgingly confess that he was a snow services technician, which elicited a wary, unenthusiastic *Oh really? What's that like?* that made him even more defensive, which usually led to his getting drunk (okay, drunker) and sulking in a corner or else insulting someone and being asked to leave. And then the confrontation with Judith later. How dare he act like that, in public, with her friends? What was he trying to prove—that he really was a loser? Which, of course, really pissed him off, but instead of exploding in anger like a hotheaded little nuke as he was increasingly wont to do, he pouted and sulked like a spoiled brat because it was true—it was true! He *was* a loser. His job was worthless, he was worthless—*everything* was worthless. A revelation and acknowledgement that also led to his thinking the unthinkable—maybe he should go back to school, or at the very least, make some attempt to look for another job.

Unfortunately, it was also at this crucial juncture that Old Dave disappeared. Rumor would later have it that he'd gone off to a tropical isle, that he lived in a thatched hut and skippered tourists around on a small schooner. The night the news broke, the as-of-yet unchristened Snowman tramped into the front office dropping cigarette ashes on the floor and splashing coffee all over the place to inquire what he and the rest of the crew were supposed to do in Old Dave's absence, but instead of the soon to be familiar *Snowman! Stop tracking up the floor! And don't you know smoking is forbidden in here?!* Evelyn sat at her desk, a nervous wreck, wringing her hands like a deranged washerwoman, her bright bird eyes caught in an unfamiliar cage, her funny little button face crinkled up like one of those microwave aluminum foil popcorn bags. Voice trembling, she informed said pre-Snowman that Gastreaux wanted to see him *immediately*, and, his own anxiety climbing, he rode the frosty, glass-walled elevator up to Gastreaux's mezzanine office, where Gastreaux himself sat in a red leather swivel chair, taking savage bites out of a huge breakfast taco over the clutter on his desk. Through a mouthful of masticated egg, potato and bacon slathered with a spicy red salsa, Gastreaux proceeded to offer him the job as Commander of Number Nine and a dollar an hour raise, *possibly* more at the end of an unspecified probationary period, keeping in mind that he would now be acting on management's behalf and should therefore conduct himself accordingly. And of course he said yes, how could he possibly not say yes. He was practically peeing all over himself like a squirming little puppy dog. He actually believed, wanted to believe, that, yes, this really was a wonderful opportunity and he really was going to do a great job and save not only the company but the whole fucking world and all of humanity and, oh boy, in exchange for that inconsequential little chore Gastreaux was going to give—*give*—him a whopping dollar an hour more. Even better, he'd inherited Old Dave's crew, he wouldn't have to deal with a bunch of greenhorns. Or so he thought. Employee turnover at an all-time high, his comrades in arms, Jippi Jaime, Hanktheredneckasshole and M'Shaka N'Baka, soon departed to take on their own crews. And in their stead, a whole new crew, not only of Mexicans but these truly alien Zolmen, or, more technically, Zoltecs (Margarito insisted on this distinction—between Mexican and Zoltec that is). On the way back to the shop one morning, he made an unauthorized detour past the house to pick up some cash he owed Jipi Jaime. He caught Judith peering out the kitchen window at the odd floral arrangement of bronze and terra cotta faces peering back at her from the SnowBile. Let me guess, she said. Snow White and his seven dwarves, right? Is that how many you have—*seven?* He had to think. No, not seven, five, sometimes six. True, he did slip once and call Bombástico "Bashful," and even odder, Bombástico gave him a wide-eyed *ooh, ooh* look, like—how did you know?

While he dug himself deeper into this rut, Judith finished her Master's *summa cum laude* and started work on a doctorate in the Department of Dialectical Ecology, and *boom*, just like a flock of pigeons exploding out of a hayloft, the pages flew off the calendar and the next one two three years disappeared in a total mind-blinding whiteout of activity. She attended seminars, served on committees, published regularly, taught upper-division courses (her students adored her, developed enormous and existentially convoluted crushes on her, turned suicidal at the least suggestion they had fallen short of her expectations). Word was out that she was working on a highly explosive dissertation with Hieroglyph (*Hugh* now), she was being recruited by Harvard, Berkley, MIT, a stellar career in academics seemed assured. Upon completion of her PhD, she began a generously funded postdoc. Six months later her dissertation was in print. It would go on to become the gold standard in colleges across the nation. Judith, however, would not. The brilliant mind, the future voice of American letters, the fiery advocate for environmental protection of the text, the *orthological ecology warrior*, dropped it all to join the team at PPP, the innocuous sounding Print and Paper Products corporation, an international conglomerate owned by the extremely wealthy and notoriously conservative Bochit brothers. A collective gasp of shock and disappointment rose like a flaming hot air balloon above the Osberg campus. This was the corporation that had converted thousands of square miles of ancient redwood forests—giant sequoias that had held the blue sky on their shoulders long before the birth of Jesus or even the Buddha—into toilet paper, hamburger wrappers. She refused to explain herself to anyone. To him, the Snowman, her lover and prospective partner in life, she only said that she could do more good working within the system, which sounded like such a total crock that he almost called her on it, except that it also seemed so out of character that he thought, wait, is this part of that conspiracy thing? (Assuming there was one, that is.) Hugh Hieroglyph was reported to be destroyed, he failed to appear at his professorial pulpit for days at a time, and when he did, unshaven, disheveled, reeking of alcohol, his discourse often deteriorating into rambling, incomprehensible bloviations on the inherent untrustworthiness—I'd even go so far as to say the *sneaking*, the *deceitful* nature of the other sex—*text*, I meant to say *text*, by which, of course, I mean the text of the other, the not-I, the alien, unfamiliar, that parvenu, pretender to the throne, the distaff half, bitch in skirts, filthy whore—I mean *brass bath, itchy shirts, chilly floor* . . . um . . . er . . .

So while the now (be)knighted *Snowman* (it *was* Nico who so dubbed him, was it not?) continued to pricketh on the plain in the saddle of SnowBile Number Nine, his lengthening tenure in the snowbiz ensured by the rhythmic hammering tighter of his coffin lid (another dollar an hour raise), Judith began her new career in an informal fab with a bunch of other brilliant and enthusiastic young men and women exploring cutting edge technologies to reclaim useful words from remaindered litera-ture, outdated fiction, prose, poetry, political and philosophical essays—stuff nobody wanted anymore. After removing viable word stock from texts through a process called lexical extraction, machines that looked like giant mechanical dentures (Judith gave him a guided tour, hard hat, safety glasses, white lab coat) shredded, masticated, digested and reconstituted the paper into institutional cereal products, pre-fab building materials, avant garde furniture and designer hygenic paper products, specifically toilet paper, facial tissues and dinner napkins. The salvaged words were sold in large batches to interested parties, mostly legal firms and government agencies. (And by the way, this recycling aspect sways him more to Judith's idea of working inside the system, which, he has to admit, he kind of is too.)

As someone said, success is a double-edged sword. Within a year, Judith had been promoted to assistant general manager, which must have been what, year six—*seven?*—of their relationship? Their schedules were completely opposite. He worked long nights, Judith long days, their paths rarely intersected, they seldom had sex. When they had time together, they argued. Why don't you quit that stupeed job? You're wasting your life. (He knew that.) You can find something better. (Really—like what?) You could go back to school, get vocational training, earn more money. Yes, I know, who the hell cares about money, right, *Snowman?* (And since when had she started to call him *Snowman?*) Well I do if it means nice clothes and good food, if it means being warm and comfortable instead of shivering all night in a *dump*. In other words, he said in this sick twisted sarcastic tone that almost sounded conciliatory at first, the status quo? That trigger having been pulled, the next second he was calling her a bourgeois bitch, a whore and a pig, words he'd never spoken to anyone before (and, yes, he probably was at least moderately drunk). As if that weren't enough, he had to continue. She wasn't even a whore. Whores made their living on their backs. She made hers on the backs of others. She worked for a corporation that exploited cheap labor in Third World countries to make frivolous products for the rich. To which she replied that he was full of shit (*sheet*, actually), he was a hypocrite (*hee*-po-*creet*), he worked for the institution too, he was comp*leeceet*. The *complicit* momentarily stunned him, but he bounced off the ropes. Yeah but he didn't give the orders, he didn't reap the profits, he was an honest, hardworking, underpaid fellaheen laborer. So just because you let yourself be trampled like a worthless little piece of sheet, that somehow excuses you, *Snowman?*

Brrrinnng! All right, break it up! Back to your corners!

At their next encounter twenty-four hours later they had ferocious sex without speaking to each other once, then crashed on opposite sides of the bed, on their cold, disconsolate antipodes, yearning deep in their souls for the warm spooning comfort of each other's body.

They resolved to work things out. Maybe they just needed more room. They looked at a number of places, argued over every one. When Judith announced she had found an apartment downtown, he complained it was too expensive, he detested the fakey neighborhood—besides, it's too small for both of us. I know, *Snowman*, that's the idea, it's for me alone, it's going to be my apartment, you aren't ever going to agree to anything I want, you don't really want to move out of that hovel, I'm not even sure you want to be with me anymore. A curtain of gloom descended upon him. What did this mean? Were they separating? Was it over? His mood sank from melancholy to morose when Judith's old friend Jon from grad school, who, okay, probably was gay, arrived in a vintage powder blue pickup with the make emblazoned on the tailgate in flamingo pink *Frod* and the house began to empty of her personal things, which, yes, he did help carry out, including the large teakwood roll-top desk that had belonged to a great, great somebody in India in the 1860s, and a mahogany armoire from a great, great somebody else in Singapore in the 1870s, as well as all the wall hangings, antique lamps, authentic Shaker rocking chair, in essence leaving the bed, or rather mattress and springs, on the bedroom floor, a broken-down couch and sofa in the living area and the kitchen table and chairs, oh yes, and her ideogram on the wall. Judith, too, looked miserable. Maybe if they had acted, if one of them had said, wait a second, this is so wrong. Instead they pouted and glared at each other like children (well, he did) while the hominess, the clutter, the frenzied zeal that had occupied the house vanished as if it had been sucked away by an enormous vacuum cleaner. Finally Judith got in the truck, possibly crying, Jon gave him a sympathetic *what can you do?* shrug and drove away, and he went back inside, sat down on the sofa at the front window, poured a glass of whiskey and lit a cigarette. And at some point tasted salt water in his drink.

And yes, it is melodrama, but what else are you going to say? They were like avulsing continents, the church divorced from the state, the planet Earth waving goodbye to the moon as it sailed off forever into the frozen blackness of space?

The first night, the first day, the first week, he felt like someone had died. He felt as hollow and empty as an abandoned coalmine. He left the house empty in the evening, he worked all night on empty, he returned to the cold, empty house in the morning empty. He had zero appetite, ate almost nothing, subsisted on coffee, cigarettes and whiskey.

No one at work noticed or said anything if they did.

One morning, collapsed on the couch, slipping in and out of consciousness, he heard a persistent scratching at the front door, maybe a branch bent by the wind. But everything's dead, there are no trees, no branches, remember, Snowman? How about a newspaper, then, blown down the street by a wintry gust? Yeah, but nobody else in the whole goddamn city but you gets the newspaper, it's all online. A vacuum cleaner salesman? Ditto (online). Raven? Not in this clime. Dreading an encounter with the chirpy next-door neighbor (Hannah? Anna?) or any human being for that matter, he pulled himself up from the couch, clomped like Frankenstein's monster to the door, swung it open. On the step sat an emaciated black cat with a torn ear, an open wound in its neck, bones showing everywhere beneath its flaccid coat and more anguish than he'd ever seen in an animal's eyes. Without waiting for an invitation, it staggered inside, its back leg dragging, tail partially defoliated, a glimpse of large black balls. He shut the door, put down an old flannel shirt on the kitchen floor, heated some milk, browned some hamburger and went to bed. And woke that evening with the nearly weightless presence of the cat lying sphinx-like on his chest, its large yellow eyes fixed on his. The cat recovered from its wounds quickly, its presence on his chest grew weightier every day. His name was Me'th, with a slight hitch after the "e," what linguists call a glottal stop, so it's pronounced as two syllables, *Me-th*, from there it's an easy leap to *methamphetamine*, which certainly fit his unpurrily bad attitude and emaciated frame when he arrived on the Snowman's doorstep that morning, but it could also be short for Methuselah, depending on how many of his nine lives he had already used up (or even, if some speech impediment was involved, Mephistopheles, which would go hand and hand with his coal black coat). Almost immediately, they became inseparable. They slept together, lounged on the sofa or couch together, ate dinner and breakfast together. Me'th jumped up on the table and dined on hot oatmeal in milk, breakfast tacos, bacon and eggs, chicken-fried steak. When something didn't meet Me'th's tastes, he sat like a statue and glowered with the contempt of a pharaoh.

The first time he and Judith got together again (she'd forgotten a box of notebooks) they sulked and snarled at each other like angry resentful adolescents, which made sex that much more powerful. Afterwards Judith wandered around the shabby little house. She already looked out of place, as if having made the decision to remove herself in body she had also detached herself in spirit. Then Me'th came in with a convulsing rat between his teeth. He had proven to be quite the hunter, whatever there was left to hunt, rodents, bugs—despite their best efforts, the authorities had *not* been able to eradicate the persistent vermin population. Cockroaches, especially, not only survived but even thrived in the cold.

By now Me'th was the size of a small panther. He and Judith eyed each other like two witches and Me'th headed for the bedroom closet. How can you live like this, Snowman? Judith said. Then she started on his job again, she knew some people, maybe they could get him something in an office. Which was all he needed to set him off. I don't *want* a fucking office job! To which she replied, You asshole, if you applied your intelligence to something good you could make a real deefference in the world. Which both appealed to some noble instinct inside him and stung him deeply. You mean like you're doing now? he retorted, his aim to inflict as much pain as possible. You don't know what I'm doing! she said (which sounded slightly ominous when he thought about it later) and headed for the door, his last happy remark before she slammed it shut behind her, Fuck you, bitch! And so end this brief rapprochement with that percussive ugliness, that triumph of the will, if such triumph means the intentional destruction of all you hold beautiful and dear in exchange for the transient satisfaction of vengeance. Afterwards, sit in the dark and drink whiskey and brood. Maybe contemplate suicide—abstractly. Half an hour later swearing to himself he was really going to do it—he was going to look for a better job, he was going back to school, he was going to find a way to use his mind. He should call Judith, she'd be so happy to hear, maybe they could get together Sunday. For what, Snowman? So you can end up fighting again? So she walks out blinking back tears and leaves you staring into the dark like a cold brute beast? And am I really supposed to believe you want to return to that stuffy, stodgy, straitjacketed suffocation in those hallowed hollows of academe? As for a better job—he'd be lucky to find a position as a mailroom clerk. Just thinking about that nine-to-five office jive filled him with mortal dread. Which, one might reasonably surmise without a degree in psychology, probably did have something to do with the fact that he watched his old man shuffle papers his entire life—but not fast enough to escape bill collectors, illness, death.

Thus began his bachelorhood. Whatever connection he'd had with civilization evaporated and went out the door with Judith. The day after her visit, his screen died and so ended his participation in the electronic community. Never an exponent of the cell phone, his only contact with the outside world now his landline (although it never rang), or stopping at the liquor store or the convenience store for provisions, where a discussion of a price increase or a particular product on display evolved into his desperately grasping at chunks of conversation while the increasingly nervous clerk rolled his/her eyes at the growing line of impatient customers.

He told himself he should get out of the house more, maybe get involved in some kind of recreational activity, or how about looking up some old college buddies. Total fiasco. Sitting in a sports bar, three wide screens blasting, these two ignoramuses, both in IT, both of whom easily earned five times his salary, citing minutely detailed statistics of this currently hot twenty-year-old hockey player, who (even the Snowman knows) is going to be a total, fifty-million-dollars-down-the-drain, has-been train wreck next year, while the precious hours, minutes, seconds of his own life slipped away. He should have made some crummy excuse, got up, walked out. Instead he got drunk, and then drunker. Soon he was shouting inarticulate nonsense about the war and poverty. You could feed a family of four for a year on our bar tab! You could build a school in Afghanishtan! Shave a bunch of shtarving children! S'like we're murderers! The other bar patrons, even his buddies, are getting uncomfortable, there's a tap on his shoulder, *Sir, you'll have to leave now*, the rest of the night lost in a black velvet lake of nothingness.

Well how's about catching an all-night matinee at the old Varsity theater, which has somehow been magically transported way the hell out on Twelfth Street (some real estate conglomerate sees this area as the next target for gentrification), the sole patron, seated in the middle row in a maroon velour folding chair, generations of chewing gum stuck to the metal bottom, inhaling the stale, musty smells of peanuts, buttered popcorn, spilled soda, mildew, smoking a cigarette and sipping from a bottle, and no rules, no regulations, no ushers in red polyester uniforms with white piping down the pant legs pointing flash-lights in his eyes, *Sir, you'll have to leave now.* The moth-eaten, water-stained velvet curtains roll back, the screen lights up to an orchestral burst of sound and he settles deeper in his seat into that other time and place, his ocular nerves bombarding soft, receptive parts of his brain with lurid Technicolor panoramas of cowboys and Indians, space aliens, a troupe of male exotic dancers, cavalry soldiers and mustachioed bandidos. It's a crazy sci-fi western directed by—who else?—Boone Weller.

On rare occasions he wheeled out the TV, long ago exiled to the closet where it talked brightly and entertained itself like an autistic child perfectly content to be banished to time out in perpetuity. Once he tripped over the orange extension cord snaking out from under the closet door, inadvertently unplug-ging the TV so that it languished in darkness for days, a lapse duly recorded and reported, he knew, to the proper authorities by the Responsible Audience Tracker in each television set, an innovation that came about with the passing of a new public program initiated by the FCC in collusion *sic* (of course the intended word was *cooperation*, but in a recurring failure of con-temporary copy editing, the writer's much more honest but also highly damaging original word choice was *not* struck—*Ted.*) with the Department of Education, which strongly encouraged citizens to keep their televisions on twenty-four hours a day with the slogan *An informed people is a warm people. Remember, stay warm, stay informed!* When he discovered his error, he plugged the TV in again and wheeled it back into the closet.

As for meeting other women, when? where? how? Six a.m., stopped at a convenience store for cigarettes, excuse me, miss, you dropped your, um, tampons? Not to mention, twelve hours a day, six, *seven* days a week on the job, he had nearly zero time or testosterone and the only *fucked* he wanted to get was *up.*

He sat at the kitchen table wolfing down his food in ragged bites (and rudely ignoring Me'th, which almost guaranteed a dead rat in his bed that night), too tired to chew, to taste, to care. Just gnaw at it until his belly was full, the food gone, drink bourbon and smoke pot and cigarettes until he sank into an alcohol and weed-numbed, fart-warmed cocoon of sleep before the next twelve-hour ordeal. Except when he couldn't sleep, when, restless, depressed, agitated—life's happening out there and he's shuttered up in this dim little hole—he wandered the brilliant, blinding, snow-white streets like a zombie, a ghoul, a vampire too hastily risen from his earthen bed, unshaven, unkempt, his face a ghastly gray-white, dark circles hanging like partial lunar eclipses beneath his red-rimmed, disturbingly bloodshot eyes hidden from the public behind a pair of cheap wraparound sunglasses so that the night was always with him in shades of charcoal darkness and penumbral luminosity. Which also added to his confusion about the time of day. He said good afternoon instead of good evening, good night instead of good morning. There was also this odd phenomenon in which all the noise and clamor of pedestrians talking, laughing, shouting, blasting boom boxes, competing Christmas carols *do you hear what I hear? . . . hark! the herald, angels sing,* the honk and blare and roar of cars, trucks, buses plowing through the slushy, snowy streets, steam rising from manhole covers, drains, heating vents, welcome waves of warm air washing over him when customers whomped open the glass doors of shops and stores—when all that faded and was subsumed by a phantom Arctic Roar. It rose above the din of traffic, it came out of the mouths of sales clerks, cashiers, mailmen, traffic cops gesturing like automatons, this constant background roar and yet no one else but him heard it. How was that possible? Yeah, but they don't have to work in it, Snowman, they don't have to listen to it howling in their skull all night long, they don't have to worry about what's lurking right behind them if they turn around or look over their shoulder. *I'm sorry, sir, what did you say?* Oops. You're doing it again, Snowman. And besides, it's not like you're the only one who feels miserable. The whole fucking world's miserable. Just walking down the street you can see everyone's miserable. People constantly slip and fall on the goddamn icy sidewalks, you can hear the sickening thud of bodies hitting the frozen concrete. A man and woman in rags herd a puppy swarm of ragtag kids ahead of them, a man in the remnants of a military uniform limps on crutches, his eyes like caverns, an old woman with wild, stringy hair in a housecoat and men's work boots shuffles along, tears streaming down her cheeks, a group of men huddle over a fire barrel in an alley. One of them glances up and the Snowman sees a frightening kinship in his eyes. On every street corner half a dozen beggars are trying to outdo the next, legless, armless, brain-damaged, shell-shocked, homeless vets, men and women who have been horribly beat up, raped, abused, blackened eyes so swollen they can barely see out of them, faces beaten into purple and red pulp, noses twisted or flattened, missing teeth. Adding insult to injury, the constant reminders everywhere, the flashing lights, signs, the adjurations, *Only 246 shopping days until Christmas!* It's like a commandment—it *is* a commandment. Thou shalt buy and consume! Thou shalt spend thy pittance and be satisfied! The tired old Christmas anthems grind on and on in stores, shops, bars, theaters, office buildings, proclaiming *the birth of God!* A *miracle!* Although what kind of miracle can you hope for when the sons and daughters of God are trampled underfoot everyday like grapes, when civic and business and church leaders fill pitchers and goblets with the blood of the poor, the hungry, the meek and call it wine? *What did you say, Mister?* It's right there in the headlines scrolling across the TV in the shop window in front of him. Under the auspices of Osberg's new *camping ban* the police are conducting regular sweeps to drive the homeless out of downtown. The churches have locked their doors. All the missions, charity wards, Salvation Army and Caritas are overrun. Families live in abandoned buildings, open fields, vacant lots, in hovels made out of scrap lumber, carpet, cardboard, tar paper. Like cockroaches they burrow themselves deeper into the cracks and crevices of city parks, storm drains, bridges, underpasses, steam and utility tunnels. Utility workers freak out every time they hear a damp cough or spot an aqueous pair of eyes looming out of the dark. Extermination squads go in with shotguns, nets, poison gas. The courts are filled with endless cases of vagrancy, public intoxication, urination, no underarm deodorant, lack of hair conditioner, littering, loitering, larceny, creating a public nuisance, a public disturbance, a public disgrace, officer, they cuss and they curse and, much worse, they smell! beat them, officer! up against the wall! shoot them, abuse them, oh, the gall! At first the wretches were glad to go to jail to get food, warmth. Now the jails are so crowded they're packed in like screeching rats, biting and tearing at each other over scraps. Rumors spread of slave labor in factories, mines. Legions of jonesing homeless Ice junkies wrapped in blankets shuffle through the streets like zombies with ghostly white eyes. It's like some kind of pestilence, plague. He's not even sure anymore if he's imagining all this or it's really happening. Oh yeah, but the proof's in the plum pudding, right? One night the Snowman's doing the shit run, he pulls this old derelict out of a dumpster, the guy hasn't changed his clothes in months, he's hobbling around in cracked boots, can barely walk. The Good Samaritan Snowman takes him to the clinic. When they finally manage to pull his boots off his feet are just shreds of raw red meat on bare bones. They're eaten up by gangrene, endless frostbite. The only thing that's keeping them from rotting altogether and killing him is the fact that they're completely frozen. The old bum knew it too, but he wasn't going to tell anyone. Because he also knew as soon as they got him in a charity ward they were going to chop off his feet, push him outside in a wheelchair with two cents in his pocket, So long, pappy, take better care of yerself. And it so happens he was right. And hovering over all this inhumanity, watching, observing, commanding all, the Great Eye. Sometimes he feels like it's watching him in particular, like it's tracking his every move. Of course everybody feels that way. That's the beauty of the Eye. This highly visible entity *is* watching everyone. Every single person and thing in its line of sight beamed back by optical nerve fiber to Police Central. Lately the Snowman's noticed this graffiti appearing everywhere. At a glance it looks like a pale green triangle. Examined more closely you can see it's the pyramid from the old dollar bill with the all-seeing eye in the truncated pinnacle, and in the center of this eye, like an odd slant of light, the figure 1%, and then in the middle of the larger part of the pyramid below, the figure 99%, and at the base the words *all wealth flows upward . . . losers.*

In stark contrast to the periphery, the center, the heart of the crystal city, is sterile, clean, the denizens are all well-dressed, they look attractive, happy, and why not, they've got great jobs, great lives, they make a ton of money and they live in this enormous atrium, warm sunshine, pockets of lush tropical public gardens—they're so dense people get lost for days, they have to send in rescue teams, EMS, there are cases where someone goes native, lives off wild fruit, berries. The humidity's so high sometimes there are brief thunderstorms, people bring out their brightly colored umbrellas and splash in the puddles. Oddly, the Great Eye seems to cast a more benevolent gaze over these inhabitants, and the Snowman's kind of got an insider's perspective on that. Following yet another raise and promotion, Judith has moved into a super high rise and, yes, he has visited it on a few occasions. Because despite this big schism between them, they can't seem to be together and they can't entirely be apart. Sooner or later one of them calls the other and after some hemming and hawing they'll make a date to eat at a restaurant or see a movie, something safe like that, although, one way or the other, they always end up going back to her place and, one way or the other, they always end up fighting, he storms out, thunder and lightning crashing about him, let death come, the heavens fall. Apocalypse! Götterdämmerung! Next time they meet, they glare at each other across this vast chasm, both hurting so badly the salt sea washes right up to the back door of their ocular portals and threatens to spill out, at the same time the whole thing's so ridiculous their faces and bodies are exhibiting all these tics and spasms and they're both on the verge of breaking into raucous laughter. Sooner or later Judith says something like, You're abominable, Snowman, or he says, Look, I know I'm an asshole. And sometimes they even have crazy sex. It's almost like a sadomasochistic thing. They torment themselves, they torment each other. And as long as they remain in each other's orbit they seem doomed. Which invites the return of an old ghost. What if none of this is true? What if (his overly active ventromedial prefrontal cortex really kicking in now, with a little help from the old atavistic-leaning reptile brain) Judith really is involved in some big conspiracy and her whole job is to make him angry and resentful toward society and keep him schlepping along this lowly path toward utter ruination even though she loves— loved—him dearly? Yeah, that'd make perfect sense, right?

Of course you realize your assignment will be very difficult. There will be times when your own emotional involvement will cost you enormous suffering, but you must never, under any circumstances, divulge any information or knowledge relevant to this operation. Is that understood?

11
By the Fire

WHO KNOWS, MAYBE IF HE had some time away from the job to relax and sort things out and in the process rejuvenate his whole being. How do you say sunshine, Margarito? How do you say summer solstice? How do you say God, paradise, eternity, vacation at the sea, beach ball, bikini? But even if he had asked for the gift of those words and Margarito had given them—*Sí, Snowman, luz solar, solsticio de verano, Díos, paraíso, eternidad, vacaciones al mar, beach-a ball*—ha, ha, just keeding Snowman—*pelota de playa, bikini!*—they would have remained inutile, abstract, because the one week's unpaid vacation he was technically permitted each year afforded him neither time nor money for any real travel, and even if he did bring up the idea, Evelyn'd squinch her bright blue bird's eyes together behind her wire-rimmed glasses and give him that pained, chewing-on-a-lemon look. Right now isn't a good time, Snowman. Yeah, well when is a good time? I don't know, Snowman, that's up to Mister Gastreaux. But don't even think of mentioning it to Gastreaux. I know we're real busy 'n all, 's just I could really use some time off now. Time off? For what, *Snowman*, good behavior? I don't get time off. Nobody gets time off. And he was such a goddamn coward, shuffling and bobbing like a punch-drunk pug and muttering, Yeah, well, sure, I can see what you're saying, if we're understaffed 'n all. Sometimes he thought of Old Dave, who, according to the latest rumors, had opened a club in a tropical paradise—*yeah, a friend of mine swears a girl he knew tended bar there*, or he's running a wilderness survival school—*yeah, a friend of mine's buddy who was a Navy Seal trains there.* It was kind of a joke that everyone called Old Dave *old* because he was probably only thirty-something when he disappeared, more or less the Snowman's age now. Sometimes he secretly hoped for a catastrophe, preferably natural, nothing that *killed* anyone, you wouldn't want that, would ya, Snowman? Just something to jam the cogs, stop the machine long enough for him to get off and figure out some kind of plan.

Santy Claus musta hoid him because on the official first day of winter a true blue norther came howling down on the city in the middle of a black moonless night. In two hours the temperature plunged to an unheard of twenty below zero as a massive arctic front funneled into the southwest, helped along by the enormous fans the Canadians had erected along their border to keep out the golem of global warming, which manifested itself in towering anthropomorphic cloud masses of warm, poisonous air that wafted over the Canadian territories and hung there like a fatally halitotic breath. Then it started to snow, real snow, frozen H_2O snow, snow that fell down from the high heavens instead of up from the cooling towers of power plants, God's own glorious gift of snow. It snowed day and night. It snowed up, down, sideways. The houses, streets and cars were soon buried in deep, muffled whiteness. Even out in the suburbs the jobsite was completely snowed under when the snow crews arrived, their job done for them by Mother Nature's winter playmate Jack Frost. An executive order came down, all snow crews furloughed until further notice. Only SnowBile commanders and their chief assistants should report for duty at 1800 hours sharp the following day.

More or less at the specified time, they're all standing around Evelyn's desk, him, Jipi Jaime, M'Shaka, Hanktheredneckasshole, a couple of newer, younger commanders and their assistants (Margarito, of course, is his man, despite Gastreaux's objection to his being not only Mexican but illegal). Shortly afterwards, the elevator descends from the mezzanine and Gastreaux waddles into the middle of the group. I'll get straight to the point, gentlemen. Which, in essence, is they have zero work to do. They're only being sent out for appearance's sake to keep the paying public happy. And forget about the SnowBiles. We ain't burning up all that fuel on them brontosauruses—how ya like that metaphor, Snowman? Operational vehicles will include only SLEDs. *SLEDs?* The commanders are all giving each other puzzled glances and shaking their heads—M'Shaka's dreads actually send a carelessly placed soda bottle flying across the room like a missile that shatters against the glass-framed portrait of the original power plant owner, at which Gastreaux rolls his eyes in a silent appeal for divine intervention.

The SLEDs (Small Light Engine Distribution vehicle) are a holdover from the snowbiz's early years when SnowBiles were accompanied by a "senior officer" who drove ahead to scope out jobsites and reconnoiter potential trouble spots. Much smaller than the SnowBiles, aerodynamically shaped, almost rocket-like, the SLEDs (more commonly referred to in the lower case—*sled*) travel at extremely high speeds on titanium carbide blades and a cushion of air that carries them about an inch above the roadway. They are also lightly armed with a small-bore deck cannon and carry two three-gallon backpacks. Technically, commanders are required to update their skills with the sleds on an annual basis, but these things have been gathering dust for years in a small warehouse adjacent to the motor pool, where the commanders and their assistants all repair now to have a gander and, hmm, raising the engine cowlings and lifting the hatches, everyone's starting to get this gleam in their eyes. After all, what red-blooded male of any race, creed or persuasion isn't going to get hot and bothered at the prospect of driving a cool piece of machinery like this?

And then, it's like a movie—it *is* a movie. The houselights go down, the curtains part, the screen lights up and there's the Snowman and Margarito slicing through the howling wind and snow in this sleek silver needle. Inside, it's all high tech warmth and comfort. They're strapped into contour seats, their faces illuminated by the soft red, green and blue of LED screens and gauges. He's got this goofy grin because, despite all the grumbling, this is pretty much like flying around in a spaceship, which is why he also feels a little nervous because, well, he is rusty on this thing and it does go awfully fast and what if something unforeseen happens? On cue, cough, sputter, sploot, the engine starts to act up. He manages to pull into an abandoned construction site before it dies completely. Now what? Not a house in sight, not another car on the road. He pushes open the hatch, steps out with a flashlight and, shielding his face against the icy blast, trudges to the front of the sled and raises the engine cowling. Nothing looks out of place, no wires loose, no obvious leaks. Of course this is a job for the mechanics, but due to recent budget cuts there's only old Smokey Joe working night shift, and it'll take him half an hour to drink another cup of coffee and bitch and moan to Evelyn about how he busts his ass and the goddamn union steward's a wimp (past tense *was*—the union disappeared with dereg, which shows you just how out of touch old Smokey Joe is—*Ned.*), and then another half hour for him to pull on his coveralls and mukluks before he even gets his saggy old ass in the seat of his mobile unit. Meanwhile Margarito has gotten out and is watching all this with that bemused smile, which, under the circumstances, almost borders on malevolent. On top of which it's cold and getting colder. The hell with this. He unloads a backpack and a torch and, employing a (very dangerous) trick he picked up from Hanktheredneckasshole (of course), shakes the tank furiously, flicks a match in front of the torch muzzle and *whoomp!* ignites a stream of bluish-orange flame that he directs against a pile of construction debris, which immediately erupts into a pretty good-sized bonfire. Heat—now for comfort. Under the front seat of the sled he finds a bottle, dusty, musty, but it's half full and it's pretty decent scotch. Treasure in hand, he settles his butt down on a legless, cushionless couch in front of the fire, uncorks the bottle for a swallow of smoky peat, extracts a joint from his pencil pocket and lights it up. All this time, Margarito has been bent over the sled engine and in fact seems to be doing some pretty serious mechanic stuff. It's only after a full minute that the Snowman realizes he's been staring at Margarito's ass, and, even more unsettling, it looks pretty damn good, firm, round and, yes, attractive. Shocked at himself, he guzzles more scotch and shifts his gaze back to the fire, his thoughts muddling around the possible meaning of this unintentional ogling when he becomes aware that his attention has now focused on the pieces of raw lumber blackening and curling in the crackling flames, and not only that, his mood has plummeted into this dark, forlorn place he has managed not to visit in a long time. It's like watching his family home burn again, like everything he knew and owned, his entire life except for the shell of a body it inhabited, has been incinerated, gone up in flames, nothing left but charred ruins and blackness. In this state he notices Margarito approaching the fire. The hood of his parka has fallen back and something weird's happening, his face is mutating, it glows like a terra cotta sun in a red-hot kiln, like a bronze mask hammered out of fire, and he's wearing a bizarre headdress made of feathers and animal fur and even shrunken human heads and in his hands he holds a human heart, its torn aorta and arteries still pumping black blood. But whose daydream is this now? Whose hot little slice of fear? This momentary bout of raw, heart-pounding terror nothing more than the product of drugs, alcohol and retinal flashes of luridly painted Maya and Aztec warriors on the walls of Mexican restaurants? Bronze and terra cotta transform back into mortal flesh. In his hands Margarito holds not a vital part of the human anatomy, but the oily, glistening sweetbreads of internal combustion, among which the Snowman's pretty sure he can identify carburetor, oil pump and possibly the solenoid. What the fuck did you do to the sled?! he sputters, more out of consternation than anger. Margarito sits down next to him, gives him a funny, almost coy look (everybody seems to be in on some big secret except him) and with mock solemnity and uncharacteristically silly word choice says, Don't worry, Snowman, I weel feex *heem*.

The wind howls, the flames roar, the joint passes back and forth, the scotch pours like honey down their throats, while Margarito, who magician-like has pulled out of nowhere a pair of channel locks, needle-nose pliers, various Phillips and flathead screwdrivers and a set of socket wrenches, screws and unscrews, yanks out plugs, caps, wires and switches, his hands black and shining with grease and oil, the big fat snowflakes falling from the sky anointing his eyebrows and mustache, which almost seems to hang askew, first this way and then that, Charlie Chaplin-like, as Margarito's face screws up in concentration. Suddenly he rises to his feet, strides across the fire-lit expanse of snow, bends over the sled again and—okay, just to verify, the Snowman's gotta take another peek, and damn if Margarito doesn't have a pretty nice ass. Which, holy shit, means what, Snowboy? That you've been in the closet your whole life and didn't know it? Or just that Margarito has a nice ass and that's that? Come geeve eet a try, *Snowman*. Margarito's full, throaty voice tunnels through the cold wind and driving snow, catching the Snowman totally off guard. He struggles to his feet like a rusty oil derrick, his body so stiff he can barely move. He's toasted on one side, frozen on the other, his eyes are watering from the smoke. He raises the hatch and settles his butt down on the cold seat as if he were sitting in a puddle of ice water. His breath hangs in front of his face like cotton candy. The windshield looks like a patch of Siberia. He turns the key in the ignition and VROOOM! the engine fires up immediately. Whooeee! he shouts. Margarito shuts the engine cowling, climbs back in the cockpit and closes the hatch. In another minute the heater's blowing hot air and the icy tundra of the windshield melts into dark wetlands. The Snowman's admiration abounds. Where the devil did he learn how to do that? Margarito explains he worked in a bus company when he was a kid, sometimes he helped the mechanic tear down engines. And the extra parts he stuck in his pocket? Oh, *those*? Hee hee hee, they aren't important, *Snowman*. It's just eco-junk greenghosts put in everything to make it burn more fuel, cost more money and break down more often. However, he can use it in his greenhouse's aquatic biodegradation filtration system. Which might have drawn an even more incredulous, *his what?* if it weren't for the fact that the Snowman has seen this very system in operation with his own eyes. (And here, sensing the opportunity for another of his interminable digressions, Boone takes it.)

One morning after work—before the blizzard hit, of course—he found the guys gathered around the Coupe. Apparently their car had broken down. Hey, Snowman, how bout you geeve us a leetle ride? And what's he gonna do, be a shithead and say—no way, José? He barely gets "Okay" out of his mouth and they're all piling in . . . three, four, five . . . eight, nine—*ten? Sííííí*, Snowman, *Heepee Haimay's* crew needs a ride too. They barely get out of the factory gate and *los guys* request that he stop at a convenience store so they can buy him a beer to pay for the ride, and of course it would be rude to refuse so he pulls in. A minute later the guys come out carrying half a dozen cases of beer. And then there's the Coupe, rocking and rolling down the snowy main street of SunnySide, arms and legs sticking out everywhere, all these drunken, bleary-eyed men laughing, hollering, crashing beer bottles out the windows, whistling at girls, just a bunch of love-starved GIs home on leave, just a bunch of college pranksters in raccoon coats and straw boaters up to the usual sophomore hijinks. They quiet down considerably when a squad car pulls up next to them at a traffic light and the officer behind the wheel and his partner in the passenger seat both give them this scrutinizing glare from behind their wraparounds. Also hard to ignore—the high-powered weaponry visible in their gun rack. During the Snowman's tenure at the Ice Factory, he has watched the police presence steadily increase here on the bad, sad, unsunny side of town where the greenghosts (almost) never go. In fact, he's entering uncharted territory as the guys steer him down one street after another through an increasingly desolate sprawl of poverty. They stop outside a large, two-story, white, wood-framed house with peeling paint and a sagging front porch and even though they've been drinking beer the whole way the guys say, Hey, Snowman, come in for sawmteeng to dreenk. He tries to explain he's gotta go but they say, Why you gotta go, Snowman? You got a girl at home? Nooo, Snowman, you don't got a girl at home. So, okay, sure, why not? Inside, men are sprawled everywhere, on chairs, couches, sofas, hammocks, the floor. There's, like, fifty men living in this one casa 'cause 'a there's nowhere else to go. They sleep and eat in shifts. One group is eating breakfast, another dinner. Shelves are loaded with gallon cans of oil, lard, twenty-five pound sacks of flour, beans, cases of beer, blocks of white cheese. Strings of garlic and red chile peppers hang from the ceiling. Bombástico's going around gobbling up scraps and leftovers and asking, anybody want to go with me to the tienda for some cheeps? Carroteeno's already snoring on a sofa with a one-eyed teddy bear in his arms. Nico's got a hot water bottle tied to his back and he's looking glassy-eyed as he intermittently puffs on one of his twisted brown cigarillos and sips beer. Some of the guys are watching a soccer match on a small blue screen TV, beamed across the border to cheer the empty hearts of millions of lonely men separated from their world, lives, families *Goal!* At least this big old ramshackle shack is toasty and warm from practically nonstop cooking, supplemented by a barnyard's worth of belching, flatulence and other naturally occurring sources of warmth.

Taking his cue, Boone returns from a digression within a digression to show Margarito giving the Snowman a tour of the greenhouse he has built out of discarded construction materials. Tubular steel frame, twelve mil plastic sheeting, fluorescent and mercury halide lamps overhead, fans, valves, PVC pipes. Margarito has created a self-sustaining water purification and thermal heating system that runs all the house's gray water and sewage through a series of sediment vats and reverse osmosis filters, then sends it gushing into hydroponic tanks bursting with vine-ripened tomatoes, zucchini, jalapeños, cilantro and oregano, thick, alien-like corn stalks bursting with multiple ears of corn. All these men produce a lot of fertilizer, Margarito says with understated humor. When he asks where Margarito learned how to do all this, the answer is deceptively simple. He read about it in an old *Organic Gardening* magazine.

(By the way, this might be a good place to discuss the current state of the farming industry. All agriculture in the U.S. has been subsumed by giant indoor factory farms. Enormous green-houses sprawl across hundreds of acres and, in some cases, entire rural counties. Artificial lighting, hydroponics, heat provided by naturally occurring methane—i.e., cattle farts. The U.S. also imports produce from Mexico but, unfettered by pesky environ mental and safety regulations, and thanks to the excessive use of chemical fertilizers, pesticides, herbicides and fungicides, as well as widespread contamination by human waste, the fruits and vegetables they grow are so toxic they glow. People hang beets and carrots, strawberries and tomatoes on their Christmas trees. Meanwhile, NASTA (which some irreverent wags refer to as the North American Slave Trade Agreement) has had devastating effects on the Mexican farm economy. Corn, which is not just a staple crop in Mexico but its heritage, is at risk not only from contamination by GMOs, but also unfair competition. U.S. agricultural dumping, in particular the sale of surplus corn and soy beans below market value (American farmers receive gov-ernment subsidies), has forced millions of Mexican farmers off the land and across the border into the U.S. And while the irony of this may escape the general public, it is not lost on the U.S. growers. Every time the Gov gets a thorn up his ass, ICE rushes in and hauls off half the workforce and an entire crop fails (keep that in mind, you Tea Pottyists). Add to that the devastating effects of Pecos Bilious, a movable vortex, black hole, the never precisely pinpointable point of intersection between earth and sky. Spawned by unnatural meteorological conditions generated by de-thermalization of the desert clime, this rogue tornado travels back and forth across west Texas, destroying wind turbines, solar farms, vast tracts of greenhouses, sucking buildings, acres of crops, cattle, sagebrush, cactus and rattlesnakes—you name it—out of one universe and blasting it into another—*Ed.*)

But all these digressions! These irrelevant details! the critics protest. Boone can only shake his head at the ignorance of these philistines. You ever read *Moby Dick*? How about *Tristram Shandy*, for God's sake!

12
The Rose

IT'S NOW JUST AROUND MIDNIGHT and they're cruising the streets of SunnySide to kill time before heading back to the shop, as usual he's bitching about the lousy job and shitty equipment and even Margarito's looking morose and defeated, his perennial optimism crushed beneath the weight of this unrelenting cold and snow—at least that's the Snowman's take, especially when Margarito keeps giving him these doleful glances. A bright pink-and-green neon glow washes over them. They're passing a cantina called the Desert Rose. A green neon cactus with pink flowers glows on the roof and another in the front window. To the Snowman's surprise, Margarito suggests they stop in and what the heck. He discreetly parks the sled in back and they clomp inside in their muddy mukluks, parkas smelling of woodsmoke, hoods thrown back. Whatever he was expecting, this ain't it. The place is packed. On the small stage a norteño band in Stetsons, western pearl snap-button shirts, tight brown or black or blue jeans with enormous silver bull or mustang or rattlesnake buckles, and dogger heel boots is furiously fiddling, pumping accordions, strumming guitars and guitarróns, and blowing red-hot trumpets while the ubiquitous tenor sings in a golden mellifluous voice and young men in similar norteño outfits laugh and howl that peculiar, vocal cord straining coyote cry *ai ai aiiiee!* and young *novios* and portly middle-aged couples dance the two-step and old men with long white mustaches and brown leathery faces click and clack dominos. The walls are covered with black and white photographs of Zapata and Villa, posters of bronze

Maya and Aztec warriors and princesses in feather headdresses, jade bracelets, anklets and necklaces. Pink, red, yellow, blue and green *papel picado* skulls, skeletons and roses hang everywhere like odd Tibetan prayer flags. Strings of gold and silver tinsel droop from the ceiling. Colored Christmas lights glow over windows. Waitresses in green, orange and red flounce and ruffles bustle back and forth with trays of food and drinks. Kids wired and tired and up way past bedtime run around laughing and screaming. A number of people wear gray donkey ears, not a few of which look dusty, moth-eaten and past their prime. Some even have on entire donkey costumes. Margarito explains it's a holiday in his country, *la Fiesta del Burro*. Or, as you say in English, Snowman, the Day of the Donkey, which, just to clarify, does not honor this hard-working beast of burden, but rather the people who themselves work like donkeys. In fact, Margarito and the Snowman have walked in on the annual confirmation party for the sons and daughters of SunnySide. As the clock strikes twelve, two rows of thirteen-year-old boys and girls march in—the girls in billowing white ankle-length dresses tied at the waist with pink sashes, the boys in western shirts with pearl snap buttons, leather belts with donkey head buckles and cuffed jeans over western boots—all solemn-faced, all wearing a brand new pair of gray velvet donkey ears on their heads. A priest in white cassock and gold stole steps forward and reads from Scripture the story of Balaam's donkey (basically, the donkey saves Balaam's ass), then goes from child to child, smudging ashes on their foreheads, consecrating these young souls in the spirit of the donkey and confirming them in eternal bondage to the earth, to endless toil and senseless labor. Afterwards the kids wander around, dazed, bashful, giddy beneath the toxic, smothering garlic, onions, hot peppers and booze-wet smooches of fat, beaming uncles, aunties and grannies.

Meanwhile, the Snowman and Margarito have found a booth by the front window, and Margarito's filling glasses from a bottle of brandy that has appeared on their table. The man on the label wears a red sash printed with the words El Residente and he's climbing out of a river onto an icy pile of greenback dollars. Below that a slogan in Spanish that the Snowman accurately understands to mean *Better to be a resident in the United States than president of Mexico*. Despite this humble sentiment, the brandy's pretty good stuff, warm, smooth, tongue and brain numbing, and they quickly down half the bottle. After which he vaguely remembers Margarito, sounding uncharacteristically drunk and almost absurdly lugubrious, telling him an unlikely story about a dead donkey. For some reason he doesn't want to pursue right now (gender issues?) he can't stop staring at Margarito's lower lip, which, now that he's noticed it, does seem unusually soft and sensuous, sort of like a piece of tropical fruit pendent beneath the shining black mustache, but there's also this uncharacteristic sadness in Margarito's eyes that he can't figure out, a look of regret or remorse that doesn't seem to have anything to do with this story he's telling.

Then there's something else that's clearly Boone's doing, because somehow he and Margarito end up in this hallucinatory story where they actually turn into donkeys. But they just look at each other and laugh. Hee hee haw! Wait until the ladies get a gander at this whang! Haw haw hee! Wait until they see that snout! In fact, the script does call for them to meet some women but they realize they can no longer fit in the sled. How are we going to get there? Easy, we'll trot, that's what donkeys are for. But what about the girls? They can ride on *our* backs for a change. And they both laugh again, Hee haw! Hee haw!

And then it's like he's been drugged, or further drugged, because now Margarito is gone and, still in his parka and mukluks, he's dancing with a woman twice his age and weight who's wearing half an inch of makeup and a lipstick smile that covers the lower half of her face. Then, apparently without any transition, he and Carroteeno, in a green fedora and black guayabera (he looks kind of like a huge leprechaun, an impression enhanced by his bowl-cut orange hair), are back in the booth

by the window playing dominoes even though he doesn't know
how to play dominoes and the whole gang is crowded around
them, kibitzing, Nico in his powder blue tuxedo neurotically
combing his pompadour into greater perfection and puffing on
one of his rustic cigarillos, Raf-I-el in some kind of swami outfit, white turban, wraparound robe and sandals, Bombástico
(who, despite his lost paycheck, has continued to gain weight,
almost as if he's absorbing calories from the atmosphere, or else
he's one heckuva moocher) in this surreal little Lord Fauntleroy
(Liberace?) costume (purple velvet jacket and short pants, black
patent leather shoes, white socks and lace, lots of lace) that would
probably fit perfectly a baby elephant and, finally, Xuan decked
out in a top hat, a vest of what appear to be human rib bones (an
ironic fashion statement indeed), a mantle of griffon feathers and
a necklace of jaguar teeth, the shining blue sapphire in his gold
tooth exposed by an oddly benevolent but also quite macabre
grin as, in a rare display of good humor, he mercilessly teases
Nico, tickling his chin and talking baby talk to him. (Nico,
by the way, is Xuan's nephew—in fact, the Snowman has only
recently discovered that *los guys* are all related, their extended
family, the Astrayas, apparently come from a small village in
rural Mexico. For some reason this is important and probably
should have been mentioned earlier—*Ed.*)

Olé! someone shouts. *Ai-ai-aiií!* shouts another. And look,
here's Merry Margarito again, arriving at the table with a girl
on each arm, and the guys are cheering and shouting, *Aiii,
Margarito!* Which one will it be tonight, Margarito?! But wait
a second. Is this the wry, reserved Margarito we've come to
know? Or is this another Margarito we've only read about in
storybooks? Oh yes, *that* Margarito. Margarito the Lothario,
Casanova, Don Juan, Margarito threading yet another velvety
red heart on the string he wears under his decidedly *un*-hair
shirt. Margarito who, in another time and place, made old
women, widows, housewives, nuns and innocent young school-
girls swoon. Margarito dragging his ass into work late with a

girl on the front seat next to him, her body still glued to his, cooing in his ear, clinging to him, the gleam of her lips and her teeth and the whites of her eyes as he tumbles out of the car sleepy-eyed and grinning and she drives away, red taillights glowing bye-bye. Margarito who—but even as Boone is about to provide further examples of Margarito's amorous exploits, an awkward moment occurs. Nico, mouthful of yellow rodent teeth fully on display in a happily drunken grin, turns to Margarito and shouts, *Aii, Maria!* Margarito's face darkens and he hisses something at Nico that sounds like *cuayatay, iidiiotl!* and then angrily pushes away the girls. This, however, seems even more out of character, and Margarito shrugs, smiles, not convincingly, and says, You see, Snowman, Nico ees my conscience.

(Due to a software error, the following outtake was unintentionally reinstated after B. W. made the cut—*Ed.*)

> *Close-up of the Snowman's face, his arctic blue eyes slide sideways as if waiting for an explanation.*
> *Close-up of Margarito's face, his warm brown eyes look conflicted as if he's struggling to make a decision.*
> MARGARITO (in an artificially casual tone): Maria is someone I know in Mexico.
> *Close-up of the* SNOWMAN'*s eyes (still waiting).*
> MARGARITO (in uncertain tone): She ees my—seestor?
> *Close-up of the* SNOWMAN'*s eyes (skeptical).*
> MARGARITO (laughs, then speaks, oddly, with a French accent): Hahaha, nooo, *Snowman,* I weel not lie to you, she eez not my seestare, she eez my . . . *cousin.*
> *Close-up of the* SNOWMAN'*s eyes (suspicious).*
> MARGARITO: Hahaha, Snowman, you are right. She ees not my cousin either. She ees . . .
> *MARGARITO ceases speaking.*

(end erroneously restored cut—*Ed.*)

Then, another abrupt transition, the guys have all disappeared and now it's just Margarito and the Snowman, both still wearing parkas, their faces bathed in pink-and-green neon from the sign in the frosty plateglass window. Margarito is still struggling to find the words to explain who this mysterious Maria really is. Finally he says, Maria is my nemesis, Snowman. She is my tormentor, my temptress, my other half.

Ma-riiii-ah, I just met a girl named Ma-riii-ah.

The name echoes through convents and monasteries, cloisters and orders, churches, chapels and cathedrals. It resonates through the red brick canyons of Spanish Harlem and the opera houses of Milan and Vienna. But not that Maria, not Mother of God, Queen of the Catholic Church, beloved saint to the billions of faithful who have worshipped her over the centuries. Not Maria, star of stage and screen, of teenage angst, melodrama, gangs, inner city turmoil, nor even Maria Callas' wrenchingly beautiful *Ave Maria* on acid (*Snowman?*). But Maria, poetess of well water and bare feet, Maria, a thousand miles away as the crow flies and a hundred years back in time.

The camera zooms in again on Margarito's eyes, which are moist and far away, and the screen fills with an image of a young woman with black hair, lips the silken red of rose petals, eyes flashing like obsidian, in a red cotton dress with green and yellow flowers embroidered at the hems of the sleeves and bodice, standing barefoot in the door of a small pastel-blue stucco house with potted pink geraniums on the doorstep and in the open window and chickens scratching in the yard. But where'd you get all that, Snowman? From the private little nickelodeon of your own imagination? A composite of all the lousy lurid Technicolor films he watched on TV as a kid, squirming in his seat and aching for the stupid love scene to be over and get back to the fistfights, gunfights, bandits fleeing across the Frío Grande on horseback pursued by carbine blazing troops in blue uniforms with yellow stripes down the legs? The camera tightens on the young woman's face. In her eyes there is a wildness, a hunger for life, for love. Her gaze is fixed on the yellow dirt road that winds across the desert past Doña Hermosa's house and out to the narrow highway, where a large, black, strangely bulbous and yet streamlined car with huge tail fins, like a futuristic vision of automobiles from the 1930s, was just passing. It looks like the Coupe. It *may* be the Coupe.

13
On His Bicycle

OF COURSE IT *IS* THE COUPE with the Snowman behind the wheel in yet another of Boone's clichéd segues that doesn't quite make sense chronologically. He's just cracked another beer and lit up one of these sweet oval cigarettes and he's feeling pretty good. Hey dog! He points at a yellow mongrel mutt curled in the shade of a large prickly pear cactus. Hi, Doña Hermosa! He waves to a little old lady clad entirely in black and seated on a flat stone, then does a double take, his head whipping back for another photo opportunity snapped up with the old cerebral instamatic. Isn't this the same little old lady he passed a hundred miles back? How the hell'd she get ahead of him? And how does he know her name? Immediately afterwards he passes another little old black beetle lady bent beneath a load of firewood. She twists her face sideways and with a conspiratorial gleam in her bright little insect eyes gives him a nearly toothless grin. *Didn't think you'd get away from me that easily, did you, Snowman?* He drives another mile or two and passes what appears to be the same black-carapaced little old lady bent over a large-bladed hoe, hacking at the shrunken, spiny, gray-green alkaloidal organisms that call this barren soil home. Shortly after that he comes upon yet another wizened, black-garbed little old lady bent over a steaming black cauldron, stirring a heady broth of toads, lizards and bat wings. Or is it only her laundry? There must be an explanation, not the same little old lady at all, but an entire colony of old ladies in black widows' weeds, an escaped convent of old ladies, old ladies sneaking down creaky wooden ladders and steep winding stairs from dusty suffocating attics where their families have kept them hidden for years. Of course it's Boone again, doing screen tests for Doña Hermosa right down to the minute the cameras roll, extracting pieces of Doña Hermosa from every spidery old creature waiting in the wings for her opening night debut and hasty exit until he gradually forms a composite, a skeletal little old bird clattering inside a cage of whalebone and black satin to simulate perpetual night, sleep in here, old lady, dream your fluttery wingflap dreams of lost youth and wake again in death's skeletal embrace wrapped in black mourning weeds, the garments she wears not just for comfort and modesty but representing an entire system of culture and belief, of life and death, sin and redemption, of endless toil, piety and faith in a god who may have little faith in her.

INTERMISSION

Intermission? But I was just getting interested in the boo . . . vie! (A voice in the audience.)

Now hold on, Boone. My old grannie always wore black and nobody died yet. Maybe eet was just easier to keep clean, you can't see the *dort*, everything's so *dorty* in this *dorty* country. Beer in hand, unsteady on his feet, Nico, in pink crocs, madras shorts and a bright-yellow surf tee embossed with the image of a Maya lord hanging ten on a surfboard, wanders in front of the camera.

Nico! You're ruining this scene! If you pull a stunt like this again I'll have the scriptwriter kill you off! (Boone's voice, off-screen.)

Totally unintimidated, Nico gives Boone his trademark ferret grin and heads toward a shiny silver Airstream with a big blue star on the side. See that, *Snowman?* After this peekchore we gonna be in a fleek with some cheek Snow White. You know her, *Snowman?* No? Hey, you want a beer? Inside the air-conditioned trailer, Xuan, Raf-I-el and Carroteeno are playing poker (three card draw?) at a table. Bombástico is feeding a baguette loaded with salami, baloney, red onions, pickles, tomatoes, three kinds of cheese (provolone, Swiss and cheddar), and dripping with hot sauce, mustard and mayonnaise into his mouth in a slow but steady conveyor belt-like process. Hey, Bombástico, you jess eat lonch, now you eateen again? Bombástico, who at this point is almost perfectly spheroidal in shape, rolls his eyes helplessly.

Nico, returning to the topic at hand, now opens the floor to debate on why old ladies in Mexico wear black, which invites a flurry of conflicting hypotheses along with the consumption of significant quantities of cerveza so that soon they're shouting and throwing beer cans at each other and comparing bad teeth— fock that shit, man, that ain't no black, that green. *Mira, cabrón*, I'll show you black! Hey, where's M'Shaka? He'll tell you about black. In the end they direct their ire at *him*. Why you come here asking dumb greenghost questions, Snowman? Why you gotta know *why* all the time? And now, to add to the confusion, here's Boone again, hammering on the trailer door. *Snowman!* What the hell are you doing in there? You've got a scene to finish! Boone's losing his mind, his whole morning already shot searching for the right spot to insert his itinerant vision of the quintessential crone of the Mexican campo, placing her in every small town, village and pueblo the Snowman drives through.

A disconnected flash shows the Snowman behind the wheel of the Coupe, heading home from the Ice Factory in the a.m. darkness. A startling apparition of flapping black wings and gleaming bicycle spokes charges out in front of him and this fierce, hawk-faced little old Mexican lady shrouded in a black shawl jerks her head sideways and glowers at him in his headlights. He's crossed paths with her before and assumes (correctly) that she's intrepidly pedaling her mountain bike through the snow to some quasi-villa in Terrancetown to make breakfast for *el Patrón* and *la Señora*, get *los niños* washed, clothed, fed and off to school, do the laundry, clean the house, make lunch for *la Señora* and her guest, Mrs. McGillacutty, greet *los niños* after school, make them snacks, prepare dinner, clean up after, then pedal back across town to the SunnySide at nine o'clock at night to take care of her own family. The Snowman senses this is foreshadowing but he doesn't know for what. (Of course he doesn't know Boone has cleverly embedded a barcoded link to a documentary about immigrant women who work as caregivers in the United States. They come from Asia, from Pakistan and India, from Eastern Europe, Latin America—pretty much every Third World and developing nation (although not so much from Africa)—and often are separated for years from their own families, whom they are supporting with their wages, while they attend to the babies, children, disabled family members and elderly parents of complete strangers.)

(Theater lights flash on and off.)

Dressed entirely in black, from the tips of the patent leather shoes pinching her toes to the black shawl covering her head and shoulders, Doña Hermosa sat on a warm, flat rock on the side of the road, completely still, not moving, nothing inside her desiring to move. Heat eddied around her like hot bathwater. Sunlight splashed over her shoulders like molten glass. Her small black eyes gleamed like raisins as she peered up the dusty yellow stretch of road, unconsciously squeezing the package of cactus candy in her skirt pocket that she had packed in the early hours of morning, the only hours that mattered anymore, when she woke in darkness and lay in bed, her thoughts slowly returning to life, aided by the sounds outside the house, an owl flapping up into the dead rattlepod tree, the coyote's stealthy swish through the jaguarbush where she dumped the meager scraps of garbage each day, that girl Maria's dog barking over in the canyon, the Cacahuatl's rooster crowing across the arroyo. *I'm alive, I'm still alive.* Would she really utter those words and with such astonishment? Was it frightening to be so old? Or was there comfort in the certainty of death's proximity, the wise old

Doña Horoscope plotting out her own life down to the last day, hour, second and finally that infinitesimally small transitional point when her candle was extinguished and she slipped out of life and into oblivion. Or was that him, the Snowman, again? Intruding upon the poor old woman's waking thoughts with his own quaking fears of mortality?

Groaning, she sat up on the edge of her bed, lit the kerosene lantern, illuminating the things around her, the blue tin cup on the small wooden table, the rough wooden armoire. She used the chamber pot. Applied a few drops of rose water in appropriate places. Splashed a handful of water on her face. Pulled her white flannel nightgown over her head and examined herself in the cracked mirror, her thighs sagging off her bones like limp pantaloons, her small breasts—thank god they were never big, she didn't go around bent over like those cows who've calved a small herd in their lifetime. Her breasts were her hidden treasures, never seen by a man, not even another woman, not since she was a child, those delicate blue veins beneath the almost translucent skin, like the snow she'd seen once high in the mountains when she was a little girl, although she couldn't remember what she was doing up there, maybe Papa took her with him to pick wild berries. She remembered kneeling in the snow and how it burned her skin and how she scooped some up in her hands and ate it and it didn't taste like anything. Doña Hermosa pulled her black woolen stockings over her bony, veined feet and ankles, dressed herself in layers of black satin, organdy and crinoline. Her small, gnarled hands laced up ankle-high black shoes. She went to the kitchen, lit the gas burner, put on water and made coffee, then sat her skinny old bones and sagging flesh down on the rough wooden chair with all its familiar knots and splinters, the big tin cup held in both hands like a child, her bright little eyes peering over the rim as she sipped her coffee in between nibbling at a piece of stale bread (same thing as toast, just not burnt), while ancient Auntie Aurora's raw red washerwoman fingers stretched across the dark horizon and raised it up like a window sash and the grand dame herself appeared, dressed as always in her colorful rags and on her hands and knees industriously scrubbing away the lampblack coal dust and other remnants of night.

No, Doña Hermosa had no fear of death. She understood the stupidity of such worries. She lived in the midst of dying every day of her life. She'd butchered hogs, shoved bone-handled carving knives between their ribs and opened up that steaming larder of tripe, liver and kidneys, she cut the heads off chickens, snakes, an occasional lizard, nursed and sat vigil with her dying mother, father, brothers, sisters, neighbors, aunts and uncles, nieces, nephews and cousins, and while everyone else around her went on dying she clattered along like an old bicycle with extra dings, broken spokes, a bent wheel, preparing herself for the day ahead, boiling water for coffee—she already has a cup of coffee, Snowman, she's starting to forget things, she's getting senile, she sits at the table like a drooling idiot mashing spoonfuls of soggy cornmeal between her toothless gums—wasn't she eating dried bread?—and gulping hot coffee, black coffee—did I already say that?—with a spoonful of sugar, but no more than that, save some for tomorrow, but what if there is no tomorrow? all right then, two spoonfuls, three, eat it all! what the hell do I care? It's not even real coffee, it's an ersatz cup of joe she's brewed out of parched corn and river bottom mud—black muck actually oozes from the corners of her mouth like a shit-eating little witch. But why does it have to go on like this? Why can't you give the old lady a break, Snowman? Why do you have to attack her every little idiosyncrasy, mock her entire way of life? Of course she's anxious, she's worried, an old woman, all alone, death so close she can almost shake hands with it, listening to the wind in the rattlepod tree, listening for someone lurking outside her door, another of those horrible greenghosts she encountered when she went out to dump the old cake tin she uses for a chamber pot in the morning. They call themselves *archaeologists, anthropologists.* Thieves, that's what they are. They steal things from her house, her yard, even her garbage pile, they bother her with their

stupid questions. Ho, Doña Hermosa! You've lived here two or
three hundred years. You're an expert on the native ecology.
Tell us, what do you call that strange insect at your feet? What?
That? It's a bug! What else do you want to know? What are you
doing now, Doña Hermosa, building a fire? Why are you doing
that? To cook my dinner, of course, to heat this pail of water
to soak my aching feet, to warm the house because suddenly it
feels so cold in here, did you bring a draft when you came in,
Mister Greenghost? But why don't you just turn on the faucet,
Doña Hermosa? Why don't you just turn up the heat? Look pal,
how many times I gotta tell ya. The lady doesn't have running
water, she ain't got any heat. Maybe if she put up a sign outside,
Sorry, Granny's gone for the day, they'd leave her in peace with
what little life she had left, that slender package of daylight
she received each day, not a day but a waiting for something to
happen, for something to change, for someone to come, and
if nothing happens, if no one comes, if nothing changes, the
entire day spent creaking around the dusty yard, scratching at
the barren patch of dirt she calls her garden, gathering dried
grass and sticks for firewood. At night go through the process
in reverse, sit in her chair and sip a hot cup of tea brewed out
of the bitter roots, berries and leaves she's been collecting from
this ruined land for so long she no longer knows their names or
whether they've been nourishing her or slowly poisoning her to
death. Maybe drink a glass of purifying water instead, not that
horrible chemical water they drink in town but a cup of good
cool well water brought up from deep underground tasting of
roots, blind amphibians and the cool, dark mysteries beneath
the earth.

Afterwards, remove the outer layers of her garments, the dry
black husks of crinoline and satin and organdy, kneel on the
packed dirt floor beside the bed to offer up her meager plea,
Let me live another day, whatever life it is, let it go on, even if
in my dreams. She lays herself out on the narrow bed and pulls
the rough wool blanket up to her chin as darkness seeps out of

the corners like India ink and gathers around the feeble candle-light—it was a kerosene lantern this morning. She extinguishes the flame with her dry old fingers, lies back and stares up into the dark membrane of night hovering against the ceiling of the bedroom—there is only one room, the bed's in the corner—until her eyes finally close and she submits to sleep, dream, some unformed terror that wakes her again in the darkness before morning.

A lizard scurried across the road, kicking up spurts of yellow dust. A pile of garbage ripened in the hot sun, melon rinds, tin cans crusted with tomato sauce, a rancid animal hide, the creature inside eviscerated, consumed by the dry desiccating heat, by an army of probing proboscises, pincers, mandibles and fangs. Doña Hermosa's nose wrinkled imperceptibly. Hoo, what a stink. High in the pale blue ether over her head Grandfather Vulture rode the air currents in slowly tightening circles, all his mechanisms of sight, sound and smell fixed on the small black bundle deposited in the middle of this vast barren land shimmering two thousand feet below. Of course it's that old fool Death dressed in the same moth-eaten buzzard costume he's been fluttering around in for the last two or three million years. When was Death born, anyway? Did Death discover itself one dark, dreary morning in soggy black diapers, still bewildered by its own power, just beginning to establish its profession, before anyone knew what Death was? Or was that more of the Snowman's existential nonsense? Or Boone again, with his heavy-handed symbolism, because sometimes a vulture is just a vulture, and poor old Grandfather Vulture, how was he supposed to know it was Doña Hermosa? He was only doing his job, patrolling the ozone, cleaning up the carrion Death left in its passing. He wasn't prepared for the violence launched his way in the form of a telepathic surface-to-air missile. The sky was placid, blue, the upper atmosphere serene, the blast when it came sudden, a silent scream, a cry of denial without words or sound that slammed into breast and wing, scattered feathers, rattled talons, beak and hollow bones. *Go away! I'm not ready for you yet, you old buzzard!* The vulture crumpled, tumbled, fell two hundred feet before he caught himself, shook out his threadbare tuxedo in midair, tested the current with the tips of his long black pinions and plunged into a thermal that lifted him a thousand feet up into the cool atmosphere. Oh what it must be like to fly, to leave behind the weight of your body and lift up from the earth like a feather, like a bit of fluff, like a—bird. Ha! Imagine that she should ever envy that wretched old bag of bones and feathers, Grandfather Vulture. But, *Díos mío!* What glory to leave behind her poor ruined body, to have all her aching joints, her arthritic wrists, elbows, hips and knees dissolve into nothing, and only her thoughts, her mind, up in the clouds and cool blue ether.

A thunderous roar split open the heavens and a jet airplane skated across the vast blue sky trailing behind it a long white spume of condensation. *Wraaak-k-k!* A catarrhous cackle escaped her lips. These damned greenghosts, always intruding upon her little world. If they weren't creeping around the yard in search of so-called artifacts to dig up and smuggle home in hidden compartments, they were flying overhead in airplanes. The greenghosts moved so fast, they leapt from one place to another in their damned time machines without knowing anything about the land or the world in between. Like that bunch of crooks that roared by just now in that big black car. Of course they were crooks, anybody who drove a car like that had to be a crook. And they were headed straight for Señor Valladoides' villa on the mountain.

13½

On His Bicycle Pt. 2

or

The Almost True Story of Maria and Margarito

DOÑA HERMOSA'S BRIGHT BLACK currant eyes followed the progression of a swirling yellow dust devil in the middle of which flashed silver spokes, red and orange plastic reflectors, colored streamers, little metal bells with thumb levers that ching-chinnnged like a cash register and a brass klaxon with a big black rubber squeeze bulb that honked like the geese that flew high over her house early in the spring. At last, it was him, Merry Margarito, always full of life and laughter, that great big smile and those shiny brown eyes, peddling toward her on that fantastic machine. During the day the enterprising young Mercantile Margarito hauled crates of vegetables, huge piles of flattened cardboard, bundles of firewood, in addition offering a cheap taxi service to travelers along his route. In the evening he washed and polished metal and chrome, touched up paint, arranged satin pillows and candelabra and rode the young girls around like princesses beneath the starry black night, and later still when they complained of the chill in the air he held them close and whispered in their ears, *moonlight and roses, mi amor, diamonds and lilies*, his warm breath as sweet as a meadow in spring as he raised the hungry, yearning mouths and soft, trembling lips to his and his agile, young hands searched beneath cotton, silk and satin for the swelling of breasts and nipples ripening into hard red berries, crept up the smooth caffè latte thighs, seeking hidden entrances and secret openings among the pink velvet petals and inflorescence of yearning clitoris, labia and even sphincter.

No! No, no, no, no, no! Doña Hermosa, you mustn't think such things. He's just a boy and you . . . It's just that she felt giddy with Margarito's warm, young body so close to hers. Imagine, he couldn't be more than fifteen or sixteen and already such a gentleman, the way he helped her into her seat. But he wasn't interested in an old lady like her. No, the rascal, the rogue, he only had eyes for the pretty young girls. Poor Doña Hermosa. She had never been pretty, no boys ever whispered sweet nothings in her ear or looked at her with longing. She had grown old and never had a man, only another man's children, the children of her poor sisters, the children she had by inheritance, default, the children she cared for while her sisters worked in the fields or earned their keep in the beds of the men who worked in the mines, the children and then grandchildren she thought of as her own. She squeezed again the package of cactus candy she had made for this occasion and the faces of her grandnieces and nephews lit up in her mind like a string of colored lights. Oh, but how she hated it when people called her pious and saintly and poor old widow, a widow by proxy, who never grew anything in her own plot. And then what? Just die? Nothing else? Exposed, finally, in her death, her poor purposeless body handled by the brewhag, a few women, or worse, shipped off to the funeral home in town. And be forgotten as soon as the mortician's lackey filled up her hole, a ragged, filthy drunk, sweating, cursing the trouble she's caused him, ready for a bottle, his only pay and consolation. Of course she was thinking that because they had just passed the church and right after that the cemetery, simple wooden crosses, headstones, a few homemade brick and mortar monuments with plastic flowers and a faded black-and-white photograph of the deceased behind a dirty piece of glass.

Doña Hermosa's heart constricted. All those poor souls, poor

Mama, poor Papa, all her brothers and sisters and everyone she had known in the village and even people she had never met but heard their names repeated among the old folks and all the names of everybody who had ever lived all the way back to Adam and Eve. But you, Doña Carmen! Don't think I've forgotten you put my poor little banty hen in your cooking pot!

Doña Hermosa issued a sigh drawn forth from all the tissues of her body. Ah well, they were all better off still, and she'd be with them soon enough, or not with them exactly. No one was buried in that poor little cemetery anymore, they were all buried in the city, where the dead now went to lie among the living. Somehow the greenghosts were to blame for that too. Everyone gathered around the greenghosts' hotels and the greenghosts' bars and restaurants, even the dead. The greenghosts brought with them all their machines, cars, telephones, televisions, vacuum cleaners, vegetable processors, things that separated you from the earth, from the past, that moved you away from your home, your family, your own grave. Who was left to care anymore how you died or where you lay? Ah well, what difference did it make? She'd be nothing, an empty birdcage filled with blackness and dirt.

Far off in the distance a black speck drifted over the hills and, with a chill, she recognized old Grandfather Buzzard again. Why was he being so damned persistent? Couldn't the old fool take a joke? Was he going to make her pay for that little slight she gave him earlier this morning?

Now what? She had been so busy digging her own grave she hadn't even noticed. Margarito had turned off the main road and they were bouncing along a bumpy, rutted lane. Ouch! That hurt. But Butterboyrito doesn't feel a thing, does he? As insensitive as a mule. Pudding-butt, if he wants to ride those little sluts around on his bicycle that's fine, they have plenty of cushioning on their fat asses, but a dried up old bundle of sticks like her? Why did he have to come this way? Oh look, that stupid girl Maria's house. Now she understood. Because there was one girl in particular, wasn't there? Doña Hermosa had heard all the gossip and rumors, she knew all the details. Margarito and Maria, Maria and Margarito, a matrimony of names. Oh lucky girl, he was so beautiful, so handsome, could such a young man really exist? Oh poor child, he was going to deal her her deathblow, he was going to break her heart. Ah, but she was so young, so innocent, how was she to know? A dumb country girl without any experience in the world, with nothing but a pretty smile and a simple red dress. There was the shameless hussy now, practically falling out of the window in anticipation and—oh my! Just like that they rush into each other's arms and kiss without any regard whatsoever for the presence of their elders. Fine, let them have their little play, she'd pretend she was napping. Oh Lord! There's Maria's foolish old Uncle Poblano, coming in from the fields for lunch. Look out, kids! Ah, but that Margarito, quick as a fox he jumped back on the bicycle and pedaled away, he was banging into every rock and hole in the road. Watch out you idiot! You almost crashed into that cactus!

Now what? The ridiculous buffoon was singing to himself, probably thinking about his stupid girlfriend. Hoo, what a racket! If her father were alive. But this stupid old Tío Poblano doesn't suspect a thing. If he had his wits about him he'd shoot Margarito's mangos off. Oh but she shootn't talk like that, shootn't say such horrible things. Although why not? Who says? The church? The scriptwriters? Just because she's an old lady, because she's so close to God or at least the grave, because she *shouldn't* throw away a lifetime of piety out of jealousy for this *child*. Stupid boy, grinning like a moron, not a care in the world. Thinks it's going to go on like this forever. No wonder, the way his grandfather spoiled him. Let the boy have anything he wanted. Even sent him to school, but they couldn't make a dunce like that learn anything. He had to be outside chasing butterflies in the meadows, chasing girls with skinny legs and big dark eyes. That drunken old fool, how could anyone expect the boy to turn out good? Maybe everyone else had forgotten, but she remembered perfectly well how Margarito had killed that donkey and ruined his whole family. The old man didn't care. He never had to work either. Found a chest of gold buried on his property. People said it was left by one of those awful conquistadores who came through five or six hundred years ago, raping and murdering, stealing gold and jewels and everything else they got their filthy hands on. Now that old drunk has this treasure hoarded away somewhere and soon it'll belong to Margarito. Some people have all the luck. Of course he'll squander it, alcohol, gambling, girls, girls who'll grow up to be fat, sullen cows smacking damp cornmeal between their palms with a bunch of skinny, hungry babies at their feet while he sits at the kitchen table sucking on another bottle of beer and yelling about God's injustices against man. But that wasn't going to happen to Margarito was it? She knew that and he knew that and everybody knew that, a boy so handsome, so quick. Marry a rich girl, that's the ticket. Better yet, a widow with a nice little bundle tied up under her bed. She'd be so grateful to have him, she'd tolerate his little adventures, and she'd be gone soon enough and he'd have his freedom. All he had to do was smile and whisper a few words in her ear, something soft and tender, something that tickled her and filled her up inside, *Moonlight and roses, my love, diamonds and lilies.* Oh, but we've heard that tune before, haven't we? Ah! The mountebank! The scoundrel! So that's what he was up to, courting her and riding her around on his bicycle so he could take everything she had. She knew it all along. Was it possible the devil himself could inhabit such beauty? Well let him have his day, he'd find out soon enough that it wasn't always so easy, there was still a bill to pay. One way or the other, my pretty boy, it all ends up in the grave.

Margarito's baby face appeared in her mind with that boyish mustache starting on his lip and those big brown eyes buried and falling apart in the ground and she felt an ache in her heart. How could she think such a thing? How wish that cold and darkness on a beautiful boy like Margarito? Ah yes, but don't waste your tears on that one. Even as a child he was a stinker. While the pious old ladies in black cackled their fervent weepy prayers to an alien god for a little bit of happiness in the middle of that vast, barren existence, little Butterboyrito was in the kitchen gorging himself sick on sugar skulls, or else terrorizing young girls in lacy white dresses with pink ribbons, setting off fireworks behind their backs, leaping at them in the dark in his fright mask, not one of those store-bought masks with big teeth and horns and maybe an eyeball falling out, but a mask made of his own exuberance and excitement when he stuck his fingers in his mouth, yanked his lips back from his gums and teeth, rolled his eyes, flapped his ears, shrieked and groaned and did everything he possibly could to expel the demon of fear lurking inside his own chest—all captured on a video taken by an uncle returned from El Norte with cash in his pockets and this magic phone that took movies. (Boone seems to be making a point here. Foreshadowing again?)

At least they were back on the main road. What a relief. It wouldn't take any time at all to reach the city now. They were passing houses, people on the street. An icy breath caressed her face. Air conditioning. They were passing the new greenghost hotel, a tall glass and steel building with blue ceramic tiles around the yellow stucco entrance to make it look authentic, although what kind of authentic was that, Doña Hermosa authentic or greenghost authentic? Not that these greenghosts would know. Look at them, strutting around in their under-wear, well, not their underwear, but those awful *shorts*, and the women, they might as well be in their brassieres, no decency at all, and they're all so horribly white and fat, you'd think they'd never seen the sun before or done any real work in their life. Of course they're all rich, they can do whatever they want, come here and run over old ladies, frighten the hens so they won't lay eggs, turn the men into groveling servants and the women into whores, and then they have the audacity to say, What's wrong, granny? Got a thorn in your ass? Horrible! Trash! Maybe it's the air conditioning that turns them into such brutes. They reek of it, cold, metallic, chemical. It nestles in their hair, in their clothes, almost as if they were air-conditioned themselves. Wouldn't that be wonderful, though, to have a nice little breeze blowing under your skirts? Oh that's naughty, Doña Hermosa! But just think, who'd care anymore if they had to wear this ridiculous costume all the time? The hell with black wool and sackcloth, she'd go around on the hottest day, smiling at her neighbors, *Buenos días*, Señora Sombra, got your air on? Sí, Doña Hermosa, the breeze is blowing from the north.

But the way people were staring at her. She must look ridiculous, an impoverished little bundle of sticks ashen with dust and her hair fallen down around her face. And it was all this stupid boy's fault, him and his stupid bicycle. He was so proud of it and it was just a rusty piece of junk. Imagine, sixteen, seventeen, a grown man. Maybe if he got himself a real job and bought a car instead of going around murdering old ladies with this contraption. But it was almost over now, all her tortures and travails. They'd turned up a narrow street crowded with small stone houses and doorways decorated with carved stone flowers and doves and statues of angels and saints. And look! Of all things! There was her sister, Ida. Ha! Big and fat as ever, although what on earth was she doing here? Not that it really mattered at the moment, because she knew it was a dream and soon she would wake. But what a joy, it was like a fiesta, and there was her niece Ana with her husband Pedro and, oh glory of God—the grandchildren! How they've grown! They were all running out into the street and shouting, here they are! They've arrived! They were crowding around and thumping Margarito on the back. What a fine lad! He's brought poor old granny to us on his bicycle! The whole time Doña Hermosa was trying to recompose herself and smiling so hard her head hurt.

14
The Great Blizzard of Aught Nine

AND STILL THE SNOW FELL. Meteorologists blamed El Niño, changes in ocean currents, solar flares, low-pressure cells and high-pressure sales. Snowflakes as big as pillows fell from the sky, enormous, mattress-sized blobs of snow. Roofs of houses, high schools, churches, civic centers, old folks homes, shopping centers and fire stations collapsed beneath the crushing weight. Radio and cell towers, light and power poles, billboards and signs over mega-stores toppled over. The ghostly white globes of the famous moonlight towers, one-hundred-sixty-five-foot-tall ironwork structures erected in the 1880s to illuminate the growing city, hovered inches above the snow like alien spacecraft. Cars disappeared beneath the snow like deep-sixed bathyspheres, their aquarium windows like peepshow stereopticons into dark shadowy interiors where silver buttons and knobs and glass dials and gauges brooded in undersea quiescence, sometimes a body, the face a mask of asphyxiated bewilderment, or even, miraculously, the whole city listening with bated breath—a survivor! Someone found alive! The sirens were going all the time, EMS, police, fire department, dogcatchers. Then even they fell silent. The streets were impassable. Nobody could get to work except by giant earthmoving machines. You'd see a hundred and fifty people in business suits and overcoats packed shoulder-to-shoulder, standing room only, in the enormous orange dump bed. Finally even management realized the absurdity of sending crews out to make snow and the remaining skeleton crews were furloughed until further notice.

The city was paralyzed. People could do nothing but sit at home in front of the TV, taunted by the familiar message constantly looping at the bottom of the screen. *An informed people is a warm people. Remember. Stay warm, stay informed!* Stiff upper lip, the Guv says. We don't need no stinking help from the Feds. Then there were blackouts, the grid went down, the power out for days, gas shut off as a safety measure. People relied on what resources they had. The more fortunate fired up emergency generators. The Snowman had never used the tiny fireplace and could only hope it didn't burn the house down. A stack of cordwood had sat rotting on the side of the house ever since he moved in. He'd stare into the flames getting pleasantly drunk and stoned while the storm howled outside, rattling windows and sending icy drafts blowing through the cracks. When the fire died down he hauled himself up from the couch and put on more wood. Then he ran out of firewood. Inspired by drink, he smashed a wooden chair to pieces in the kitchen, splinters flying everywhere, big gashes in the linoleum floor. Plenty of wood to burn, eh, Me'th? He ripped molding from the baseboards and ceiling. Time to get started on that remodeling project, no, Snowman? *Arbeit macht warm!* Nicht wahr, meine Herren? He's shouting out loud and roaring with laughter at his own stupid jokes. Gasping for breath, he collapses on the sofa in front of the fire. A persistent chirring sound draws his eyes to a tiny creature on the hearth. It's a cricket, and not only a cricket, but a cricket in top hat, tuxedo and tails playing a fiddle and now it's singing in the most amazing golden voice a classic Sid Ney tune *Then I wish upon a starfish.* Hmm, what's up with that, right? It occurs to him that it might be some kind of electronic eavesdropping device, one of those insect bots intelligence agencies are using now, or even scarier, roboticized insects, rigged up in tiny headgear, transponders, cameras, electronic signals coming from the void, telling which muscle to do what, left foot forward, right foot forward, left, right, left, right, marching to the tune of a different drummer, aren't we, boys? Because *of course* the government's going to be interested in *you*, right, Snowman? All those vital secrets harbored in your bank vault brain? More likely it's his—shall we say, *vivid?*—imagination, a wrong turn on the pharmaceutical highway, his mind racing at the speed of molasses out there in the Dalian hinterlands of sanity.

By now the fire has burned down again, nothing left but cold ashes, and he's hunched up like a troll in the dark caverns of his thoughts, his arms wrapped around himself for warmth, slipping in and out of stuporous fragments of consciousness and dream. Through a muffled gray light he can see around him things or the skeletons of things, great creatures, rusty cars, machines, factories, rivers turned into icy blue serpents, everything frozen into stillness and silence beneath the snow, the entire planet become a frozen white marble, like the eye of a dead fish floating in the black ocean of space. The scene changes and he's lying in a four-poster canopy bed next to Ebenezer Scrooge, or no, he has actually *become* Ebenezer Scrooge and now this ghastly monstrosity has entered his bedchamber and stands before him rattling its chains and stinking of rotten plum pudding, pine wreaths and the grave. He hears himself beg, *Please, spirit, are these things that have come to pass, or presentiments of that which is yet to come?*

> And a choir of angels sang
> *Wonderful!*
> and
> *Magnificent!*

How do you say snowbound, snowblind, snow loco, stir crazy, cabin fever?

Finally, the great storm passes, the city returns to normal, the snow crews carry on as before, but something's happened, a change has occurred, there's an attitude in the air, the snowmen are no longer met with cheery greetings from homeowners or waves from passing cars. *Au contraire.* Now hostile glares dart at them from every angle. People shout obscenities and make vulgar hand gestures. There are rumors of eco-nut snipers in snow-white parkas perched on rooftops waiting for snow trucks to stop at traffic lights, which does add a certain cowboy cachet to the snowbiz. The truth is, people are fed up with snow. Yeah, sure, here in the southern climes, the snow was initially welcomed as a novelty. The famous Waterloo Springs, where twenty- and thirty- and even forty-something nymphs used to swim topless in the pristinely clear water, was converted into an ice skating rink. The sleepy but steeply hilled little community of Timberly just south by southwest of Osberg transformed itself into prime ski country. But that love affair has long since dried up. People have only been waiting for an opportunity to vent. Now they openly blame the snow industry for all their ailments and woes. The general populace spends all its time in overheated houses, offices, schools, staring at screens and eating enormous quantities of comfort food almost nonstop. The per capita consumption of alcohol exceeds that of water. Depression is universal, likewise prescription meds. Morbid obesity is a national epidemic. The health of the body politic has plummeted, life expectancy is practically troglodytic. All fine for private healthcare providers (with wealthy clientele) and mortuaries—who never have a bad day. Adding to the headache, heating bills are outrageous, utilities over the top—costs for maintenance of the infrastructure are astronomical. The cold forces the pavement through an endless freeze-thaw cycle, buckling streets, breaking pipes, producing huge moon crater potholes. On the SunnySide entire families are regularly asphyxiated by kerosene stoves or smoldering charcoal burners they use to heat their homes, or else they perish in roaring infernos that ravage their flimsy tarpaper and plywood shacks in minutes. Intrepid VBS reporters are on the scene, fanning the flames of public outrage. *Homes, families, communities consumed on the pyres of poverty and ignorance!* Uncle Bob's got a panel of noteworthies on his show to discuss the public's loss of faith in the snow industry, the staunch Tea Potty Republican, Mississippi Senator Strumplin Snoops, the Reverend K. James Fallible representing the religious community, and, on behalf of all the science guys (and all you purty little science gals, too), none other than ICIN's own Roger Wilco. But no sympathetic softballs lobbed their way tonight. The usually placid Uncle Bob's just as pissed off as the rest of the citizenry. He's mercilessly grilling Senator Snoops. You can hear him over the radio, jamming his big stumpy forefinger in Snoops' inbred, porcine face and shouting at him the question a lot of people have been asking themselves lately. Why the hell do we make snow if it only causes everyone such misery?! Hmmph! Senator Snoops snorts at such ignorance. Everyone in the whole wide world knows darn well and good why we make snow. The very greatness of this nation was founded on snow. If snow was good enough for Jesus and Abraham, it's good enough for us. And that is why it is so *vital* that we continue to make snow. Hmm, this line of reasoning sounds weak even to his weak-minded constituency. At which point Roger Wilco, speaking in a decadent nasal drawl, steps in. Hmmm, yesss, well, it is an interesting *hypawwthesis*. Completely untrue, of course. You have to understand the chemical *commmpozishun, mawlekewls* of hydrogen and carbon, not to *mennshion* oxygen, impossible to explain *reahhlly*, a matter of science, I'm publishing a paper next month. Uncle Bob's frustration audibly growing, he looks to Reverend Fallible for guidance. Even over the airwaves you can see his gleaming blue eyes, in fact, frighteningly blue, you don't want to look into those eyes, you just wanta smile and get your ass the hell out of his vicinity. Sometimes in order to preserve life it is necessary to extinguish life! There are not enough loaves in the field nor fishes in the sea to feed the masses! We are the chosen people! We must reclaim what is ours from the heathen! Close the gates on the barbarians! We live in a gluttony of fornication! Sodomy is all around us! Horrible bestial acts involving organs and orifices! Sausages!

Mmmmmph! At which point there are shouts and sounds of a scuffle and Uncle Bob, FCC regs and radio etiquette on his side, takes control of the mike again. Despite his heroic efforts at restoring a modicum of reason and order to the forum, the entire radio audience scattered across the cities and hamlets of this great nation are joined in a collective sea of gloom and confusion from which even Superman would be helpless to extract them. Until, that is, Uncle Bob brilliantly resolves the issue by asking one of his innocuous-enough-sounding questions in his trademark "slightly baffled" voice. Gentlemen, could this crisis be related to the *illegal immigrant problem*? Which results in a huge exultant chorus. It's the *ILLEGAL IMMIGRANT PROBLEM*!!!! (*I-I-aieeee!*) Thereby unleashing a barrage of unabashedly racist accusations, threats and calumnies that until this moment had been simmering unspoken beneath the surface of public discourse but now explode in a bleating denunciation of the primary culprits, those brown-skinned denizens of those torpid southern latitudes, those cucarachas, mojados, wetbacks, beaners, spics, spans, *animals*. They infest our cities, our towns, our countryside! They take our jobs, our cars, our flat screen TVs, our women! And boy does Uncle Bob have his thinking cap on tonight. He's already seized on the theme of his next program. Tomorrow night on VBS, "Our jobs, Our way of life!"

The immigrant population, legal and "illegal" alike, quickly feel the backlash. ICEmen raid welding and auto body shops, construction sites, restaurants, nursing homes, dry cleaners, maid services. States, cities and municipalities enact ordinances, extrajudiciary restrictions. It gets so bad that even natural-born-and-bred American citizens of any race, religious belief, creed, gender orientation or ethnicity except your pretty obvious hetero white guys are afraid to leave their homes and only go out when absolutely necessary. Panicked employers, afraid of hefty fines and public boycotts, lay off all undocumented workers. The snowbiz, comprised almost exclusively of Mexicans now, resists this trend, although the irony of hiring Mexicans to keep out Mexicans has worn thin in popular opinion.

One night the Snowman comes out of a convenience store to find a pair of beefy, ex-high school linebacker goons from the SilverSpoon Police Department roughing up Nico. Goon number one's hoisting Nico off the ground by his collar and snarling in his face, Hey, sunshine, what'choo doing in this part of town? Nico says nothing. He hangs in the air, fists knotted at his sides, beaked face defiant. But what's up with Bombástico? He's bouncing up and down like an agitated weather balloon and going *ooh! ooh!* And no wonder. A streetlight's LED white phosphorescence illuminates a scarred bronze face, the blue gleam of a sapphire in a gold front tooth, a black obsidian blade held at the level of a man's throat. (On screen, this scene transpires in a jerky, handheld shot. Apparently Boone, who "just happened to be on the spot," filmed the whole thing without any effort to intervene. Not so of our intrepid Snowman.) At the exact instant Xuan's knife hand begins to arc through the air on its fatal trajectory, the Snowman steps in. *It's all right, officers, he's with me.* Even as he says it, he realizes how stupid this sounds. In fact, goon number two stares into his manic, bloodshot, chemically unbalanced eyes like *Who the fuck are you?!* then actually says *Who the fuck are you?!* He shrugs, glances down at the senior Snowman's patch on his shoulder. Yeah? The cop snarls, his narrowed porcine eyes suggesting he's not entirely convinced by this putative symbol of authority. Well in the future make sure you keep your monkeys on a tight leash around here! As the SnowBile pulls back onto the highway, Nico exuberantly yells out the window, *Fok you!*

The race baiting hits closer to home when, on another night, he finds Margarito apparently trying to separate Xuan and M'Shaka from a battle of the titans between SnowBiles Number Nine and Number Eight. And they are titans. Xuan seems to have grown about two feet taller, he's this totemic giant with blood red scars running down his face like indelible warpaint, the blue sapphire in his front gold tooth gleams like a penetrating particle beam and those huge biceps bulge like eighteen pounder cannon balls. M'Shaka, too, looks like some kind of tribal god carved out of mahogany, his dreads are the lion's mane, his beard the pharaoh's envy, even in his big puffy parka he looks like he could bench about seven hundred. Which is why it seems odd that he has redirected his ire at Margarito, who's maybe a third his size at best. What's the matter, Marguh-*ree*-toh, you don't wanta fight? You hate the greenghosts so much, here's your chance. And while the Snowman's pretty sure that's what M'Shaka said, he's also pretty sure he said it in Spanish, which causes this little hiccup in his head, like *huh?* At the very same moment you can see M'Shaka's and Margarito's eyes register the Snowman's presence and, *bam*, just like they've practiced this scene a hundred times before, they back off, joking, throwing jabs and fake punches at each other.

At the time this confrontation almost seemed funny, M'Shaka, face black as ebony, referring to himself as a greenghost, except he looked so darn serious, gone his usual ultra-cool struttin' and jivin'. And when had he ever heard Margarito, or any of the guys, for that matter, express hatred for greenghosts? When he made an offhand comment about this incident later, Margarito brushed it off as a misunderstanding. In fact, there's a scene at the Rose. (There's some uncertainty whether this is the same night as the Day of the Donkey celebration, or another night. Boone originally intended for the entire movie to be set in a bar, everything told in a conversation between Margarito and the Snowman using flashbacks—*Ed.*) Margarito is sitting across from him, a look of profound sadness on his face, his eyes like pools of melted chocolate, and he's saying, we are pacific people, *Snowman*, we do not want to fight. Then there's a painful image of himself, tears in his eyes, his voice breaking, completely drunk obviously, as he tries to apologize to Margarito, like everything—the cold and snow, the bigotry and discrimination, this whole fucked-up existence—is somehow all his fault. He even starts to sound a little bonkers here, like one of those wild-eyed psychos you run into on the street who just happens to choose you as his confidant. I am the precise point in the fulcrum upon which it all resides. I am the pinprick in humanity's hide through which this evil virus entered. I don't know how it happened but I know it's true. A chill that has passed through the front window has prompted them both to put up their hoods and they somewhat resemble monks confessing their sins to one another, but rather than offering compassion, Margarito's expression grows dark, his eyes fierce. His reply is unusually harsh, his disdain a cudgel to the heart. Isn't it rather grandiose to imagine yourself such an important cog in this scheme, Snowman? Don't you think some higher power might be at work here? Oh yes, I know, you greenghosts use the word God all the time, you invoke God, you shout God, God, God. You think this entitles you to a special place in heaven as it is here on earth. You believe you are the chosen ones and everybody else be damned. The truth is, you greenghosts aren't any worse than anybody else, just a little more afraid, a little crazier, a little farther from God, no matter how many times you say the word *God*. This is the way it always is in troubled times, Snowman. The hatred, the anger, the urge to strike out. Because somebody has to take the blame for the cold and the misery. Somebody, but not you, Snowman. It is true you are a greenghost. You cannot be different than what you are. But you did not cause this to happen. You are but an instrument, one of many in this great wheel of life.

To the Snowman's ears this sounds a little like Buddhism, and why not? Moogoogairitopan's ancestors carried with them the knowledge of the Buddha's coming ten, twenty, thirty thousand years before he came, they endured the Buddha's truth of long suffering and hardship on their ancient journey across time and space, vast continents, barren planes, frozen bodies of water, the bitter cold, the vast black night boiling with stars, the unrelenting heat of day, the thousands of miles they traveled along that ancient pan-American highway, from the Inuit's barren whiteness to the Inca's mountain fastnesses, surviving earthquakes, volcanoes, inundations, cohabiting in caves with saber-toothed tigers, bears, learning to hunt down and kill giant mastodons.

It also occurs to the Snowman that Margarito's English has improved markedly, his accent largely disappeared, his vocabulary grown expansively—the eloquence that comes with spiritual lubricants, perhaps?

Margarito gives him one of those oddly coy looks—really, it's almost like he's flirting, the big brown eyes, the long, soft eyelashes, the full, sensuous lips curled in a playful smile. But his tone is anything but playful. Greenghosts think we are stupid because we don't speak their language. Can you speak the lingo of angels, *Snowman*? of Genius? of God? My people were here first, *Snowman*. It was they who taught the fathers of your fathers' fathers how to live here, how to survive, how to grow food, how to hunt and fish, how to use the fruits and seeds, the roots, bark and leaves of native plants, they who offered for free the land next to theirs, the prospect of good neighbors. But that wasn't enough, your people took our land too, our homes, our lives. But now you see we are beginning to reclaim what is ours. You think you can stop us, but how can you put up fences against the wind, or the migration of butterflies? How can you stop the millennial progress of a glacier?

Uh-oh, looks like Boone's climbed up on his high horse again. In yet another heavy-handed detour, he allows Margarito's little homily to swell into a full-blown speech that sounds straight out of *The Grapes of Wrath*. Cinema sleuths even claim that in one frame, Rosasharn can be seen hovering in the background like an unwanted shadow.

We will come anyway, *Snowman*, despite the hunger in our bellies, despite the fear in our hearts, despite the contempt we feel from the greenghosts who look at us as if we are filthy animals when we stand at the freezing day-labor sites begging, not

for handouts or charity, but a job, *Snowman*, a job that none of
your people want, backbreaking labor for lousy pay, living in a
rundown hovel with twenty-five or thirty or even fifty other men
with barely even space to lie down at night, sending home what
money you can to help your family and make it so your children
don't have to work like you do, so they can go to school and
learn how to be something other than a dumb donkey, so your
wife whose face you barely remember doesn't have to kill herself
with her own regimen of unrelenting labor. Each time you see
her she appears thicker, duller, older, that beautiful young girl
you had wooed with the urgency of spring floods, of roan stal-
lions galloping after chestnut mares, fading ever farther into the
abyss of memory. And every day, week, month, year is the same,
the same lousy job, the same lousy pay, only on Saturday nights,
when the stars explode out of the black night and the music in
the cantina swells and flows over the dark countryside for miles,
only then think about a beer, one good beer, but only think
about it because the first one tastes so good and the other men
are all having another and there's some kind of card game going
on and you just feel like laughing and having fun on your only
night off, so sure, why not, give me another, and then another
and another until your paycheck's gone and you owe somebody
everything you'll make the following week. And what do you
put in that letter home then? Dear *familia*, work doan go too
good this week, they doan pay us nawteeng, so nawteeng ees
what I seend you, maybe next month—love, Penurio. Or else,
maybe you go to the payday lender and borrow five hundred
bucks at fifty percent interest, but—too bad Petunia or Pedro
or whatever your name is, the boss has to cut expenses—you
don't work next week so now you owe seven hundred fifty dollars
and somebody's threatening to hurt you. Is this what we sought
when we left our homes to come here? To work like donkeys and
maybe even die here in this land that is not our own?

As if Boone isn't already beating a dead horse (okay, ass), here
he inserts documentary footage of roadside memorials around

Osberg, white wooden crosses festooned with plastic flowers, ribbons and banners to mark the exact spot where the whole transplanted family, Papa and Mama and half a dozen niños and niñas, ran off the road and into oblivion wrapped in the metal embrace of their hurtling junkyard as they crashed into a concrete pillar, bridge abutment or other civic monument to inertia, where cousin Primo coming home from his third job of the day fell asleep and crashed into a King Kola truck and died in a rain of broken glass and foaming brown effervescence, where uncle Tío wandered out onto the interstate late one night drunk and daydreaming of a sandy, rocky path he used to follow through the desert to a dark green cleft in the mountainside where water spilled out into a deep pool surrounded with lush vegetation and all the animals in the desert came to drink and got run over by a tractor-trailer hauling designer bottled water drawn from a tap in the back of a used furniture shop on Calle Octubre 32 in Mexico City. There are even rumors the bodies are actually buried right there under the snow beneath the crosses. The screech media jump on it immediately. They don't even bury them properly! They just dump them on the roadside and leave them to rot! It's unsightly, it's unsanitary, it's a national disgrace! There's even this strange TV commercial (funded by the Bochit brothers, it is revealed later) that shows copper and bronze and terra cotta masks pushing up through the snow in pools of blood, and then some kind of chain reaction as the snow begins to melt everywhere.

But what's gotten into Margarito? Why is he so upset? How to explain these inexplicable fits of bad temper? Sometimes they last days, he comes to work grumpy, irritable. Despite Margarito's generally sober demeanor, the Snowman suspects he goes on periodic benders. Once he muttered something about stomach problems. And, true, he does seem to spend an inordinate amount of time in convenience store restrooms, which could also be attributed to shy bladder.

15
Suspicion

AROUND THIS TIME, GASTREAUX gives him a special assignment. Roger Wilco, ICIN's top R&D man, is in town, he wants to go out with a crew at night to observe the technology in the field. You're such an intellectual, *Snowman*, why don't you give him the tour?

Right off the bat he pegged Roger as a privileged preppy prig. Pale, boyish face, freckles, tousled sandy hair, tortoise shell glasses, *bowtie*, a red and green scotch plaid parka and L.L.Bean dress overshoes. Hands clasped behind his back, Roger blinked at him through the thick lenses perched on his thin nose as if he were examining a bug, then kicked one of the SnowBile's eight-foot-tall tires. I made these. Yeah, so what, just because you can't cook Jell-O right, that makes you a genius? he thought but didn't say. And now he was going to have to babysit this jerk for the next twelve hours, which meant he'd have to be on his best behavior, which also presented him with the unwanted prospect of a long, painfully sober night ahead. By the time they pulled out of the factory gate, his contempt for this *asshole* had swollen into such great proportions that he couldn't resist the urge to put him down in front of the guys, he started making all kinds of stupid, uninformed pseudoscientific criticisms of Roger's tires and that *Wolverine* snowblower thing and various aspects of the snowbiz itself that Roger dismissed like flies with a few simple facts and statistics and then unexpectedly added, I like you, *Snowman*, you're funny. Would you care to try one of my experimental drugs?

Gotta give it to that Roger. Not only was he a fucking genius, he manufactured some truly superior pharmaceuticals. Half an hour after ingesting Roger's nostrum, the Snowman's pretty well convinced he's not only watching but actually starring in Sid Ney's animated classic *Phantasma*. The whole crew has taken on this kind of cartoonish, funhouse-mirror appearance: Xuan looks like Goofy, Nico—maybe Woody Woodpecker, Bombástico definitely looks like Bashful, Carroteeno—Grumpy, of course. And Raf-I-el? Oh, maybe this anime character with henna hair and blue face who's so hot with the kids these days. Somewhere along the line he also realizes that Roger (who, it also occurs to him now, bears an eerie resemblance to Tommy from the junkyard, albeit a cleaned up, bespectacled version. Pure coincidence? Or that cheapskate Boone's notorious penchant for employing the same actor in multiple roles?) is speaking fluent Spanish with the guys, in fact, Margarito's asking Roger all kinds of questions in that somewhat coy, even alluring manner and not only that, Roger seems totally infatuated with him, which for some reason really irks the Snowman. The camera's panning back and forth between Roger's pale, inebrious face and Margarito's bright, surprisingly alert eyes (considering he's also participating in the experimental drug test—maybe he got the placebo) in a way that lets us know Roger's divulging some very interesting stuff. There's even this epiphanic moment—frantic piano, the plot thickening—when the camera lingers on the Snowman's face so we can see his suspicions awakening, hmm, what if Margarito's stealing trade secrets or something? That'd make plenty of sense, right? Then it gets even more interesting. He's pretty sure he hears a word in English, *cryogun*, which must not be anything like the iceguns they use because, if he understands correctly, instead of Icine it apparently shoots out some kind of ionized gas (*gas ionizado*) that immediately turns to ice anything it hits. Roger cackles, You could kill a dinosaur with one of these things.

Five minutes later this conversation is completely erased from his memory. All he retains of this night is an oily blur of images that includes Roger and Nico chasing after each other with the torches and laughing hysterically. He's also left with a fuzzy sense of something not quite right in the world. He tries to shake this feeling, but now his antennae are up, his spider senses tingling. Some things here just don't add up. Like the night he found Margarito tapping away at the onboard computer, the guys crowded around him. Strange red, green and blue hieroglyphs covered the screen. He didn't even know the computer could do this graphics stuff. When he expressed his amazement, Margarito smiled that friendly, open, *nothing to be concerned about, Snowman* smile and explained that he was showing the guys how to perform their jobs more *effeeshently*, and even that silly mispronunciation seemed uncalculated. Except that Margarito seemed to know more about all these machines than the people who designed them. Zol*tech*, right?

On top of that, Gastreaux has been on his case about missing stuff. And another thing, Snowman, this fucking inventory. As soon as we get something in, it disappears into that pile of shit you keep in the motor pool and we never see it again. You got some kind of black market thing going on? Your Mezkins building rocket launchers out of it? And what's he gonna say, Ummm, no, actually . . . hydroponic gardens?

Another thing. Why are the guys so damn deferential toward Margarito? Even this diminutive they use, *M'Grito*, like my lord, my liege, my prince, my king. All very interesting because Margarito's ability to speak English alone wouldn't carry much weight with them. Nor is he physically imposing. And he can't be a day over twenty-five—okay, maybe thirty (he does have kind of a baby face, despite the lustrous mustache), so it's not like some wise elder thing. And yet there is something lambent and real in his eyes, a *nobility* about his presence.

He also remembers now that Nico, lips loosened by a quantity of beer, eyes glazed, slurring his words, had started to tell him a story about Margarito and out of nowhere Xuan's thick, heavy hand clamped down on Nico's shoulder and, grinning fox-like, the blue sapphire gleaming lethally in his gold tooth, he said, Having a leetle chat with the Snowman, Nico? Not telling heem any lies, are you? Nawteeng that will make him think badly about us, I hope. Doan want to involve Meester Snowman in our family affairs, do we, Nico? Someboddy might get hurt.

Oh, and while we're at it, there's this other issue that's been bothering *Meester* Snowman. The last time he went to Judith's place he smelled a popular men's cologne—apparently it's a mix of whiskey, diesel fuel and grizzly bear piss—it's even called *Grizzly*. Everyone, even *los guys*, even Margarito, is wearing this stuff. Oh, that was an associate, it's easier to meet here. Easier to fuck here, you mean, he almost said, but again managed to hold his tongue because after all she was a single adult and it was none of his fucking business what she did, right, Snowman? Although actually it *was* his fucking (even though they aren't doing much of that anymore) business. How could it not be his business when there was still this huge gaping sore between them, despite the fact that she seemed to be happily, constructively going on with her life while he kept on dredging this rut he was in deeper and deeper? So maybe it's no surprise that one evening soon after this last development he drops by again to return a bracelet Judith must have dropped behind the stove long ago, but right before she answers the door he hears someone speaking in a soft throaty voice that sounds oddly familiar, and then when she does open the door, a little warily it also seems, there's that familiar cologne smell again and, uh-oh, just like that, all kinds of cogs and gears start grinding away in his brain and in a mighty leap paranoid jealousy transforms into crazy speculation and then ugly, indiscriminate anger—Judith barely gets the door closed and he's already interrogating her, in fact outright accusing her, What—are you even fucking that *wetback* Margarito?! His eyes are leaping all over the place for a sight of this treacherous Zoltec, Mexican, whatever the fuck he is. Judith's eyes in turn blaze like cobalt 60 in a linear accelerator.

Her whole being radiates utter contempt. Her voice when she speaks is as frigid as arctic ice water. *It's my maid*, Snowman! And at that precise moment he actually catches a glimpse of— yes, it's clearly a woman, Hispanic, in some kind of domestic outfit vacuuming in another room, who calls out just then in Spanish, *Está bien, Señora?* And oh shit oh fuck, now he feels like a total idiot, loser, moron. Of course he should apologize, say, I'm sorry, I don't know what I was thinking, but—nascent rage turned to self-righteous outrage, the next instant he's attacking Judith's bourgeois indulgence, accusing her of exploiting the working class, abusing minorities, I mean—a *maid?* To which Judith responds, cool as an ice cube, I pay her well, *Snowman*. She has health benefits, an IRA. What about you? A leaden weight crushes him down into the carpet like a squashed bug. Here he is, stuck in his stupid job in his stupid lousy life, and there's Judith, a big muckety-muck, and even her fucking maid's better off than him.

Here for some reason there's a disconnected scene in a laboratory, centrifuges, kilns, spectroscopes, microscopes, beakers, burets, Bunsen burners, glass tubing. Two women in safety goggles and white lab coats are involved in a fairly animated conversation, both speak with accents and—okay, the one definitely sounds like Judith (or-*ee*-gin, *seemp*-to-mah-*teec*), but the other? He hears her identified as Doctor Juana—Mexican apparently. Oddly, her voice is familiar too, maybe she's someone famous, he's seen her on TV. The putative Judith and "Doctor Juana" seem to be particularly interested in some kind of "*enzyme*."

One other thing of note. Despite this unhappy schism in their relationship, from time to time Judith, thoughtful as always, drops off bundles of shredded paper for him to use as cat litter. One night he could have sworn he caught Me'th reading rather than peeing in his box. Which raised three possibilities. One, Me'th could read. And two, there was something readable in those shreds. Out of curiosity he examined a handful of confetti. The paper had been cut vertically. There were no sentences, not even words, just disconnected and oftentimes bisected letters. And this stuff came from businesses and offices all over the country. The odds of piecing together even the smallest intelligible morphemes were nearly impossible. Even with cloud computing, nanotechnology, thousands of nerdish computer engineers feverishly pushing the envelope, it'd take incalculable hours and access to masses of this stuff to even begin to hope to find a match. Only a lunatic would try such a thing. That was the third possibility. He pulled another shred from the bundle.

But this is already starting to sound too fond, too funny, too much like some tired little drawing room comedy. It's pretty clear Boone is floundering in this sea of disparate pieces. The audience is beginning to die on him, he's dying in front of them, the Snowman's somewhere out there dangling in the cold winter wind.

But don't worry, folks, Boone's about to turn that around. He's pretty sick of the direction this thing's taking himself. He despises his crew—everyone, lighting, cameramen, scriptwriters, soundmen, grippers—they're all ambitious young hotshots, they don't give a shit about tradition, the most pathetic of the lot, the special effects guy, for whom Boone has acquired an enormous reservoir of opprobrium. Stuff that used to cost millions, take months to build, entire sets, huge lavish scenes, the guy does it all on his laptop in a couple of hours. In a particular fit of pique, Boone, disdaining the scriptwriter's profuse apologies and explanations of how he was trying to achieve subtlety, scrawls across the page in red lipstick, *Subtlety my ass! I don't wanta put them to sleep! I wanta kick them in the teeth!*

16
The Man

THEN, SMASHING BOTTLES, shouts, a blade flashes, someone
screams and we're back at the Rose as Boone continues to hijack
the chronology. Mercurio, the new man on Jipi Jaime's crew,
who only a minute ago was laughing over a very scary incident
in his journey to *el Norte* that in hindsight seemed very funny,
lies on the wet floor in a spreading crimson pool. A man stands
over him with a bloody knife, his eyes wild, his face anguished,
a curse escaping his lips, *Puto!* Then Xuan is at the man's back.
Gracefully, almost intimately, as if he were embracing a lover
from behind, he reaches around and places one hand on the
man's chest, with the other smoothly, gently even, draws his
obsidian blade across the man's throat, separating flesh like
silk, opening up that obscene, widely grinning second mouth,
blood gushing out like paint, the man collapsing to the floor,
convulsing, making horrible gurgling noises. And all you can
do, Snowman, is sit paralyzed with horror, trying to convince
yourself it's all untrue, a bad dream, that there will be some kind
of reprieve, who knows, maybe God will intervene.

Boone? Are you there? Can't you cut this scene? It's just
ketchup, right, Boone? Wasn't this supposed to be a comedy?
Not now, Snowman, we're shooting. But this is murder, Boone.
Someone just got killed. *Trust me, Snowman.* Trust you? Boone,
you've got a reputation for unhappy endings. *Relax, Snowman.*
It's cinéma vérité, remember? Just act naturally.

His natural reaction would be to run screaming, Help! Help!
Murder! Mayhem! Call the cops! but when he suggests this

possibility, Nico shakes his head, *Nooo, Snowman,* the police only cause *más problemas.* Even more disconcerting, he discovers Margarito was the man's actual target. Why would someone want to kill Margarito? When he asks this question (how do you say *murder, assassinate, kill?*), Margarito seems to have lost his patience with the how-do-you-say? game. He also seems to have regressed in his English language skills. Forget about eet, Snowman. Eet ees not eemportaunt. But it's important to me. But why, Snowman? Why must you know everything? Not all answers are the ones you want to hear.

And then, just when it seems like Boone's got this mooovv . . . ook (*mook?*) up and running again, there's a technical snag, and it's almost certainly due to Boone's perennial problem with chronology, because even though the Snowman knows the following scene would almost certainly have to have occurred on another night (he clearly remembers that the next evening the guys showed up at work like nothing had happened, a new man in their midst, whom they introduced as Chupiter, Mercurio's replacement), it seemed to him like the same night, in fact he vaguely remembered the lights dimmed and a kind of theatrical scene change took place, stagehands hauled off the bodies, or maybe they even got up and walked off themselves, others waltzed around with mops and buckets, scrubbing the floor, rearranging chairs, tables. Then the lights came up again, the place was nearly deserted, almost everyone had gone home. He and Margarito sat across from each other in the booth. But something seemed missing, as if a package of time with all the events it contained had disappeared from the universe, or the film had caught in the projector, then jerked ahead again.

At a table next to them sat an old man. Nearby a boy, his grandson most likely, an unkempt little mongrel pup, maybe five–six, climbed up on bar stools, crawled under tables among puddles of spilled beer, dropped food, bright-eyed, antennae-waving cucarachas already feasting at their own banquet, drooping pant legs, fat female thighs squeezing like lumpy oatmeal out of fishnet stockings, everything in life still a mystery, one minute happily chattering to himself, oh boy, is that a spider climbing up that man's leg? And he doesn't even know? What if it bites him? Will he die? The next minute his lower lip trembling, eyes welling with tears, ready to cry like a little baby because of a remark some drunk made to him, not even a word of reproach, just something small, mean, meant to hurt him for being so young, for being so stupid and naïve, even the waiter bending under the table to scold him, *aii, mijo*, what are you doeen down there? You mossn't play on the dirty floor! Now he's sitting at the table, fidgeting. You can't blame him. He's tired, wired, he should be home in bed. The old man, his grandfather, seems to have nodded off in a drunken stupor and is totally oblivious.

Margarito, who has also been observing this scene, pours more brandy in their glasses, takes a large swallow. One night he and his grandfather came into town to pick up supplies. Afterwards Grandpa wanted to offer a prayer to Santa Agave at the cantina, but one prayer turned into two and then three, a litany of praise to the blessed saint of mezcal. Pretty soon Grandpa nodded off. (Boone has pulled some old wino off the street for this scene. He figures if he needs to develop the Grandpa character later he can easily find a replacement.) At a table across the room sat a man with raven black hair and mustache and a hawk face. A black patch over one eye partially hid a jagged red weal that extended from his brow, down over his cheek to his jaw. Margarito had heard people call him *El Matador*, but he called him the Man. When he and Grandpa went into town for supplies he almost invariably saw the Man standing on a street corner or coming out of the cantina or the barbershop. He watched carefully the way the Man peered up at the sun as if it were an unfamiliar entity or rubbed a freshly shaven jaw still burning with witch hazel. Sometimes when Grandpa was in a shop or conversing with an old friend, he followed the Man at a distance. He knew all his habits, affectations, the crooked black, foul-smelling cigars he smoked, the gold watch he carried in his vest pocket, the gold rings he wore on his left hand, the sinister hand he clinched and unclenched as if it ached to unholster a gun. Sometimes he suspected the Man knew he was following him. They said he had an eye in the back of his head, that his boots left cloven prints, that the ground caught fire beneath his feet—these latter two claims, at least, he had disproved. He was fascinated by the Man's brooding masculinity. That's what a man should be, someone who was tough, who experienced adversity and came through unbowed, unlike the other men in this miserable little village. They were already worn out, defeated, their lives crushed by years of backbreaking labor interspersed with rare moments of passion, the drunken brawls, the precious moments of release and even joy in bed with a woman—nothing he knew about then, of course. People stepped off the sidewalk when the Man passed, afraid of his power, his presence. A cloud of whispers followed him down the street, buzzing around him like mosquitoes, stinging and biting and injecting him with their insidious poisons. Maybe not now, but in months, years, they'd weaken him, bring him to his knees, see him tried, judged and hanged. Maybe someone even more violent and ruthless than the Man would do the job for them. Then they'd forgive him, love him, raise him to sainthood, claim his misdeeds as their own, all his women, gunfights, jailbreaks, murders. Somehow Margarito knew that one day he and the Man would actually meet, that he, Margarito, would be recognized as someone special, someone who had already been given the mark, designated as an acolyte in the brotherhood of real men. The Man would anoint him with a few strong words, important words, words that'd guide him through life and give him direction when he doubted himself, when he sank into the morass of mundanity. And now that time had come. He felt the Man's single good eye fixed upon him, staring at him. Ah, Margarito, my little friend, it is you, isn't it? I've been looking for you all night. Were you hiding from me? Suddenly he didn't want to meet the Man anymore, he no longer wanted that eye to notice him, recognize him, call him by name. He said, let's go home now, *Abuelo*, it's late, I'm tired, I've got school tomorrow. But Grandpa didn't want to leave, he was enjoying his drink, maybe he even knew what was going to happen next, he was in on it all along, a secret and cruel ritual of manhood carried out by the men of the town.

A chair shrieked on the wooden floor. The Man crossed the room to their table. Do you mind if I join you? Grandpa was drunk, gregarious, Oh no! Not at all! An honor! Please, Señor, sit down! Margarito! Move over! Make room for the gentleman! The whole time the Man watched Margarito, rotating his head on his shoulders like a hawk to keep Margarito in sight of that ugly, evil *good* eye. By now Grandpa was on the verge of passing out. Margarito urged him with his eyes, Please, Grandpa, wake up! But Grandpa only chuckled and waved his hand in his sleep, brushing away Margarito's pleas like flies. This was the moment the Man had been waiting for. His hand crept across the table, leathery and reptilian, and clutched Margarito's thin wrist. So pretty, like a pretty little girl, the Man cooed in his face. The stench of whiskey and rotting meat flooded Margarito's nostrils. The Man's face twisted into a rictus grin. Pulling Margarito closer, he peeled back his eyepatch like the velvet curtain of a private little theater of horror. *Look!* he snarled, forcing Margarito to stare into the oozing red wound. A hot, oily mass slid through his bowels. He felt himself falling into a deep, dark void. Then he saw himself trudging across a vast barren whiteness. He was cold and shivering and a howl like that of some great beast echoed behind him. He woke with his face buried in his arms, the Man gone, Grandpa snoring contentedly, his beard-stubbled face crushed into drooling bulldog slumber. The bartender helped him drag Grandpa out to the wagon. Fortunately, the horse knew the way. The next day Grandpa didn't remember anything. He came out and found Margarito standing alone in a field, staring up at the big empty sky. Maybe he thought, Ah, the boy misses his mama. He went over and placed his heavy, callused hand on Margarito's shoulder, offering reassurance from an empty reservoir.

Margarito finishes this story just as the boy at the nearby table sits up and stares directly at him as if photographing him, imprinting him on his mind. Margarito swallows his brandy, pours another one. He saw the mark in my eyes, Snowman, and just as surely as the Man marked me, now I have marked this boy. You're smiling, Snowman, you think it's funny. More superstition. Everything in this world is connected, Snowman. One thing does not move without moving another.

Sandalwood man, Moogoogairitopan, Metamargarito.

17
Adios, Muchachos

A YOUNG WOMAN COMES IN, thin, high cheekbones, snow melting on the shiny black river of hair pouring over her pink wool coat. She glances around, the points of light in her eyes like dim candles flickering at the end of a lifetime of crushing poverty, then goes directly to the table where the old man and the boy are both sleeping now with their heads in their arms. She shakes them awake, gets them to their feet, pushes them outside, admonishing the old man in an urgent whisper *pero, piensa en el niño, Papá!*

Molten chocolate and arctic blue, Margarito's and the Snowman's eyes meet and for a moment there's a kind of mutual plunge into the abyss. Margarito struggles to speak. He says "I" and his lips move as if forming a word that seems to begin with the letter M and at the same time a face blooms on the screen like a calla lily in a pool of black ink, the eyes flashing like obsidian, the soft full lips parted like silky red rose petals, the perfect white teeth bared as if to bite—even through that celluloid medium there is a palpable sense of wildness, of yearning and hunger for life, for love. Margarito's eyes veer off to some distant place and he begins to speak in a monotone, as if he is repeating lines scripted for him by the passing of time, the repetition of events, like a jaded stage actor who has played the same role in a long-running but second-rate play. Each time he returned to her he felt that hunger in her mouth, in her kisses, in her warm body against his. He felt it swallowing him and consuming him, the voice of the *madre*, the *tierra madre, madre de maíz, madre de los niños, los niños que serán, tus niños.* That's what the women in my country mean when they use the word love, Snowman. *Babies.* Because that god of yours doesn't pass out contraceptives at the church door, he doesn't put IUDs, sponges, gels in women's vaginas. He puts babies, lots of babies—babies in the caramel-sweet *leche* of their breasts, babies floating in reed baskets in the deep black rivers of their hair, babies in their hungry mouths, babies in the lies escaping from the sweet, soft fruit of their lips, babies in their cunts, in their bellies, in the cradles of their arms practiced almost from their own infancy at cradling babies. Babies crying and clutching at you and pulling you down into the abyss. Ask me, Snowman, how do you say marriage, Margarito? How do you say matrimony? How do you say wedded, bound, imprisoned? That is when it all begins and ends, Snowman, when you get married, married to the woman you love, married to the land, the poor earth of that wretched country. You get married, you have babies, you work hard, you hope the drought doesn't come, you hope nobody gets sick, you hope there's enough food on the table for everyone to eat, you hope the damn donkey doesn't die, you hope *los políticos* and *los ricos* and *los narcos* and *los militares* and *la policía* leave you in peace. You grow older, your back more bent, nothing changes, you accomplish nothing, gain nothing, you merely survive. And then the drought does come, your beans and corn shrivel up and die and the damned donkey dies, and your babies get sick and begin to die and maybe you even die. Or maybe you scrape together enough money to pay the coyote and you leave all that behind to come here, to the land of opportunity, *el norte.*

Hey, everybody, Margarito's eyes roll around the empty cantina. Look, I'm here, I made it, I'm in the North. His eyes meet the Snowman's again. Yes, Snowman, you hear the bitterness in my voice, you think I am not acting like myself. You are right, Snowman, I am not acting like myself. Is this what living among the greenghosts does to you, Snowman? Blind you? Maim you? Make you lose sight of the truth? Fill you with coldness and darkness until you think that is the only way of life? Margarito raises his brandy. The orange firelight gleams on the rim of his glass and in the black bristles of his mustache, on the moist swelling of his lips where a slight tremor has begun, and in the muddy brown depths of his eyes welling now with tears. That's it, the mask Boone wants, Margarito in his great sorrow. The critics howl at Boone's unrelenting heavy-handedness, but the movie-going public loves it, thanks in large part to Margarito's spectacular performance. When was the last time a male actor dared such naked vulnerability? And how to explain this concurrent urge he, the Snowman, feels to offer comfort, to place a reassuring hand on Margarito's shoulder, to say words he hasn't formulated yet and would probably never say if he had. How do you say *Friendship*, Margarito? How do you say *Loyalty*? *Trust*? But those aren't the words he's really looking for, are they? How do you say *Love*? Why is it always so hard to find the air in his lungs to get that word out, to admit it into his vocabulary? And then what? Are you crazy, Snowman? *Love*? Men don't talk about that. Or, who knows, Aw, gee, Snowman, I didn't know you felt that way. But that isn't what he means either, is it? *Is it?* Finally it's too much even for Margarito and he glances away, almost as if he's hiding something. What doesn't he want you to see, Snowman? His weakness, pain? Or his derision, because you're just another stupid greenghost so full of empathy and compassion you don't even know you're getting snowed under again?

A car starts up outside, its brake lights pour red ink over the frosty plate-glass window. Across the street, in the shared parking lot of the Taquería Los Altos and the mini-multiplex auto glass repair shop, martial arts studio, hair salon and tarot card reader, people have been steadily gathering, men, women, a few children, all Mexican, stamping their feet, rubbing their gloved hands together, blowing steam. A big new bus with the word *Tornado* on its side pulls into the parking lot and the people begin to board, sometimes there's a hug with a family member or friend, goodbye, *adiós*, see you in a month or a year or never again. Every morning at six a.m. the bus pulls away from the city and heads south loaded with survivors of the crusades, middle-aged women with careworn eyes carrying plastic garbage bags filled with clothes, presents, sad-eyed young women with babies in their bellies, old men with rugged, weathered faces, bright-eyed young men in denim jackets and cowboy boots with some money in their pockets and the attitude of conquering heroes—*Ai-ai-aiiii, muchachos, vamos a ver a las mujeres y la tierra, vamos a comer la comida de nuestras madres, vamos, muchachos, a la casa.* You see, *Snowman*, going back down is easy, you just pay your money and get on the bus. Nobody cares about some Mexican crossing back into Mexico.

The jukebox pushes out a tune of sad and lonely men. The bartender places the chairs upside down on the tabletops, sweeps his way into a little well of light with a straw broom and, like a mime, disappears into the shadows. The Snowman reaches for the bottle but Margarito says, no, Snowman. No more drinking now. Let's go home, we have work tomorrow. Margarito smiles and for a moment his old cheerfulness seems to return. Look, *Snowman*, the sun is rising. The sun is always good, isn't it, Snowman? It means warmth and hope, it means a new day and a new life.

And then that sun disappeared. That sun packed up its bags and got on the bus and headed south for the winter. And he pushed his way out of the theater, out of the artificial summer, the last remnants of illusion and dream shattered by the suddenly too bright, too cold, too sterile light.

He didn't need a phone call or a carrier pigeon or even Evelyn's bright little bird's eyes in her worried little button face to give him the news. Where before he had approached the Ice Factory each night with that growing sense of dread and anxiety, only to be met by Margarito's beaming, incandescent smile and that unfettered optimism, *we can do eet, Snowman!* now there was this: a black hole. When he spoke aloud to fill that void, no voice spoke back. How do you say *cave, chasm, abyss*, Margarito?

Without Margarito as intermediary, the guys soon reverted to their taciturn selves. When he asked, How do you say *camel, crocodile, kangaroo*? they shook their heads, Who knows, Snowman? Go ask God, maybe God knows, and then stared at him out of their impenetrable bronze masks. When he made an attempt at conversation or launched into one of his stoned, disjointed dissertations, they listened in polite but clearly disinterested silence. Now what? Endure this isolation for the next weeks and months and possibly even years?

Had he known that another change was in the making he would have happily contented himself with the status quo. Approximately two months after Margarito disappeared, the Snowman walked into the front office and found an old scene being reenacted. Evelyn frantic, Gastreaux apoplectic. *Los guys* hadn't shown up for work, no one answered the phone. Evelyn was riffling through applications, scheduling interviews. She hoped to get somebody tomorrow or the next day. For now he'd have to take out a patchwork crew. She'd already paged Hank, Jaime and M'Shaka—they were coming back in. Gastreaux's last words: It's gonna be a long, cold night, Snowman.

18
Snowman's Blues

RUDDERLESS, COMPASSLESS, DISORIENTED and sailing ever deeper into terra incognita, he cast a frayed lifeline toward a familiar but ever more distant shore, and recoiled in horror. Judith, that jinn of hers, that demon within her, that hurtling locomotive of brilliance and ambition that ran over, crushed beneath, shoved aside any obstacle in her path, recently promoted to executive manager, her long locks shorn, the thick black storm cloud he loved to put his hands in reduced to something between a pixie cut and a gladiator's helmet. He pouted like a child, he told her he hated it, even as he noticed how it seemed to sculpt her features, make her ears, nose, cheekbones, mouth and chin more defined, her neck longer, the strange blue of her eyes more alarmingly radiant, her face more alien, something like the bust of the Egyptian queen Nefertiti. Also gone, the laid-back earth tones and natural fabrics. She dressed now for boardroom combat, black leather jacket over a black kidskin bustier, black body-fitting kidskin pants, black stiletto heels that could easily punch a hole in a man's skull, a black leather and platinum-latched handbag that suggested surface-to-air capabilities and an array of earrings, necklaces and bracelets that gleamed like arcane martial arts weapons. He said he hated her outfit too, even as words like *tough* and *seductive* and *hot* jammed his brain. It was like she was a totally different person, like he'd just met her for the first time in his life. He wanted to seduce her, make love to her, explore her. He wanted to discover her strengths, her weaknesses, her secrets. Too late, the die cast, his adolescent invectives irretractable. Thanks, *Snowman*, you always had a way with words—her sarcasm cold, flat, indifferent, like a sword blade left lying on a battlefield. At which point this attempt at rapprochement, détente or anything less than unconditional surrender was hopeless. Confess to this figure of puissance and pulchritude that he felt like a sad, lonely little mouse? No way.

For reasons he didn't understand, this dismal encounter served as the inspiration to visit his mother. He remembered when he was a child and the snow began he was fascinated by this cold cotton fluff falling from the sky. He also remembered his parents' reaction. The old man was ecstatic. His transfer to the southwest office was like being exiled to a prisoner's colony on a desert isle. He hated the heat, longed for the cold northern winters of his youth. His mother, on the other hand, born in the south, was only too happy to return to that torpid clime. Then the snow started and she was forced back into a frozen hell she thought she had escaped forever. She couldn't accept it. The house was cluttered with old photographs, sunny meadows alive with the buzz and drone of bumblebees and dragonflies, quiet green ponds, screened-in porches crowded with gladiola and hollyhocks. She kept the thermostat at a sweltering ninety degrees. The old man'd say, We've got to accept reality, Margaret, the snow is here to stay. By now she had begun to mutter and talk to herself. She claimed the snow was part of a conspiracy. One day he came home from school to find her wandering around the yard in an absurd Little Bo Peep costume, pink and white ribbons and bows, thermal underwear peeking out from under ruffled petticoats, applying her watering can to long ago withered flower beds, meticulously pruning dead weeds as if they were prize roses. After she returned home from the hospital she seemed better. Then she disappeared one night. The police found her almost frozen to death, lying in a snow bank. This time she was in the hospital longer. When she came home she sat in a drugged trance, completely lethargic, or else crept about the house like a zombie. And then the fire. He was in his junior year in high school. He was walking the half-mile home from the bus stop when he heard the sirens. Oh boy, at last some excitement in this boring little burg. When he got to the top of the hill he could see up the street to the corner where his house stood. First he saw the fire trucks and then the flames. There was no way to know if it was an accident. The neighbor who had called 911 kicked in the front door. *Your mother was sitting in a sofa in front of the fireplace, flames all around her. She gave me this strange smile when I entered but when I tried to make her leave she became hysterical. Then Tom Collins across the street came in and together we managed to drag her out of the house.* Unfortunately, the girl . . . Little Sis was in middle school, her day ended sooner, the bus dropped her right at the door. She must have only been home a few minutes, upstairs in her room listening to tunes a new friend had downloaded for her, the world outside blocked off by her earbuds. After that his mother was permanently institutionalized. The old man essentially gave up. He died a year later and he, the future Snowman, went to live with his grandmother, finished high school, college, started grad school, his emotions hidden behind a wall he erected brick by brick against all overtures of intimacy, truth telling or sympathy. It was hard to visit his mother the first time—and the second and the third and every time without thinking *You killed her.* She didn't recognize him at all this last visit. He barely made it out of the hospital without breaking down. Salt water welled in his eyes the whole way home. But please, Snowman, stop or you'll make me melt. There won't be anything left but a carrot and a few lumps of coal. Here, Mother, burn these to warm your dreams.

Despite the Snowman's adamant demands, supplications, beseechments—practically down on his knees, begging—Boone insists on including the above scene. The film is now all in black-and-white with a distinct noir feel. A cigarette smolders in an ashtray, the smoke drifts over a glass of whiskey. A bluesy tenor

sax plays in the background. The Snowman sits in the sofa in
front of the window chain-smoking and methodically sipping
whiskey, each belt of booze, each nicotine nudge spaced according to some circadian death wish, five, ten, thirty second inter-
vals of poison between the breaths of clean air, lymphatic flushes
of the liver and pancreatic systems, subtracted from the sum
total of his existence—yeah, that sounds real good, Snowman,
you oughta write it down somewhere, not exactly a diary, but
an obituary in daily installments, these vital hours, minutes,
seconds ticking away while you lie on the couch like a living
corpse, sucking life into this dying butt, which is another joke,
right? Resuscitating a fucking stick of cancer. This goddamn
paralysis, all you can do is watch the world pass before your eyes
and mourn that passing rather than take action, weighed down
by the absolute meaninglessness of your life, the imminence
of death, whether in ten or twenty years or two minutes. And
talking to yourself no less, eh *Snowman*? Another habit picked
up out of the lost-and-found bin of neuroses, pathologies and
psychoses. Knowing he should drag his ass to bed and get some
sleep before he has to begin this madness all over again. But even
after he crawls under the covers and passes out with the ceiling
an ectoplasmic blur spinning overhead, Me'th's chartreuse eyes
burning with palpable disgust from the foot of the bed, he tosses
and turns ceaselessly, he has disturbing dreams—snakes writhe
at his feet, eagles tear chunks of flesh from his bare chest, he
falls naked into a huge clump of spiny cactus. At one point he
sees Margarito at the very center of the earth, naked, his bronze
body gleaming with sweat as he shovels enormous quantities of
coal into a roaring furnace that provides heat and energy for
the entire planet. Then it's no longer Margarito but a beautiful
young warrior woman with a strong sinuous body in iridescent
blue and green and gold plumage and jade necklace, anklets
and bracelets (this transformation, he decides lucidly while still
asleep, is probably the super-ego's objection to a naked man) and
now he's bent backwards over some kind of stone altar and she's

straddling him, he can feel himself inside her, she's hot and wet and huge, he feels so inadequate he's straining, yearning, urging his dick to be bigger than it is. Nevertheless, sex has never felt so intense in his life, his entire body is an erection. But then, just as he's about to come—and really, he feels like a fire hydrant about to burst—she raises a gleaming black blade overhead and plunges it into his chest. He wakes gasping for breath with a piss hard-on.

He repeats this routine every morning he comes home from work and even the rare nights he has off he does nothing but drink and smoke until morning when—numb, dumb, mumbling unintelligible monosyllables to himself, to Me'th, to the toaster oven, the first golden sunlight streaming in the window—he passes into oblivion. This Grand Canyon of a rut he'd dug for himself, somewhere along the line having managed to rationalize its ruttedness, to kill whatever resistance lay inside him to the madness of continuing in this rut, the struggle for life somehow sublimated, reduced to a barren insect existence of utility and function, and that sublimation added up to what, the last ten years of his life, and those entire ten years could be edited into a ten-minute script that represented what, the noble toils of mankind? The Trojan wars of blue-collar drudgery? Yeah, he was such a goddamn titan, a warrior of the working class. That's why he was abusing himself and his health and letting his mind rot. That bright light bulb of intelligence and curiosity in his brain slowly dimming into the cavernous recesses of troglodytic existence. What the hell happened? He was on some kind of path, trajectory, then he fell off. All those years he believed or tried to believe and then no longer believed—in anything. Maybe that was also when he began to lie awake at night with that horrible, writhing dread that made him clutch at his chest and his skull, fearing heart attacks, strokes, the complete disintegration of his liver, pancreas and kidneys into a soggy hemorrhaging pulp because of too much nicotine, caffeine, too much drugs and alcohol, when he pulled the blankets over his head and hid like a child and felt death crawling over him, insinuating itself down his throat and up his asshole into his stomach like a huge oily black worm until he felt like he was going to shit himself in bed and still he was afraid to get up and go to the toilet for fear he'd shit out his own guts. Fear, that's what they taught you, Snowman, fear your heartbeat, your pulse, the thing beating in your chest like a caged animal, fear your motivator, your warden, headmaster, proctor, monitoring how you do your job and act in society and the way you live your life and how you say good morning and good evening sir and how do you do ma'am? Maybe that's why he could only sleep during the day, tucked away in his warm little cocoon, in the warmth and security that life was going on around him—because night reminded him too much of the coldness and nearness of death. When he was a kid he used to lie in bed and stare into the darkness, his childish mind already buzzing with adult fears of some great looming catastrophe, the whole world always just ready to collapse upon him. But when did death become something less abstract, not just a theoretical possibility or even a probability but an undeniable fact as evidenced by the recurrence of death all around him, when he actually said to himself inside his skull, inside his brain, inside the *I* of his I—*I'm* going to die, and in that moment those words attained their true value, death transformed into a great fathomless void that could not be wrestled with and finally overcome like an enemy, that could not finally be embraced in one's arms like a friend after years of resistance, that could not be dissuaded by any amount of words, prayers, incantations, abject pleas, penitent tears or pathetic offerings of treasure, because what can anyone offer Death that Death will not claim as its own in the end? That preoccupation with death that made him withdraw from the life around him, because it really wasn't death he was afraid of, but life—the sheer impossibility of life—with all its horrible little organs and valves pumping away inside him ready to rupture and burst at any second. Everything suddenly seemed so delicate, so fragile, anything, a needle or shard of glass could puncture that membrane that sustained him and all his vital fluids, his *aqua vitae*, ninety proof preferred, would gush out on the ground, leaving a big puddle of ice water and residual ethanol where he, his life, his corporeal self, used to be. And he was going to live with that fear for the rest of his life? And call that living, call that life? And anytime anyone asked, put on a big act and say, No, I don't feel the cold, no, I'm not lonely, no, I'm not afraid of dying? Did Judith ever share that fear? Did she ever, in her determined march forward to success, second-guess or in any way doubt herself, her purpose or goals in life? Did Margarito share that fear? Would he ever admit that fear to anyone else? He looked at Margarito's bronze and terra cotta-hued face so unlike his own and attributed to it other powers, animal maybe, even supernatural, but certainly nothing that betrayed normal human fear. And yet he was almost certain he remembered Margarito saying once, Why shouldn't I be afraid, Snowman? Why won't you *allow* me to be afraid? If it happened, Boone must have edited the scene.

Was it just him, his lot, to live alone in this bleak, isolate cell, an alien among aliens, the true abominable snowman? He'd read about these guys called *Polyarniks*, a special breed of Russian meteorologists who essentially disappeared into the arctic vastness for yearlong stretches by themselves to observe and record the elements. People said, How the hell can they stand it? Would anyone guess that they craved this solitude? That, in fact, they derived great satisfaction and sometimes even doubled up in laughter at getting paid for being underground men, hermetic, ascetic, invisible men—*steppenwolves*? That this obsession of theirs was legitimized simply by recording how warm, how cold, how much precipitation on a given day, 365 days a year, thirty–forty years of their lives? He thought again of the Frankensteinian monster fleeing across the arctic ice floes from the torments of humankind. Or, returning for a moment to his putative Viking heritage—what if he had simply never understood that it was all for the glory of battle, to raise to his lips the ram's horn and blow out all his loneliness and fear in a cry of triumph even if that triumph meant great folly and even death? His loneliness deep, aboriginal, as if his tribe had exiled him into the wilderness with no hope of redemption, as if he were the last man on earth and now the monster was coming for him. It wasn't supposed to be this way, everybody was supposed to be in this together, united by a common bond, faith in God, trust in humanity, *something*, instead of everybody in their hermit cells, in their Neanderthal caves, separated from each other by the cold and snow and the layers of insulation they built up against the cold.

Here Boone rather haphazardly inserts what becomes an iconic film clip. In the black of night the Snowman stands on a limestone ledge on the face of Mt. Bonal, drunk, leering like a gargoyle, howling against the howl of the cold wind whipping his hair around his face, the orange glowing embers of the city of Osberg sprawled like the hub of a galaxy to the east, the white caps on the black ice-fringed lake six hundred feet directly below, swaying on his heels, just lean forward an inch . . . a fraction of an inch . . . another fraction . . . until his body reaches a precise geometrical position in relation to gravity's pull beyond which there is no return. And then into the arms of God.

God God God. Why does he keep saying that? The mantra of desperation, of helplessness, hopelessness. Does God feel sorrow and remorse for all the little tortures he she it has devised for us—his her its own children, does he she it wrack hiserits brains, wring his womanly beard in her hands, Why did I kill that one and sicken those? Why feast here and famine there? Although what god is that? Whose god? The purportedly Christian but— let's be honest—more like Old Testament tyrannical God of the honorable Reverend K. James Fallible? The God of Zol? Margarito's silent and unspeaking God who came to him in his dreams one night with a great flapping of wings, shedding shimmering gold, green and fiery red scales and clutching a writhing serpent in its beak? Or the Snowman's God, the God of nightly news, the oracle of the airwaves, the Uncle Bob God?

Oh, but Snowman, it's all a joke, ya see? It's just for laughs. No need to get serious on us now, Snowboy. We liked you better when you were funny. What's all this talk of corpses and dying?

By this time he's strung out, emotionally raw, ragged, tears streaming down his cheeks, all those uncried tears from years gone by released now in wellsprings and even torrents. Then he sees his toes down there wiggling in their thick, damp socks and breaks out laughing at this further absurdity.

I mean, seriously, he was killing himself because he was afraid of dying? Really, Snowman, that's fucking idiarctic. Kind of like a man searching for his own corpse.

It was usually when he reached this epiphany for the forty-six-hundredth time that he'd manage some kind of resurrection, free himself of all the shit and laugh it off. If you're gonna kill yourself anyway why are you so worried about dying? Besides, you don't really want to die, do you, Snowman? You want to live. Open the damn windows and let in some air. Quit breathing that foul tobacco shit down in your lungs. Quit boozing and drugging and wasting your life. He'd clean himself up, shave daily, watch his diet, go to work feeling ten years younger and twenty pounds lighter, he'd notice Clarisse checking him out more, even Evelyn, Lookin' good, Snowman. He'd tell himself, Okay, Snowman, we're just gonna do this shit a little longer while we save some money and figure things out, and then we're getting the hell out of Dodge. That lasted a week, maybe two. He may have even gone a month. Sooner or later his resolve faltered, a sweet, fiery glass of bourbon glowed on the mantel of his imagination, the smoky, peaty fire of a glass of scotch called to him from the pages of an outdoor magazine, and how much better would that be accompanied by a pint of locally brewed stout or porter or amber ale? As Old Dave once said after one of his own many failed attempts to go on the wagon, *I . . . felt . .*

. so . . . good . . . I . . . wanted . . . to . . . get . . . drunk. The first
drink was like the return of an old friend. It was such an old
friend he'd already forgotten it and was halfway through his second boilermaker before he even realized. By then he was on a roll
and no stopping this train now, buster (choo choo). That night
stagger into bay number nine with a furious, head-pounding,
gut-roiling hangover that only showed signs of abating after the
application of several over-the-counter pharmaceutical products
as well as certain under-the-table anodynes provided to him for
a relatively modest fee by Jipi Jaime. He'd tell himself, Okay,
Snowman, we were just letting off a little steam, now it's time
to get serious again. Then Gastreaux started getting on his case
about another discrepancy in his inventory, or the new guy on
the crew fucked up royally and now he was going to have to
eat shit for it, or maybe he did call Judith and didn't get two
sentences into the conversation before he was angry and calling
her names and then *Slam!* (well, *click*), so that by the end of the
night he was seething with so much anger and resentment he
needed something to take the edge off. He'd smoke a joint, pour
some whisky, light a cigarette and *boom*, just like that—back
in the routine.

And oh yes, he knew. He knew he knew he knew that maybe
just maybe he should try to get some kind of help, talk to a
professional. You mean like a job counselor, right? Or one of
those people who help you organize your life better? Wait a
second, you don't mean a shrink, do you, Snowman? Oh sure,
let's hop on over to the shaman's tent and rattle bones with the
witch decoctor and he'll sure as tootin' fix you up. No matter
what the ailment, there's a magic potion, a prescription, that's
the ticket, and so what if you grow an extra arm in the middle
of your back and a lizard tail out your ass?

They tried to make me go to rehab, I said, no, no, no.

19

Further Suspicions

STONED, NEUROTIC, HE DIGS into another box of shredded paper. He has become obsessed with the possibility of actually matching disparate shreds with their partners. Oddly, despite the many reasons for her not to, Judith has continued to drop off sacks of shredded documents, ostensibly for Me'th's cat box, even though by now half the house is packed floor to ceiling with boxes of this shit, and the thing is, he's determined to get through all of it, and yes, it does occur to him that this may have been intentional on Judith's part—that is, she's stoking his addictive nature by dumping all this on him, even if he can't figure out why or to what end. Is it simply basket-weaving? Does she hope to redirect his obsessive behavior toward something less destructive? What if, going back to that conspiracy thing, she's exploiting this unique talent he doesn't even know he possesses yet that enables him to accurately extrapolate swatches of text based on extremely limited data, kind of like absolute pitch or tonal recognition whereby a single note, even the first vibration of a note, resonates an entire melody? A single morpheme, a phoneme even, might trigger, for example, the Gettysburg address or the preamble to the Constitution or even larger chunks of text he's never encountered before. What makes this talent so unique (still supposing, that is) is that it's not something your average computer can do, because it isn't just quantitative, i.e., sifting through a finite range of possibilities in a given field (the universe?) and reducing it to binary code. It's a constantly morphing matrix of infinite data scattered across an infinite spectrum of fields of human experience filtered through the infinitely adaptable soft machine technology of human sensory organs, including the imaginary and speculative (imagine a machine imagining): politics, the social milieu, the tech industry, film, literature, music, jazz, scat, scatology, the common vernacular, that's some bad shit, man, that's some goooood shit, plus the air temperature, sun or cloud cover, the sweet, yeasty smells from the bakery across the street, spilled gasoline (the possibility of an explosion, a childhood memory of a man in a uniform at a gas station), car exhaust, dog shit, a dropped slice of pizza, what you're going to eat for dinner, what the Prince of Wales ate for breakfast, the war, the war, the war (anger, vengeance, pain, suffering, death—DEATH—madness)—*everything* any average human being might think about or encounter at any single second of any single day. And he can pull all of that out of a single word, even a simple vowel or diphthong. Of course there is the distinct possibility this is all delusional on his part, and, filtered through Boone's camera lens, its veracity is even more suspect. Nevertheless, one day, eyes blurry, hands shaking, his whole body kind of thrumming like an electric dynamo, he aligns a "d" and an "i" side by side and the phrase "distribute the product through central hubs" pops into his head, followed by what sounds like a list of GPS coordinates, which stream at him so fast that even with his newly discovered super power, he can't catch half of it.

A disconnected shot shows the green glass spires of the PPP corporate tower. Then a boardroom where a bunch of government suits are listening to a PPP representative (whom we can't see but it sure sounds like Judith) describe the operations of their paper products division. Recycled paper is shipped to Mexico, where it's bleached and sterilized in huge vats of a whitening agent. The whitening agent? Derived from a genetically modified plant cultivated in arid climates as a biofuel alternative. The bleached paper is then re-con-*stee*-tuted into various commercial products

that are shipped back to the United States, as well as to Asian
and European markets. Of special note, this bleaching process
produces a "waste product," which, as you know, has also proved
to be of value. Two birds with one stone, as they say.

Coincidentally, the following morning he strolls into the office
to pick up his paperwork, as usual dropping cigarette ashes and
spilling coffee, but instead of Evelyn's perennial chastisements
he finds her frantically searching her desk. She looks terrified.
Fearing his own involvement, he grabs his paperwork and starts
to walk away when Evelyn calls out, *Snowman!* Rushing over,
she yanks an invoice from his stack, but not before he spots the
phrase *waste product* and a figure that, if he has read correctly,
is in the millions. Mighty valuable waste, no, Snowman? Of
course he immediately begins to obsess—what the heck could
this waste product be? The answer seems right at the tip of his
nose but he can't put his finger on it (the answer, not his nose).
And why is it that every time he enters the office now he feels
Evelyn's bright blue bird eyes watching him? For the first time
he senses that maybe it isn't just his imagination. I mean, what
if poor old Mom wasn't crazy?—well, not completely anyway.
What if there really is a conspiracy? Some dark power or force
that controls every aspect of existence, that smiles and shakes
hands and goes to church on Sunday while signing orders that
release armies of psychopaths into society, biological machines
with microchips shoved so far up their assholes a sizable bean
fart couldn't dislodge them, their minds filled with horror-house
images of razor blades, nylon stockings, writhing bodies. An
icy chill slices across the grain of his fears, laying open bundles
of nerve fiber like sheaths of telephone wire. *Snowwwmannnn?*
There an echo in here?

One night he noticed a door ajar in the tank house. Like a
chunk of cheese in a mousetrap, a wedge of warm yellow light
invited him inside and, dumbass that he was, and despite the
sign on the door that explicitly warned in bright red letters

DANGER! KEEP OUT! he thought, why not? And immediately regretted his rashness as he stepped through a kind of
airlock into a large room and stopped, awestruck in the presence of the gleaming ten-thousand-gallon stainless steel tanks
of Icine, over which danced a glimmering blue aura. A men-
tholated smell of eucalyptus poured into his sinuses, filling his
brain with images of doctors' offices, hospital scrubs, the silver
flash of surgical steel. Then he was floating away, he was drifting
among the angels, they all wore blue gossamer wings and carried
tinfoil wands with confetti and sparkly stuff coming out of the
ends, and they all had such sweet, such sad and melancholy,
chubby wubby wittle cupid faces, and they were, the angels
were, all smiling at him and calling to him in angelic falsetto
boys' choir voices, *Snowwwmannnn, Snowwwmannnn, you're
dyyying, Snowwwmannnn,* and for a little while it seemed like a
good idea, it seemed all right just to let go and die like that, but
then he remembered something, he didn't wanta die, he wanted
to live, you decided a long time ago, remember, Snowman? To
live, I mean? If he could just take off this damn blanket, it
was so heavy it was suffocating him, he struggled to push it
away. Then he was awake. He lay flat on his back on the cold
ground with big fat snowflakes melting on his face, his heart
beating furiously, his head pounding like he'd been brained
with a sledgehammer, and M'Shaka's black bearded face bent
over him, hood back, dreads splayed everywhere, his eyes a tor-
mented photo album of too many dead faces to remember, his
booming voice somehow cool and calm and yet urgent, C'mon,
Snowman, breathe that fresh air! The big black hands shook his
shoulders again. You gotta wake up now, you gotta get back
on your feet and get to work or they'll fire your snow-white ass
faster than you can say cock-a-doodle-don't. M'Shaka N'Baka,
to whom he probably hadn't spoken a hundred words in all the
years they'd worked together, and even then it was mostly 'Sup?
or What's happening? or even, disconcertingly, Yes sir! when he,
the Snowman, first took over the crew and M'Shaka responded

reflexively as taught in the military, that or it's his indoctrination in southern courtesy, particularly black folks speaking to white. M'Shaka N'Baka, whose face went in an instant from some kind of threatening gorilla mask as seen from a distance measured not just in feet or inches but decades, centuries of bigotry and hatred inherited from the Snowman's own southern genealogy as well as the cold winter canyons of the segregated northern city he was born in, to a handsome Nubian warrior prince come to save his Anglo white ass from his own stupidity, employing some of the impromptu medical skills he picked up in combat, M'Shaka N'Baka, a.k.a. Funky Freddie, as he was known back in the day as a badass nineteen-year-old kid zootsuiting around town rapping and dealing, a.k.a. Shake'n'Bake when he started using too much of his own product and lost control of both himself and his market. Brain half-fried, he shook like he had Parkinson's and he owed a lot of money. He hopped on a bus for Atlanta and safe haven with his grandmother, who, with boundless love in her enormous bosom, nurtured him on chitlins, ribs, fatback, sausage, grits, black-eyed peas, buttermilk cornbread and peach cobbler, as well as a lot of hard physical labor "volunteered" through her church (practically every waking moment of his life now is accompanied by weeping, tearful prayers, testifying, readings from the Gospels and cries of Hallelujah!), so that in a matter of months he had regained much of his varsity halfback physique and a much clearer mind, albeit bathed in the light of Jesus. With few other options, he went down to the recruiter, where he barely recalled enough of the fifth-grade education he'd acquired over twelve years of school to fill out the application. Lance Corporal Washington, Frederick, who, while he, the Snowman, was in college getting stoned, fucked up and fucked for the first time in his life, was humping an M4 carbine and about seventy pounds of gear along rivers and canals and through fig and olive, orange and date palm groves in the stench of garbage and rotting bodies in temperatures that climbed above 120 degrees. Sergeant Fred Washington, who lived through bomb blasts, machine gun, rocket and mortar fire, who learned how to seal holes in his buddies' guts with pieces of poncho and even his bare hand. You know what it's like to shove your fist into a hole in a man's gut, *Snowman*? Big grin. Jus like bustin' a virgin cherry. Before he could reply, if he could have even come up with a reply, M'Shaka was saying (in a fairly lame attempt at black dialect by Boone's white hipster scriptwriters), Hey, hey, hey, Snowchile, no need to get dee-fensive, you didn't want yo white ass in that nasty ol' war nohow.

Later they said there was a leak in one of the tanks, a rotten gasket. That was the official explanation. Ever since just a whiff of Icine was enough to send the angels singing inside his head, *Snowman in excelsia, Snowmanodelphia, oh man, it's hell for ya, we sure hope things end well for ya, Snowman, we really do.*

For the following week he wore dark glasses to hide the white film over his eyes. Evelyn just shook her head. Clarisse looked at him with more interest.

20
The Blue Heart Beat

AFTER THIS INCIDENT M'SHAKA seems to have adopted a primitive I-saved-your-life-now-I'm-responsible-for-you attitude toward him. He even has the sense M'Shaka is trying to protect him from some unforeseen danger. He clearly remembers M'Shaka saying, You already in trouble and you don't even know it, *Snowman*. But maybe M'Shaka meant his emotional state, because he also told him he needed to get out among people more, and even talked him into going to an all-black club on one of their rare nights off. But you gotta promise me, Snowchile, you cain't go in there looking like some kind of hillbilly, the brothers gonna think I lost my mind. Put on some civilized clothes, hear? In a box of his father's things he finds a midnight blue Hawaiian shirt with a flamingo-pink orchid print. Your father really looked like something. His mother, in a rare sentient moment, her eyes misty, drifting back thirty, forty years in time, before the big freeze set in, before he was born or even conceived. Oh, he was a real romantic. You wouldn't believe the letters he wrote me. And then after the war he was working all the time and going to school at night and . . . and that was the end of that. Along with the storied shirt, a swell pair of white linen trousers with pleats and cuffs and a gold watch chain with nothing on the end but dreams, and a big-shouldered suit jacket, maroon, with black velvet lapels, and a heavy duty Edward G. Robinson tough-guy overcoat that may also have been the old man's but maybe his Uncle Albert's. He parks the Coupe on Twelfth Street, crosses beneath the blue neon glow of the Blue

Heart Beat, saunters past the big black doorman with a ruby in one ear and a very large and surprisingly pink hand proffered for the expected gratuity. And yeah, he's hip, he's hop, he knows that jive, yo, bro', gimme five, *slap!* And while the nonplussed doorman's going *Say, what'choo doin', fool?!* and examining his hand like it has betrayed him, the Snowman's strutting past the two linebacker bouncers in black bowlers, tuxedo vests and bared biceps the size of bowling balls, who stare with theatrical surprise at the empty celluloid frame he has just occupied while, continuing his Hollywood red carpet stroll, he directs a leading man wink and nod to the blonde bouffanted hatcheck girl, whose spaghetti-strapped gold sequin evening dress takes a death defying plunge into chasmic caffè mocha décolletage, and *blam* walks right into the noise and music and smoky blue haze illuminated by misty will-o'-the-wisp red and yellow and green lights, gleaming bottles, glasses, mirrors, TV screens. Men in lime-green, grape-purple and lemon-yellow polyester suits and ladies in bright tropical plumage, stiletto heels, tons of makeup and super-coiffed hairdos pack the bar and the small tables at the edge of the crowded dance floor, talking and laughing and raising glasses while couples dance and twirl in the spotlight and the tenor sax honks and croons and the electric guitar weeps and moans and the electric organ cries and laments except that now—now there's this liminal moment when all these black faces turn and stare as if inexorably drawn to the glowing beacon of his incongruously white face. A maître d' in black suit and tie approaches him like a foreign ambassador, May I help you, *sir*? For a second he actually considers making a run for it when he hears, *Whooeee, lookee here dis nigger*, and freezes because even though he looks more like an albino than a mulatto (relatively speaking) he also knows that right now he's the nigger in question, but, ha ha, it's okay after all because it's M'Shaka beaming at him with this big friendly smile and a look of genuine affection, and suddenly everything's cool, it's down, it's chill, this white dude's with M'Shaka so he's gotta be all right, right? And

M'Shaka's buying drinks—a very pricey single malt scotch—
and his diamond rings are clinking against his glass and the
Snowman's eyes are kind of bugging out because the stones are
huge, I mean, it's gotta be plastic, right? He's just gotta ask, you
get that stuff discount or what? M'Shaka laughs, oh man,
Snowman, you are a blast. By now he's had a couple of drinks,
his mind's kind of lolling in a tarn of smoky highland peat when
he hears a chair squawk and this beautiful dark smoky creature
with liquid brown eyes, huge, tarantula-like eyelashes, a red
stone in her nose and large gold hoops in her ears seats herself
next to him and in a sultry voice says, So this is the Snowman
you were telling me about, Freddie (M'Shaka's homies apparently still address him by this diminutive). Hi, Snowman. I'm
Tropique. You don't mind if I sit here, do you? I thought not.
Say, anyone ever tell you you look like Billy Bob Bengay? *Huh?*
No? Well I think you look *exactly* like Billy Bob and he's my
favorite actor. *In that case.* Tropique leans closer and, batting
those enormous eyelashes, says, Aren't you going to ask me to
dance, Snowman? But—oh no! He's only danced with a girl like
two or three times in his entire life and one of those times was
in a dreaded seventh grade music class. He's so flustered he's
sputtering apologies, excuses—he doesn't really know how to
dance all that well, his lumbago's acting up—but despite his
protests, there he is, up on his two left feet, stomping and shuffling like a hog farmer at a hoedown. Why, Snowman, you lied
to me, you do too know how to dance, Tropique purrs as he
crashes into yet another couple. A slow number comes on and
then he and Tropique are dancing close, the warmth of her body
against his, her smooth cheek and her perfume and the smoke
and the lights and the tenor saxophone and then they're kissing
and oh boy, he's getting a hard-on and thinking wouldn't it be
incredible if—and it is incredible, because it's Tropique herself
who suggests they go somewhere less crowded and just like that
they're heading for the door, M'Shaka grinning at them like a
proud matchmaker, You two lovebirds leaving already? And

everything seems to be singing along until he leads Tropique to
the Coupe. You driving this thing for real, Snowman? Which,
completely missing her sarcasm, he takes as a compliment,
explaining that the Coupe is a classic, one of a kind as—gentleman that he is—he creaks open the passenger door for her and
quickly crunches it shut, effectively blocking any attempt on her
part at escape, then hurries around and climbs behind the wheel,
starts the engine, lets out the clutch and they rumble down the
street, the cold wind blowing in various pinholes, rat holes, mice
holes and black holes. Tropique's wearing a leopard skin evening
parka but she shivers furiously, Brr, Snowman, don't you have
any heat? He keeps saying, Wait, wait, it'll come on any moment,
there, you feel that? He's waving his hand under the dash but of
course it's his imagination. I've got an idea, Snowman, Tropique
says. Let's not go back to your place, I'll bet it's like your car.
Besides, her place is nearby. It's this new upscale condominium
plunked down on top of a small parcel of land until recently
occupied by four of the original homesteaded houses in this
neighborhood, wood-framed bungalows with large covered front
porches for visiting on hot summer evenings built at the end of
the nineteenth century—it took the bulldozer about an hour to
smash all four of them flat. They pull up to the curb and
Tropique jumps out. Hurry, Snowman, I'm freezing my ass, and
they run up the stairs to the lobby, enter the elevator's welcome
warmth and creak up to the second floor. Her place is real
swank, leather chairs, couches, designer lamps, tables, chairs.
She gets them drinks, rum and cokes (he's not really into the
sweet stuff but what the heck), puts on some music, lights a joint
of what turns out to be some very potent pot and the next thing
he knows, they're making out and it's real hungry, passionate
kissing, he's thinking, hoo, baby, Snowman, this can't be happening, things like this *never* happen in real life, not in your real
life anyway, Bogart maybe, or Gable, Fonda, Peck, Clooney,
Brad Pizzoccheri—*James Bond*, for chrissakes. By now he's also
pretty well trashed. He vaguely remembers Tropique asking him

some odd questions, has he heard anything about Margarito? And where again in Mexico did he say Margarito was from? But, wait a second, how does she know about Margarito? Oh, you know, *Freddie* told me how down you were because you lost your crew, especially this guy, Margarito. I guess you liked him a lot, huh, Snowman? Tarantulan eyelashes flutter. *Huh?* What did she mean by that? And why this solicitous attitude? Weren't M'Shaka and Margarito about to tear out each other's throats not too long ago? But then she says, Let's not talk about that, and they start to kiss again and he's feeling even more aroused. Tropique even says something that, in any other circumstances, would sound totally laughable, Ooooo, yeah, Snowman, you're red hot, you're making me melt. But just as suddenly she stops. Say, Snowman, you ever hear about some kind of *waste product?* *Wha . . . ?* Now his antennae are up and the old paranoia's really kicking in again because something's definitely not kosher here. But then he thinks, C'mon, Snowman, that really is crazy. *Everybody* can't be involved in some big conspiracy against you. Nevertheless, now he's more circumspect, which must be pretty apparent to Tropique because suddenly there's this strange *anti*-attraction between them, in fact, Tropique says she feels tired, which is clearly an invitation for him to leave.

Then there's an odd transition—somehow he's back at the Blue Heart Beat (the night still young, etc.?), engaged in a stoned philosophical discourse with M'Shaka on the nature of death, a subject that would seem to give the upper hand to M'Shaka, who has seen a lot of very ugly death, but no, not that kind of death, not physical death, the Snowman interjects, but death of the self, the soul, the thing that says *I am.* Rastafar-*I*, Snow*mon*, M'Shaka says in a tone that suggests humor but also solemnity, then launches into a brief dissertation that suggests some confusion between the vestiges of a profoundly Christian upbringing, a war-weary nihilism and his growing involvement in a modern pan-African belief system whose brightly colored robes and banners are planting themselves in the gloom of ghettoes across the nation like rainbows potted in gold. No one knows if it promises the passing of one storm or threatens the arrival of another. Interestingly, as M'Shaka expounds on this subject, once again he seems to transform before the Snowman's eyes into a handsome warrior prince—he can almost see him in a leopard skin and holding a spear. It's probably the pot.

The nightclub ambience now gives way to a bright, reve-latory morning light and—okay, Boone's really wigging out because now they're in church. This big black preacher Rev'rend Relahable's wiping sweat from his brow with a white handker-chief and bending and swaying and raising his hands to the heavens as the organist plays "Rock'a My Soul in the Bosom of Abraham" and every voice in the choir is united in soaring praise to the Lord and the pews are rockin' and rollin', ladies in extrav-agant pink and lavender, turquoise and vermillion silks and satins and fabulous feathers, flower- and fruit-ornamented hats and gentlemen in tailored black or dark blue suits and brightly colored silk ties are clapping and swaying, he and M'Shaka are in the last pew and he's kind of tapping one foot and humming out of tune but M'Shaka's rocking and swaying and really belt-ing out this classic in a beautiful baritone. M'Shaka gives him this sidelong ironic look and says, The Lord works in mysterious ways, Snowman.

The scene changes again and now they're at M'Shaka's place. He lives in a small wood-frame house not that far removed from the Snowman's dwelling. Inside there's a huge flat screen TV, vel-vet paintings on the walls and a very large extended family that it doesn't seem possible could all fit in this little house, M'shaka's sister, Shoshanna and her three kids, M'Shaka's wife Daneesha, his son Arthur, glasses, round face, bright intelligent eyes, a younger sister Swaneika with enormous brown eyes and shiny black pigtails knotted with red and blue rubber bands, another son, Jasper, who's maybe four–five years old and runs around laughing and tugging at people's arms, as well as a bunch of brothers, sisters, aunts, uncles, nieces and nephews and, finally, the family matriarch, Mammy (don't get your britches in a hitch just yet), a little old lady who smiles widely at him out of a little brown walnut face and big window-frame glasses, when she says something to the Snowman, he doesn't understand at first that she's talking about *her* memories of the Civil War, she's like a hundred and fifty, two hundred years old—no one knows, she's so old they don't even remember whose mammy she is. Then there's another attempt by Boone's crew at authentic black dialect when M'Shaka's little boy Jasper runs up and loudly announces, Don't touch that man, Daddy, he freeze yo ass off. M'Shaka says, Hush yo mouf, boy, where you hear that foolishness? From you, Daddy. At which point Daneesha calls out, Y'all stop that bullshit an' come on in here and eat this mess fo' it gets cold. Then everybody's sitting down at this huge table loaded to the ceiling with food, everybody's chattering and passing steaming plates of pork ribs, fried catfish and chicken, black-eyed peas, mashed potatoes in brown drip gravy, cornbread and johnny cakes, batter-fried okra, relishes, collard greens, mustard, dandelion and turnip greens swimming in pork fat, boiled crawdads, ham hocks, pigs feet, hush puppies, hominy grits and drop biscuits, peanut soup, baked yams and manioc, sweet potato pie. The Snowman's appetite's as big as a refrigerator, he can't wait to dig in. In fact, in a classic faux pas, he's just shoveling a forkful of black-eyed peas into his mouth when Daneesha says, let us now offer a prayer of thanks, and everyone holds hands as Daneesha launches into a fairly lengthy but also clearly heartfelt prayer with a lot of thank you Jesuses and hallelujahs throughout and a cacophony of amens at the end, then everyone's jamming elbows and cramming food in their mouths and yakking away. Daneesha's sister, LaMarchessa, an enormous woman in a shimmering paisley dress and way too much "Le Celeb" perfume with a huge bosom and massive arms swinging as she passes him yet another helping of black-eyed peas and more fried catfish and how about a slice of pecan pie, and by the way, Mister Snowman (in keeping with Southern tradition, men are often still addressed by their "Christian" name preceded by *Mister*), I'm sure Rev'rend Relahable would welcome another member into his congregation. And then—it must be an overload of stimulants—but he's pretty sure he remembers M'Shaka saying, Hey, Boone, my man, come on, do we really have to eat all this shit? I've been a vegan for five years. And get rid of those tacky velvet paintings and that cheap-ass big screen TV, and I sure as hell hope you don't have a Cadillac parked out front. And by the way, what great big four hour epic period piece and sentimental portrayal of the slave owner did you steal this jive-ass *Mammy* from? And, *poof,* just like that, the Snowman's back home in his own bed and the alarm clock says it's time to go to work.

21
Fed up

MEANWHILE THE SCENE AT WORK has taken a new turn. In response to public sentiment (firebombings, sugar in the gas tank—and, true, a few nutcases have taken potshots at SnowBiles) the company starts laying off Mexicans and hiring card-carrying Americans, i.e., white guys, oh yeah, and a token number of black dudes. Only thing is, you'd really have to be nuts or desperate or both to take a job like this, e.g., our Snowman (prolonged exposure to Icine has been known to cause the sensation that one is losing one's mind—probably because one is), so the applicants mostly arise from the bottom of the gene pool, Troglodytes, Neanderthals, brain-damaged vets (sorry, guys—and gals), plus your usual drunks, bums, *Icers*. Barely ambulatory, they drag themselves through the night like zombies, their reflexes operating at about three percent. They stand around the valve couplings, inhaling the vapors. They scoop up handfuls of Icine-laced air and blow it in his face, laughing like gaping idiots, Ah-haw-haw, c'mon, *Snowman*, try some, which tends to angrify him pretty quickly because by now he's had his lifetime quota of Icine. This new hiring policy proves so disastrous, ICIN quietly goes back to Mexicans, but these guys are not at all like *los guys'* comic troupe. These are serious thugs—do-rags, bandanas, crude, blue-inked prison tats (including full facials), nasty scars, lots of bling and piercings (pretty much like Maori warriors). They throw gang signs like kids playing rocks, scissors, paper, he's pretty sure most of them are carrying heat, he feels like he's riding around in a prison van. To make a bleak situation bleaker, Gastreaux announces that his nephew, Gordon, will be assigned as the Snowman's assistant crew chief. The *Snowman* suspects *Gordie* has been hired specifically to keep an eye on him. In one week, Gordie goes from, Gee, I can't tell you how excited I am to work with you, Mister Snowman, to, Gee, Mister Snowman, that's not how it says to do it in the Operator's Manual. Does my uncle know you don't follow company regulations? Golly, Mister Snowman, is this a bottle of tequila under the front seat? Surely you don't drink on the job? And I really don't think you should ingest illegal substances on or off the job, Mister Snowman. Gosh, aren't you supposed to key the mike and make contact with dispatch before exiting company property, Mister Snowman? And golly, shouldn't the spatial locator sensors already be on, Mister Snowman? And gee whiz, didn't you forget to turn on the warning lights, Mister Snowman? Gordie isn't a spy, he's a gadfly, Chinese water torture, mosquito buzz and bite. And what the fuck's this *Mister* Snowman *shite*? About this time he notices Gordie giving him a totally creeped-out look. Golly, Mister Snowman, who are you talking to? And who *are* you talking to, Snowman? God? The night lurking out there like some great black beast to drag you down into hell? The goblins of your imagination trying to tear the wings off your already doomed flight? Driving in to work this evening, he had plotted to hoist this twerp Gordie by his own petard. Citing those very same outdated company regs, he figured he'd jump in the sled and cruise the back roads getting totally trashed and let Gordie worry about the job. Only thing is, the goddamn sled's back at the shop all banged up, its runners out of alignment, the front air foil smashed in, after the new guy Hector, on his own initiative, decided to demonstrate to the other newbies how to do wheelies, and now, to top it off, Evelyn's bespectacled, middle-aged voice full of crisp secretarial efficiency and an edge of menopausal bitchiness has just come sing-songing over the airwaves, Morning, *Mister* Snowman. Boss wants to see you in his office when you get in. Don't ask me what it's about because I'm not supposed to say. Rage spreading through his brain like a wildfire, and in complete violation of company policy, not to mention Gordie's whining and whimpering, he turns the SnowBile around and heads back to the office, rumbles through the front gate, screeches to a halt in the parking lot, jumps down from the cab, stomps up the stairs, bangs through the front doors and, hood thrown back, bluebottle goggles pushed up on his forehead, boot buckles jingling like sleigh bells, parka flapping open and furiously puffing on a cigarette he doesn't even remember lighting, he storms past Evelyn—who raises her startled bluebird eyes from her screen and stares into his bleary, bloodshot eyes, into that caffeine-nicotine-psalt-alcohol and dope-driven madness and still persists, *Snowman*, how many times have I told you not to smoke in here? And where are your mukluks? Why are you wearing those ridiculous . . . but leaving Evelyn with her mouth open and making unintelligible popping sounds, he ignores the elevator and stomps up the helical, free-hanging concrete stairway to the mezzanine in a tornadic vacuum of accumulated slights, insults and suppressed rage that sucks open the glass door to Gastreaux's office *whomph*, scatters papers everywhere and actually knocks Gastreaux back in his swivel chair, still clutching a MacWhaler triple-decker fish sandwich in his hands, his mouth cranked open to take a gargantuan bite. His cold, dead, fish eyes widen with mock surprise. You look upset about something, Snowman. Are you upset? Surely it's not because I asked you, and very politely, I might add, to come have a little chat with me? Gastreaux takes a huge bite out of his sandwich and, dropping gobs of tartar sauce in his lap, masticates furiously, his wiry black eyebrows jumping like crickets. He had seen himself shouting in Gastreaux's face, denouncing the lousy job, the crummy pay, the abysmal working conditions. He had intended to raise the red banner of labor rights and solidarity, threaten to re-unionize, start a public campaign. Instead he launches into a relatively innocuous complaint about his lousy crew and now he's got this boy scout Gordie shoving his nose up his butt. Gastreaux takes another huge messy bite out of his fish sandwich, chews ferociously and says through a spray of fish and tartar sauce, Look, Snowman, I ain't causing you trouble. It's you who's making trouble for me. You think I'm mad because one of your guys wrecked the sled last night? No, I ain't mad about that . . . like *hell* I'm not mad! We ain't got shit in the budget for that kind of contingency. Gastreaux shoves the final bite of MacWhaler in his mouth, chews quickly, fiercely, looks around for something to wipe his hands on, finally decides his pants'll do fine, after which he pushes himself up from his chair, waddles around his desk and pokes a fat sausagey forefinger in the Snowman's chest. Look *Snowman*, you come in here shouting like a fucking maniac, you spoil my appetite and you can't even come up with one lame piece of shit excuse for your fuckups? Can you explain to me why I don't fire you right now?! Gastreaux's eyes bulge like billiard balls, his face has turned crimson, he's actually exuding heat. The temperature begins to rise in his office. There just happens to be a large thermometer on Gastreaux's desk and the red line of mercury soars upward. Ice melts on the walls, the ceiling begins to drip, beads of emerald green ice water trickle down the large plateglass window overlooking the lobby. So now the Snowman has to drag his defeat back downstairs past Evelyn, her stunned little button face riven with confused matronly seductive hormonal urges (did she really say, *You need a woman, Snowman?*), and back outside to the SnowBile crouched like a giant white jumping spider, its headlights burning through the falling snow, his door still hanging open, Gordie's smug, prissy face up there waiting for him to climb behind the wheel again so he can start in with his whiny, obsequious protestations. A wave of boiling hot madness surges through the Snowman's brain and right here is when he makes the most fateful decision of his life, because instead of climbing back up behind the wheel of the SnowBile like a dutiful little puppy dog schmuck and picking up his route an hour behind schedule and nothing ahead of him but an endless horizon of cold black nights and utterly meaningless labor, he hears this voice in his head say *Oh Snowman, you gotta go, man,* and he just keeps on trucking. Gee, where ya going, Mister Snowman? Gordie calls out. Hey, are ya coming back? Whata I do with the truck? Hey! By then he's climbing in the Coupe, sputtering and fuming with indignation—*Mister* fucking *Snowman?!*—and cursing Gastreaux in his mind while marveling at all the mordant, in fact utterly brilliant rebuttals he couldn't come up with on the spot but which are now flooding his brain. By the time he turns onto his street, the realization of what he has done has begun to twist and swell into something bordering on raw panic. What *has* he done? More importantly, what's he going to do now? He passes the pink house where Moses, in a pink housecoat and a pair of knee-high, faux caribou skin mukluks, has worn a muddy brown track in the front yard in his neurotic, Ice-driven mad-dog circles. And that's why you gotta go, Snowman, he tells himself in rebuttal to his doubts. He pulls up outside his little ramshackle shack, hurries inside and begins to pack. He hasn't traveled in such a long time he doesn't know what to take, he's just stuffing shirts and pants and underwear into a duffle bag. The whole time Me'th's sitting on the sofa, watching him with growing suspicion, then alarm. Hey, Snowman, what's up? Why aren't you at worrrk? Why all the hurrrry? I'm taking off, Me'th, I'm going on vacation. Mmee-yii-don't-know-about-that-Snowmaaan. My mind's made up, Me'th. I hate to leave you like this. Now's the time to put some of those feline survival skills in practice. Just close the cat door behind ya when you go out, tell your friends not to spray the goddamn walls, and, please, don't leave little critters rotting all over the place. So, this is it ol' buddy, goodbye and so long, hope to see you again someday, parting is such sweet sorrow, new horizons lie ahead, better to have tried and failed than not to have tried at all. By the time the Snowman's done bloviating, Me'th has already jumped down from the sofa and banged through the cat door. If the idea was to make the Snowman feel guilty it's working. With a leaden clunk at the bottom of his soul, he locks the door behind him. The utilities and other bills will keep on paying themselves ad bankrupticus, the house will continue in its cold, uninhabited decay. He gets behind the wheel of the Coupe, stops at an ATM, takes a pretty good chunk of cash out of his meager account and turns onto I-35 headed south, nagged by the suspicion that he's following a path set out for him by some greater power. But maybe it's just the Eye, following his flight with a skeptical, even disapproving glance.

22
The Border

OHHH, MEXICOOOO. It was a song on the radio, it was a soundtrack playing in his skull, it was the melancholy yodel and whine of a diesel locomotive rumbling through a tiny desert town in the middle of night, it was the coyote's yip and howl in the pale moonlight, it was a lonesome old cowpoke drifting south of the border on a broken down pinto without a watering hole in sight.

This is what he knows of the border.

In crackling, lurid Technicolor, a band of Indians in bright red warpaint and feathered headdresses splashes across a shallow, toilet-bowl-cleanser-blue river on horseback, followed by a blur of U.S. cavalry troops, Mexican bandidos, desperados, revolutionaries, train robbers, bank robbers, drug smugglers, federal marshals, bounty hunters, vigilantes, hordes of college kids on spring break.

I don't remember how it happened exactly. Somebody said Hey you wanta do something different this weekend? and somebody else said Like what? So we got in Jerry's car and drove four hours down to the border and walked across the bridge into a blast of heat and sunlight in this dirty little board, tin and adobe town. I think some of the streets were even dirt. I remember me and my buddies careening in and out of dive bars, Mexican music on the jukebox, glugging bottles of beer, shots of tequila, in the streets con men flashing bags of weed, trays of rings, wristwatches. An old man with a thick white mustache, shaggy white eyebrows and brown leather face tried to sell me a mummified human hand. Smiling broadly, he demonstrated

that it could be used as a backscratcher. Women in lingerie
leaned out of doorways, Hey, greenghost, hey, boy, you wanna
date? I remember smoking pot and drinking more tequila and
these dingy little rooms with blankets over the doorways, they
don't even want you to take your clothes off, just take it out and
push it in, if you can find it in the folds of fat, they're all kind
of fat and nasty, I can hear Bugsy's girl saying, C'mon, horry
up, ain' you feeneesh? Somehow I got lucky, I ended up with
this dusky little rose with big sad eyes. She said her name was
Margarita. Like the drink, I said. She gave me a tired smile and
led me down a hall and behind a curtain. I remember taking off
all our clothes and she folding me in her arms and legs, in the
smells of sweat and perfume and musty sex and moving up and
down on top of her while I rambled on about how I was going
to do something really great some day, she seemed amused, she
stared into my eyes and said in English, Yeah? So when you
gonna do all these great things? Turned out she was earning
her way through college, prostitution paid better than working
in some stupid motel in the middle of nowhere. Afterwards my
buddies were going, Geez, what took you so long? You go for
seconds? Later staggering drunk, puking over the railing of the
international bridge into that oily black slough sliding below.
The cold hit me like a bucket of ice water. A single day in the
hot sun and I'd already forgotten what that kind of cold felt like.
At least it revived me a little. I still don't know how we made it
back to Osberg, all of us hungover and sick the next day. Every
time I take out the picture postcard of that little jaunt I keep
stored away in the dusty archives of my brain and examine it
more closely I find myself tripping over certain unwanted details,
the garbage in the streets, the raw sewage in the gutters, sick
scrawny chickens scratching at the dirt, the mangy dogs wandering among the filthy stalls of the wretched little market, the rancid putrescent smell of rotting meat that slams into your brain
like smelling salts, the underlying hatred and resentment in the
eyes and in the voices of the people. And my little Margarita,

did she too hate me, despise me? Wasn't there something more, something dark and real in the smoldering grottos of her eyes when she pulled me down on top of her?

The following is narrated by an anonymous male voice with a heavy German accent:

The international Border between Mexico and the United States stretches approximately two thousand miles, or slightly more than three thousand kilometers, from Imperial Beach, California and Tijuana, Baja California, on the Pacific coast, to Brownsville, Texas and Matamoros, Tamaulipas, on the Gulf of Mexico. This somewhat transitory and at times even illusory border dividing Mexico and all of South America to the South Pole from the United States and all of North America to the North Pole has been made solid and real in the form of a twenty-foot-tall metal wall that physically separates the two countries. This is not the first of such walls.

Images appear on the screen of China's Great Wall, Hadrian's Wall, the Maginot Line, the Atlantic Wall, the Berlin Wall, the walls around Jericho and Jerusalem. The narrator continues:

This wall cuts off not only the flow of people in either direction, but the normal migratory movement of jaguars, gray wolves, ocelots, Sonoran pronghorn antelope, black bears, fox, coyotes and many other animals, blocking them from seasonal mating and feeding grounds. Add to this the clearing and destruction of hundreds of thousands of acres of wildlife habitat for additional roads, airports and staging areas manned by the U.S. Border Patrol. This damage is compounded by both drug and human smugglers' routes that crisscross ranchers' and local residents' land, leaving behind trails of garbage and destruction. Residents hear gunshots at night, they find dead pets, the bodies of illegals who have been raped and murdered. Running gun battles erupt between Border Patrol agents and drug smugglers.

One of the worst cases is the town of Roma in Starr County, according to the U.S. census, one of the poorest areas in the nation. In bygone days people smuggled rustled cattle, bootleg alcohol. Now it's mostly drugs (and guns, but more on that later) and the feds have gotten purty darn interested, to employ the vernacular. Roma residents say everything is aboveboard but how to explain all this money plowed into the local economy? In an otherwise dirt-poor border town, business is booming. A meat processing plant, convenience stores, car washes, body repair shops, steak houses and seafood joints, beauty salons, a gym. At the end of the growing season, DEA agents set up roadblocks and stop everyone entering or leaving town. Thirteen thousand pounds of pot are seized in three months. In a single sweep, the feds arrest eighty people, all locals, all seemingly regular citizens—ranch hands, mechanics, hair stylists, etc.—and charge them with involvement in drug smuggling. The defendants, most of whom are too poor to afford legal council, are afraid to speak out for fear of retaliation from drug dealers. Everyone in town's terrified. No one will give their name to reporters. One man interviewed in a front yard scattered with old washing machines, lawn mowers and car parts is visibly angry. "This here shit's been goin' on for years. Government never gave a damn. Now they pick on innocent people—little people. Meanwhile them crooks up in Washington get away with murder." Even the county judge appears nervous on camera. Stuck between a hard place and a harder place, he says diplomatically, "We must crack down on criminal activity . . . (*pause*) . . . that hurts the community." His mustache drooping, damp with sweat, he smiles at his little linguistic coup, and then becomes more assertive. "But we also must be careful not to persecute innocent people."

Much of the Mexican side of the border has become a vast no man's land disputed by drug cartels, used by coyotes as a launching site for the hundreds of thousands of illegal immigrants hoping to cross into the U.S. They come from Mexico, Central and South America, from Asia and the Middle East. They come on buses, in pickup trucks, vans and tractor-trailers, they come on bicycle, on foot. They ride through the interior on the roofs of

freight trains, young men, old men, children, entire families—
you'll see freight cars with entire living room suites on the roof,
couches, sofas, TVs, dinner tables, they set out place settings and
dinnerware and eat their meals as if they were at home in the
casa. There's a geriatric car, old men play dominoes, old women
knit sweaters. A nursery car, cribs and playpens with pooping,
peeing, crying, screaming, giggling infants and toddlers in this
open-air *ferrocarril* daycare. But things aren't entirely rosy for
our travelers. Even here on top of this hurtling beast, gang members lurk, terrifying and extorting the other riders. The natural
elements, too, are their enemy. Tropical deluges, scorching sun.
Sometimes women in the villages they pass through toss food
and water up to them, take messages or words of greeting to
pass on to families left behind. People tumble off the trains at
night in their sleep, they're whacked off or smashed to death by
overhanging tree branches, iron trestles on bridges. They arrive
at the border with broken arms, legs, scars, wounds, missing
limbs, tales of rape, assault, murder. Almost thirty percent of
the women (including girls) have suffered some kind of sexual
assault in their travels. Those fortunate enough to survive their
journey to the *frontera* are still at the mercy of the coyotes who
promise to ferry them across the Frío Grande in rubber rafts
and guide them through the frozen expanses to sanctuary in
el Norte. At this point, many simply turn themselves in to the
customs agents on the American side, hoping the overcrowded
bureaucratic system will eventually release them into society on
temporary visas. Those are the lucky ones. Now all they have to
do is find two or three grossly underpaid jobs with exhausting
hours and backbreaking labor to buy the cheapest, unhealth-
iest food they can afford and pay the inflated rent in shitholes
without flushing toilets, potable water or heat, and still maybe
send some money home.

(At this point it is no longer clear if the narrator is expressing
his own sentiments, or Boone has taken the reins again—*Ed.*)

So important to the Mexican economy are these modern

day *braceros* (they contribute over a hundred billion dollars per year to the gross national product of Mexico, approximately ten percent) that, in a uniquely Mexican cultural adaptation, over the Christmas holidays, Mexican police escort huge caravans, in some cases the entire populations of villages, from border cities to their homes in the interior. Despite this protection, many of these returning economic heroes still face extortion, rape, murder, kidnapping and imprisonment from cartels, common criminals and the police themselves.

The border between the state of Texas and Mexico stretches approximately 1,250 miles or two thousand kilometers along the Frío Grande, from the vast smoky industrial ditch of El Paso and Juárez, through desert, canyons, sumpy pockets of subtropics inhabited by a hundred or a thousand or fifty thousand or a million people to the twin cities of Brownsville and Matamoros, where, during periods of drought, the river dies into the white sandy beach before it reaches the shimmering aquamarine waters of the Gulf.

"The cities of Ciudad Juárez and El Paso . . . constitute the largest border community on earth, but hardly anyone seems to admit that the Mexican side exists . . . we have these models in our head about growth, development, infrastructure. Juárez doesn't look like any of these . . . a nation that has never hosted a jury trial, that has been dominated by one party for most of this century, that is carpeted with corruption and poverty and pockmarked with billionaires is perceived as an emerging democracy marching toward First World standing . . . Juárez, home to 350 foreign-owned factories, is an exhibit of the fabled New World order in which capital moves easily and labor is trapped by borders . . . Juárez is in your home when you turn on the microwave, slide into a new pair of blue jeans, make your toast in the morning, watch your kids playing with that new toy truck on Christmas morning . . . Juárez is a world of slums, teenage rape and murder victims mummifying in the desert, brutalizing labor practices, declining real wages, drug addiction and a million people crowded into sun-blistered board and tin shacks."

The above information the Snowman lifted almost verbatim from an unattributed source (Charles Bowden, *Harper's*, August, 2009—*Ed.*) for a paper in his undergraduate political science class.

He also remembers driving through El Paso once with his parents when he was a child. He looked across a wide concrete culvert and saw what he understood to be Mexico. The sprawling mass of shacks and hovels looked like endless mounds of garbage. People lived there.

At six in the morning and halfway across the international bridge between Laredo *viejo y nuevo*, he slams into a wall of heat and humidity, a foggy gray hallucination of cars, trucks, buses, clouds of exhaust fumes, men pushing carts and bicycles loaded down with ten foot stacks of collapsed cardboard boxes, street vendors selling chewing gum, peanuts, tacos, coffee, soda, slices of papaya and watermelon. In the northbound lanes cars are backed up all the way down to Mexico City. Throngs of pedestrians, both Mexicans and U.S. tourists, surge forward, among their ranks purveyors of a large and sometimes unlikely underworld economy, petty thieves, hardcore criminals, housewives, timid old ladies from Kalamazoo, Michigan, smuggling exotic plants, animals, artifacts, jewelry, pharmaceuticals, including AIDS and cancer treatments unavailable in the States, steroids and, of course, street drugs, principally pot, meth, heroin, cocaine and *Ice*.

For comic relief Boone includes a scene where this guy is smuggling both bricks of pot and fighting roosters in secret panels in his truck. Unfortunately for him, with the traffic backup he doesn't cross the border until dawn and—yep, you guessed it—the roosters start crowing and—uh oh—an alert border agent gets curious.

At one point the traffic comes to a complete halt and he gets

out of the Coupe to peer over the bridge. Thirty feet below, he
can see the roiling waters of the Frío Grande, a turgid, oily green,
orange, red and black serpent seething with all the poisons it
has imbibed along its course—sewage, industrial sludge, agricultural runoff, chemicals, petroleum products, seeping nuclear
waste. Clumps of river willows and cottonwoods, giant reeds and
cattails, even palm trees miraculously thrive on the south bank.
The traffic starts moving again and he jumps back in the Coupe.
Ahead of him the highway actually seems to pass through a
large white building on which he reads *Puerto Fronterizo Nuevo
Laredo*. He's feeling like a schoolboy on his first field trip until
he screeches to a halt in front of a contingent of heavily armed
Mexican soldiers and police. An officer in an orange vest directs
him into a parking lot where another man in uniform points
him toward an entrance in a gray concrete building outside
which a long line of people is gathered. Poor saps, he thinks.
They probably lack proper identification or something like that.
I mean, all he's gotta do is hand over his IUD, a quick computer
scan, an automatic debit on his checking account, a printout,
and he's on his way, right? So how is it he ends up at the back of
this very same line, exiles, expatriates, tourists, businessmen in
various states of disarray—heavy winter coats folded over arms,
damp, steaming cardigans and bermuda shorts, miniskirts and
anoraks, ski outfits and bikini tops—there's even some kind of
clown act, red noses, fright wigs, baggy trousers, giant flapa-
doodle shoes, their makeups running so badly they all look like
they've been crying. The border between Mexico and the United
States isn't just a line of demarcation between two nations, it's a
portal between alternate dimensions. A yellow line painted on
the gray cement floor leads this ragtag crowd on a zigzag course
through a maze of sweating, shadowy concrete walls. (Cinema
sleuths will later accuse Boone of simply splicing in frames from
The Cabinet of Doctor Caligari—Ed.) Along the way this cop
seems to take a particular interest in the Snowman. The guy's
a real sad sack, sleepy eyes, strange mustache (paintbrush-like

tufts at the corners of his mouth), sallow face, potbelly, shabby gray uniform, shirt spattered with salsa, trouser-fly torn (here, too, Boone has unabashedly spliced in cuts from the famous comic actor Cottonfloss's last and largely unknown American movie—a disastrous flop, which also tells you how disastrously out of touch with current Mexican cinema Boone is, the obvious choice having been the more contemporaneous comic genius Exspirito—*Ed.*), only that big black revolver hanging down his thigh in its well-oiled leather holster to remind everyone this is serious business, especially since this cop's staring right at him and it's a good thing for his dark glasses because he just now remembers he's also very stoned and very likely has at least one joint stashed somewhere on his person, which probably explains why he has been masticating this wad of chewing gum like a horse with a hank of fresh green alfalfa. Even worse he's starting to sweat like a pig (which, of course, they don't do) beneath his parka, but if he takes it off now that'll make him seem even more obvious. Too late. The cop is approaching him, he's giving him the old up and down. He opens his mouth, exhales a toxic cloud of garlic and decomposing meat and in a raspy, conspiratorial tone says, *Sayyyyy*, ain't you Beely Bop? Ha!Ha!Ha! Yeah, sure, I seen all your peekchores, *Abominable Snowman of the North, Attack of the Mutant Platypuses . . . Heyyyy*, the cop glances around. This ain't nawn of that candied camera ees eet? Hola, Mama, ees me, Adalberto! Look, Meester Bop, a beeg eemportant eemissary of good weel and foreen culture should not haff to wait forever een line. For only five dollars American I weel be only too happy to expedite your case. Pure extortion, but it beats waiting half a day. He hands over the five bucks and the cop escorts him down the line to an open office with squeaky floorboards that smell of polish and disinfectant. Big wooden fans turn slowly over a long counter with Plexiglass windows, behind which men and women in suits and ties wait with tired disinterest for the next customer. A young man in glasses and sweater vest hands him a stack of forms to fill out. But don't you have IUD? he objects. Of course we have IUD, señor, the young man says in perfect English. So what's the problem? the Snowman persists. The young man's female colleague leans over and smiles brightly as he replies, It doesn't work. After filling out said forms and paying another thirty bucks for vehicle registration, he's sent to a desk where a matronly woman with a large mole next to her mouth and a black bouffant that looks like it's made of plastic peers at him over cat's-eye glasses. All right, Meester Snowman, what's your beezness here? Tourist. Toureest? Where are you visiting. *Chopahuac*, he replies. Oh? What you are goeen to do in Chopahuac? He thinks it best not to mention Margarito again and says, Sightseeing. The woman's eyes narrow. And what makes you think there are any sights to see in Chopahuac, Meester Snowman? The whole time she has been pecking at an ancient looking manual Royal typewriter missing the letter W, clack-clack-clackety-clack. All right, Meester Snowman. She stamps the bottom of the form. Welcome to Mexico. Outside he finds the Coupe completely exposed to the world, doors wide open, hood and trunk up and yet another cop practically peeing himself with excitement as he rummages through the back seat. Oh *shit*, busted. He lights a cigarette, takes a couple of huge drags and steps forward, Can I help you, officer? The cop glances up at him. Sayyy, Meester, thees ees a very nice car. I know some peoples who weel be eenterested to buy heem. Not for sale, he says, greatly relieved.

He exits onto a street packed with shabby shops, stores, pedestrians. Indian women sit on the sidewalk with babies in shawls, begging. There's trash everywhere. Humid yellow light suffuses the gray morning, the sun trying to come up. His stomach growls and he remembers it's dinnertime. He parks the Coupe, changes some money at a *cambio* and goes into a funky little diner where the guy gives him a steaming plate of eggs and some kind of meat smothered in red sauce with refried beans, white rice and soft corn tortillas on the side. It tastes great, it fills an emptiness in his soul and revives his flagging spirits—and let's just hope you don't end up on the side of the road shitting out your guts, Snowman. Bright beady eyes and waving antennae draw his attention to a cockroach the size of his thumb playing hide and seek among the salt and pepper shakers. It almost looks like the damn thing's trying to communicate with him. He swats at it with a menu and it disappears behind a sugar dispenser, but not before the film audience hears a tiny voice cry, *Hey, Snowman! It's me, Carlitos, your contact in Mexico!* (Kind of like, Horton *Doesn't* Hear a Who.)

Laredo disappears behind him in a scattering of stucco homes, tire repair and welding shops, mesquite trees and cattle grazing behind barbed wire. He drives beneath a blinking yellow light and the Coupe bangs over a mound of asphalt. A black and yellow highway sign shows a series of such mounds and beneath that the word TOPES, which he confuses in his mind with the Spanish word for *mole*, which figures, right? Giant fucking moles burrowing under the road, heaving up oil pan and shock absorber-destroying bulwarks against foolhardy speeders. It's a border-control checkpoint but these guys wave him through with barely a glance and he's off again through grasslands, mesquite and rattlepod trees, their thorny branches clotted with plastic bags, like huge flocks of ragged-winged translucent birds, then widening bands of sandy white desert.

His old, worn, folded and refolded roadmap indicates he's approaching the city of Monterrey, which doesn't prepare him for what lies ahead beneath a dense brown layer of smog at the base of a steep, saddle-shaped mountain. He spends the next two hours circling in bumper to bumper traffic, honking horns, smothering exhaust, warehouses, factories, office buildings, billboards promising brighter floors, healthier babies, tastier soda, the finest beer, glimpses of drab pink and yellow stucco houses in densely packed neighborhoods, soccer fields, baseball diamonds, street signs, phone lines, kids on medians selling *chicles*, bottled water and sodas, newspapers, jumping down to wash windshields. It's kind of like a dirty, smoky displaced Pittsburgh or Detroit or other northern industrial city from a hundred years ago. In fact, American logos appear everywhere—Walmart, McDonald's, KFC (*Kain't Fucking Cook*, the Snowman remembers M'Shaka saying of the venerable fried chitlin chain), Target, Sears.

He finally manages to get out of town on a highway that runs along the base of a towering mountain carpeted in scrub brush, prickly pears, spiky Joshua trees and anthropomorphic (kind of like James Arness in *The Thing*) saguaro cactus—it's really quite striking, until he comes around a bend and the scene changes completely. Dust, diesel fumes, clanking machinery. Huge trucks, bulldozers and giant earthmovers roar and growl everywhere. The entire back half of the mountain looks like it's been chewed off. It's some kind of mining town—there are hundreds, maybe thousands of board and corrugated metal shacks incongruously painted bright red and green, yellow and pink. He pulls into an EXPEM gas station and up to a pump where a thin, tobacco-skinned, tubercular-looking guy in greasy brown coveralls with lanky oily black hair, scant mustache and slightly oriental eyes leans against a pump with a cigarette in the corner of his mouth. He's dirt poor and barely literate, but at the moment he's also a perfect sage, a master of the language and culture and a keen social critic to boot, and in a minute he's going to interrogate the poor old Snowman with the most sublime koan ever put to fledgling acolyte, *diesel or unleaded?* And if he doesn't want to sound like a complete moron he'd better have a reasonable-sounding response at hand which is really just the very simple, *Lleno, por favor*, but when the moment arrives, not only does he not have to betray his ignorance, he doesn't have to utter a single word. The guy makes eye contact through the windshield, jerks his thumb in the air and, grateful, he nods his head like a bobble doll, yeah, sure, fill it up, splash a coupla extra gallons on the ground if you like, I'll pay anything, just don't ask me something I don't understand, then watches in horror as this guy advances on the Coupe holding the nozzle of the fuel hose aloft like the head of a cobra while dripping a trail of high octane piss on the ground at the same time he's dropping ashes from the cigarette he's furiously puffing on. His eyes are filled with orange sheets of flame and the angels' voices are screaming up into the heavens and you just know that the very next second an explosion of heat and light is going to turn him and the Snowman into burnt matchsticks. But that's just his paranoia again, just his own modest attempt at screenwriting, because this guy's no voodoo zombie on a mission of death, he's just another beat-down working stiff and fella' heathen who's managed to live long enough not to give a shit. He's seen it all, drug smugglers, outlaws, corrupt cops, star-crossed honeymooners one tequila sunrise too many away from a divorce, tits and ass and crotch-obsessed frat boys and co-eds, gawking, hugely misinformed tourists *What language did you say they speak here, George?* But is he mistaken or does he see a faint gleam of recognition in the guy's eyes. I know, *Snowman*, you aren't like the rest, you didn't come down here looking for drugs or women, or, who knows, maybe you did, but something else too. All right, *Snowman*, I'll help you along your path, I'll fuel your dreams. He places twenty thousand pesos in the guy's brown, creased and oil-stained hand and he's on his way again, only now he wisely enters the toll highway, or *cuota* as it's called, which, he assumes, more or less correctly, has something to do with *quota*, although in this case it simply refers to the fee one pays, the tollbooth a row of airless glass boxes occupied by courteous young men and women in officious black ties and white shirts guarded by a squad of very serious-looking young soldiers with unmistakably hostile expressions in their gleaming black eyes, who, up close, he sees now, are also armed with extremely vicious-looking weapons—the new FX-05 Xiuhcoatl carbines. (*Xiuhcoatl* literally means "turquoise serpent" in Nahuatl but is commonly called the "fire snake," a pretty good metaphor—*Ed.*). An hour

later he sails through Saltillo and further industrial sprawl—
and, if he had stopped to explore, a long history of manufac-
turing (especially textiles: blankets, serapes, hammocks, etc.;
as well as world famous ceramic tiles) and exits onto the old
two-lane highway heading south. The narrow, twisting road
quickly begins to climb into the jagged, oddly white topog-
raphy of the rocky yucca- and cactus-stubbled Sierra Madres.
It's like one of those dreams turned nightmare where you're
driving along this bucolic country road and suddenly the road
begins to bend upward until you're almost driving at a ninety
degree angle, the car can barely move and you're in danger of
tumbling over backward at any moment. Worse, he's creeping
along behind an EXPEM tank truck, which also creeps him out
because, well, Mexican regulations being, shall we say a little
iffy?—what if the damn thing explodes? He passes a little black
car stopped on a narrow pullover, hood up, steam pouring from
the engine, a greenghost couple around his age standing next
to it. He considers stopping to give them a hand, even though
he doesn't really want to, but fortunately he sees another car
has stopped, a Mexican family, and a man, the father probably,
is approaching the greenghosts with a plastic jug of water. He
continues to climb this ghostly white mountain, misty shrouds
of fog envelope the Coupe, and then he's going over the top. An
altitude marker tells him he's at seventeen hundred meters—a
little more than a mile high. Immediately after, he swoops down
the other side several hundred meters until the terrain levels off
again and the highway cuts through a forest of Joshua trees,
prickly pear, barrel and cholla cactus. In the distance he sees
what look like snow-covered pyramids but it's a vast range of
mountains. And—this is a surprise—now he's passing through
what seems like thousands of acres of red delicious apple trees
growing under green shade cloths. And there's something that
looks like a coyote flattened into a tan and gray splat of fur and
bones in the middle of the highway and some kind of large,

dead lizard thing. And a whole bunch of other insignificant details both he and the viewing audience have suffered through for nothing because, as he later learns, it all ended up on the cutting room floor.

23
Stripped Mall

AND THEN, THAT'S RIGHT, BOONE insists on squeezing in yet another absurd scene (you can *never* have too much comic relief, he snarls). Strung out along the highway ahead the Snowman sees crude, hand-painted signs announcing *Precios más bajos! Qué locura! Todo afuera!* in front of rustic stalls constructed out of sticks, plastic tarps and burlap sacks. And *Indians*—men, women, children, most in rags, here or there a blue t-shirt or a red skirt, some completely naked, bare skin gleaming like buttered copper. They hold up painted gourds, hand-woven sisal baskets, striped and spotted fur pelts. Rattlesnake skins are splayed over poles like flattened bicycle tires next to reddish-brown strips of drying rattlesnake meat, tethered hawks hang upside down from their perches like dazed acrobats or stand up on their great yellow talons, wings outstretched, yearning for the sky. He's been so shamelessly gawking he lets the Coupe drift off the road and the rear wheels plough up to the hubcaps in the sandy soil. He guns the engine but the wheels spin futilely. He quickly shifts into reverse and back to first, trying to rock the Coupe loose. No luck. He's stuck. He gets out to look for something to dig himself out. A car whines by, Mexican faces wide-eyed with horror. A distant rumbling leads his eyes south toward the swollen purple and white cumulonimbus clouds towering above the mountains. No sign of lightning. The rumbling grows louder and he lowers his gaze. Through his sunglasses he sees that the most distant group of Indians has begun to run toward him, and then the group ahead of them turns and also begins to run, and then the group after that, exactly like dominos, their bare feet pounding the ground like the beating of hollow-log drums *boom-boom boom-boom* that quickly Dopplers louder *Boom-Boom Boom-Boom* and they're all shouting *Tur-eest! Tur-eest!* Meanwhile the same process is occurring from the other direction, one group of Indians after another turns and begins to run toward him, feet pounding Boom-Boom Boom-Boom, voices shouting *Tur-eest! Tur-eest!* Until all the Indians, north and south, are running toward him, BOOM-BOOM BOOM-BOOM and shouting *TUR-EEST! TUR-EEST!* Then he's turning and running, in fact unabashedly fleeing toward the Coupe. He jumps in and slams the door just as the *indígenas* swarm around him, clutching at him through the open windows and chanting *TUR-EEST! TUR-EEST!*

He would later learn from Doone's fact check girl that these are descendants of the Lost Merchants Tribe, a semi-nomadic people who, according to legend, have continued to live in this barren cauldron of a valley waiting for the return of the legendary and long prophesied giant metal bird to plop down out of the sky and into their midst bearing an endless clutch of cargo, air conditioners, vacuum cleaners, wristwatches, washing machines, televisions, radios and refrigerators promised to them by their elders ever since the day a giant, lumbering C-17 Globemaster on a secret supply mission to the tyrannical but useful despot of an unnamed Latin American country strayed off course and fell out of the sky into this valley, where it burst open like a giant seed pod spilling out cases of scotch, cigars, jewelry, lingerie, suitcases packed with hundred-dollar bills, as well as a crew of dead greenghosts. While awaiting the arrival of this treasure the Lost Merchants have survived any way they can. The men scavenge the desert for rabbits, iguanas, horned toads, armadillos, coyotes, ocelots, locusts, crickets, lizards, snakes. The women turn the fur, skins and bones, horns and fangs into hideous masks, dolls, necklaces, bracelets and culinary curiosities they sell to—some would say force upon (the word *extortion* certainly comes to mind)—the few cars that stop. In fact at this very instant a visibly angry and totally naked young gentleman is poking a sharp wooden stick in his face. *You geeve me mawney, tur-eest!* He turns the key in the ignition, *va-room!* stomps the gas to the floor and pops the clutch. The rear wheels spew sand and gravel and, thanks to the weight of the *sales associates* in back, the Coupe fishtails onto the highway and speeds away. But just when he thinks he's escaped with his hide intact he begins to pass yet another column of troop carriers loaded with serious-looking young soldiers, their dark Indian faces like copper masks, black eyes shining menacingly, all armed with those damned fire snakes. A mile further a semi-tank truck roars toward him. He spots the blue I on the ivory-white spoiler over the cab, the driver's rigid, determined face behind the windshield. The rig slams past, its wake force nearly knocking him off the road *Whuh!* Another Icine truck follows behind it, and another—a whole fleet of Icine trucks *Whuh! Whuh! Whuh!* Then another column of military vehicles. The logical part of his brain does a quick little two plus two (Icine plus soldiers) equals—one helluva protection agency. Something doesn't make sense here and it's giving him the heebee jeebees, enough that he unconsciously pushes the accelerator to the floor until he's roaring down the highway at well over a hundred miles an hour.

Oh Jesus, what are you doing, Snowman? You gotta slow down, relax. You can't get bent out of shape over every little nit and gnat. You're on vacation, you don't have to rush anywhere. Which, of course, is a signal for him to pop another beer, and how about another belt of tequila and a hit off that joint and now let's light up another cigarette and there, that's better, now he's mellow again, he's cruising along in that big screen, Technicolor panorama, that vast ochre sandbox scattered with cactus, cattle skulls, rattlesnakes, scorpions and lizards curled up in narrow crevices of shade, slipping deeper and deeper into the celluloid stream of a movie or dream of his own making. He can actually see himself driving across the desert behind the wheel of the

Coupe, just like he *is* in a movie. How did they do that? The answer's simple. Satellites. Boone's got this twenty-something superstar cyber-hacker who, as much as Boone hates to give these young punks credit, certainly knows his stuff. He's pulling down images from this spycam a hundred eighty miles overhead, filming the Snowman's every move, 99% resolution down to the square centimeter, they've even got a shot of him picking his nose. As a backup, Boone's paid RTF students on spring break (of course they're convinced this is their big break in cinema—fools) to sit on the roadside in nowheresville Mexico with EyePhones® and digital cameras on the very slim chance they *might* pick up images of the Snowman's passing. Look look look! It's him, right? Hey, Jimmy, Lois, you see him? Yeah, we've got him in focus now. Okay, keep an eye on him. Okay okay okay, here he comes, he's coming in. Watch out! What happened? I don't know, something flew off the car and hit the camera lens. A bottle cap, I think.

24
Motel Seis

A RELENTLESS RINGING TUGS at his consciousness. *C'mon, Snowman, answer the damn phone.* He wakes shouting *Hello! Hello!* into the rotary phone on the dash at the very instant he realizes the Coupe is heading straight for a boulder as big as a house and without a second to spare steers back onto the highway, still clutching the phone against his ear, the phantom ringing disappeared back into another dimension, the line dead, nobody there, but nobody just in time. Boone probably had an explanation for that too, atmospheric disturbances, electromagnetic waves from nearby power transmission lines. Hot air pours in the window. His armpits, crotch, his whole body is crusty with dried sweat, his butt's sore from all this sitting, his asshole itches, his head aches. He pops open the glove compartment, which, oddly, he has never examined before. Gotta be some kind of analgesic in here, right? Can't inherit somebody else's headache without aspirin. He digs among yellowed business envelopes, bottle openers, obsolete maps, string, loose nuts and bolts, a plastic pickle. Then he's staring directly into a black pubic patch, a moist pink cunt, above that, crowned with a copper scrub pad of hair, the face, mouth open, *Give it to me good, Snowman.* He recognizes the famous porn queen Mona Moondrake. Hey, Mona, ya didn't see any aspirin in there, did ya? Ho, what's this? A brown prescription bottle with a child-proof cap, that's what, and whazzit say—codeine? HaHaHa, Snowbum, just what the doctor ordered. Wash a couple of these little fellows down with warm beer, light up a cigarette—and then you wonder why your head hurts, Snowman? And while this palliative soon has its desired effect, you'd think he would have known better because five minutes later he's drifting off again. And no wonder. Normally he'd be home in bed right now, snoring away the sunlit hours like a blood-sotted vampire, or rolling over under the covers with only the tiniest nightmare mechanisms at work deep inside his sleeping brain reminding him that in another two or three hours he's gotta get up, get ready, go back out into the cold black night and face that roaring Godzillic horror.

He can't make himself stay awake. He unscrews the cap from the thermos, raises it to his lips and gets a mouthful of cold coffee grounds. Oof, no, Snowman, not coffee, sleep, that's what you need, pull over somewhere, catch some zzzs. But where the hell's he gonna pull over in this wasteland? Through the plasma of heat waves quavering over the highway ahead he sees—palm trees? A bloody oasis? Of course it's not a real oasis. (In a moment of extravagance, Boone had envisioned this grandiose, pan-oramic, Technicolor Hollywood production: camels, caravans, flapping tents, sheiks in flowing silken robes and shining silver scimitars gorging on figs, dates and pomegranates fed to them by voluptuous, veiled maidens.) It's a faded billboard over a ragged green and yellow thatch of palm trees that shows a woman in a red one-piece bathing suit diving into the kidney-shaped pool of a motel called The Oasis. He swerves into the gravel parking lot in front of a long, low, flamingo pink stucco building and shuts off the engine. The parking lot is completely empty except for the Coupe. Not much business obviously. Weary travelers in search of an inn stolen away by the modern new motels on the toll highway twenty kilometers to the east. Which means rooms should be cheaper, at least. He isn't particularly keen on shelling out a bunch of money just to catch some zzzs but he figures he'll get a hot shower, maybe a swim in the pool, followed by twelve hours of solid sleep to make up for his accruing longitudinal jet lag. He stuffs the bottle of tequila in his bag and on unsteady

land legs jingles across the blinding white gravel, past the swimming pool, which is empty. A large prickly pear cactus grows out
of a crack in the deep end. The fabric in the deck chairs is torn
and rotting. The manager's office is bright, airless. Hot yellow
sunlight streams through a dirty, cracked window. A half-empty
bottle of Coke-a-Cola with a green plastic straw sits warm and
fizzless on the counter. He raises his hand to bong the silver bell
on the desk just as a young woman appears in a shadowy archway. She's wearing a short black skirt, an orange blouse. The top
two buttons are open, revealing an edge of black lace. Her face,
framed in a river of shining black hair, is the color of caffè latte,
her nose aquiline, her slightly almond eyes black, shining. She
looks vaguely familiar. *Tiene cuartos?* he says. A smile parts the
young woman's lips. He hears her words but not their meaning.
He digs his finger in his ear. *Cómo?* The lips move again. *I said,
aren't we a bit overdressed for this climate?* Her English is perfect.
He wonders why he should find that strange. Please, she says,
pushing the registry in his direction. He fills out his name, citizenship, mode of transportation and destination, *Chopahuac*,
on which the woman's eyes linger before she hands him his key.
Wait, she says as he turns to leave, and hands him an orange.
Compliments of the establishment. Hmm, kind of a pauperish
offering, he thinks—it's like she just pulled it out of her lunch
bag or something. He goes back outside, follows the series of
red doors to number nine. It isn't locked, nor will it lock behind
him, which probably explains the chair next to it. He wedges it
under the doorknob just to be sure. Dim light filters through the
faded orange drapes. A lurid black velvet print of a toreador and
a woman in a lacy black gown with a red rose between her teeth
hangs over a queen-sized bed covered by a dusty brown-and-
white cabled bedspread. Hot, dead air slumps on his shoulders.
He glances up at the ceiling fan. The large white metal blades
are fuzzy with dust. Exposed wires point down at him from
the motor. He gropes for the switch. The fan creaks, squeaks,

the blades begin to turn, slowly at first, then faster and faster, making a loud whomp whomp whomp sound, like a giant bird taking to flight. Suddenly he feels exhausted. He sits on the bed and lets himself fall back on the soft mattress. The room seems to be surging forward or else he's surging forward, his mind still inertially roaring down the highway in the Coupe. Thick hot air swirls around him. The fan goes whomp whomp whomp on the ceiling. The exposed wires make him think of snake fangs. He sits up, unscrews the cap from the tequila, takes a swallow, shudders, lets his head fall back on the pillow. Something with lots of feet scurries into a crack in the wall. He pictures it crawling on his face while he sleeps, biting and injecting him with poison. The dim light in the room seems to vibrate. The faded orange, water-spotted drapes glow like a hazy August sun. Something gleams behind the ceiling vent—a camera lens? He hears garbled sounds, electrical buzzing and pops, like someone adjusting a microphone. Then someone is calling to him in an androidal, computerized voice, *snowwwmannn . . . we're waiting for you snowmannn*. The angels again, promising him respite from the heat, from the cold, from life, death, everything. He senses a presence in the room, a shadow or weight hovering over him. He tries to open his eyes, to wake up, confront this thing, but something hot and heavy holds him down, it's smothering him. *Aren't we a bit overdressed, Snowman?* The girl from the front desk is straddling him. She has taken off the orange blouse and black skirt and underneath she is wearing this absurd strapped and buckled rubber foundation wear from a 1950s Sears catalog. He can feel himself penetrating her, she's moist, hot. Now she's completely naked except for a flimsy costume of red and blue macaw feathers, patches of jaguar fur and jade earrings and bracelets. She raises her hand overhead. In it she holds a black obsidian blade. The blade begins to descend in a slow arc. Then there's the sound of a motor. A plane is coming, its propellers churn toward him through heavy snow squalls. Then he sees that the fan overhead is spinning at an impossible speed, it's breaking loose from the ceiling. In a shower of plaster, it crashes down on his face.

He snaps awake, his heart pounding, a red blur receding from his eyes. Hot rivulets of sweat run down his face. His erection strains against layers of clothing. How long has he slept? He rolls his head in the direction of the faded orange drapes illuminated by a nearby star arcing across the afternoon sky. An hour maybe. He thinks about getting up to pee but his eyes refuse to stay open, his brain is shutting down again. In a childish tantrum he throws off the parka, kicks off his boots and collapses back on the bed into further sleep and dream.

It's cold, night, he's holding a huge hose between his legs and shooting out sheets of snow into the black sky. Then it's an enormous cock ejaculating a great orgasmic stream of semen.

He wakes again. The sun has moved another hour in the drapes. He closes his eyes but can't sleep. It occurs to him that he and Judith never stayed in a motel together, in fact, never went anywhere. And whose fault was that, you old stuck-in-the-Snowbum? All work and no play, right, you Nerdly Ned nose-to-the-grindstone don't-go-nowhere stakhanovite? But now we're going somewhere, right, Snowman? He fumbles around for his cigarettes, lights one up and lies on his back watching the smoke drift toward the ceiling, where the fan shreds it like cobwebs. But, yuck, a cigarette isn't what he really wants. His mouth is dry and tastes like shit. He feels dirty and itchy and disgusting. He glances at the door to what he supposes must be the bathroom, then sits up, throws his legs over the side of the bed and stands, rocking on his heels as the blood rushes from his head. His arms feel stiff and heavy as he begins to peel off his sweater, shirt, jeans, damp thermal underwear, T-shirt, jockey briefs and stinking wool socks. Almost phosphorescently white, he pads across the carpeted floor to the bathroom, which, to his pleasant surprise, looks clean, although the empty light socket and exposed wiring over the shower stall disturb him. Another urge suddenly arises and he sits down on the toilet. An American movie fanzine lies on the floor. Celebrities' drug habits, sex habits, social, political and religious habits. Wait, what's this? A full-page glossy of Boone Weller and a story about a mysterious new film being shot in an unknown location, rumored to be the long-awaited (by his very few dedicated fans, at least) sequel to *The Abominable Snowman of the North*, starring none other than William Bengay. Also in a starring role, Mona Moondrake, ex-porn queen and recent returnee to the hallowed and holy folds of the church. There's even an official release from the Vatican. "Pontiff says Ms. Moondrake has an important message to disseminate." Odd word choice for the Holy See, the Snowman thinks, but, hmm, taking a closer look at Mona's photo, she's actually quite attractive, striking pale green eyes, the copper curls, maybe he shouldn't have been so hasty in blowing off Boone, taking into consideration, of course, Mona's previous profession and the likelihood she's carrying ten thousand or so sexually communicable and possibly even terminal diseases, on top of which actually *doing it* in front of a whole bunch of people, light and sound men, camera men, the director, scriptwriters, editing assistants, the janitor for chrissakes. *Oof,* that hurt, his hemorrhoids are coming out, and what a stink. He searches for the toilet paper, then understands why the magazine is there. Feeling a little icky, he tears out Boone's picture, presses the stiff, glossy paper against the aching volcanic rim of his soiled rectum, then dutifully drops it in the wastebasket next to the toilet, provided specifically for that purpose as he understands the handwritten note above it to say. When he flushes the toilet, however, it only gurgles weakly, leaving the evidence of his presence floating in a rudderless circle, nor is there a lid for him to hide his deed. Remembering his original mission, he steps under the shower and turns on the hot water. A tepid, sulfur-smelling trickle drips from the showerhead. He turns the other faucet and a stream of ice-cold water shoots out. Yeow! He jumps out of the shower stall, then reaches back in, turns off the

cold water and turns on the hot water again. The showerhead
hisses and sputters and a perfectly temperate stream of water
emerges. Great. He goes back under and starts to soap up his
hair, under his arms, his crotch. Oh man, that feels so good. The
water stops. He twists both faucets. Nothing. He tries the hot
water again. An ice-cold stream pummels his face and chest. He
endures this yogic torture long enough to rinse off most of the
soap, at which point the water stops for good. Still, he feels
significantly revived. He dries off with a towel, goes back to the
bed, opens his bag and pulls out a clean pair of socks and underwear, a Hawaiian shirt with green palm trees and orange flowers,
a pair of jeans and a pair of floppy gray sneakers with broken
shoelaces from a long-ago attempt at a routine at the twenty-
four-hour gym. By the time he's done dressing he feels like a new
man, except for this terrible thirst. He feels like he could drink
a gallon of water but all he's got is tequila, which seems abhorrent at the moment. He could get some water from the bathroom
but it's gotta be swarming with germs, microbes, bacteria, right?
Then he sees it, the orange, that diminuitive solar body, miniature celestial king, like a happy little beachball full of sweet,
tangy, Florida warmth and sunshine. And yum, it's delicious, so
juicy and sweet and citrusy, full of vitamin C, minerals, trace
elements. He can actually feel the sun's golden goodness flow
through his veins. Hmm, maybe this signals the beginning of a
change in his life, healthy diet, get some exercise, stop ingesting
all these toxins. He grabs his bag and goes back outside, shading
his eyes against the blinding hot afternoon sunlight, dumps his
stuff in the Coupe, grabs the thermos and heads to the drab little
cafe across the parking lot, where he's surprised to find the girl
from the motel office behind the cash register in a faded brown
uniform, strands of oily, unkempt hair falling around her face.
Her demeanor has changed completely. She looks tired, worn,
resentful. He asks her to fill his thermos. *Cómo?* she says in a
surly tone. Confused, he says, I'm at the motel? Number nine?
I just talked to you a coupla hours ago? She shakes her head, *No*

hablo inglés. He squeezes his eyes shut, opens them again, hands the thermos to her. *Por favor, lleno? Café?* The girl closes her eyes in sullen feline acknowledgement and fills the thermos from a stainless steel pot on a heating coil. He has this odd sense that she resents him personally, the way a jilted lover might. Of course he can't know that, until about two hours ago anyway, Boone had been considering her for a very important role. He drops a thousand pesos on the counter, returns to the Coupe and pulls back on the highway. Cellophane pink and orange light strikes mesas and buttes and sends their purple shadows across the distant slopes of a long, low mountain range where dark green clumps of yucca, lechuguilla, Joshua trees, prickly pear, hedgehog and saguaro cactus gradually disappear in darkening shades of violet and then blackness as he drives on into evening and the edge of night and that melancholy and despair that always come with the approach of night. What the hell is he doing here? Where is he going? What made him think it was a good idea to walk out on his job and his life and drive off into the unknown. Oh, but we're not going to let it get us down this time, are we, Snowman? We're going to get wired and awake and lively ourselves up, okay? *Okay?!* He opens his thermos and pours out a steaming cup of coffee, his taste buds already swelling in ardent expectation of dark, fresh-roasted coffee. What he gets is instant. But out of a jar or a can, pulverized, powdered, freeze-dried, cold-brewed, hot-brewed or rebrewed, it's coffee, and it's hot, and there has to be some caffeine in here, enough, at least, to further jangle his already frayed nerves. See, Snowman? We're feeling better already. Let's crank up the volume. And completely forgetting his resolve of only an hour ago, he takes the psalt shaker off the dash, dusts the pocket in his fist with white powder, snorts it left-nostril right-nostril up his nose. An electric jolt temporarily short-circuits his brain, followed by the not unpleasant saline drain from his sinuses down the back of his throat, and suddenly he's a lot more awake. Now what we need is a little herbal application to smooth things out. He lights his roach, takes a deep hit and—*ahhhhh*—exhales a pungent cloud of blue smoke. Another hit and his brain sails off with the HMS Bounty around Tierra del Fuego. He returns to port with the roach burned out between his fingers and his appetite soaring and boy oh boy, one of those cream-filled Kay Milagro chocolate cupcakes sure sounds awfully good right now. So good that he wolfs it down in two bites and starts in on another. But now he needs a hefty swallow of tequila to cut the fatty sweetness, and then, to cool the smoky fire searing his throat, a lone bottle of beer miraculously discovered submerged in the icy slush in the cooler (When, where or how he obtained this ice he doesn't remember. Boone?). He pops the top and—oh God, that's so good, he guzzles half the contents in one swallow. Christ, wha'd I do with the cigarettes? Jesus, watch out for that curve. Now we're feeling better again, aren't we, Snowman? A little better anyway. He has the sense he's climbing a winding mountain road. Inexplicably the radio lights up, sparked to life by a signal bouncing out of Mexico City a hundred or two hundred miles somewhere over there. Red-hot trumpets, brass bells gleaming like halos, pour their molten gold into the black night and the angels raise their voices in angelic ecstasy, crying *alleluia* and *hosanna in excelsis* as he inhales all kinds of holy smells, goat meat roasting in little adobe huts over fires of ocote, mesquite and piñon, hot candle wax and sweet aromatic copal flickering and smoldering inside churches and home altars, the herbal smell of dried vegetation in the surrounding countryside. He hears coyotes yapping, jackrabbits squealing, crickets chirring, the distant music of a late night fiesta in the firelit pocket of a village he can see glowing in a distant valley.

An hour later the radio has died, the music disappeared, dried up into the deep black pool of night. He stares into the darkness ahead, eyes blurry, thoughts groggy. A coyote leaps into the brush, a huge bird flaps up into the night sky. An apparition materializes on the roadside, a strange man riding a strange horse. Oh, now he sees. It's a man in a red papier-mâché devil mask with horns and black goatee and he's wearing, or actually kind of standing in, a pink papier-mâché horse costume with black polka dots and paper streamers. You can see his legs, bare and very muscular, sticking out of the belly. The man and the horse bow their heads in unison as he cruises by at a very cautious five miles an hour. Then he's inside some kind of tunnel with rough-hewn stone walls and bare lightbulbs strung out every twenty feet or so. The air is dusty, dank and smells of the bowels of the earth. Things pop out at him like a house of horrors, monster masks, mummies, horned devils. Bats fly past him. A witch on a broom. It's like an umbilicus into another world, like he's fallen down a giant rabbit hole, like a night *in* Bald Mountain. Everything has begun to spin. What's going on here? Boone! he cries out, and again, Boone! But no answer comes. Boone has clearly lost control himself. The plot's all over the place, impossible to resolve in the already bloated three hours' running time the producers have given him. It's every man for himself. *Help!*

REYoung was born in Pittsburgh, Pennsylvania and lives in Austin, Texas in a limestone cave deep beneath the city. He is the author of *Unbabbling*, a novel also published by Dalkey Archive Press.